Mr. and Mrs.
Medal of Honor

Mr. and Mrs. Medal of Honor

—A Novel—

John J. Klobnak

St. Louis, Missouri

ISBN: 978-0692912270

Dedication

For Robert W. May, Esq.
1947-2017

Contents

Prologue

Southeast Syria

July 1187

It was the proudest day in the young life of Nuri al-Khairalla. Just a few months after his twelfth birthday, his father, Sheik Abbad al-Khairalla, ruler of the tribe, had told Nuri that he'd be allowed to accompany the warriors into the coming battle with the infidel crusaders in Jerusalem. The announcement meant Nuri was a man. No longer would he be left with the women to fetch sticks for the fires and watch his younger siblings as they played in the hot sun.

Nuri had learned his lessons well in preparation for this day. He'd easily mastered the martial arts skills he'd need in battle. And time and time again, he'd been knocked senseless learning the use of the combat pole and during the ``*raqs-e çûb,* or stick dances, the warriors held while preparing for raids. The scars on Nuri's small hands were from lessons on the close-quarters use of the Khanjar dagger he now carried on the left side of his belt. Perhaps most important, he'd become one with his horse, and woe be to any infidel standing on the ground when Nuri's sword whipped through the air as he blazed by at full gallop. He feared neither infidel nor death. He did, however, fear his father.

As he said goodbye to his weeping mother and envious younger brothers, Nuri tried to be brave. Any display of emotion would be viewed as weakness and might cause his father, a tough man and strict disciplinarian, to send him back in shame. He climbed onto his camel, more suited than his horse for the long desert ride ahead, and hoisted his sword into position on the saddle.

The small caravan—Nuri, his father, and four other sheiks from neighboring tribes—left the camp just as the moon began to rise. Nuri fought the sniffle of a young boy trying his best to be a man, but his fear that his tears would be seen was groundless. The arid, desert air sucked moisture into itself so quickly that his tears evaporated into the night, satisfying the unquenchable thirst of the desert.

There was little talking among the group. Talking took energy and sometimes caused the speaker to swallow blowing sand. Nuri asked his father several times where they were going, and each time the sheik uttered a few words demanding the boy's patience. Mostly, Nuri's father just stared into the endless distance. After three days, Nuri stopped questioning his father, and he, too, peered into the distance. But Nuri wondered why they were traveling in a direction he knew to be away from the site of the coming battle in Jerusalem, which he knew was in the direction of the setting moon.

As the caravan stopped to rest on the fourth day, Nuri's father called to him. Nuri crawled under the lean-to his father had made with a blanket and two short tree limbs to keep out the blazing sun.

"You are wondering, my son, where we are going. This is natural."

"Yes, Father."

"What I am going to tell you was told to me by my father and to him by his father. Someday, you will bring your son here and reveal this to him; but you must never reveal this place to anyone other than your son who will succeed you."

"Reveal what, Father?"

"Tomorrow, we will enter a sacred place. It is a place where our ancestors have gone for centuries to plan our battles against our enemies and to ask Allah to bless our plans. This place is a hidden oasis where it is said that Mohammed, the Messenger of Allah Himself, peace be on His holy name, stopped to take refreshment on the way to battle."

"But, Father, I have, at your instruction, read the holy Quran several times. I have studied it with you and with the imams. I have never heard a story of the Messenger stopping at a hidden oasis."

"It is true, my son, that you have been a good and faithful student of Allah's holy word. It is also true that there is no account of this story in the holy writings of the Messenger. A book made from all the paper on Earth cannot even begin to describe the power and knowledge of Allah. Allah has given us all we need to know in the Quran. I can tell you only what was passed on to me by my father, and to him from his father. Because it is not contained in the Quran, I cannot guarantee its truth. It may be only legend—only Allah knows.

"But that is not important now," the sheik told his son. "What is important is that tomorrow you will enter this secret place and witness the planning of our battle against the infidels, those who crusade against us and Allah."

****

On the fifth night, Nuri saw a stone edifice rising out of the desert, glistening in the moonlight. Nuri had never seen mountains, but he had heard stories of them. These hills, however, were much shorter than he had imagined. Some of the large rocks had rounded tops, but most were squat and chopped on top, perhaps the height of a few large sand dunes. They were nothing like the huge peaks with frozen water on top that the traders from the Orient had described when he encountered them on their travels. As they neared, Nuri saw rocks that crumbled down the sheer sides of cliffs so steep that no camel could ascend them and no man climb them.

It was not the majestic site he felt would have been worthy of a visit from the Messenger. Still, the rock hills painted a stark contrast to the flat desert that surrounded them for as far as he could see.

The limestone formation came into sharper and sharper focus the nearer they moved, and as the rocks grew larger, Nuri was hypnotized with curiosity. The rocks glowed ever so slightly as the moon toyed with the western horizon.

"Hurry," his father urged. "We must enter the oasis quickly. It is forbidden to enter once the sun is visible."

They whipped the camels to a trot, circling the rocks until they came to a large boulder. Slowly, the boulder, which sat on a bed of thin logs, began moving sideways. Instructed by Nuri's father to dismount, the group led their camels through a dark, tight maze of rocks until Nuri saw an opening and heard the boulder slide closed behind them.

The hooves of the camels clomped loudly over the hard stone surface. The tight pathway was open to the sky but hidden from the view of passing

11

travelers. Nuri wondered how many had gone by, oblivious to the entrance and what lay behind. How many of his ancestors had trod the same stones?

As the caravan passed a final, narrow turn, the camels snorted in anticipation. Nuri smelled the water, too, just as he saw lush palm trees, reeds, and grass surrounding a shimmering pool of water. A group of sheiks was camped around it, sitting near several small fires. Some were sleeping; others were talking quietly near glowing embers.

Nuri stayed close to his father as they led their thirsty camels to the pool. Walking carefully into the water, Nuri bumped into a man whose robe was drenched. He saw the man pick up a heavy wooden box, carry it to the water, and then submerge at the back of the pool. But rather than wonder at the man's strange actions, Nuri's thoughts were only of how good the cool water felt on his skin after so many days in the hot desert.

Immersing himself, Nuri felt almost reborn. As he stood up in the pool, he saw a short but regal man with a long beard standing at the edge of the water. Staring at the stars and holding a Quran to his breast, the man seemed in deep contemplation. Awestruck, Nuri realized the man was the mighty Kurd, Salah al-Din Yussuf ibn Ayyub, ruler of the Islamic world. Nuri was standing in the presence of the man known to all as Saladin, a warrior who inspired fear in the souls of godless infidels everywhere.

Chapter 1

Afghan-Pakistani Border

February 17, 2008

I figured this was going to be another big waste of time. My spotter and I were being assigned to provide intelligence and sniper protection to a squad on a mission to ambush Taliban insurgents bringing in men and equipment from Pakistan. That wasn't the waste of time. A cable-news crew would be embedded with the squad, so it appeared that our mission was to shoot promotional video, not terrorists.

The news crew—Robert Meyers, a thirtyish, telegenic reporter; a nervous, chain-smoking producer; and an overweight cameraman with a serious case of Dunlap Disease—had been sent to get footage of Meyers in a war-time setting. My spotter, "The Dart" Bevins, had looked up Meyers on the internet and learned that he'd likely get his own cable-news show after the presidential election in the fall. Meyers showed up wearing a tailored, military-style uniform with epaulets on the shoulders that made me feel like saluting. Not the military salute, the single-digit version.

At the mission briefing at our base camp, the producer had insisted that The Dart and I pose with Meyers while he pointed at a map. I guess the producer wanted to make it look like the soon-to-be-anchorman was giving us some tips or something. Knowing there was already a price on my head because the Taliban and al-Qaeda had a visceral hatred of all snipers, I started to object. But the captain flashed me a don't–you–dare–embarrass–me glare, so The Dart and I just gritted our teeth and stood there compliantly. I wanted to kick The Dart when after the photo shoot, he pulled out his cell phone and asked me to take a photo of him with the TV star to send to his parents in Arkansas. I had no way of knowing then that the photo would later go viral.

The Dart and I departed from our base camp first. We rode under a tarpaulin in the cargo bay of a beaten-up civilian pick-up truck to a spot about two miles from our target. As the truck neared a curve on the narrow mountain road, it slowed and we jumped out with our gear.

It was two in the morning, cold, wet, and very quiet. We sat on the cold ground until the truck's taillights were out of sight and then scanned the terrain with our night-vision equipment. Silently, we made our way to the path where the squad would join us in a few hours. We saw nothing.

We crawled the last half mile to a spot down an escarpment a little less than a quarter mile from the Pakistan border. We eyeballed the path that sloped below us, then crossed the border into Pakistan, and finally disappeared behind a ridge.

After setting up our equipment, including my Barrett M-107 .50 caliber sniper rifle, The Dart and I scanned the area below using our night-vision equipment. Again, we saw nothing. After about an hour, we reported to a lieutenant at our base camp that it appeared clear but we had no visibility of the far side of the ridge. The Dart suggested using a drone to check, but the lieutenant said he'd have to get permission from the Pakistani government—which meant it wasn't going to happen.

About an hour before sunrise—as The Dart was using his calculator to figure how many days, hours, and minutes we had left on our tour—we received word that the squad, news crew in tow, had been deposited by its truck and was on the way to our location. Once the squad was in place below us, it was a waiting game.

We didn't have to wait long. We all heard the sound from around the ridge before we saw it. A mule—or maybe it was a burro, I could never keep them straight —was clomping loudly up the stone path, loaded to the gills and led by a muleteer in his mid-teens. I could see through my scope that several Rocket Propelled Grenades and boxes of ammunition hung off the animal.

The sergeant commanding the squad sent two men to grab the young mule driver. When the men got within about five feet, while the news camera rolled, the mule-bomb blew, taking out our two guys and the teenage terrorist. The explosion was a signal to the fifty Taliban fighters hiding behind the ridge to enter the battle. Somebody had set us up: We were the ones being ambushed.

There was no time to wonder how they'd known we'd be there, and we'd never have the answer. Probably some army lawyer had to file an environmental impact statement with the Pakistanis. There was no way to know. Although trying desperately to return fire, the squad was badly outmanned and outgunned, and had given away its position.

The Dart and I started selecting targets and taking them out as quickly as we could. We nailed six of them, slowing the rest. But when a Toyota pick-up came around the ridge with a .50 caliber machine gun bolted to the roof, about a dozen Taliban were able to cross the border. About ten more terrorists were using the truck as cover as it moved toward the border, raking the squad.

The Dart, who could go from fun-loving jokester to all-business spotter in the blink of an eye, doped the shot for me, and I got the driver, stopping the truck. I then got the man on the machine gun and put a round into the engine block, which started a fire under the hood. As another fighter jumped into the bed of the stalled truck and tried to fire the machine gun, I nailed him and then put a round through the gun, rendering it inoperable.

The Dart said he saw there were explosives in the bed of the truck, and the bad guys were unloading the boxes off the back before the fire reached them. The squad continued to take a pounding from mortars and automatic rifle fire. It was clear they were trapped. Hearing Sergeant Paul Jenkins radio back to base for help, I radioed down to him that I was going to try to take out the explosives behind the truck. When it blew, I told him, he should use the explosion as a diversion to move his men and the cable-news guys back.

I changed magazines, inserting one with incendiary rounds, reset my scope to account for the new ammo, gave Jenkins a countdown, and fired into the stack of explosives. The massive blast took out all the Taliban within twenty feet of the truck, and the concussion knocked the rest off their feet, at least momentarily. The squad and news crew moved up, reaching the top of the plateau behind us, and began returning fire more effectively from their new elevated position.

Until that last, fiery round, The Dart and I'd been hidden from the Taliban fighters' view, camouflaged by our Ghille suits. Now, they turned their mortars in our direction, bracketing our general location with unrelenting mortar fire. Just as I heard the extraction chopper radio that help was five minutes out, a mortar round landed to The Dart's left. I felt a searing heat in my leg and called out to The Dart, asking if he was okay. No answer.

I rolled over to check on him. He was still breathing, but his eyes were closed. He'd absorbed most of it. I radioed Jenkins that we'd been hit and I was bringing out my spotter. As I stood up, hoisted The Dart over my shoulders, and carried him the remaining hundred yards to the squad, shots were pinging all around us. I tried my best to move behind rocks, scrub brush, anything I could use for cover; but I was losing steam and felt my boot filling with blood.

As I nearly reached the plateau, I felt something slam into my back. I'd been hit in the shoulder by an AK-47 round. My brain told me I had to go down despite the whizzing bullets, but the weight of The Dart told me I had to keep going. Just as I began to lose my legs, a medic appeared to take The Dart from me. I was starting to lose consciousness, and Sergeant Jenkins rushed out helped me the rest of the way to safety.

The last thing I remember before being loaded into the chopper was the cable TV reporter, Meyers, following the stretcher I was on, pointing at me with great animation, and jabbering into a wireless microphone. I saw his lips moving, but the morphine injection I'd quickly been given prevented me from hearing, or caring, what he was saying.

Meyers's reporting that day would not only lock up the cable-news program for him, but would win him an Emmy as well. And not long afterward, his reports would earn me something even greater.

Chapter 2

National Security Agency, Fort Meade, Maryland

February 19, 2008

"Find anything interesting today?"

Colonel Richard Mareing, commander of the National Security Agency's Kirkos Project, shivered a bit as he walked into the chilly room full of flickering computer monitors.

"Usual same old," replied Frank Bono, a civilian employee who was jockeying one of NSA's most powerful super-computers from his cubicle in a secluded corner of the sterile building. Bono was a genius-level nerd who'd graduated from Cal Tech and then joined an internet startup where he'd become an overnight millionaire. NSA had recruited him to work on top-secret Project Kirkos after 9/11 and the dot-com meltdown, when Bono had become an overnight former millionaire. A data-mining program fed information from millions of sources into the super-secret computer that Bono often joked was powerful enough to run Google all by itself. Bono was looking for clues to identify and locate high-level al-Qaeda operatives.

Even the CIA director, who often went head-to-head with NSA over turf issues, admitted that the proprietary computer program had been enormously successful in supporting what still passed as the war effort in Iraq. Bono was running a program he had written that ran satellite photos and phone calls against historical terrorist events.

"But there *was* this," said Bono, a huge grin appearing on his face as he passed a photo to Mareing.

"What is it? Looks like a pile of rocks."

Bono tapped his keyboard, bringing up a series of satellite images. Mareing could see the rock pile that appeared in the photo, but now he could see people on the screen. Bono flashed through a montage of date-stamped imagery showing the rocks, each time with people gathered around a small pool of water inside the rock formation. Mareing noticed the dates and knew the significance of the images before Bono told him.

"Five days before every major Islamic terrorist attack, there are people here. The rest of the time, there's no one. I've gone back as far as the attacks on the Marine barracks in Beirut, the *USS Cole*, and our embassies. And, of course, here you see the picnic on September 6, 2001."

"Any idea who they are?"

"Yes, sir. I ran the database of known AQ communications we've archived against the dates and other imagery on the subjects who traveled to the location."

"Where is this, anyway?"

Pointing to the coordinates on a map hanging on his cubicle wall, Bono said, "Western Iraq, the Syro-Arabian desert, east of Jordan and south of Syria."

"This was back before AQ knew we were onto them," Bono continued, "and they were still careless enough to use cell and satellite phones, and, of course, email."

"So, who are they?"

"Sir, I think we just stumbled onto AQ's executive board room." The computer geek moved his cursor over a tall, bearded man, then enlarged and super-focused the image.

"That colonel—and my pal Kirk and I say this with one hundred percent certainty—is the most wanted dude in the world: Osama F. bin Laden."

Mareing collapsed into a chair, still staring at the photograph. "You're sure?"

"One hundred percent means I'm *absolutely* sure, and ol' Kirk here confirms it. Sir, we have identification programs capable of picking him out on New Year's Eve in Times Square."

"Hey, don't even think that. So you're saying that this rock pile with its little pond is some sort of what, meeting place where the terrorists gather before major attacks?"

"It's an oasis, and I can only tell you the facts. The facts are that they've met at this location five days before every major terrorist action over the past two decades. I can't promise you that they'll do it again, but our probability models say that the odds are about ninety-six percent that they will."

"Who else knows about this?"

"You and me. That's it. Oh, and ol' Kirk here, of course," Bono said, tenderly patting the computer with which he had developed an almost anthropomorphic relationship.

"Frank, did you take a shower this morning?"

"Yes, sir. Just like every morning. I take great pride in my hygiene and grooming."

"Good, because unless I miss my guess, you and I are going to be making a surprise visit to the Oval Office before we go home tonight."

"Whoa."

"And Frank, I don't think that 'dude' bin Laden's middle initial is F."

"Sir, you have your middle name for him, and I have mine."

Chapter 3

Fort Benning, Georgia

September 21, 2008

The pain in my left leg had subsided, or maybe I was just getting used to it. I still had to use the cane I'd received during my stay at the military hospital in Germany, but I seemed to have depended on it less over the past few days. Sometimes, I could forget about my injury, but the pain always returned, along with memories of how shrapnel had come to reside permanently in my body.

I was officially a short-timer with only five months to the day left in my hitch with the U.S. Army. I'd done my time and tasted my revenge, and I'd forever carry the scars as a reminder that revenge usually has a high personal cost. I'd served two combat tours, first in Iraq as part of the surge and, most recently, in Afghanistan. That was enough revenge for me.

I'd enlisted a little over three years ago to avenge the death of my father, who was unfortunate enough to be in the London Underground when it was hit by al-Qaeda terrorists. My dad died in that attack, and the emptiness I'd inherited was filled by a desire for vengeance, which I'd been able to more than satisfy as an army sniper.

That lucky mortar round, launched from inside Pakistan, had inflicted a severe wound to my left thigh. The metal shards the doctors couldn't remove would set off airport metal detectors for the rest of my life. By contrast, the wound in my shoulder from a round from a Taliban AK-47 had healed nicely, and despite a little residual numbness from the scar tissue, it seemed unlikely to be a long-term problem. At least that was what the surgeons had told me. I'd served my time, and I was counting the days to my release.

After returning from Afghanistan via Germany, I'd undergone additional therapy at Walter Reed. It was there that I'd learned that the lame-duck president intended to award me the Congressional Medal of Honor for what they called "exceptional bravery above and beyond the call of duty" during the Taliban assault. I'd never expected to receive anything more than another Purple Heart, because I'd viewed the exercise as a total failure: My spotter had died.

One day, as I was watching some lousy daytime TV game show in my room at Walter Reed, a brigadier general who worked at the White House walked into my hospital room, came to attention, and saluted me. I tried to grab my cane and get to my feet before he figured out he wasn't in General Patton's room by mistake, but he asked me to please be seated. He actually said, "Please."

The general told me that the president, in his role as commander-in-chief, had taken the highly unusual, personal decision to award me the Medal of Honor, bypassing the normal military protocol. I'd read it could take up to eighteen months for a Medal of Honor investigation to be completed, and it hadn't even been six months.

He explained that the usual process had been fast-tracked because of the overwhelming outpouring from so many Americans and from leaders on both sides of the political aisle. They'd watched the footage of the mission shot by the embedded news crew, which had run for weeks. I should have suspected right then that something was up.

The first thing I learned is that you don't *win* the medal: It is *awarded*. It made sense. Who in their right mind would want to enter a contest like that? Had it been bravery or reflex on my part? It didn't really matter. Whatever it had been—and despite the best efforts of a great army medic and army surgeons in Afghanistan and later in Germany—my spotter, a kid who'd become like a little brother to me, couldn't be saved. He'd lingered for almost three months before succumbing to his wounds.

The brass at Walter Reed hadn't been very happy when, during the middle of my therapy, I'd demanded to be briefly discharged to travel to Jonesboro, Arkansas, to attend The Dart's funeral. Sergeants don't generally get to demand much in the army, but Medal of Honor recipients apparently can. I now hoped to not be around long enough to get used to this special treatment.

The trip to Arkansas had been painful, both physically and mentally, but I'd never have been able to live with the regret of not attending my comrade's memorial, which drew most of northeast Arkansas and was even broadcast live by the local television station.

****

An MP in the guard shack tapped on my windshield, bringing me back to reality. As I entered the gates of Fort Benning—the home of the U.S. Army Sniper School where I'd been trained—I put an 800-mg ibuprofen in my mouth, reached for the Styrofoam cup in the cup holder of my ancient Subaru Outback, and washed the painkiller down with a slurp of the now-warm, watered-down Coke that I'd bought a few hours earlier at a gas station along my route.

As I drove my car to the visitor parking area, I couldn't stop wondering what the army had planned for me during my remaining five months. The corporal who'd shared a room with me at Walter Reed had said they'd probably want to take me on a publicity tour to capitalize on the medal and use me to help recruit the next generation of grunts. I was as much a capitalist as the next guy, but I really didn't know how I'd feel about using my friend's death as a marketing tool for the army.

I was looking forward to a quiet tour in some low-pressure, make-work job followed by a quiet discharge. Two tours and too many kills to count had satisfied my lust for retribution. I had enough of revenge and wanted to have the rest of my life back. It was time for my war to be over, but I should have suspected that what I wanted and what the army had in mind for me were polar opposites. After all, the U.S. Army wasn't famous for giving much consideration to what its soldiers wanted.

After pulling into a vacant spot and turning off the engine, I thought about leaving the cane in the car, but the leg was throbbing too much after the long drive from Washington.

Maybe when they see the cane, they'll realize I'll be of little use anywhere except behind a desk and just put me out to pasture early.

The staffer at the front desk directed me to a captain about my age who checked my orders and gave me directions to my CO's office. I was formulating reasons why I didn't want to do any press junkets as I limped into the office of my new commanding officer, Colonel Ansley Hunt.

Surprisingly, the buzz-cut, graying officer was standing, awaiting my arrival. Colonels usually didn't stand as sergeants entered a room, and I figured it was out of respect for my having been tapped for the Medal of Honor. But Hunt was also smiling, which was curious. Sometimes, you could conduct an entire meeting with a full-bird colonel and never see him even lift his eyes to look at you before you realized you were dismissed. I wondered what was up.

Putting aside my slowly mounting questions, I came to attention, albeit with a small, residual limp in the left leg, saluting as crisply as I could with a bullet wound in my shoulder.

"Sergeant Novak, welcome home to Fort Benning, son. How's the leg?"

"Coming along, sir. The cane is still helpful."

"Good, son. That's good. Please have a seat. Take a load off that leg."

"Thank you, sir."

Hunt took the chair behind his desk, motioning for me to choose one of the two chairs in front. He was about fifty with the physique of a thirty-five-year-old and was probably on the bubble for either one star of silver or the army's golden boot out the door.

Glancing around the office, I saw that it was a cut above the typical army space. Hunt had somehow scored a wooden desk instead of the standard-issue gray metal military office furniture. Flags stood at attention behind the desk, and Hunt's walls were covered with framed photos of comrades, certificates of achievement, and other memorabilia of a long military career. In the middle of the wall, to the left of his desk, was a chrome-plated Barrett M-82A1 .50 caliber sniper's rifle that had been mounted on a polished oak board and inscribed with the names of the men Hunt had led into Iraq in 1991, way back before my time.

"A real shame about your spotter, Bevins. He was a good kid, and those Southern boys always make great spotters. I always figured it was from all that duck hunting. Who knows? I mean, the first day of duck season in Arkansas is nearly as big as Christmas." Hunt had a Southern accent that had been diluted by twenty-five years of moving around the world with the army. I guessed Alabama, but I could have been wrong.

"The Dart was the best, sir. It really is a waste that he's dead."

"I guess you've had time to think about this Medal of Honor thing. Quite an honor, Novak."

"Yes, sir. It hasn't totally sunk in yet, but I understand it's a very high honor."

"The highest. So, sergeant, I guess you're wondering what we have in store for you."

"The captain outside said you have a project for me, sir, but he didn't say what. I guess I am a little curious."

"He couldn't tell you because he doesn't know. Very few people know what you'll be learning over the next few weeks.

"Now, son," he continued. "I understand you've got only a few months left, and with your package I'm not going to even try to sweet-talk you into staying in the army."

I was silent while Hunt paged through my personnel file.

"You've been an enigma to me since the first time I read your jacket. You enlisted at twenty-five. You have two college degrees, including an MBA from the country's top-ranked business school. Your IQ is in the top one percent of the army population. You refused a chance to attend Officer Candidate School and became an enlisted man taking orders from shave tails five years younger and thirty IQ points lighter than yourself."

"I had my reasons, sir."

"Yes, yes. Your father. I know. We had a lot of men enlist after 9/11, not so many after the attack that took your father; maybe we're just getting too used to it. Not many of the volunteers lost their fathers at the hands of the terrorists like you, but a lot of them wanted a piece of the bad guys."

"Something like that, sir."

"Well, I guess you got your wish."

"In spades, sir."

"If you'd taken the OCS route . . ."

"I'd have ended up holding some general's coat, sir, with all due respect."

"You're probably right, son. I respect you for that more than words can express, and I also respect you for not barging in here, demanding a medical discharge. You've done your part. You've done everything we've asked and more. I mean, hells bells, you're going to receive our nation's highest award, and I hate to ask you to do even more. But something's come up, and we need you. I can't tell you everything today, but I can tell you it won't stop you from receiving your discharge on time. And you'll be doing your country one huge, final favor."

Although curious what Hunt was getting at and wishing he'd get there faster, I said, "Yes, sir. Thank you, sir."

"Times have changed, Novak. The country wanted revenge after 9/11, and maybe we got a little too much. Maybe we didn't learn the lesson of our involvement in Vietnam—you can't fight wars from the White House, and don't get me going about consulting lawyers before opening fire and all this politically correct crap."

"I understand, sir."

Hunt stood, walked around the desk, and stooped to put his arm on my shoulder. I could feel the schmooze traveling through his hand and into my bullet wound like an electric current.

"Look, son. It's complicated. The public wants us out of Iraq, and what the people want, they're going to get. But it looks like the new president is going to be the wrong guy, 'cause he's running on walking away from Iraq a lot sooner than we planned. All indications right now are that he's going to win, so within six months of his inauguration, it's likely that we'll be declaring victory and getting the hell out."

Hunt took a deep breath as if getting set for the long haul. Then he continued.

"That's not breaking news, of course. Once he's in office the feeling is we'll start bugging out as fast as we can move our gear down to the big boats in Kuwait. But you and I know plenty of bad guys are still in Iraq, and although we'll still have drones and from time to time the Special Ops boys will drop in for a visit, we won't have the same access we've had in the past to go after them.

"I realize, Novak, that this isn't making a lot of sense; I just want you to know your country has one last job for you. The president is serious about not running out the clock and disappearing back to his ranch. Before he leaves office, he wants to put as many strategies as possible in place to minimize the enemy's abilities.

"Yes, sir, I think I understand," I said. But I didn't really.

"I want you to take a break and get in shape, Novak. The docs over at the hospital will be giving you the once-over tomorrow, so keep all those appointments and get a lot of rest. We'll talk again soon."

"Yes, sir. I appreciate it, sir."

"Do you need anything for the trip to the White House for the ceremony?"

"No, sir. My gear caught up with me at Walter Reed, and I've got my dress greens. I'll have plenty of time to get them cleaned and pressed."

"General Borchers is arranging for us to fly up on a C-37A. That's the army version of the Gulfstream V, you know."

"Thank you, sir. That'll be a whole lot more comfortable than the C-17 that brought me home from Germany."

"Well, we don't get many Medal of Honor recipients; so let's say you've earned it."

"Thank you, sir."

"Is there anyone you want to invite to the ceremony?"

"No, sir. My mother died during childbirth and, well, you know about my father. I don't have any siblings. My uncle passed away a while back. I've got a couple of cousins, but I was never close to them. And I've kind of lost track of most of my friends."

Hunt nodded as if he'd just heard the information for the first time. As I figured out later, my lack of any real personal ties was one of the main reasons I'd been selected for the mission.

****

After spending an uneventful evening in the surprisingly spacious private quarters that Colonel Hunt had arranged for me on the base, I received a message from Hunt's office ordering me to report to the base hospital. I'd been in the Fort Benning hospital with a sprained ankle the last week of sniper school. The ER doctor had wanted me to stay overnight, but I knew I'd probably be washed out of the class if I did. So a nurse taped up my ankle, and I hobbled through the last few days of the program.

On this visit, my first stop was with a general surgeon who checked out my leg and shoulder. Next was a visit to an orthopedic surgeon who evaluated the limp. Both doctors seemed pleased with my progress. Of course, the pain wasn't keeping *them* up at night.

The third doctor was Lieutenant Colonel Eugene Bode, MD, an army psychiatrist. I figured Bode, who appeared to be in his early fifties, for a lifer because most army doctors never reach the rank of lieutenant colonel before bolting for the financial lure and prestige of private practice. The shrink had trained at the Mayo Clinic, according to a diploma on the wall behind him—which made me wonder even more why he hadn't taken his army pension and installed himself in some cushy private practice. His speech was so sonorous, I almost nodded off during his questioning, which made me think he might have been better suited for a residency in anesthesiology rather than psychiatry.

As he questioned me, Bode made numerous notes in his file, and he ticked off each notation after I answered each question. I wondered what another psychiatrist would make of his habit.

"So, doc," I asked to break up the tedium of the exam, "why was I sent to see a psychiatrist?"

As I'd half-expected, he shot back a question rather than an answer. "Why do you think you're here?"

"I didn't give it much thought, because I just found out about this appointment a few minutes before I got to your office."

Changing the subject, Bode asked, "So how are you adjusting to life since your return to the States?"

"Well, other than a trip to Arkansas for a funeral and the drive down here from Washington, I've been at Walter Reed the whole time. I haven't had time to experience much of the outside world."

"How are you getting along after losing your spotter? I know snipers and spotters have a special relationship."

"The Dart and I were very close."

"The Dart?"

"Oh, sorry. That's what we called Richard Bevins, my spotter."

"Why was that?"

"Honestly, I didn't know until I went to his funeral and one of his friends told me. Well, you know the nickname for Richard, and I think he was kidded about it quite a bit when he was younger. Sometime during his early teens, he and his father were restoring an old Dodge Dart. Apparently, there was some sixties TV show with a detective who drove a Dart, and his dad loved the show."

"Yes, *Mannix*. The show was very popular."

"Anyway, he bragged about how he was going to drive the thing when he got his license, and I guess he talked about it so much that his pals started calling him The Dart. He seemed to like it. I guess it reminded him of home while we were over there."

I noticed I was twirling my cane and decided to set it down before the shrink read something into it.

"Are you having any problems with feelings of guilt over his death?"

"Well, I wouldn't call it guilt so much. I mean, I didn't order us into a situation where we were undermanned, and I didn't leak the mission to get us set up by the enemy. But I can't honestly tell you that I haven't often wondered why the shell landed on his side instead of mine."

Bode pushed his eyeglasses back up to the bridge of his nose and turned the pages of my file using the eraser end of a pencil. "Sergeant Novak," he said, "you're a very intelligent fellow. Your Stanford Binet IQ test results are near genius level."

Bode paused and waited for me to respond. But, I'd learned brinksmanship in negotiating from the best minds during my time at business school. Never show weakness by breaking an obvious silence challenge, the experts had advised. Bode blinked first.

"How eager are you to begin life after the army, sergeant?"

"Staring out the window of an army hospital gives you a lot of time to think."

"So, any plans?"

"I suppose I'll go back to work eventually, I just haven't decided where. I guess I blew my chances of becoming an investment banker at a big firm. I spent a year as a grunt at a bank, then business school followed by the big offer."

"And the big offer you chose after business school was to join the army. Any regrets?"

"Are you asking if I regret not taking a job with a starting salary of $300,000 a year plus a big bonus, or if I regret killing dozens of people?"

"Touché."

"Look, doc, I knew I'd probably never get the big Wall Street job if I joined the army. I hoped I'd kill somebody on the other side and maybe make a difference in putting al-Qaeda out of business. But I found out that killing people who weren't the people who put those bombs on the subway train my dad was on wasn't the same as killing the people who did. It was war. I'm a soldier, and I can live with what I did. But I can also live without doing it anymore. So yeah, I'm looking forward to resuming my life."

"It looks like you'll have a lot of latitude in choosing a career."

"Sir?"

"I see that in addition to being a very bright, educated young man, you're worth almost eight million dollars. Most people in your comfortable position would be begging for a medical discharge."

"My dad was a fairly successful man who lived a frugal life. After my mom died, we lived relatively simply, in a nice neighborhood with good schools. After I sold our house after dad's death, liquidated all his accounts, and cashed in his life insurance and the grant from the congressional-victims fund, it added up to more money than I ever imagined I'd have. I invested it wisely, and it's just been rolling over in a few bond funds since I enlisted."

"So, theoretically, you don't have to work. You could just retire."

"Doc, the terrorists took my dad. They're not getting my ambition, too."

"So, one last, totally hypothetical question: With all you've got going for yourself and after all you've been through, what if you had a chance to actually get the people responsible for 9/11 and the London attacks?"

Without hesitating, I told Bode, "I'd pay eight million bucks for the chance."

Chapter 4

The White House

September 25, 2008

The flight to DC was quick and the aircraft as luxurious as I'd heard. During my year as a grunt for an investment bank, I'd flown on private jets several times on road shows for deals. Most companies used them to hit three or four cities in a day while peddling IPOs and stock offerings. But most didn't have access to a G-5, which was my current ride.

A lot of my MBA brethren were probably forced to take the bus since the recent market crash following the collapse of Lehman Brothers. With the wave of layoffs that was sweeping Wall Street, there might not be any jobs for me five months from now. There was no debating that it was bad timing for me. But I'd never forget what Al Silverman, the legendary AC Collins & Sons market guru, told me once: "The time to buy is when you feel like you want to puke." Americans were puking as if there was a mass stomach flu epidemic. I was glad I still had my money in bonds, knowing there would be some great opportunities to pick up. I hoped I'd have some time to focus on my investments, but hopes, I would soon find out, don't always work out.

The only uncomfortable part of the flight was being in such close proximity to the brass that accompanied me on the luxury jet. The army was big on reflected glory, and right now I was the mirror. I was, however, anxious to meet General John "Borch" Borchers, the army's so-called Sniper's General. One of the last men drafted during the Vietnam War, he had become a sniper and been sent to Vietnam just as the U.S. was withdrawing its forces. Sniper school lore said Borch was one of the last men off the roof of the American Embassy in Saigon, where he kept the Viet Cong at bay while the choppers rescuing the last groups of Americans transported them to naval ships just offshore. As the story went, the general barely caught the door frame of the last Jolly Green Giant leaving the embassy roof and hung on in midair until he was pulled in by the crew. After the war, having decided to make the army a career, he enrolled in Officer Candidate School, going from private to major general. But Borch fell asleep shortly after takeoff, so I figured I'd missed my big chance to swap war stories with a legend.

I assumed we'd land at Joint Base Andrews, but the army luxury liner touched down at Reagan National and taxied to a fixed-base operator away from the main terminal. It was sunny and unseasonably warm for a late September day as we exited the plane and descended the air stairs to the waiting government SUV with its Secret Service team standing smartly nearby.

Once at the White House, the Secret Service made us go through a metal detector, which the shrapnel in my leg set off. One of the Secret Service agents whispered something to the guard, who came around and shook my hand. I assumed the TSA didn't handle the scanners at the White House. An agent led our entourage to a conference room, told us to make ourselves comfortable, and left, closing the door behind him.

A few minutes later, an attractive, twenty-something woman who I figured for the daughter of a big contributor entered the room. Everyone stood, and I felt the sharp pain knife through my leg. I wondered if I'd made a mistake leaving my cane on the plane.

"Gentlemen, I'm Karen Keller, from the president's Office of Protocol. The president is, as you'd expect, very busy. I know you all understand how important it is that we keep him on schedule, and I appreciate your cooperation.

"Which one of you is Sergeant Novak?" she asked, clearly oblivious to the difference between stripes on a sleeve and stars on a shoulder.

I struggled to my feet again and identified myself. The efficient aide went through the agenda, step by step. The ceremony, she explained, would take about twenty minutes.

"You're from where, Kansas City, Missouri?" she asked me.

"Close, ma'am. The St. Louis area."

"Yes, of course. Several local television stations from, uh, St. Louis are here, and the local newspaper's Washington correspondent asked for an interview. A few news-radio stations would like you to call them for telephone actualities, and there are the usual members of the national press corps. The press office will bring them here, one by one, in a few minutes. We've told the TV guys they can each have five minutes with you; we'll give the newspapers ten. We've already distributed fact sheets with the background of your story. I see you're staying over in Washington and that you'll be appearing on several national TV programs tonight."

That was news to me, and I looked at Colonel Hunt, who told the aide, "Yes, ma'am, the army's press attaché has that all under control. I know Sergeant Novak will make the president and the army very proud.

I wasn't sure how I liked the idea of being on TV.

"Did I mention that we'll hold the presentation in the Rose Garden? The president loves the Rose Garden, and since he leaves office in a few months, this might be one of his last chances to conduct an event there— what with the weather so unpredictable. When I announce from the back, very loudly, 'Thank you, Mr. President,' that will be the signal that the ceremony is over. Then, we'll usher you back here, where the president has asked me to give each of you a memento of your visit to the White House. Afterwards, a Secret Service agent will escort you to your vehicles.

"If anyone needs anything, just lift the phone receiver, dial the operator, and someone will find me. I'm going to alert the press secretary's office that they can start bringing up the media. Congratulations and good luck, Sergeant Novak."

****

Most of the interviews were quick and pretty lame, and most of the members of the press pleasant and professional. General Borchers said he thought it had gone well while Colonel Hunt labeled one young St. Louis TV reporter, John Towell, an "asshat" for asking how many innocent civilians I'd murdered?" I'd pretty much heard every imprecation in the army's vast lexicon of profanity, but I had to wonder what an asshat was.

I asked a porter circulating in the conference room for a Coke and sneaked another ibuprofen, praying that the leg would hold up during the ceremony. Just before three o'clock, we were escorted to the Rose Garden, where members of the press and several uniformed White House military staff were forming an audience. A podium displaying the presidential seal stood ready. A well-dressed woman grabbed my arm and introduced herself as my senator from Missouri. Before I could say anything, she grabbed my hand, struck a pose, and, after a camera flashed, disappeared. As I was led to my position on the dais, I noticed the parents of my late spotter in the front row. The Dart's mother was sobbing, and her husband was gently patting her back. Not knowing what to do, I made a small nod in their direction, and they nervously waved back.

Sensing movement behind me, I turned to see the secretary of defense and the chairman of the Joint Chiefs walking toward me. The two men shook my hand in turn and expressed the standard bureaucratic congratulatory greetings. A loud female voice from the rear announced, "Two-minute warning." Those still standing quickly took their seats, a guy I guessed was a lighting engineer made a last-minute check of the podium with some kind of meter, and the conversation became more hushed. A bank of video cameras on tripods that had been aimed at me turned toward the Rose Garden entrance, and the president walked briskly into the garden, pumping hands all around.

The president walked right up to me, bigger than life, and looking directly into my eyes, said, "Sergeant, this is one of the proudest days of my time in office. Let me say on behalf of a grateful nation that we are all in your eternal debt."

I knew the man was a politician, but he was so sincere that I believed him.

"Thank you, sir."

The president paused briefly for the cameras, crossed the few feet to the podium, and launched into his remarks.

"Welcome to the White House. The Medal of Honor is the highest award for valor our nation can bestow. The medal—part of a cherished American tradition that began in this house with the signature of President Abraham Lincoln—is given for gallantry above and beyond the call of duty in the face of an enemy attack.

"On February 18th of this year, on rough, mountainous terrain along the Afghan-Pakistani border, U.S. Army Sergeant Travis Novak risked his life and suffered severe wounds during an assault by an enemy of overwhelming numbers. Armed with only his rifle and bleeding profusely from a mortar shell that had also mortally wounded his spotter, Corporal Richard V. Bevins Jr., Sergeant Novak kept the enemy pinned down long enough to allow his comrades to evacuate to safety. Then, as the enemy forces crossed the border, charging their position, Sergeant Novak carried Corporal Bevins over one hundred yards of rough terrain, stumbling only once when he was shot in the shoulder by enemy fire. Sergeant Novak would not leave his friend and comrade behind. He let others make their way to safety before he left his position.

"Sergeant Novak killed seventeen terrorists that day, including one high-value target. A precisely placed, incendiary shell fired by Sergeant Novak also blew up a truck carrying a large cache of explosives, delaying the enemy's advance and depriving them of materiel they could have used against our troops in Afghanistan.

"At this time, I would like to welcome the many distinguished guests who have joined us today, including the vice president, secretary of defense, secretary of the army, and chairman of the Joint Chiefs. I regret deeply that Sergeant Novak's parents are no longer living and cannot be here today. I know they would have been very proud of the Sergeant, especially his father who, as I think everyone knows, died during a terrorist attack on the London Underground.

"Sergeant Novak, a shining example of the best America has to offer, has served his country and comrades with honor, courage, and distinction. Sergeant Novak was an excellent student. He was a national merit scholar who attended Duke University on an academic scholarship even though he had many offers of athletic scholarships for football and lacrosse. Despite several lucrative offers to join elite Wall Street firms after graduate school, he decided to enlist in the United States Army even though his academic credentials entitled him to attend Officer Candidate School. Sergeant Novak wanted to make sure he saw action against the people who had attacked our country on 9/11 and who were responsible or his father's death.

"I now ask that the citation be read for the presentation of the Congressional Medal of Honor to Sergeant Travis Sumter Novak. Colonel, would you please do the honors?"

The president motioned me to join him in front of a blue and gold backdrop, and we stood at the side of the podium as a military aide read the citation repeating the events of that day in Afghanistan. Then the president took the Medal of Honor from another aide and placed the distinctive blue ribbon around my neck, resting the medal on my tie. The two of us posed for pictures, after which the president returned to the podium.

"I have one other item today," the president said. "Mr. and Mrs. Richard V. Bevins Sr., Would you please step forward."

The Dart's parents, visibly stunned by the president's request, joined me on stage at the president's side.

"You have already heard about the events of that day in Afghanistan. Sniper teams comprise a sniper and a spotter, both of whom are indispensable to the team's success. Even after the enemy had identified their well-hidden location, both Sergeant Novak and Corporal Bevins made the decision to stay behind and keep the enemy pinned down long enough to allow their comrades and an embedded TV news crew the chance to withdraw safely. It was a decision that cost your son, U.S. Army Corporal Richard V. Bevins Jr., his life. Accordingly, it is my great honor to present the nation's second-highest award for valor, the Distinguished Service Cross, to your son posthumously."

The military aide read the citation, and the president presented the medal to Mrs. Bevins. After more photos and more tears, and as the president was being led from the room, a loud female voice from behind the audience announced, "Thank you, Mr. President."

*****

I was still making uncomfortable small talk with Mr. and Mrs. Bevins when the protocol blonde gently but firmly took my arm and excused me, saying I was needed inside. Little Miss Protocol gathered up the rest of the group that had flown together from Fort Benning and led us to the conference room. There, a Secret Service agent pulled Colonel Hunt and me aside.

"Gentlemen, if you will please follow me," said the agent while leading us away from the conference room. I was hoping this diversion wouldn't cause me to miss out on the memento the woman had mentioned earlier. I'd heard that the president often gave guests cuff links, and I still had a few French-cuff shirts from my days at the brokerage in storage back in St. Louis.

The agent led us silently through the halls of the White House, stopping at the desk of a secretary who told us the president was waiting for us in the Oval Office and asked us to go in. The president was on the phone, his coat off and his tie loosened. He was less formal than at the ceremony but still bigger than life.

The president motioned us to a sofa and finished his call. Two men in army uniforms who were seated in armchairs got to their feet and introduced themselves. Colonel Richard Mareing explained he was with the NSA; Major R.J. Shay said he worked with a group I'd never heard of, ATEC. The president joined us in the sitting area, sat down in the armchair closest to the sofa, and told us to be seated.

"Sergeant Novak," the president began, "I meant what I said out there today. You're a hero, and this country owes you more than it can repay. Still, we're going to ask you to do one more thing for our country—something that could be very dangerous. If you don't want to do it or feel you can't, I'll understand and will still feel the same way about you. But if you decide to pass, you must keep secret all that you hear today— from anyone. Is that clear?"

"Yes, sir."

"Colonel Mareing will tell you about a top-secret project and what we have in mind for you."

Mareing —an athletic but studious-looking guy in his early forties clearly on the fast track to general—stood and pointed a remote at a high-definition television.

"Thank you, Mr. President. The top-secret project is called Project Condo. It was set in motion by a NSA computer called Kirkos, Kirk for short. Kirk is an extremely powerful super computer, a *very* powerful computer that's essentially a data miner. But unlike the typical data miner that just runs basic searches looking for information, Kirk can aggregate millions of pieces of information and run it against other data points to look for trends. Kirk's new probability algorithm can evaluate the data, determine if there's a pattern, and predict future behavior with remarkable accuracy. In early February, Kirk identified this."

Mareing hit a button on the remote, and a picture of a rock formation popped up on the TV screen.

"What you're looking at," Mareing said, "is a limestone formation in Anbar Province in western Iraq. There's a large cavity in the middle and that pool of water is an oasis. The thing is, from the desert outside, this rock formation looks solid. But inside it's the size of two football fields. The rock walls are sheer, and unless you're an experienced mountain climber, there's no way up; and from the outside, it appears that there's no way inside. Furthermore, it's in the middle of nowhere, with nothing but desert for many miles in any direction."

Mareing pressed the remote again, and several black-and-white satellite photos began to flash across the screen.

"Here's what Kirk found. Exactly five days before every major terrorist attack for the last two decades, the satellite has picked up people inside the rock formation—which we're calling 'the rock pile,' or just 'the pile.' We don't know the identity of all the people who have attended all these meetings or the significance of five days. But we do know that this man attended every one of them."

Mareing switched to another slide showing a close-up of a bearded man.

"This man is, without question, Osama bin Laden. We don't know why they assemble at the rock pile, but we have some archived phone calls that refer to something called the sanctuary. We assume that's what al-Qaeda calls the rock pile, but we've found nothing that tells us the significance of this location."

The president raised his hand, and Mareing instantly yielded the floor. Looking straight at me, a deadly serious look on his face, the president took up the story.

"Sergeant Novak, if the polls are right—and my people think they are—the other party is going to win the election. It's no secret that they want to accelerate our withdrawal ahead of our current agreement with Iraq. Next year, our options will be much more limited than they are today. Our plan is to put a man inside this pile of rocks in case the group returns. A significant level of chatter from the terrorists suggests something big is being planned very soon."

Turning to the major beside him, the president asked, "Major Shay, would you please tell the sergeant what we have in mind?"

I knew Shay's type. The dress uniform couldn't hide his Ivy League pedigree. He was slim but muscular, my age perhaps a few years older, and probably a marathon runner. A pronounced scar, maybe combat related, ran over his left eye. The scar confused me as most Ivy Leaguers usually found a way to avoid combat, at least outside a Wall Street boardroom or the Princeton Club's squash courts.

"Sergeant," Shay began, "it's an honor to finally meet you. I'm with an army unit you've probably never heard of; very few have. Some who know us jokingly call us the Farmers because we work on a farm. Our official name is ATEC, for Army Tactical Engineering Corps, and our job is to solve unique problems confronting the military. Most people think DARPA is the country's military mad scientist, but its work has become too public for projects like Condo. So, the military turns to ATEC for projects as sensitive as this one. Our people are scientists, engineers, mathematicians, architects, and doctors, as well as a non-science types whose aptitude tests exhibit high creativity. We like people who have struck the word *impossible* from their dictionaries."

"Having been assigned this project, we had to figure out how a sniper could be inserted into the rock pile and stay there indefinitely, undetected. There's really no place to hide—and even if there were, the temperatures are so extreme that no one could last very long. We'd have to continually keep supplying fresh forces, which would be a problem in view of our impending withdrawal, not to mention increasing the likelihood of detection."

Shay removed a cloth cover from a mock-up of the pile that sat on the coffee table in front of the sofa.

"Do you see any place where a man could hide?" Shay asked me.

After studying the model about fifteen seconds, I shook my head. Shay reached down and lifted part of a limestone cliff. The small piece that came off in his hand revealed a living area modeled to scale.

"What we've done, sergeant, is fabricate, for want of a better word, a condo built right into the pile. We sent in engineers covertly. We made sure no one came within sight while we were there. We used precise, scientific instruments to learn everything about the pile, from its dimensions to its elevations and color variations right down to the last rock. Because the pile is so remote and the people we're looking for don't visit it often, we figured they wouldn't notice that we built up this flat area here by a few feet. The condo is about sixty feet above the floor of the pile, and from the inside of the pile, it's indistinguishable."

"You've already built it?" I asked Shay.

"Not only built it, but moved it on site in western Iraq. The president made its completion a priority, and we've literally worked night and day to get this done. We're installing the systems now and are still working on a few of the mechanical details. But yes, it's on site waiting for us to put it into service."

"Why not use drones to monitor the pile, then call in an air strike?" I asked.

The president stood, pointed at bin Laden's mug on the screen, and said, "Son, what I'm going to tell you is so top secret, so closely held, that perhaps less than thirty people in the world know. This man, bin Laden, is only a figurehead—a puppet run by a shadowy figure whom we've never been able to identify. We have a few voice tracks from years ago when he gave bin Laden his instructions, but we don't know who he is. He and his boy, bin Laden, have cost this country and the world greatly. If possible, we'd like to capture him.

"Yes, we could drop tons of bombs on them, but we'd never be sure. We've equipped this condo not only with state-of-the-art weaponry, but also with highly sensitive microphones and cameras. We want to listen before we take them out. Worst-case scenario, we want their corpses identifiable, so his buddies can't keep sending out messages on the internet that use his persona to instill hatred.

"Sergeant, this job needs someone with your skill set. You're an expert sniper; you're more than intelligent enough to understand the complex equipment in the condo; and, if I might suggest, you've got a personal reason to want to do this job. Now, as I already said, no hard feelings if you turn me down."

I looked into his eyes and said, "Sir, with all due respect, I don't have any living family. There's nothing that would prevent me from taking on this assignment."

The president nodded solemnly as if the thought had never occurred to him.

I stood and faced the president. "Mr. President, I have only one favor to ask. My enlistment is up on the twenty-first of January. I'd like your assurance that I can return to civilian life when my enlistment expires."

"Sergeant, we're both short-timers; my hitch as commander in chief is up the day before yours. But I'll issue an executive order directing the army to release you from duty exactly on the day and time your enlistment period is finished, no matter what the circumstances. As of that date, you'll be a civilian. You'll receive a copy of my order in writing. So, do we have a deal, son?"

"Sir, after that medal today, I don't know how I could turn you down."

"Look, sergeant, you earned that medal."

"No, sir. Not this medal," I said, pointing to the Medal of Honor on my chest. "I mean the one you gave to The Dart's parents."

The president shook my hand and as we all rose and moved to the door to leave, the president called me back.

"Sergeant Novak."

"Yes, sir?"

"It's customary for presidential visitors to receive a small memento of their visit. Of course, very few leave with the Congressional Medal of Honor. But I want you to have something else as well."

The president unfastened two solid gold cufflinks emblazoned with the presidential seal from the French cuffs of his stiffly starched shirt and pressed them into my hand as the White House photographer snapped a photo. Then, rolling up the cuffs of his shirtsleeves, he made one more promise.

"I'll send you that photograph with my signature and today's date as a provenance, so when you pass these cuff links down to your son, he'll know exactly where you got them."

Chapter 5

ATEC Farm, Rural Maryland

September 26, 2008

The next morning, after an early breakfast, a driver took Colonel Hunt and me to Ronald Reagan Washington National Airport, where we met up with the pilot of an army helicopter idling on a remote tarmac. The pilot told us our destination was about forty minutes away and asked us to board the chopper.

It will be great to be in a helicopter that isn't taking incoming fire for a change.

Once strapped in my seat, I gazed out the window and was surprised to see the possessions I'd brought with me to Fort Benning being loaded into the chopper. Several bags and boxes had apparently been gathered from my quarters there. When I saw my Remington hunting rifle being loaded into the chopper, I had to smile.

"You must have been pretty confident that I was going to accept, sir," I said to Colonel Hunt.

"I told them you'd do it. But if you hadn't stepped up, you would have been sent to a very chilly outpost at the North Pole to serve out the rest of your tour. We can't take any chances of this getting out; we can't trust anyone—even a holder of the Medal of Honor."

"I understand, sir."

"You'll be restricted to the ATEC facility until deployment. When you return to the States, you'll be debriefed and then sent back to Benning for separation. Do you have a home in the States, Novak?"

41

"No, sir. I sold my father's home several years ago. Finding an apartment was one of the things I was planning on doing over the next few months. I've got a few things in storage back in St. Louis, that's it."

"Well, Uncle Sam will be providing you with free room and board for the next few months."

After about forty minutes, true to the pilot's word, we started our vertical descent. An isolated farmhouse and four unusually large barns were all I could see.

The chopper touched down on a helipad that had been carved like a donut hole out of a farm field surrounded by dense woods. From the landmarks we'd passed during the ride, I guessed we were somewhere about sixty miles north of the U.S. Capitol. Major R.J. Shay had emerged from a Humvee parked by the helipad and was making his way through the prop-wash, motioning for Colonel Hunt and me to get into the vehicle.

"Welcome to The Farm," Shay said to me in greeting.

"I thought The Farm was in Virginia and was run by the CIA."

"That's their farm," Shay said. "This one belongs to the Department of Defense. We do a little better job of keeping ours a secret, which makes it easier to get those billion-dollar agricultural subsidies from Congress."

Shay's driver pressed a remote-control switch, activating a huge sliding door on the barn nearest the farmhouse. As the Humvee pulled in, I saw the barn was a cover for a passageway to what I suspected was an underground facility.

Shay led us to an electric golf cart, where he and Colonel Hunt took the front seats and I took the seat facing the rear. He guided the vehicle onto an open-sided freight elevator and pushed a button, starting our descent to a large area about forty-five feet below the barn that spread out several subterranean acres. I saw that there were three elevators besides the one we'd taken—doubtlessly, one providing the connection to each of the other three barns above.

Huge ceiling lamps brightly lit the area. Offices lined the walls, and a large work area filled the middle, reminding me of the jet fighter assembly lines at Boeing back in St. Louis. Several hundred people were scurrying all over the floor, unphased by our arrival.

"With satellite coverage so pervasive, we have to do our work underground. We have several flatbed trucks that do nothing but transport things back and forth to Andrews. Most of the time, the boxes on the flatbeds are empty. And we keep changing the shapes of the boxes to keep the other side wondering what we're doing. We'll give you a quick briefing, then take you over to the condo," Shay said.

Shay drove the cart along a driveway marked in neon yellow striping along the edge of the mammoth room, stopping at a set of glass doors. "You'll be bivouacked in the staff-housing unit until you're deployed," he told me.

After a quick visit with the commanding general of The Farm, who reiterated the president's warning about secrecy, Hunt and I rode in silence as Shay drove up to what looked like an unstable pile of rocks; it was set on a metal platform and looked like it might topple over any second. The structure was about twelve feet tall and about the size of a large living room except there were no straight lines. The sides had too many angles to count. The top was flat in one part though curved in another, and the left side sloped at a forty-five-degree angle. The rock pile was mainly grayish-white, but the sloped area on top was black.

Stepping off the golf cart, I looked up at the structure. "I thought you said it had already been installed in Iraq."

"The real one has. This is the prototype we used to perfect the one you'll live in over there. We'll use this one to get you acquainted with how the Iraqi structure works."

Shay led us to the platform of a hydraulic cherry picker, like the type used by electrical utilities for work on power lines, which took us up to the flat surface of the mock-up. It looked just like rock, and the material even felt like rock. But I knew it had to be something else because it would be impossible to mold rock into such precise forms.

"This is our loading dock. It's also the main entry point, although there is another way out.

Shay punched something into a control pad, and I watched as a four-feet-square steel door covered in the fake rock material disappeared in a space above. As we stepped closer, Shay threw a switch, which opened a second large door, this one on the flat surface we'd just walked across.

"This is the storage area for the propane tank that fuels the generator," Shay explained. "The generator is right behind it. When necessary, a chopper lifts the old gas unit out and another chopper drops in a new one."

Closing the hatch, Shay motioned us inside.

****

I ducked to fold my six-foot frame into the four-foot-square doorway. Feeling a twinge in my leg, I wondered why they hadn't put in a bigger door or maybe tapped actor Verne Troyer for the short-list for this job instead of a full-grown sniper.

"We built this hatch to accommodate every piece of equipment inside; unfortunately, it isn't the greatest for people."

No kidding.

As we entered the condo prototype, I saw that the walls were painted white and had been designed to match the topography of the irregular rocks on which it would sit in Iraq. The control console and window to the left would look out into the cavity of the pile toward the oasis. Shay explained that the console's array of color screens monitored cameras positioned throughout the pile and out into the desert. The monitors would turn on automatically if the outside sensors detected any movement.

"A 20-kilowatt generator is hidden outside under the dock, under the main hatch. If the motion detectors pick up movement outside the pile, the generator will shut down. We built the condo to run on battery power. The generator can run the entire thing, but it's used only to charge the batteries. We want to run it as little as possible because although we have an experimental muffler on it, it's quiet, but not totally soundproof."

"When you get over there," Shay continued, "you'll notice that the side of the outer wall of the pile below, where we fixed the condo, is blackened. We chose that area partly because it has a line of sight to almost every square inch of the pile, but also because we installed solar panels disguised as part of the vein of black rock. Even if you get right next to it, which you'd need a sixty-foot ladder to do, you probably wouldn't notice. It can get windy up there, so we've hidden some wind catchers in several strategic spots. The wind is shunted through these vents, which turn turbines sending power to the batteries."

"That's pretty amazing," I joked. "Did Al Gore help you out here?"

Shay laughed—but not too hard. I suspected he might be a Democrat. Or maybe he was still sore about Gore taking credit for inventing the internet, which had been conceived by the Defense Advanced Projects Research Agency—or DARPA, as it's usually called—where Shay had said he'd been assigned when he entered the army.

"And if all that fails, the stationary bike is also hooked up to the grid. In fact, if you lose battery power, you can throw a switch and power the main gun console and communications system directly from the exercise equipment for a short time."

I walked to the console that sat in front of the long, narrow, panoramic window. Shay slid into the chair in front of the console, which looked like one of those high-end recliners that Relax the Back stores sell.

"This will be your home base in the condo. This chair can be adjusted for working at the console, monitoring cameras, or engaging targets."

Shay pushed a lever, and the chair swiveled ninety degrees to the left. He pressed another lever, and the chair collapsed into a bed.

"You don't want to get too far from the console at night. If you doze off and we need you the chair will vibrate you awake. We'll also be monitoring the sensors from our base in Kuwait, and we'll be in constant contact via satellite. The chair might not be that great as a bed, however."

"Hey, it's a whole lot better than sleeping on the rocks in Afghanistan."

Shay swiveled the chair back so it faced the console. "This center screen is the control for the condo's offensive capabilities." Shay pointed to two rectangular boxes attached to the ceiling on opposite sides of the control panel.

"Inside these cases are identical remote-controlled Barrett M-107 .50-caliber sniper rifles." Shay got up and flipped down a panel on the rifle case on the left, exposing the specially configured M-107.

"The rifles sit here, in this apparatus. It allows the gun to move up or down, left or right, covering everywhere in the cavity of the pile except within about ten feet directly under us. If you need to take out someone down there, grenades can be deployed to neutralize the situation. There's a second M-107 in the other case on the opposite side of the control panel. They'll alternate, but both will be precisely aimed at the same target."

"You with me so far, Novak?"

I nodded that I got it.

"The apparatus is set on a rail that allows for the recoil, and the rifle automatically returns to the firing position. Spent shells slide into a containment compartment. By the way, there's an armory built into the wall right behind you. There, you'll have cases of various flavors of .50-caliber ammo and a regular M-107 in the off chance you need to hit something these guns can't reach. You'll also have two M-4s with a case of ammo and a couple of Sig Sauer 9-mm pistols, as well as a variety of grenades.

"Don't forget my Remington 30.06."

45

"Yeah, well, you'll have to bring your own ammo for your Remington, but I don't guess it matters if you want to do some plinking when it gets boring."

"I haven't shot it for a while. My dad gave it to me when I was twelve. We used to go hunting every fall back home."

"Yeah, sorry about your dad; that sure was tough."

"Thanks. So what else does this condo have to offer a lone, crippled guy against the world?"

"I'll get to that. First, let me show you how this works. When you engage a weapon, say you want to use the M-107s, you enable the appropriate switch on the control panel, and the system will open small, hidden doors to the outside. We only need enough room for the .50-caliber round to exit safely. Your window looking out into the cavity will be closed, of course, so you'll have to rely on the cameras. You acquire your target with this joystick, using the digital reticle, just like a video game; then, you'll release the safety, press the red button, and the shot will be delivered right on target. We know you snipers always work with spotters, but we couldn't accommodate two people. So we did the next best thing and digitized a spotter."

Shay punched a button on the console, the screen came on, and the five letters DARTS, for digital acquisition recognition targeting system, popped up.

"At ATEC, we always name our devices. We thought you'd like the name we came up with for this."

"The Dart would love it. Thanks a lot."

I spent a few minutes inspecting the Barrett M-107, checking the fit inside the case. It was a weapon that I knew intimately. It was a loud weapon, clearly why they'd put them in soundproof, fireproof cases.

I'd never seen anything like this setup, and I was impressed. Something like this could put snipers out of work, although the cost of dropping these condos into every situation would be a little pricey. As I played with the controls of the huge leather chair, Colonel Hunt quietly crept in and put his paw on my shoulder.

"Son, I'm going to shove off," Hunt said. "I've already had the nickel tour. It's an amazing set up. No army sniper has ever had a hide like this. You and I will speak again when I return before you deploy. How long do you think, major?"

"ATEC engineers are working night and day to finish up," Shay answered. "We can't chance delaying this. We've been lucky that only a few small groups of Bedouins have passed by during the construction, but Private Murphy's Law is always with us. In view of his few remaining months in office, the president wants this show on the road yesterday; he's afraid his successor might cancel the mission."

"So, you're saying the new president won't know about this?" I asked.

"Our orders come from the commander in chief, and until those orders are countermanded by a new president, we'll carry them out to the letter. Although a small group of intelligence guys know about the pile, the only people who know about the status are the president, his chief of staff, the people located here, and Colonel Hunt—perhaps the bravest man in the project, maybe next to you, Novak."

"Don't worry about me, men," Hunt said. "This is bigger than all of us."

Confused, I asked, "What do you mean, sir?"

Shay jumped in to explain. "The colonel's a sure thing to make general, but if the new president finds out we've stonewalled him, well, I'd say Colonel Hunt, as project leader, won't have much support for promotion and will probably be encouraged to find a new line of work in the private sector."

"Now, don't you worry about me," Hunt said quickly. "I've been in the military my whole adult life, and I can take care of myself. We'll notify the new president at the right time. We can only hope all this campaign rhetoric is forgotten once he starts getting his daily briefings and understands what we're dealing with. Anyway, if we nab the big prize, hell, they'll probably skip the one star and give me all four. We'll talk soon—and don't you have any big parties in my fancy condo. This is the most expensive place you'll ever live in."

"Sir, would you hold on to this for me? I don't think I ought to take it along." I reached into my backpack and handed the colonel the Congressional Medal of Honor.

"Novak," Hunt said, "you do this right, and you might be one of only a handful of soldiers in history to be awarded two."

****

Two weeks had passed quickly at The Farm. I'd spent hours and hours going over the condo's many systems and in briefings on everything from desert weather to how to solder a wire to a circuit board. I was trying to absorb all the plans and back-up plans—and back-up plans to the back-up plans—in case the automation failed during the months I'd be spending in virtual isolation. To say my head was swimming would be an understatement.

"Let's look at the climate-control systems now," Shay suggested at the start of another day of training. "We had to do a little creative engineering here, and it still isn't as perfect as we'd like. But it should keep you fairly comfortable. You'll be going in October, when the temp can fall as low as fifty at night and rise into the eighties during the day. In the summer, as you know from your time in-country, it's red hot."

"I was hoping an expensive crib like this would have A/C."

"Well, it does—sort of. You see, since we can't run the air conditioner off the generator because of the noise, and the battery system doesn't have the capacity, we had to come up with an alternate solution."

"And what's that?"

"Do you know how refrigeration works?"

"Not really. I just turn the thermostat up or down, and it always seems to work."

"It's a little more complicated. Did you learn about the Venturi effect at any of those fancy schools you attended?"

"Sounds familiar. But look who's talking about fancy schools—Major MIT."

Ignoring my comment about his prestigious graduate alma mater, Shay launched into an explanation of the Venturi effect.

"Simply put, refrigeration works by forcing coolant through small pipes that narrow. As the coolant is compressed into the narrowing pipes, the molecules are forced into a smaller space, removing the heat and causing the temperature of the coolant to drop. The cold gas cools the pipes, and fans blow the cold air created into your house or car. That's what we've tried to do here. We drilled through the limestone beneath the condo, almost one hundred feet down, where the temperature is a constant fifty degrees. We're using powerful fans that will pull air in from outside, compress it down through the tapered pipes, and then blow it back up through the vents in the condo. It's not perfect, but we've been able keep the place near eighty degrees during the summer. So you won't get too hot, and the computers should be protected from overheating. And in winter, the fifty-degree subterranean air is a lot easier to heat than the thirty-five-degree air outside."

"Sounds good."

"You'll also have a refrigerator, which will run off the generator; our passive solar and wind systems are dedicated to running the lights, computers, and cameras. There isn't enough juice to run the fridge, but it's super-insulated; and instead of a freezer section, it has a very efficient ice maker that will create large blocks of ice that will keep it cool for several days as long as you don't leave the door open very long."

"Like an old ice box?"

"Yeah, I guess you could say that. You'll also have a small microwave, but you can run it only while the generator is running. And as far as water's concerned, we'll ship in drinking water, both bottles and those large office-type dispensers; but we've also run a small pipe into the oasis pool. The pipe intake is in the deepest part, about seven feet down, so no one should see it. The pipe goes under the sand, and we used the same material that we used to build the condo to encase it, as it travels up along the cliff to the water system. The water goes through a purification system, so it's potable, but it doesn't taste very good. Then it goes into a large storage tank. The system will activate every time the generator runs and automatically refill the tank, so you should have plenty of water to take a shower every day. You need to try to cook and shower while the generator is on, so the batteries and the water tank are always topped off.

"The latrine and sink will drain out a pipe we camouflaged down the outside of the cliff. It runs to a septic containment tank a hundred yards outside the pile. Unfortunately, we couldn't accommodate a washing machine, but we found an old-fashioned washboard that you can use to wash your clothes in the sink. Just hang your clothes to dry on the shower rod in the bathroom. Obviously, there's no hot water, so you'll be taking cold showers, but there's a small heater in the ceiling over the shower stall. Best we could do.

"We need to talk about food soon, plus anything you want to take with you—books, electronic equipment, CDs, whatever. I've prepared a list, but if there's something special you want, we need to get that here to ship out with you. So think about it, and write down what you'd like us to get for you."

"Yes Sir," I replied. I couldn't resist asking, "So, I put the frozen pizza in the microwave and then jump in the shower?"

"Funny, but yes. Let's get some chow and call it a day."

We had a fast, fairly forgettable meal during which we spoke little. Back in my stark, sterile quarters deep under the Maryland farm field, I sat comfortably on the bunk, trying to remember everything I'd seen and heard so far. I was amazed at all the thought that had gone into the condo and the mission, and even more amazed at how far the project had come in such a short time. The weapons system was incredible, and the chance of any force being able to overcome the condo very slim.

The politics of the situation, however, were quite another matter. With a new, yet untested government in Iraq, I was sure I didn't want to get caught. Those Arab states didn't have the same tolerance for illegal aliens that we seemed to have, and I couldn't claim to be undocumented with all the classified documents I'd have. But I quickly put those concerns out of my mind. All that was for the politicians to worry about. I just wanted my discharge, and they could do whatever they wanted with the rest of their war. The new president would probably love the idea anyway—unless he was as timid as some had suggested.

As I drifted off to sleep, I figured, worst-case scenario, I'd be very bored for a few months, rehab the leg on the exercise equipment, and then quietly leave the army and get on with my life.

****

My tour guide, Major Shay, began the next day with an overview of the condo's communications system. We were on the top of the rock structure when Shay kneeled and ran his hand over a dish-shaped indentation in the roof that looked just like limestone.

"This is your satellite dish," he explained. "It blends in, and you could probably walk over it and not notice what it is."

"Does that mean I can get DIRECTV?"

"Sorry, no. We can't risk them wondering why a new customer is in the middle of the desert. You'll be in constant contact with us at the condo command center. Everything is scrambled and encrypted, of course. Your dish will receive, but your transmissions can't come from here directly to the bird above. With all the intel-gathering capabilities these days and us leaving the country, who knows who's going to be allowed to roam around the Iraqi countryside."

"How do I transmit back to base?"

"You'll transmit from inside the condo, but your signal will be microwaved in bursts to a smaller rock formation about a few miles away. There are several limestone formations nearby, none as substantial as the pile, but this one is about twenty feet high; and we've built in a camouflaged microwave receiver to pick up your signal and transmit to a satellite uplink. It will shut itself off and activate only when you key your mic or telemetry is received. There's a back-up radio system if the satellite system goes down or is compromised."

"What about internet access?"

"You have a MacBook, and it will be configured to work via satellite. It won't be exactly like real-time surfing, but it will be better than nothing. You'll enter the links you want and hit "send." Your signal will follow the same microwave-to-satellite route, and we'll route the net back to you. Sorry, you'll have no live streaming. You'll be able to check email, although it will be monitored. It's important for you to be vague in your communications to the outside world. If we feel you're giving anything away, you'll get your message back."

"Understood."

"We also have a short-wave antenna built in, so you can listen to broadcasts from around the world. It can also transmit in an emergency if the other system goes down. I'm not sure there's much local radio fare that will interest you."

"I don't think they carry St. Louis Cardinal baseball games in Iraq," I quipped.

"Don't worry. You'll be back by spring training. You'll also have emergency transmission equipment if things get bad; but don't use it unless you have to bug out."

"Got it."

"There's also a low power system to keep you in contact with us and the systems when you leave the condo for any reason."

"Sort of like Wi-Fi?"

"Yeah, sort of, but on a different frequency. It'll work up to a quarter mile around the pile. Hopefully, you won't be going any farther than that. We don't want to risk using a walkie-talkie that could be picked up by the other team."

"I understand."

"We've converted a new iPhone for you and linked it to the condo's systems. Of course, you can't make outbound calls, but the guys here have loaded it with a selection of songs and games. I hope there's something you'll like. If there's an alert from the sensors or if we need to contact you, the music, game, or whatever you're doing will be overridden, and our message will play through to the device. If somebody somehow manages to grab you, they won't be suspicious because it looks just like an iPhone. We can remotely wipe it, download normal civilian software, and track it by GPS."

"I've really wanted to see one of those new iPhones."

"You'll be able to pay bills and manage your brokerage accounts, and run your life, like you would normally. Just remember that someone will be monitoring every transmission. We've vetted everyone who's going to be involved in this project, but when you get back, be sure to change your passwords."

"Okay. No problem."

"We've done everything we can to keep you in contact with us and the outside world but without giving away your position."

"It's sounding more like being a kid again and getting grounded, with my privileges taken away."

"Yeah, but you'll have some great toys in your room."

****

I was summoned to The Farm's infirmary, where I was greeted by an attractive army nurse of about twenty-five—First Lieutenant Chris Winter, RN, her name badge read. Things were beginning to look up. Leading me into an exam room, she told me I'd be seen by several doctors who would collect medical data that they'd use to monitor my health during my isolation in the condo in Iraq. Then she told me to take my clothes off. I sometimes have that effect on women, regrettably, it's usually in a doctor's office.

After she left the room, I stripped to my boxers and sat impatiently on a paper-covered exam table. About fifteen minutes later, Nurse Winter returned.

"Sergeant Novak?"

"Still right here, ma'am."

"Sergeant, this is Major Skip Sallee, the project's medical director."

"Yes, ma'am."

I shook the major's hand as the nurse attached a blood pressure cuff to my arm and inflated it. Sallee said he'd done his residency at Duke, which made me relax a little more. We chatted about Duke's chances in the upcoming basketball season while Nurse Winter disconnected the blood pressure cuff.

"One eighteen over seventy; pulse is sixty-five," Sallee reported.

"Is that good?"

"Yeah, it's fine. Sergeant, we want to get some data on you to establish a baseline. A complete medical telemetry system in the condo will allow us to remotely perform any number of tests in case you develop a medical problem while you're there. Of course, we have video cameras, so we'll be able to see you, and the condo will be stocked with a complete inventory of pharmaceuticals and medical supplies that should take care of most minor situations. We're also going to want you to take some special vitamins every day, to make sure you get all the nutrients you need. If anything serious comes up, we'll extract you from the condo by helicopter."

"How does the remote monitoring system work?"

"It's pretty simple. You'll hook youself up with sensors that will relay biometric data on everything from your body's temperature and blood pressure to your heart rate. We can even do a remote EKG."

"Kind of like that old TV show, *Emergency*, where the paramedics would send patient information right to the hospital?"

"Yeah, kind of like that, although we've made lots of progress since then. We can even do blood work and urinalysis. If you come down with something, we can more than likely treat you with the drugs we have on site. Of course, it's unlikely you'll catch anything because you'll be there alone.

"Today, we want to gather data that will show us your stats in a normal environment so we can recognize any abnormalities in the future. We have your army medical packet, which has longer-term data, but this exam will be much more thorough. It also will reflect your recent surgeries for the mortar and gunshot wounds."

"I see."

As the comely nurse drew several vials of blood, the army doctor checked my wounds.

"You're healing nicely," the doc said. "How much residual pain do you have?"

"The shoulder's pretty much healed; I have some numbness but not much pain. The leg still hurts a bit. They gave me Vicodin, but I try not to take it unless the pain gets bad because it makes me nauseous sometimes. A couple of ibuprofen seems to knock it down."

"I understand. We'll have everything you need for that. But I worry that you're going to have a little stiffness in both the shoulder and the leg if you don't continue to move around and work out a bit. There's also the danger of blood clots if you don't move your legs enough. So, we have a stationary bicycle and a treadmill on site, and you need to use both daily. You'll also have a small set of weights, which will help with the shoulder strength. And I want you to take a baby aspirin daily as added protection against blood clots."

"Yeah, they told me I have to do my part to recharge the batteries."

"Well, you've been through a lot and this is a stressful assignment, so I want you to take care of your batteries, too. I want you to get out of the condo when you can and move around a bit.

"No problem, doc."

"You and I will go over the telemetry equipment before you leave. There are also DVDs that will explain everything in case you need a refresher."

Then I saw an ophthalmologist from Johns Hopkins, Frank O'Donnell, MD, who confirmed what the sniper school had already determined: my vision was 20-10 in both eyes, and I had exceptional peripheral vision.

A radiologist ran a cat scan and MRI, and then I returned to the exam room and was reunited with Dr. Sallee and Nurse Winter. The army nurse left with a tray of samples, leaving me to my final duty: peeing in a cup.

"Is there any chance you could send along a nurse, Nurse Winter, maybe, to keep track of me?"

"Sarge," Sallee responded, "I think that would be way too long a first date."

****

I was poring over the manual for the weapons system in the cafeteria when Major Shay spotted me. He pulled out a chair and sat backwards facing me.

"Is your head spinning yet?" Shay asked.

"A little," I told him. "It's like cramming for finals."

"Yeah, but this test has much higher consequences if you flunk."

"Now you sound like an instructor at the sniper school at Fort Benning."

"I was going to try to get this next part in earlier, but those doctors took all day. We still have a little time left; let's go check out your ride."

"My ride?" I asked as we got in Shay's golf cart for the short ride back to the condo.

Patting the dash of the golf cart, I said, "I can't say much for your ride."

"Well, it's sure not a Corvette, but it beats walking around this place."

Shay pulled up on the outside edge of the condo in an area that would face the outer cliff of the pile looking out into the desert, and I saw an opening in the outer wall that hadn't been there before. We rode the cherry picker up to the top of the loading dock. I was a bit puzzled as Shay walked onto the storage area, and I followed him down into the space for the generator and propane tank.

"In the event you have to bug out and the rescue chopper still hasn't arrived, there's a compartment back here behind the propane tank. What do you think? It came back this morning; we had to send it out for some tweaks."

"Are you kidding me?"

Tightly stuffed inside the storage compartment, behind what looked like a rolled-up version of a giant erector set creation, was a Blackwater Light Strike Vehicle. The LSV was a souped-up dune buggy that was being tested by all branches of the military for special operators. An army captain sitting in the passenger's seat of the LSV introduced himself as Steve Klingel.

I squeezed through the tight space and sat in the driver's seat, checking out my ride while Captain Klingel began describing the buggy.

"She'll do one hundred flat out, and there won't be much out in the desert that will stay close."

"How big are those tires?"

"Forty-one inches. They were the biggest problem we had with making the buggy work with the escape system our engineers designed," Klingel explained. "But a ground vehicle was something the president insisted on, so we figured it out."

"How do I get this buggy down to the ground? From what you told me, the condo is almost fifty feet in the air."

"See that roll of carbon fiber?"

"What's that? A radio antennae or something?"

"Or something. That's how you get it down. Listen carefully. Once it's down, it's down. You have to throw this switch here on the wall. It will fire ten small explosive charges that will jettison the outer wall plate. You'll be looking out at a fifty-foot drop, straight down. Now, you have to trust me on this: it works. The LSV's tires are set very tightly in a pair of tire guides. You simply drive forward very slowly, and this carbon-fiber tracking will unroll in front of you. As the weight of the LSV pushes it ahead, the vehicle will slowly descend, and you'll drive right off at ground level. For every two feet you drive forward, it will descend a foot. It's a steep decline but perfectly safe. The transmission and braking system are automated to keep the LSV from pushing the track too quickly. So by the time you get it unrolled one hundred feet, you'll be on the ground."

"Wait a minute. You think I'm going to drive this thing off a fifty-foot cliff?"

"That's the deal, Sergeant Novak. And as long as you have a few spare minutes, let's give you a chance. We've done it plenty of times here, although the drop here is only fifteen feet. But once you understand how it works, the height over there won't phase you at all."

As I was trying hard to rattle off a good reason for deep-sixing a drive off a cliff, the captain explained that the LSV was armed to the teeth.

"It has a top-mounted, general-purpose machine gun. And there's even a surface-to-air Stinger missile bolted down in the back that you can use in the event of an air attack. We saw in your file that you've qualified on the Stinger. Plus, you can take whatever you can grab out of the armory here in the condo."

All this is incredible—like something out of science fiction.

"There's a locator beacon and radio, so if you have to didi, we'll be able to find you and get help there quickly. Just make sure no one shoots off this little box here." Klingel pointed to a black box with a small antenna bolted to the LSV's dash.

"Didi?"

"Sorry, I've been hanging out with some of the Vietnam vets here. *Didi* is Vietnamese for scram. Make sure you don't break this little transmitter, or we won't be able to find you in that big desert. It's GPS operated. You simply press this button, and it will direct you to a prearranged rendezvous site. If you can't make your way to the primary site, press choice two for the alternate. We'll be tracking you, so we'll know which site you choose."

"So I just didi right off the side of a cliff?"

"It's pretty simple actually. If you take and do what I tell you, you won't have any problems. Hopefully, you never have to use it, and today's ride will be your first and last. Think of it as a day at Six Flags."

"OK. Let's do it, I guess." Snapping the NASCAR-style safety belt, I asked, "Does this have an ejection seat?"

"Now you're thinking like an ATEC engineer. Hit *START*.

The engine quickly rumbled to life, and I put my left hand at the ten o'clock position on the steering wheel, stepped on the brake, and eased the shifter into *DESCEND*.

"Now get your hand off the wheel," Klingel instructed. "Take your foot off the brake, and let the buggy do the work."

I slowly removed my foot, and the buggy eased forward. There was no lurch, just a gentle start, as the huge tires bit into the carbon-fiber grate, and the buggy moved slowly toward the opening in the wall. But even moving so slowly, it somehow seemed like the buggy was moving too fast. As my right leg involuntarily attempted to hit the brake, Klingel's left hand shot out and grabbed it.

"Sorry about that, Sarge," Klingel said. "Everyone's brain has this thing about not wanting to go off a cliff, and yours is no exception. But remember, I won't be there the next time. Just remember to keep your foot off the brake."

"Yeah, I'll try."

The buggy moved forward smoothly. The giant erector-set-like contraption snapped into a straight plane below us as the coiled circle moved in front of the buggy, getting smaller as I drove. Then the buggy took a steep downward direction, away from the top of the pile.

"Great," Klingel exclaimed. "Now we're almost to the end. Put your hand on the shifter and when you hit the floor, shift into *DRIVE* and floor it."

As I followed his instructions, I heard the end of the track flex upward and scrape the back of the buggy as it sprung back up. Klingel explained that the reason for flooring it at the end was that once the tires exited the track, explosives charges would disintegrate it a few seconds later.

"Perfect," Klingel said, removing a small video camera that he had attached to the roll bar behind the seats.

"You gonna put that on your Facebook page?"

"That would easily get me life in Leavenworth," Klingel said. "No, this video will be on your CondoTube page."

Everybody in the army thinks he's a comedian.

"All your training here has been videotaped, and you can watch it again when you're in your real condo if you forget how to do something."

"You guys are pretty sneaky."

"That's what they tell us, Sergeant Novak. Now, if you can be as sneaky for the next few months, all this expense and preparation will be well worth it—and you'll live to tell the story to your grandchildren."

Chapter 6

Syro-Iraqi Frontier

September 28, 2008

The dilapidated shack was a far cry from the metropolitan home in Damascus where twenty-eight-year-old Adad Haneef lived with his parents. Haneef sat on a makeshift chair, reviewing the instructions he had received the previous evening. As he replayed the directives in his mind, his right hand went to his jacket pocket, and he grasped the new Apple iPhone that the courier had delivered to him. Haneef had read much in the last year about this new, remarkable device—the brainchild of the son of a Syrian immigrant — and he was curious about its capabilities.

Haneef had been educated at the École Nationale de l'Aviation Civile, the national school of aviation in Toulouse, France, one of the top aeronautical engineering programs in Europe. An instrument-rated pilot, Haneef frequently flew his father's personal Cessna 340. But despite his love of planes, Haneef had turned down his dream job with Airbus after his studies to return to Syria to join the revolution.

Born to the privileged, mercantile class of Muslim parentage, Haneef chafed at his country's system of political royalty. Although his parents were well respected in the palace of President-for-Life Dr. Bashir al Assad, Syria's ophthalmologist-turned-dictator, Haneef would never have the chance to lead his people. The young revolutionary cursed the mistake of birth that prevented him from pursuing a path that he considered himself born to follow.

Haneef secretly admired the U.S. system of democracy, which allowed anyone to become the country's leader regardless of family background. If the polls were correct, the upcoming U.S. presidential election would certainly prove that. But democracy would not be so necessary, he thought, if the right man were in charge — and he considered himself that man. Haneef planned to use the fame of his impending attack against the infidels to overthrow the good doctor when the inevitable caliphate revolution occurred and gain power for himself.

Haneef toyed with the iPhone, tempted to unleash its power. But he didn't dare turn on the device. And even if there weren't drones circling, on the alert for stray signals, there wasn't a cell tower within fifty miles of the encampment where he and his comrades worked day and night, awaiting their orders.

Tomorrow, I will obey my instructions by driving to the designated location to activate this device and receive our orders. Once I succeed, President Assad can go back to making the country safe from cataracts and glaucoma, leaving the vision of Syria's rightful place in the world to those with true vision.

****

Early the next morning, Haneef left the encampment and got behind the wheel of a dusty Chevy Aveo that had been liberated from a Jordanian hospital parking lot a month earlier. He drove nervously, aware that the iPhone he carried had a sophisticated GPS system that the CIA or the Israeli Mossad could use to track his location and unleash drones or the special operations forces that lurked throughout the Middle East. Although he knew such tracking was impossible while the iPhone was in its current off mode, he had lost too many comrades to smart bombs to take even the possession of an iPhone lightly.

After about thirty minutes, Haneef neared the small outpost village of At Tanf. When he saw a cellular tower, he stopped the car and in fast succession hit the phone's power button, selected the settings control, and switched on the signal. After hearing the iPhone's chime signaling that an email had been received, Haneef disabled the transmitter, powered off the device, and drove back toward the base.

As he drove, he checked for signal bars on the burner phone he always carried with him. Seeing none, Haneef pulled into an ancient cemetery, turned off the car's engine, and walked into a cavernous mausoleum that would provide additional shielding from cell signals. Sitting in front of the vault containing the bones of a long-forgotten saint, he cautiously pressed the power button on the iPhone. No cell service. It was safe to read his mail.

Having memorized the contents of the email message, Haneef found a crack in the rock wall, high above the crypt. He reset the phone to its factory settings to forever remove the message, cleaned it thoroughly with an alcohol wipe to remove any DNA, and shoved it into the crack as far as it would go. To ensure that the phone would not be discovered, he pounded a small wedge-shaped rock into the crack. Haneef's instructions had been to destroy the device. But one day, during his campaign for the presidency of Syria that would be assured by the success of this mission, he hoped to convince an enterprising broadcast journalist to return with him to this spot so he could reveal this artifact of his personal jihad against the infidels. It would make great television.

****

The next morning, after a fitful, sleepless night in his small cot at the shack and aided by two helpers, Haneef pushed his latest custom-designed, remote-controlled aircraft to the opening of the storage building behind the shack.

"Let's be quick," Haneef told them. "We want to get the drone up, do our tests, and get it back inside before it can be picked up by radar or satellite."

Haneef had become interested in ultralight aircraft when he read a news report about how Mexican drug cartels were using the motorized hang gliders to ferry marijuana across the U.S. border. The skeleton-like frames of these small crafts were hard to pick up on radar, especially during flights above heavily trafficked highways. As long as the Mexican aero-mules stayed above the high-tension power lines and didn't overload them, these lightweight planes worked.

In designing his own plane, Haneef had calculated that he could make the craft about three-quarters the size of a commercial ultralight and eliminate the need for a pilot by using easily available remote-piloting controls, making the plane even more impervious to radar detection. But Haneef had something much more deadly than smuggling drugs into America in mind.

The men pushed the aircraft to the end of a short field. Haneef pressed the start button on a remote control and listened as the engine coughed to life. Within a few seconds, the small but powerful engine was purring like a Toro lawn mower, and his two assistants were keeping the craft steady by holding down the struts connected to the wheels. Following Haneef's directions, the two were taking care with the struts, which were connected to a trigger latch that would release the landing gear as soon as the craft left the ground.

Haneef had designed the craft to be as stealthy as possible, and wheels hanging down would reflect too much radar energy. Anyway, the craft would not be making a return landing.

The small plane rolled away, reached its takeoff speed, and rotated into the sky. Haneef allowed the plane to ascend to about seventy-five feet before turning it back toward the field. As the plane came directly overhead, Haneef activated the strut control and the wheels fell to the ground.

Haneef ran the plane through several other tests, including a test of the video camera housed in the nose, and then brought the craft in for a soft-belly landing. The men retrieved the struts and wheels, reattached them to the fuselage, and towed the plane back to the shed.

His craft again safely hidden, Haneef headed for his car and drove toward the main highway and a cell signal. Taking his burner phone from his backpack, he dialed air traffic control in Damascus, entered an extension, and asked, "Does the weather look stormy in the East?"

"I thought I saw a large flock of birds on the radar a while ago, nothing else."

On hearing the response, Haneef smiled and disconnected. He didn't have the exotic composite materials of the infidels, but now he was assured that his small, well-designed craft with its homemade radar-absorbing paint would not trigger any radar alarm bells. But such efforts to thwart alarms were really just overkill. The ultralight could take off in less than 200 feet, on any straight, paved road near a target. At its cruising speed of sixty miles per hour, its target would be history before air defenses could be summoned.

Now, Haneef's big task was to assemble the required number of aircraft and get them near the designated targets. Although the design was sophisticated, the craft could be made from off-the-shelf parts, readily available anywhere in the world. He would need only time and a warehouse facility to assemble the ultralights.

Haneef assumed the first target would be Israel. He could fly right over the border, no problem. The target information and the payload would arrive soon. Then the infidels would bow down and beg for peace, and he would be forever acclaimed as the Syrian hero of the Islamic revolution. Of that Haneef was certain.

Chapter 7

Westminster, Maryland

October 16. 2008

After grabbing my wallet and Oakley' Flak Pack, a smallish, heavily-padded backpack designed to protect laptops and other breakable electronic items, I followed Shay onto the giant freight elevator, and we walked to his civilian sedan parked outside the faux barn. Shay got into the driver's seat and motioned to me to get in.

"You mean there's not a big security detail following us?"

"We don't want to attract too much attention. I told them you were good people. And let's face it, you're the last guy who'd want to blab anything about this. It's your butt on the line."

"So, I can buy anything I want in Westminster?"

"Anything personal, you'll have to pay for. But as for foods, snacks, and things like that within reason, the president said we should make sure you'll be comfortable."

"I need to stop by my bank. I haven't had a chance to go to the bank in a couple of months. I can get a few bucks for today, and I need to move some cash into bonds. I've been meaning to get to it, but you know . . ."

"No problem. I'll drop you off there, and then we'll run by anywhere else you want to stop. I need to pick up a couple of things for myself as well."

Shay gave me his cell number in case we got separated and then asked, "You have your cell with you?"

"Yeah, but it doesn't have much charge left."

I was a bit embarrassed when I pulled a four-year-old Motorola flip phone from my shirt pocket.

"They won't let you take that with you, not that it matters. There's no cell service within a hundred miles."

"How will I get by without being able to text?" I asked, feigning desperation.

"Somehow, I think you'll have a way to get your messages through. And let's keep an eye on the clock, because we need to get back to The Farm by three o'clock. There are a few more things you need to be checked out on. I know I told you it would be a few more weeks before you deployed, but we received word yesterday that there's been a significant increase in chatter. We'll be shipping out sooner than we expected."

"How soon?"

"Could be any day now. We'll caravan over to Andrews and catch a transport with all our stuff, including what you buy today. We'll touch down in Kuwait, and then we'll chopper in with the first resupply, assuming the boys at the pile are ready.

"Okay. By the way, what's this 'we' business?"

"I'm going in with you. I'll spend the first day there with you to show you anything we missed during your training. I'll catch the last chopper out, after it brings in the water supply."

"I thought you said there was an oasis there."

"There is. You'll see. Concentrate on your shopping list right now. And I almost forgot to mention that the brass is throwing a little going-away dinner for you tonight at the house."

"The house?"

"The farm house near the barn. It's a real house, and the general actually lives there. So don't spoil your appetite by eating too much junk food today. I hear they're going to have a really great cook."

****

Shay dropped me off in front of a branch of my bank in Westminster, Maryland, a historic town the sign said had about sixteen thousand residents. On entering the branch office, I walked to the first teller window, pulled my identification out of my wallet, and told the teller I wanted to withdraw $9,500 from my checking account—an amount below the ten-thousand-dollar threshold that would require the bank to notify bank regulators and Homeland Security.

The teller called her supervisor, who double-checked my military photo ID, driver's license, and passport, and asked if I was the Sergeant Novak who had received the Medal of Honor. I said I was, and the supervisor, who said she'd seen me on CNN, shook my hand and thanked me for my service and sacrifice; and asked me to pose for a picture the teller took using her cell phone.

Of course, my having received the Medal of Honor didn't stop the supervisor from taking time to check my account balance, which was just north of eighty thousand dollars. Nothing beats having cash during a stock market meltdown. Satisfied, the supervisor authorized the withdrawal.

My bank business done, I asked the teller if I could use a telephone to call a taxi. I didn't know if the spooks at ATEC were monitoring my cell phone, but I wouldn't have put it past them. The teller offered to make the call for me, so I thanked her and walked toward the side entrance, where she said the cab would pull up and called Shay on his cell.

"It's taking a little longer than I expected. They need to confirm a few things with my branch in St. Louis. The teller says there's an optical store on Baltimore Avenue, and I want to pick up some new shades. How about meeting me there? I also want to get a haircut; I hear it's hard to get an appointment over in the desert."

Shay agreed to the meeting place, and I exited the side door, jumped into the waiting cab, and asked the driver to take me to the nearest AT&T store. The driver said there was one about a mile away. I pulled my backpack on to my lap and removed eight innocent looking screw-in rivets from the bottom. A shoemaker in Kabul had modified the backpack's canvas lining to allow access to the foam padding inside the bottom. The Afghan craftsman, who said he'd had a lot of experience making false-bottom luggage, had hollowed out the heavy padding, allowing me to secrete credit cards, cash, and other flat items from anyone looking for something of value. I put a thousand dollars in cash in my pants pocket and hid the rest, along with my passport, inside the foam.

A few minutes later, the cab arrived at the phone store, and I told the driver to wait. Fortunately, it was a slow time of the day, and a clerk approached me right away. I told her I wanted to buy an iPhone, and she took one from a display and started to explain the features.

But I was pressed for time, so I cut her off, provided the necessary information, and paid in cash for one year's service with unlimited data, including an overseas package. After checking the service, I threw away the box and charger, keeping the ear buds. You can never have too many ear buds. I turned off the power and concealed the device in the backpack's false bottom.

After a fast ride to the optical store, I paid the taxi driver, rushed into the store, and bought a pair of Ray-Ban˚ Wayfarers in what was probably record time. I was wearing the Wayfarers and checking myself out in a mirror when Shay walked in.

"Trying out for a role in a remake of the *Blues Brothers?*" Shay quipped.

"Always wanted a pair of these."

"Well, you look cool. But let's get a move on. After we get your stuff at Walmart, we can grab lunch before your haircut and then head back."

We drove to a nearby Walmart, where I put shaving cream, razor blades, toothpaste, and a month's worth of candy, cookies, and other snacks in my shopping cart. I picked up a cheap digital camera and several media cards, which Shay told me I'd have to pay for.

"Remember, you only need a month's worth of stuff. We'll bring in whatever you want on the monthly resupply. If you pick up much more, you'll have to sleep outside. Oh, and those media cards will have to be checked when you return from the mission. Scenic sunrises over the pile are fine, but pictures of the control panel will be confiscated and digitally exiled."

"Okay, but I want to make a stop in sporting goods."

I pushed the cart to the sporting goods department with Shay in tow and asked a white-haired clerk for twenty boxes of 30.06 ammunition.

"That's an awful lot of expensive ammo," the clerk said. "What the heck are you hunting?"

"Just breaking in a new gun, getting ready for deer season," I lied.

"You know, there's a limit of one deer," the clerk warned. "How many shots you figure that's gonna take?"

Beating me to a response, Shay answered, "The way this guy shoots, twenty boxes will be about right."

"You really should get some training with a gun before you go out hunting," the elderly clerk advised.

"I'll do that. Thanks very much."

I declined the clerk's offer of a hunting license, saying I had one. Of course, I didn't mention that my license had been issued by the president of the United States. I paid for the ammo with my American Express Platinum Card, wanting to conserve the cash, and we thanked the clerk for his speedy service and started moving toward the checkout at the front of the store.

"I'd think a guy with your dough would have the American Express Black card," Shay joked.

"Not much to buy in the mountains of Afghanistan, unless you want dope or a mule."

Or a great deal on a false-bottom backpack.

We were almost out of sporting goods, when I noticed a small portable folding chair and threw it in the cart. Then I picked up an inflatable air mattress and added it to the top of the pile.

"You planning a float trip on the oasis pool?"

"I want a back-up in case I can't sleep in that chair."

****

Shay refused to leave me alone in the barber shop, knowing the propensity of barbers to be inquisitive. He was right. The guy whose chair I'd sat in, Bruce, used every joke in the world to get me to tell him about myself, but I didn't bite. After I got the standard-issue short, military cut, I paid and tipped the comedian.

Next door, at a restaurant that was bustling with locals, we grabbed an empty table near the front window. Despite Shay's earlier warning about not spoiling dinner, I ordered two appetizers, crab dip, and a basket of wings while we perused the menu.

"I think I'm going for the crab cakes," I told Shay. "Where I'm going, there won't be much in the way of seafood unless there's fish in that pond."

"Well, if you want to be fully prepared, we need to run back to Walmart and get you a fishing pole."

"But then I'd need an Iraqi fishing license. I guess I'll just have to be happy with all that canned tuna we bought at Walmart.

The waitress took our orders, the crab cakes for me and the seared salmon for the lean major.

"I thought you'd get the ribeye, major. A guy who stays in shape like you do could easily get away with it."

"As I get older, it gets harder and harder. It's not like college anymore, when I could eat as much as I wanted and whatever I wanted."

"And drink . . ."

"And drink, of course."

Shoving the menus to the far side of the table, I said, "You know, major, ever since we met at the White House, I've felt like I've seen you somewhere before. Were you ever in Iraq or Afghanistan?"

"Nope. I think I mentioned that I went straight to DARPA's Fellowship Program right out of OCS. Then I was a project manager there for a few years, and I've been assigned to ATEC ever since. You weren't the only soldier who knew a general."

Shay had obviously done his homework on the strings I'd pulled to get into sniper school.

"I swear I've seen you somewhere. I thought that maybe you got that scar on your forehead over there."

Shay touched his forehead, feeling the long scar tissue. "This? No, it was combat all right, but not the kind you're talking about. You really don't remember, do you?"

"Remember what?"

"About nine years ago. The NCAA lacrosse quarterfinals? Duke vs. Yale?"

"Yeah, I remember the game, but . . ."

"I went to graduate school at MIT, but I went to undergrad at Yale. I played attacker for the lacrosse team. I was a senior that year. You'd have been what, a freshman? Thirty-seconds left, and I broke free; and then this brick wall wearing number 5 checked me into the next week. The butt of his stick knocked off my helmet and put a twenty-stitch gash in my forehead as a souvenir of the game."

"It was a clean hit, major."

"That's what they told me when I woke up. I didn't remember much about the plane ride back to New Haven. My head hurt so bad, the next week I got a B on an engineering test.

"I'm surprised you didn't kill yourself."

"Hey, I've seen your grades. Summa cum laude. Not so shabby. That was my last collegiate game. I've haven't touched a stick since."

"Well, we lost in the semi-finals anyway, and I never played in the finals. So *now* you tell me I'm going on a potential suicide mission, and my minder is the guy I knocked out of the biggest game of his life?"

"I promise, on my honor as an officer and a gentleman graduate of Yale, that you're in the best of hands. *Lux et veritas.*"

"Light and truth?"

"The Yale motto. I'm impressed with your Latin skills, Novak."

"The one benefit of attending the Barrington School for Boys and Girls growing up. They believed in Latin, starting in the fifth grade. Since my time there, they've probably let their hair down and now offer French and Spanish as well."

We were laughing when the waitress arrived with our appetizers. Pointing to the TV over the bar, she asked, "Did you fellows hear the news? Looks like the guy who's going to be our new president says he's going to start pulling U.S. troops out of Iraq, perhaps on day one."

After we'd placed our entree orders with the waitress, I told Shay, "Now, I guess we know why we're going in early."

****

Shay found a news/talk station on the car radio, and we listened to callers cheer and lambast the announcement all the way back to The Farm. Those who praised the decision said the U.S. should get out of Iraq faster to save American lives; callers in the opposite camp said an earlier U.S. exit showed disrespect for the Americans who had died there and signaled the terrorists that after keeping their heads down for a few months, they'd be able to move right back in.

Shay and I talked about the agreement by our current commander in chief to leave Iraq by the end of 2011, and how the brass thought al-Qaeda would be so diluted by then that they'd no longer be a factor. A flaming nation-builder, Shay argued that the Iraqi government just needed more time to take full control of the country and that after living so long under Saddam Hussein's oppression, the Iraqi people longed for a democratic government. Of course, Major Shay had never served in Iraq, as I had, and his view had been shaped mainly by his studies at Georgetown University, where he was pursuing a doctorate.

I tried to explain that once we pulled out, regardless of when, Iraq would devolve into a sectarian civil war. Having lived there a year, I considered it inevitable. But arguing with Shay was like trying to convince a child that a dime was worth more than a nickel even though the nickel was bigger. I gritted my teeth, reminding myself that I'd be done with the military in a few months.

Once we arrived at The Farm, we dropped off my shopping bags in my quarters, and Shay told me to head over to the mock pile. Still rattled by the announcement and clearly worried about how it might affect the mission beyond the decision to depart earlier, Shay was going to check in with the general.

Chapter 8

Karbala, Iraq

October 16, 2008

Second Lieutenant Maggie Taylor's body armor chafed her neck. Even though the sun had gone down, the heat was still oppressive. She'd seen enough of Iraq to last six lifetimes and was counting the days until she'd go home.

The attractive twenty-four-year-old archeology major and recent graduate of Tulane University's ROTC program had read the news about the possible early withdrawal on the *Drudge Report* before leaving her base early that morning. If the election went the way everyone was predicting, her tour might end earlier than she'd expected, which would be excellent.

When Taylor had told her tearful mother that she was headed for Iraq, she'd promised to return with a Persian carpet for the foyer of the family's Garden District home in uptown New Orleans. Before leaving Joint Security Station Hussayniyah, she'd mentioned the promise to her Iraqi interpreter, asking if he could recommend a store nearby.

Taylor was second in command of a token military police unit of eighteen MPs that had been left in Karbala to patrol the ancient Ukhaidir Fortress about fifty God-forsaken clicks away. Built in 775 AD, it was one of the country's archeological treasures. Having inspected her unit's presence at the fortress, Taylor was heading back to the base.

Her driver, Private First Class Glenn "Spanky" Stafford, a nineteen-year-old from Orlando, Florida, was seated next to the smarmy Iraqi interpreter they called Sammy. Sammy had been chattering in Arabic on his cell phone all day, and it was giving the lieutenant a headache. She wished they'd gone out without the loquacious Iraqi—or even better, that she was fluent in Arabic and didn't need an interpreter—but their orders required an interpreter to accompany them on all patrols.

The streets were quiet and the shops were closing for the night when Sammy pointed to a carpet shop at the end of what passed for a shopping district in Karbala. Grabbing at the steering wheel, Sammy instructed, "There, pull over. My cousin has the best carpets in Iraq. I told him you seek a nice carpet, and he promised to give you a very good price. Soon his store will have a website, and you can tell your rich American friends to buy carpets from him."

"Okay, Sammy, but it's gotta be quick," Taylor told him. "We're due back in twenty minutes, and I don't want them sending out the cavalry looking for us."

"What is this cavalry? A new American weapon?"

"No, it's kind of an old one. Let's get in and out fast, OK?"

"As you wish. You will see that my cousin has beautiful carpets and a great price for such a beautiful woman."

PFC Stafford, who'd been in Iraq for barely two months, nervously pulled up in front of the shop and instinctively reached for his M4 in the back of the Humvee. Sammy jumped out and opened the door for Taylor. The young officer saw a smiling man of about forty standing outside the store, smoking an unfiltered cigarette with a long ash. The man made a low bow and a sweeping motion with his arm, welcoming her to his store and then holding the door open.

As Taylor took in the vast array of carpets and artifacts, she heard a muffled shot outside. Whirling around to face the door, she saw PFC Stafford slumped over the wheel and Sammy running inside, a small-caliber automatic pistol in his hand. The shopkeeper's strong, cigarette-stained hand went quickly around her neck, and a 9-mm pistol was pressed firmly against her temple. As Taylor struggled to reach her sidearm, a veiled woman with hard, determined eyes jabbed a needle into her arm. A fog quickly enveloped Taylor's brain, and she crumbled atop a carpet she noticed would go perfectly with the drapes in her parents' foyer.

Chapter 9

The Farm

October 16, 2008

After spending the rest of the day learning more about the condo's systems, I took a quick shower and put on a clean uniform. When I exited my quarters at eighteen hundred hours sharp, Major Shay was outside in the golf cart, ready to drive me to the dinner at the general's house.

"Hop in," he said.

"You know, most guys join the army and learn to drive tanks. The Yale man drives a golf cart. It just seems right."

Shay laughed.

"I feel like I could spend another month learning about the condo. There's so much to digest."

"You'll do fine. You've pretty much got it down cold. And, remember, everything's on DVD in the condo, so you'll be able to fill in any gaps."

"OK, sounds good. You know, a general has never thrown a dinner party for me before."

"Don't get a swelled head, Novak. It's only a barbecue with a few guys you've worked with on the project. And Colonel Hunt caught a ride back, so you'll see him, too."

"Great. I didn't get much of a chance to talk to him before he left."

Shay drove the golf cart onto the freight elevator, the platform rose slowly to ground level, and we emerged from the barn as the sun was setting. Shay guided the cart along an asphalt path that snaked to the rear of the farm house about three hundred yards away. As we skirted the front

74

of the house, I noticed four black Chevy Suburbans parked up against the house and several Humvees crawling along the fence.

In the small area at the rear of the house, lit by about ten Tiki torches, several picnic tables covered by white tablecloths were overloaded with heaping trays of hors d'oeuvres. As we got out of the golf cart, an aroma that emanated from a large grill triggered a familiar olfactory memory.

"Smells like pork steaks."

"Pork steaks?"

"A St. Louis favorite. Pork butt sliced into steaks slathered with sweet barbecue sauce. I haven't had 'em for years, and never outside St. Louis."

"Like I told you, they brought in a special chef who really knows his stuff."

Colonel Hunt emerged from a group of about a dozen officers and technicians that was milling around casually, cocktails and meatballs on a toothpick in hand, and hurried to greet me.

"Good to see you again, Novak. I hear you've about got it down."

"Well, sir, it's a lot to learn; I wish we had more time here. I hope I won't let you down."

"No, no, son. You won't. Listen, before I leave tonight, I want to talk to you privately. But first, I want you to meet the chef we brought in for your big soiree."

As Hunt and I walked toward the grill and I marveled that a man like Colonel Hunt would use a word like soiree, I saw the back of a grey-haired man in a white dress shirt, apron strings tied behind him, turning meat on a charcoal grill. I was shocked when the president of the United States suddenly looked over his shoulder, meat turner in hand, and greeted me warmly.

"Well, it's our guest of honor. Good evening, Sergeant Novak."

"Mr. President, this is a surprise, sir."

"Let's say the medal you received a few weeks ago has certain privileges. Hope you like pork steaks, being from St. Louis. I had 'em when I stayed over at a friend's ranch near there one night during my first campaign eight years ago. I liked 'em so much I made the guy ambassador to Belgium. But they're a little on the fatty side, and the first lady is pretty strict about my diet. So sometimes when she's out of town, I have the White House mess whip up a few. This time, I had a good excuse to take matters in my own hands."

"I'm speechless, sir."

"Novak, I've got a little more grilling to do here, something I'm looking forward to doing more when I leave office in a few months. You go get yourself a drink and have a deviled egg and a beer, whatever you want. The dinner bell is gonna ring in a few minutes. After dinner, I want to talk to you privately for a few minutes, son."

"Yes, sir.

Dusk had stolen what little fall heat was in the air, and the group went inside to the dining room. The president led us through the buffet line and I followed, with Colonel Hunt and the general whose house had been commandeered by the top guy in the military food chain right behind.

After everyone had been to the buffet line twice, the president stood, struck his knife a couple of times against a water glass, and asked for quiet.

"Friends, I come here tonight to thank you for the herculean effort in completing this project. I'm truly amazed at the ingenuity you've displayed and your dedication in getting this project designed, built, and installed. Y'all know the importance of what we're doing and the importance of secrecy. Your efforts have given our country its best chance of putting an end to terrorism and restoring peace. I toast you all."

The group stood and clinked glasses against bottles of beer and even the president's Diet Coke. Then, raising both arms to still the cheers and applause, the president continued.

"Friends, I also want to toast the man who will take your efforts to Iraq and hopefully catch the people responsible for so much misery and suffering. I present the recipient of the Congressional Medal of Honor and our guest of honor, Sergeant Travis Novak."

The president grabbed my arm, lifting me out of my seat and sending an electric shock down my injured leg. I clinked the president's glass and raised my own to the men at the table.

"Thank you all for everything. I know I still have a lot to learn, so I hope I don't screw up too badly. I'll be counting on you all while I'm out there, and I know I can depend on you."

There were more cheers all around and a few shouts of "good hunting." The president thanked everyone for coming, and the stewards immediately began clearing the tables. No one had to wonder if the evening was over.

The president put his arm on my shoulder and asked me to walk with him to the general's library. One Secret Service agent held the door open while another whispered something into his lapel and closed the door behind us.

The president sat down on a sofa, setting a leather-bound portfolio on a small side table and then motioning me to sit beside him.

"Novak, here's my end of our deal. This is an executive order that I'll sign here in your presence. You'll receive a signed copy for your files. Please read it and see if you're in agreement."

The president handed me a sheet of heavy stationery on which *The White House* was embossed, and I silently read the order:

> Be it known by these presents that Sergeant Travis Sumter Novak, U.S. Army, who distinguished himself on the battlefield in defense of his country and for his exemplary service was awarded the Congressional Medal of Honor by this grateful nation, despite two combat injuries, has volunteered to embark on a critical yet dangerous mission on behalf of his country. Sergeant Novak's enlistment in the United States Army expires January 21, 2009, and I hereby order that Sergeant Novak shall be honorably discharged from the United States Army at 12:01 a.m. of the date of the expiry of his enlistment, local time at the place of his then-current assigned location. Sergeant Novak shall not be required to be discharged according to military regulation or custom unless convenient for him. Moreover, in recognition of his service and sacrifice in the conduct of a dangerous mission deemed above and beyond the call of duty, Sergeant Novak shall be relieved of all subsequent military obligations, both inactive and active reserve. Following his discharge, Sergeant Novak shall have his choice of any available military transportation to reach any destination of his choice. Further, Sergeant Novak shall be eligible for all benefits, pay, and other emoluments earned by him during the time of his service. This order shall become final unless reversed before the date of his discharge.

After a few minutes, the president asked, "How's that sound, Novak?"

"Sounds great, sir. Thank you very much."

"Now, you know my replacement will be coming in on January 20. It's sort of sport for one administration to reverse many of the presidential orders of its predecessor. So I'm going to tell them that the army asked you to undertake a special mission, and that you asked me for the favor of ensuring your ability to leave the army on time. Hopefully, they won't pursue it further—and we're only talking about a few hours given the time difference anyway. I doubt that the new administration will want to be seen as insulting a holder of the medal."

"Yes, sir."

"Let's hope this order is overlooked by the new administration long enough for you to do your job. If they get wind of the condo, they'll probably pull you out anyway, so I can't foresee that they'll mess this up for you."

"Yes, sir."

"More to the point of your mission, there's a bunch of chatter out there—both human and electronic intel. We're hearing voices on cell phones that we haven't heard for a long time. The bad guys know that barring an election miracle, the new president is going to pull our troops out, and they're getting emboldened. Kirkos, that NSA computer, is predicting a major terrorist event in the next few months. There's a new rash of car bombings and suicide bombers all over Iraq and the Middle East. The success of your mission can change all that. I've done all I can to make sure you're safe over there, but you know the risks."

"Yes, sir. I've been there before."

"I know, son, but the climate is different now that the bad guys know we're leaving. We knew an earlier pullout was their intention if they won, but nobody dreamed they'd start so soon. They're even calling the Pentagon, telling the secretary of defense what orders are going to be issued the minute the man's hand comes off the Bible, and not a single vote has been counted yet."

The president pulled out a small, silver replica of the Medal of Honor and handed it to me.

"Novak, I want you to wear this while you're over there. Put it on your dog tag chain."

The president turned the medal over in my hand, and I saw ten numbers engraved on the smooth surface.

"I'm not much of a code man, not like those guys at the NSA or the CIA, but I did this one myself. This is a phone number. The area code and the three-digit prefix are reversed. So the second group of three digits, 412, is actually the area code reversed. The first three digits are the prefix, also in reverse order. Then you simply reverse the last four digits. If you ever find yourself in a bad spot, call that phone number. A man will answer. Tell him who you are and what you need, and, hopefully, I'll be able to get help to you. After January 20, I'll still have some friends in high places. Understand, Novak?"

"Yes, sir. Let's hope I never need to use it."

"Right, Novak. Let's hope. Look, I've got to get back to the White House. The press hears I'm gone without telling anyone, and who knows what they'll make up. When you get back, I want you to come to the ranch for another barbecue, understand? When you get home, call that number and tell the man how we can contact you."

"After months of MREs and canned food, I'll think of little else. Thanks again for everything, Mr. President."

There was a sharp knock on the door, and a Secret Service agent carrying a phone entered. The president identified himself and listened for a few seconds. Then he said, "I'm leaving here now. Keep me posted."

As he returned the phone to the agent, he gave me a fast update.

"The bad guys snatched a female lieutenant, an MP, near Karbala. Got to get back to the White House. Good luck, sergeant."

We shook hands hurriedly, and the president exited through the rear patio doors. As he did, Colonel Hunt entered the room carrying a large box. We heard the roar of Marine One touching down and then taking off only minutes later.

"All right, Novak. It's crunch time. We head out in the morning."

"We?"

"You think I'm going to send you on a mission like this and risk my military career without seeing this place myself? I'm going in with you and Major Shay, and then I'll camp out in Kuwait for a while until I see everything's going smoothly. I've taken a leave from the sniper school, where the word is I'm having some surgery and taking time off to recover. I hope I have a job to go back to when this is over. So right now, you're the only member of my brigade."

"I understand, sir."

"Who knows how this is going to end? Maybe you'll sit out there in that condo and stare at that oasis for a few months, bored out of your skull, and then come home."

Handing the large box to me, Hunt said, "One more thing, Novak. I had the boys at Benning make a little something for you."

I set the box on the sofa and opened the lid to find a sniper's Ghille suit loaded with fake stones the same color as the rock pile in Iraq.

"Wow," I exclaimed as I removed the suit from the box for a closer look. "I'll blend right in with the rock pile wearing this camouflage suit."

"All the electronic crap we've installed in the condo is great, son, but who knows if it'll work as advertised when push comes to shove. That fancy video game gun gives you any trouble, you pull on this suit, grab that loose M-107, and rock and roll."

Chapter 10

Joint Base Andrews, Maryland

October 17, 2008

The sun was just coming up as our caravan halted at a remote tarmac at Andrews and parked beside the massive C-17 Globemaster. A wide metal ramp extended from the open tail section of the idling plane.

The truck that had transported our group's luggage and personal equipment, along with the equipment that the technicians would set up at the pile, backed to a spot near the C-17's cargo hold. At the direction of a loadmaster, a forklift began transferring the pallets, securely shrink-wrapped with opaque plastic to keep their contents secret from the crew. As the forklift released each pallet in turn, the loadmaster shoved the pallet down the rails in the floor and secured it in place.

All the personal items that I'd assembled for my stay at the pile were on one of the pallets. I carried only my backpack containing a shaving kit and some condo operating manuals that would help me pass the time on the nearly fourteen-hour flight.

Shay had told me that we'd be met by an ATEC truck and forklift on the tarmac in Kuwait.

"We'll land, and the truck will back up to the plane. When they tell us they're done unloading the gear, we'll exit the plane. Until then, we stay on board. Our guys already in Kuwait will be at the landing site to meet us. Got it?"

It was a pretty simple concept. I got it.

****

The C-17 was a versatile, flying warehouse that could be configured to carry just about anything, including troops. In addition to the ATEC technicians, a spare flight crew was on board to relieve the first group of pilots during the nonstop flight. The crew and the loadmaster, who would guide the offloading, had been instructed to maintain their distance from the passengers and to ask no questions.

The members of the ATEC contingent were dressed in civilian clothes to give the crew the impression that we were a team from the CIA. How ironic, I thought, that the team was disguising itself as CIA agents to reduce suspicion. I wore jeans and a polo shirt, the same clothes I expected I would launder at the condo and wear on my discharge, if I wasn't relieved before then.

Before our departure, I'd been issued a wardrobe of army camouflage uniforms and boots whose coloration would blend with the faux stone of the pile. An ATEC lawyer, Captain Chris Carenza, who didn't have to tell me he was from St. Louis, had briefed me on the importance of wearing this uniform at all times. I was surprised Carenza, who was a few years my senior, was an army lawyer. The last time I'd heard about him he had scored the winning goal in the NCAA soccer finals. But, he didn't want to talk about his athletic career, he was all business. After the U.S. pulled out of Iraq, he warned me, there was no telling what the government there would look like. If I were captured out of uniform, the Iraqi government could accuse me of espionage. I wondered exactly what else they could possibly think I was doing in a high-tech stone hut full of cameras and satellite uplinks. I knew if I were captured, I probably wouldn't be coming home.

There were many more seats than our group needed, so everyone spread out. I picked a seat, reclined it a bit, and reached instinctively for my laptop. But along with my other possessions, it was now in quarantine.

Major Shay was already sawing logs, so I pulled an operating manual for the condo's water supply system out of my backpack. I was reading about the purification system when the reality of my assignment hit me hard. Since the president had asked me to volunteer, I'd had little time to think about the mission and the long isolation in store for me. But as an army sniper, I'd disciplined myself to relax, wait, and endure both uncertainty and the unknown. Relaxation was like peeing; it was a good idea to do both whenever you got the chance. So now was a good time for me to settle back.

The cargo area was a little warmer than I'd have liked, and I could hear the hypnotic sound of air rushing over the aircraft's giant wings. The powerful jet engines droned, creating a soothing blanket of white noise. I closed my eyes and reflected on how I'd come to this point in my life.

****

After graduating from Duke with a bachelor's in finance, I'd worked as a junior analyst—code word for galley slave—in the investment banking department of my dad's brokerage firm. One of the firm's clients had been a retired three-star general whose firm was making an acquisition, and I was on the project team. The general had played lacrosse at West Point, and we hit it off. After the attack that killed my dad, I confided in him that I planned to enroll in the MBA program at the University of Chicago Graduate School of Business the next year and then enlist immediately after receiving my degree. I explained that I wanted to extract personal retribution for my father's death so those who were responsible would remember my name— just as I would forever remember theirs.

The general commiserated with my anguish but thought I'd change my mind about enlisting when I saw the opening offers for Chicago MBA grads. But my emails to him during my studies at Chicago convinced him of my sincerity. He tried to persuade me to attend OCS, but I told him I was determined to be a sniper — to see the enemy in my sights and personally pull the trigger. I asked him if he could pull some strings so I could enter the elite sniper school as soon as possible. I knew that, at my advanced age, I'd never get the chance unless I moved into the program very soon after basic training and AIT—which was pretty much unheard of.

Fortunately, my two degrees allowed me to enter the service as an E4, which would satisfy the major objection an ordinary enlistee would encounter. I'd been committed to being in top condition when I reported for duty, so the army would have no excuse to deny me my chance for revenge. Along with my daily training regimen, I'd spent time every weekend at a shooting range in the southern suburbs run by Vito Modica, a retired Marine sniper. By the end of the academic year, I understood all the mechanics and science of shooting, and my marksmanship with both the M4 carbine, the rifle I had to master to qualify, and the Barrett M107 was spot on.

A week after graduation—after turning down several offers from prestigious investment banks and hedge funds, and even an offer to work in Washington, D.C., at the Securities and Exchange Commission—I reported to Fort Leonard Wood, Missouri. My drill sergeants pretended they weren't impressed by my physical conditioning, but as a four-year NCAA Division I athlete, I was in a lot better condition than the average enlistee. I got the expected "college boy" taunts from the drill sergeants. But at the end of basic, my drill sergeant told me if my college had any more men like me, he'd love to have a whole platoon of them.

Within six months of finishing basic training, the general had pulled his strings, and I received orders to report to sniper school at Fort Benning. While soldier after soldier washed out of the program, I persevered, graduating near the top of my class. I was given a two-week leave and told to report for duty in Iraq, supporting a group of operators out of Fort Bragg.

We'd flown to Iraq on a chartered 757. The sight of hundreds of GIs carrying their rifles on board a commercial airliner would have given any would-be hijacker a coronary.

The heart attack that my father had suffered during that terrorist attack and that had immediately sucked all life from him was the reason I was on that flight. It was also the reason I was on this one.

****

I was deep in thought with my eyes closed, but I sensed someone move into the seat next to me. I opened my eyes to see Colonel Hunt, shook away the cobwebs, and listened to his whispered directions.

"Son, the condo is a very high-tech piece of equipment, and if someone in authority gives the order, it can be taken over remotely and locked down tight—or even blown up. You know how the military and the spooks can be. I told them you're a patriot, and that this was unnecessary, but I was overruled. Confiding in you like this, my neck's on the line. But I won't have one of my men, especially one wearing the Medal of Honor, treated like that without knowing the situation."

"Thank you, sir."

"Son, if I ever give you an order that's prefaced by my saying, 'I am your direct commander,' you know to get the hell out of there and get out quick. Understand?"

"Yes, sir. I appreciate you telling me. Thank you."

What else haven't they told me about this mission?

Chapter 11

Karbala, Iraq

October 18, 2008

Unconscious since her abduction from the carpet store the previous day, Lieutenant Maggie Taylor awoke groggily to see two eyes peering at her from behind a dingy burka. She slowly raised her hands to her pounding head, trying to get to her feet in the same movement. Both efforts were futile. Her headache was unrelenting, and her left ankle was chained securely to the wall.

Sitting up, Taylor saw the man Sammy had claimed was his uncle standing guard at the door of the small room, an AK-47 at the ready. A checkered scarf covered his nose and mouth, but she easily recognized his tobacco stained hands.

Unlocking the chain with a key she had taken from her pocket, her female captor pointed to a putrid bathroom whose door hung on a single hinge. "You move, now," she commanded in halting English.

As Taylor emerged from the bathroom, the female guard shoved her roughly back to the floor and reattached the chain on her ankle. Then, the woman turned, walked to a tray on the opposite side of the room, and placed it on the floor within Taylor's reach.

A bowl of cold, pasty rice, the heel of a stale loaf of bread, and a cup of lukewarm water occupied the small tray. Parched and ravenous, Taylor drank the water, scarfed down the bread, and tasted the putrid rice before spitting it on the floor.

The phony carpet merchant slapped the taste right out of her mouth. "Eat, whore," he shouted at Taylor. "Soon you will be on trial for your crimes. Your soldiers are leaving you. They cannot help you now. You will pay for your crimes against Islam. You will pay soon for your crimes against Iraq."

"I don't appreciate being called a whore," Taylor yelled back at him and spit in his face. The last thing Taylor saw as she lapsed back into unconsciousness was the butt of the AK-47 as he smashed it into the right side of her head.

****

Eight hours later, Taylor opened her left eye, which unlike the right was not swollen shut. Her head still throbbed mercilessly, and she smelled the damp concrete floor, which hadn't seen a broom since the Hammurabi administration. Across from where she lay, a sink with a single faucet dripped loudly, and she caught a musty odor emanating from the mold growing on the bare wood where a tile backsplash had once been. A bare, Al Gore-style curlicue bulb hanging from the ceiling, dead still in the breezeless room, provided the only light in the small, dark room.

Tugging on her leg, she found it still chained to the wall. As she rolled onto her side and struggled to sit up, she noticed that her vision seemed obscured and put one hand to her face. Her kidnappers had put a hijab on her head. She wondered if it was for religious reasons or to cover the contusion on her scalp.

Taylor's superiors had urged her to wear a hijab while on patrol, a respectful gesture that they said would facilitate better communications with the locals. But Taylor, a Missouri Synod Lutheran, decided that wearing a hijab would be blasphemous and chose instead to wear her helmet, much to the chagrin of the politically correct captain who ran her MP unit.

From her sitting position, she listened intently to the sounds outside the building. Voices emanated from the other side of the closed door, and traffic noises suggested that a busy road was nearby. She heard the call to prayer and concluded she must be near a mosque. But in Iraq, that didn't narrow it down much. Every few minutes, she heard a helicopter buzzing overhead and was heartened that a search for her was apparently underway.

87

No one who knew Taylor would describe her as cool under pressure. Nonetheless, she did her best to remember what she had learned in her escape and evasion training classes. But with her leg chained to a half-inch eyehook securely cemented into the masonry wall, she could do little else but hope for the best. Knowing that hope wasn't a great strategy, her eyes flooded with tears.

Reflecting on how she had gotten into this mess, she rebuked herself for stopping for the carpet. She had been only months from joining the parade south to Kuwait. Just a couple of months to go. But her foolish determination to find a carpet for her mother had cost her driver his life. How would she possibly explain to her superiors that the boy had died so she could shop for a rug? She could be bound over for court martial for such stupidity. But at that moment, she would have gladly traded an army stockade for her damp, filthy prison.

Taylor was sure that the terrorists would use her capture for a propaganda campaign, so her story—complete with video—was doubtlessly flooding the U.S. and international media. By now, her poor mother would have been told of her kidnapping and would be a wreck; her dad would be loading his guns and trying to buy a ticket to Baghdad. And her uncle would be unleashing all his clout as a congressman from Louisiana to get the Pentagon to pull out all stops to ensure her rescue and safe release.

She considered telling her captors that her uncle was an important man in Washington but then thought better of it. But with no weapon and no cavalry on the way, she would have to buy time to give the army a chance to find her by playing the cards as they were dealt and looking for an ace.

The knowledge that the army would never leave her behind reassured her. They always said that no one would ever be left behind. That was it, she thought. If the president announced that he wouldn't start the withdrawal from Iraq until she was released, the bad guys would give her up in a heartbeat. Yes, there was a simple solution. The president had probably already made the announcement and Pentagon officials were negotiating her release. One way or another, it was going to happen. She told herself she just needed to hold on as she passed out again.

Chapter 12

Ali Al Salem Air Base, Kuwait

October 18, 2008

We touched down in Kuwait and were directed to a remote hanger. The Globemaster taxied to the giant sliding hanger doors and did a one-eighty to position the rear cargo doors facing the hanger. Once the big engines were shut down, the crew's loadmaster opened the rear cargo hatch, and intense heat instantly engulfed the interior of the hold where we still sat.

Major Shay assembled our group, and we walked down the ramp and into the huge hanger that ATEC had commandeered. Several Chinook choppers were parked inside. I'd been inserted into the field by a Chinook on numerous occasions, so I knew these birds could lift something like twelve tons.

Shay led us into an office where we were greeted by several ATEC staff and offered cold drinks. Then Colonel Hunt and I followed Shay into a darkened room, secured behind a strong door with biometric locks. Live video feeds from the pile were being projected on a large screen, and two technicians stationed at a console were switching between various scenes and talking to other technicians in the condo.

"That's what you'll be looking at for the next few months, Novak," Shay said. "Everything you'll see there, we'll see on this screen. We'll know right away if there's a problem or you need help."

"How far in-country is this place?"

"As the buzzard flies, about two hundred sixty miles. In the Chinook, the condo is about two hours from here, depending on the winds; the

Blackhawks are a little faster. We have F15s in Saudi that can be there in minutes, but hopefully, that won't be necessary."

"Let's hope."

A full-bird colonel who looked like a former linebacker waved at us from across the room as he made his way toward us. Colonel Hunt stepped out and shook the man's hand.

"Dennis, good to see you again. This is our boy, Sergeant Travis Novak. Novak, this man will hold your life in his hands while you're in Iraq. Colonel Dennis Svoboda is the boss here at Condo Control. Dennis and I go back to ROTC at Texas A&M. You're in the best of hands—but don't get in any poker games with him."

"Novak, I'm proud to meet you. We're going to take good care of you and make sure you have everything you need to do your job."

"Thank you, sir."

"It looks like the last group of technicians will be finishing up by the end of the day," Svoboda said. "We're hoping to be able to get you fellows out to the condo early tomorrow morning, assuming they get done with their punch list."

Having figured on at least a couple of days to kill before heading out, I was shocked by this report.

"We'll give you a little tour here in Condo Control, and then you boys can get some chow. Novak, you're going to want to supervise the palletizing of your gear and supplies. Unless something goes wrong, we won't return to the condo for about a month, so make sure you have everything you need."

"Yes, sir."

Colonel Svoboda led the tour, showing us all the video feeds and telemetry. There were screens monitoring the temperature, winds, and humidity, along with camera angles. I knew that all this data would be fed into a computer to control the guns. Motion sensors would sound an alarm and switch on the cameras if an intruder came within a mile of the place. Well-hidden, sensitive shotgun microphones could be trained on conversations anywhere inside the pile.

Svoboda spent the most time talking in front of a screen dedicated to the battery capacity.

"This is one area we need you to watch closely. As you were told at The Farm, we want to run the generator only when it's needed to charge the battery systems. We'll try not to let it get below fifty percent. But if we get company in the pile, we'll have to depend on the solar and the small wind collectors; together, they might provide only about thirty percent of our requirements, depending on the sun and wind, of course."

"I understand, sir."

"First couple of days you're in the condo, we'll work you hard about watching the power meters. There's enough propane to run the generator a couple of times a day, which should be more than we need. But I don't want to risk ferrying out a new tank to the condo. It's a long flight carrying a heavy load, and once a month is about all we want to risk."

"Yes, sir. I understand."

****

We finished our tour of Condo Control and found our temporary bunks— not as nice as the digs at The Farm but adequate for one night. Shay and Hunt left to check on things, leaving me alone in the dorm-style cubicle.

I was eager to try out the iPhone I'd bought during my shopping trip in Maryland which I couldn't use in the underground facility at the Farm, and I pulled it out of my backpack. I knew I wouldn't be able to use it in the condo to make phone calls or send text messages, but it would be nice to be able to play games without the prying eyes of the Condo Control patrol.

The iPhone displayed one bar of cell service, so I logged onto the Apple App Store, opened an account with my American Express card, and ordered some programs—mostly games that didn't require Internet access—some utilities, and Google Earth. I was amazed at the phone's GPS system, which located me to within a few feet. I turned off the GPS system and powered it down, returned the phone to my backpack with the cash and my passport, and went out into the main hanger.

Our gear was being unwrapped from the pallets, and I watched as my possessions were transferred into smaller storage bins with inflatable rubber tires. I was told that supplies would come in on a large pallet and be lowered onto the loading zone. I'd have to wheel these carts into the condo, and then wheel the empties onto the pallet for evacuation.

Finding my Remington 30.06 rifle and the ammo I'd purchased, I decided I'd carry them with me on the copter. No sense taking the chance of it getting smashed en route.

Major Shay joined me and provided an update on the departure plans. The engineers at the pile would be done around nine in the morning, so we'd head out at 7 a.m.

Then Shay and I walked together to the mess hall, where Colonel Svoboda and Colonel Hunt waited for us for an early steak fry dinner. Hunt produced a cold case of Bud Light from the insulated duffel bag he'd smuggled in with him and swore us all to secrecy about the condo and the beer.

With a 7 a.m. departure the next day, after declining an invitation to play poker with Colonel Svoboda, we called it a night at 9 p.m. and retired to our bunks. But I spent a sleepless night, tossing and turning in my bunk, and thinking about all that had happened during the day.

This clearly isn't going to be the featherbed assignment I was hoping for to take me to the end of my enlistment.

Chapter 13

The Condo, Northwestern Iraq

October 19, 2008

There were six copters in our entourage: two Blackhawks and four Chinooks. We'd fly in on one of the Blackhawks, while the other flew shotgun. One of the Chinooks would remove the large propane tank, and one would bring the replacement tank shortly after our arrival. A third Chinook would bring in the pallet with my gear and supply bins. The last bird would bring in water for the pool. It seemed like overkill to me, but Shay said doing it all quickly would help avoid detection.

Our pilot radioed back that we'd be arriving a few minutes early; so I'd be able to watch the unloading process, which Shay said was pretty idiot-proof. Thanks a lot. We'd practiced the drops using a block and tackle many times back at The Farm, but a Chinook hovering above is a lot different from a chain hanging from the ceiling.

Before we left, Shay had made me empty my pockets and dump out my backpack. He said it was nothing personal, but they wanted to ensure that nothing gave away the condo's existence. I was slightly insulted by the search, but I'd prepared for it. The secret compartment in the backpack, where I'd hidden my iPhone and cash, worked perfectly.

They'd let me keep my wallet and the pair of jeans and polo shirt I was wearing. I'd given my keys to Colonel Hunt, who would take charge of my Subaru back at Benning. The rest of my things were in storage at The Farm.

I carried the backpack onto the chopper along with the Remington and wondered what my old friends on Wall Street would think of my carrying a canvas backpack to work instead of an expensive leather briefcase. We took off quickly, and I tried to close my eyes to grab a nap. But sleeping on a Blackhawk is pretty much impossible. The trip was uneventful. No RPGs, no AK-47s, nothing for our gunners to engage—just wind gusts and thermal bumps on our almost two-hour hump over the desert.

When the pilot radioed back that we were five minutes from the pile and cautioned that it would be a bit dusty on the descent, we buckled even tighter. He was a man of great understatement. He flew downwind, made a base leg turn, and came in from the south with the pile's elongated east and west sides abreast of the chopper. As he put the copter down inside the pile, sand blew in every direction, including inside the open cabin and behind my new Ray Bans.

Shay exited the chopper door, with me following him and Colonel Hunt behind me. The irregularly shaped sand and rock-strewn pile was bigger than I'd expected and more oval than rectangular. We walked a lap around the enclave, and Shay showed me the secret passage to the outside.

The three of us went back inside the pile and walked to the oasis pool. Shay pointed out where the water line was buried. Some desert oasis pools, he explained, received their water from underground streams and rivers. Others were simply collection points of limited rain runoff and condensation. He said the spooks had reviewed satellite imagery going back over thirty years, and the pool had always been here. But the water's source hadn't been determined. It was there, Shay said, and that was all that mattered.

****

I knew the condo was on the south end, but I couldn't see it from where we stood in the center of the floor of the pile. Then someone in limestone-colored fatigues waved from what I recognized as the loading zone; his fatigues blended with the stone so well that I'd never have spotted him if he hadn't waved. The condo, I knew, would be to the left of the loading zone. Just as it had been described to me, it was indistinguishable from the surrounding limestone.

The man threw down a sturdy chain-link ladder to us sixty-feet below and waved us up It was a long climb. As I stepped onto the loading zone, I saw that the storage cavity was wide open. Looking inside, I could see that the man had disconnected the generator's gas tubing that ran the gas into the generator.

"Hey, you must be Novak," he said. "I'm Trey Mudge, the utilities engineer. Great to meet you."

Glancing at my hunting rifle, he said, "Not sure they have deer season in Iraq, Novak?"

Another army comedian. Before I could respond, we heard the first Sikorsky hovering above, ready to lift out the propane tank. The cable the copter had lowered dangled a few feet above the storage area opening.

Mudge and I climbed into the storage hold, landing a few feet from my new dune buggy, which was behind a much larger erector-set track than I'd seen at The Farm. I noticed that the storage hold had somehow been chiseled out of solid rock and had steel I-beams supporting the roof, which was opened by an electric motor. The roof recessed into a track when the hold was opened, then slid back to fit tightly when closed. It looked like a large sunroof.

"Watch closely, Novak," Mudge said. "There are hooks on each corner of the steel base plate. When they lower the cable, you hook it on the chains coming from each corner of the steel pallet. Then radio up when you're set and help guide it up so it doesn't bang off the sides. You've got about five feet of clearance all around. When it's suspended, it'll swing, so you have to control it. It has to clear only a few feet up. Then make sure you stay down here until it's clear. It can still swing in the wind once it's out of the cavity and you don't wanna get smacked."

"Got it," I said.

Mudge radioed up for the cable, and the operator lowered it the last few feet. After showing me how to attach the chains to the main line, he told me to radio up to say we were ready. Although it all went smoothly, I was a bit nervous at the thought of doing it by myself the next time.

About five minutes after the Chinook disappeared, we heard the next copter. I climbed up and back onto the loading dock and saw it approaching, the replacement propane tank on the heavy steel pallet in tow. We reversed the process, dropping the new unit into the same spot. I unhooked the cables, and they were lifted out. Mudge watched as I reengaged the gas tubing; it was idiot-proof. The now-empty Chinook first circled, then set down on the floor and shut down its engines. Without missing a beat, the team of engineers began loading their gear for extraction.

95

The next Chinook carrying the supplies I'd need during my stay in the condo arrived a few minutes later. The big bird slowly lowered a large pallet loaded with a dozen storage bins of various sizes and configurations onto the flat surface of the loading zone. Mudge watched while I unchained the cargo, wheeled the bins to the side of the loading zone, and lashed the empty bins to the pallet. The inflatable rubber tires on the bins made the job of moving them quick and easy, and the wheel locks kept them in place.

The unloading and reloading had taken just five minutes after I'd detached the chain. It's so simple that even a Chicago MBA could do it. I radioed the copter to drop the cable, hooked it to the pallet, and watched as the empty bins disappeared into the sky.

"Hey, Novak," Shay yelled from the squatty door. "Come on in and take a look at your new crib."

****

Mudge and I stooped to enter the condo. The temperature inside was comfortable, probably about eighty degrees. At least I wouldn't be here to try out the Rube Goldberg cooling system during the one-hundred-plus degree summer days. Mudge showed me the small heater that would kick on during generator runs and said the insulation should keep the interior bearable, if not a bit nippy, on cold nights.

I walked over to the command console and looked out into the floor of the pile through the eighteen-inch high tinted window. Shay explained how to lower the armored faux-stone window shade to hide the view from anyone inside the pile.

I watched the activity inside the rock cavity from the window. Several technicians were loading their equipment onto the chopper, and a lone technician at the far end of the floor was setting up what looked like a target.

"We're going to let you get a few real shots with the fifties before we leave," Shay explained. "It's important for you to get the feel for real after practicing on the computer simulator at The Farm. We'll get everyone out of the line of fire in a few minutes and let you take a few pops."

Shay grabbed a small step ladder and climbed up to open the hatch in the ceiling that contained the fifty calibers as Mudge prepared to leave.

"Novak, everything here in the condo is all set. If anything goes wrong, you should be able to fix it with our remote guidance. There are tools and spares here for almost every contingency. If we run into something serious that isn't fixable, we'll have to drop someone in; but we want to avoid that at all costs. The thing you need to watch more than anything else is this power monitor."

Mudge pointed to an electronic screen mounted above the console. It looked like two old-time LED thermometers.

"Watch this like a hawk, Novak. This bar is your battery reserve; this other bar is your propane level. It's important for the power to stay at or above fifty percent, so conserve the best you can. Run the generator when you need to, but not more than twice a day unless it's absolutely necessary. Without power, this place is just a big pile of rocks."

I thought to myself, power or no power, this pile of rocks contains one of the world's most feared weapons: a U.S. Army sniper.

"I'll give it my undivided attention," I assured Mudge. "After all, what else will I have to watch?"

Mudge shook my hand, packed up some stray tools, and wished me luck as he stooped to exit and descend the ladder to the floor of the pile.

Shay, who had been talking to the men on the pile floor over the condo's wireless network, motioned me to the control chair.

"Okay, sniper. Let's try it out."

Sitting down in what was doubtlessly the fanciest leather chair any sniper had ever used while setting up a shot, I powered up the gun's Nintendo-like screen and zoomed in on the target.

The condo's system was much simpler than using a traditional sniper scope, which requires the spotter to make some complicated computations, called "doping the scope". A sniper's scope has a mil-dot reticle—commonly called a crosshair. We snipers use the mil-dots to adjust our aiming to account for factors such as spin drift and windage. This system had a simple crosshair. All I had to do was indicate where I wanted the bullet to hit, and the computer—fed by data from the pile's cameras, thermometers, anemometers, lasers, and the range finder—instantly did all the hard math.

Back at The Farm, Major Shay had told me that Dr. Frank O'Donnell, the ophthalmologist from Johns Hopkins who had examined me had adapted the guidance for the laser used to perform LASIK surgery to develop the condo's gun targeting system. He and his team had figured out how to keep the laser beam focused precisely where it needed to be, despite the eye's involuntary, saccadic movement. The condo's gun system could track even a running target with great precision. It was pretty slick.

The target I was practicing on was a three-foot-square white sheet with a black dot the size of a penny in the middle. I could zoom right into the small black dot. It was truly amazing. With this system, I could direct a bullet straight into a target's eye—and even perform my own eye surgery.

Shay radioed a warning to the technicians on the floor, and the men took up safe positions. I flipped up the safety and pulled the trigger on the joy stick. I'd have lots of free time in the condo to try to come up with a better word than *bull's-eye*.

Chapter 14

Malakand Road, Western Pakistan

October 19, 2008

The cab pulling a flatbed down the lonely road was decorated with the colorful lights, decals, and festive decorations that typically adorned Pakistani trucks. It was owned by a shell corporation whose traces disappeared in the Isle of Wright. The green "jingle" truck was old, not unlike the many other experienced, smoke-belching big rigs on the road. Close examination, however, would have revealed that the tires were new and the engine and drive train had been recently rebuilt.

Chained to the flatbed trailer was a large, steel shipping container. The bill of lading the driver carried identified the contents as generators bound for Mingora, northeast of Peshawar. But any official who stopped the driver and demanded to see the cargo would have been summarily executed by the al-Qaeda security detail that trailed behind in a chase car.

Not built for speed, the big diesel had been upgraded with an extra-capacity alternator and additional batteries to power the compact quarters inside the container, the mobile command center of Osama bin Laden. For almost three years, bin Laden had used the big rig to move around Pakistan clandestinely and with impunity.

No traffic was evident for miles as the driver downshifted at a designated landmark. The hydraulic brakes loudly expelled compressed air and brought the truck to a slow, rolling stop. The driver turned on the light in the cab and began consulting a map, a prearranged action designed to draw the eye of anyone who happened to be on the dark road to the driver,

99

away from the man in black who moved quickly from the side of the road to under the flatbed. A trap door opened in the floor of the trailer, and the man climbed inside the dark container, where he was immediately checked by bin Laden's security against a digital photograph, searched, and told to sit.

Asu al Hamwi, al-Qaeda's second-ranking man in Syria, had traveled for days, stopping at each designated waypoint to receive directions to the next and for the person meeting him to ensure that the high-ranking terrorist was not being followed. Expecting this to be another such stop in his journey to see the sheik, he shuddered when a large hand gently touched his shoulder.

"Peace be unto you, my brother. I am he whom you have travelled so far to see."

Feeling his heart almost beating almost out of his chest, al Hamwi responded, "Salam. Thank you, my sheik. It is a very great honor."

"Come, my brother. We have much to discuss and little time."

The two men moved cautiously in the dark container to a small seating area at the back. Al Hamwi hoped Allah would let him live long enough to tell his grandchildren of his meeting with the sheik, but he doubted they would believe him. Al Hamwi would have given anything for a camera so he could take a picture with the sheik, but that would never have been permitted. He carried no papers, no computer drives, nothing on his person that might reveal his message.

Al Hamwi began his briefing by telling the sheik about the stealth ultralights that Adad Haneef had designed.

"So you are saying these small craft cannot be seen by radar?" the bin Laden asked.

"Yes, my sheik. We have tested the craft several times using a man in air traffic control in Syria who has reported back to us. Only once did the radar detect a signature, and the traffic controllers thought the signal was triggered by a flock of birds."

"And the cargo capacity?"

"These craft usually hold an adult man, but a somewhat smaller design was required to make them invisible. Our tests show that we can safely carry ninety kilograms without stressing the craft. And the cargo will have to fit inside the specially shaped container that will keep it in stealth mode."

Al Hamwi recited the dimensions of the cargo hold, and bin Laden took copious notes on his laptop.

"How will you get the aircraft into America?"

"That is the best part, my sheik. We will build them there using materials and components that are obtained locally. Haneef will have to be smuggled into the country and a small facility secured for the assembly. Of course, the cargo will have to be brought across the border as well."

"That is not a problem. Their southern border is like a sieve. We can get anything and anyone we need into Texas or Arizona, even California, with almost 100 percent certainty."

"Yes, my sheik."

"Let us say we can get Haneef and the cargo into the country. How will these aircraft be transported to the target cities?"

"His design is ingenious, my sheik. Once the parts are fabricated and the radar-absorbing paint is applied, the parts literally snap together. They do not need to be built to withstand multiple takeoffs and landings, so we can cut a lot of corners. A disassembled craft can easily fit inside a small panel truck. There are plenty to choose from in America, and they can be delivered near the targets, then snapped together, loaded with the cargo, fueled, and wheeled onto any straight road for the short takeoff. Once airborne, they will be only minutes from the targets. Even the Americans do not have the capability to react that quickly."

"You have done good work, my brother. Go now and proceed with your planning and testing. Assume the cargo will conform to the maximum weight you have quoted. You will receive details about getting Haneef into America; we need to get him there as quickly as possible. We also will activate a sleeper cell in America, which will provide the facility and vehicles you require. There can be no leaks, you understand?"

"Yes, my sheik. The two men helping Haneef will be disposed of before we leave Syria."

"And Haneef?"

"Once the operation is over, he, too, will be eliminated, as you requested. We have planned for the Americans to discover his remains in the aircraft assembly facility. He is a very smart boy with no trail to us. But he has not been discreet in speaking of his personal plans. He thinks he will get all the credit for the attacks, and the Syrian people will rally around him when the revolution comes. He sees himself as his country's next president. But his overblown ambitions fit into our plan well; the Americans will see him as having personal motives for the attack."

"I assume our Syrian brother, president-for-life Dr. al Assad, would not approve of Haneef's ambitions. We will leverage that as well and perhaps extract a few Syrian pounds for our efforts. We will meet again soon for the final targeting and approval. The funds you require will be delivered to your account in the Cayman Islands. Use the money carefully, and do not draw suspicion. Your plan is a good one. It is important that we hit the dogs on their own land. Make it so, and go with Allah."

Once al Hamwi had been redeposited on the side of the road, Abu Ahemed al-Kuwaiti, who had been listening to the report, said to bin Laden, "It sounds like a good plan. But why would we want the Americans to believe this Haneef is the responsible one? Why not claim the credit for ourselves?"

"There will be credit paid to us, my brother, just not the type you describe. Abu, the Americans have seized all my assets. I must beg the prince for money to do everything these days. Sure, a few of the oil sheiks still help us, but with all the payoffs and the cost of ammunition and explosives going through the roof, and with my three wives, we are barely getting by. The prince has a fortune stashed in a vault somewhere, but he won't tell me where it is. He says with all the people who are searching for me, he is afraid they will water-board it out of me. So we sit here like beggars."

"The prince has me living in that slum in Abbottabad. 'It's worth a million dollars; be happy!' he says. How can I be happy? I am stuck there night and day with three families crammed in, always at each other's throats, with no Internet, no cable TV, no phone, no pool, nothing. I tell you Abu, I am afraid of that place. We are just blocks from the Pakistani military. The prince says, 'Don't worry; it's all handled.' I trust them about as far as I can throw a 500-pound bomb. But I have a plan."

Chapter 15

The Condo, Northwestern Iraq

October 20, 2008

After spending my first night in the reclined command chair bed, I awoke with a stiff neck on top of my usual aches and pains. It was more comfortable than a sleeping bag on the dirt, but not much. Orienting myself, I realized I was alone, two hundred fifty miles from the nearest friendly forces, and would be for a while.

Major Shay had left with the engineers just before a Chinook lugging a huge bladder of water like one that would be dropped on a forest fire arrived to fill the pool. These people sure thought of everything. As Shay's chopper lifted off, it hovered a few feet above the ground to blow the sand around, covering up their footprints in the sand. Shay gave me a large palm frond to drag behind me when I went down onto the floor, so my path to the ladder would be hidden. Not high-tech, but it would work.

After the group's departure, Control put me to work. The prop wash from the copters had deposited sand in some of the surveillance cameras installed around the pile. So I blew off the lenses using a can of compressed air. But it wasn't quite as easy as it sounds. The cameras that patrolled the exterior of the pile were on the outside ledge of the high, cliff-like walls, and reaching over to clean them took mustering more than a little courage.

Before turning in the previous night, I'd spent a few hours going over the night-vision systems via remote with Colonel Svoboda at Condo Control in Kuwait. Then, alone in the middle of the desert in a high-tech hide atop a pile of ancient rocks, I was suddenly exhausted. Figuring that the boys in Kuwait would wake me up if anything happened, I'd decided to turn in early.

I got up, stretched the soreness out of my back and leg, and checked in with Condo Control. Colonel Svoboda, who apparently never slept, told me all systems were performing at acceptable levels. He walked me through the protocol for checking for daytime visitors, and we did a quick check of all the cameras, motion detectors, and other monitors. Before signing off, we decided it was safe to run the generator. I flipped a switch on the console to fire it up, and it began humming in the storage hold outside the condo. The batteries had used about forty percent of their capacity during the night, according to the power meter. Now that the sun was coming up, the solar systems would kick in adding to my power reserve.

While the generator was running, I made myself three fresh eggs and four strips of bacon on the electric hotplate; a small exhaust fan took the smoke who knew where. Knowing that the fresh food would keep for only about a week, after which I'd be stuck with canned goods and MREs, I savored the eggs that much more. Some toast would have been nice, but a toaster would use too much power. So I satisfied myself with a couple of slices of white bread chased down by a cup of coffee that I made in a rechargeable, battery-powered, single-serve coffee maker, something I'd never seen.

I heard the water pump running and taking in water from the oasis pond. The system would filter and purify the water before pumping it into the elevated tank, which fed the faucets by gravity. I glanced at the power reserve monitor above the control panel as the indicator for the capacity meter moved up toward 100 percent. The entire system would be charged in ninety minutes. Then I plugged in my rechargeable equipment—including my laptop and army-issued iPhone communicator—so they wouldn't drain the condo battery packs once the generator powered down.

I took a fast shower, knowing the pumps would replenish the water I used, and dressed for the day before beginning what would become my daily routine. Glancing at the outside thermometer display, I saw that it already read seventy-seven. A red-blooded American, I'd already switched the selector option from Celsius to Fahrenheit. The weather monitor reported a chance of strong winds from the north but no rain. I decided to postpone my first trip outside until around noon, hoping the winds would hold off. The cooling system was struggling to keep the temperature under eighty with all the electronics running; I lowered the setting to try to get the temp as cool as possible while the generator was running.

After logging onto what they called Internet service, I downloaded my sanitized email and a few news sites. The whole country back home was apparently buzzing about the elections, and it seemed Americans were amazed about how fast the man they'd already anointed as their only hope said he'd move the U.S. out of Iraq. Although some speculated that he wouldn't withdraw immediately after his inauguration, it was an open question until he was sworn in.

I scanned a sports summary and took my time reading a news story about the female solider being held captive by AQ. Some Chicago television preacher had flown to Syria to try to persuade the government there to help secure her release. Insulted, the Syrians had told him that they maintained no contacts with AQ; so he left empty-handed—and no doubt angry that he wouldn't get the publicity he'd expected.

The hum of the generator stopped, and a small green light lit up on the console, indicating the generator had ended its cycle. The battery meter read 100 percent.

I unplugged my now-charged MacBook laptop from the system and opened my email, which I hadn't been able to check for weeks. There were a few emails from friends and high-school pals who'd seen the reports of the medal ceremony; some from members of my old unit, still in the hazard of the Afghanistan National Golf Club; and one from a University of Chicago professor in the business school. A message from BigEagleCIC popped up as I was reading the message from my former professor. I didn't recognize the sender's name, but I opened and read the message.

> Sergeant Novak:
>
> You may not be aware that the president isn't supposed to use email—something to do with record keeping. But I'm almost out of here, so I thought, "What the heck?" I had my daughter open an account for me so I could wish you luck.
>
> I greatly appreciate what you're doing for your country; you're a true hero, son. Our job is not done there, and it won't be until we catch the men responsible for all this killing. Right now, they're threatening to kill a young lady soldier unless we start pulling out even before my successor moves into the Oval Office and I release all their pals at Gitmo.

I hope your mission works out as that computer is predicting. If you need anything, don't hesitate to let me know. You can write to me at this email address. Please know I will do everything I can to keep you safe, son.

Sincerely,

CIC

****

About two hundred miles east, three days after her capture, Lieutenant Maggie Taylor would have killed for a Tylenol to quiet her throbbing head. Still in the small, squalid concrete room, still chained to the wall by her ankle, Taylor was weak from inactivity and losing weight due to the sparse, inedible meals her captors provided. She ached from the rifle butt she'd taken to the head, the beatings that had followed, and the repeated slaps she'd received for trying to remove the hijab they'd forced her to wear.

She longed for a bathtub or shower. When she was allowed to use the filthy, disgusting bathroom, she tried to wash herself; but with the chain on her leg, she could barely reach the sink without the chain being removed.

Taylor was still hopeful that the president would demand her release by threatening to abort the planned withdrawal. But she was so exhausted that she forgot that it wasn't the sitting president who'd promised to withdraw U.S. troops from Iraq. Her capture had obviously been well planned. That slime-ball interpreter, who'd accompanied her almost every time she'd left the base camp, had set the whole thing up. So how they'd accomplished her kidnapping was clear. But why had they grabbed her? What did these people expect to get from her?

Then she remembered. It wasn't information that they wanted; it was terror. They'd captured her because they could use a female soldier even more effectively than one of her male counterparts to terrorize America. As Taylor started to cry, the door to her prison suddenly slammed open and the woman, her feeder, entered the pitch-black room and switched on the dim light bulb. She carried a sturdy wooden chair, which she set against the wall facing the door.

"You sit," she commanded. But Taylor just lay there, staring at the woman through tear-stained eyes.

Again the woman screamed at her, "You sit!" Taylor remained motionless.

The woman left the room and returned a minute later with a heavy leather belt, which she used to lash savagely at the imprisoned soldier. Rolling away from the strikes, Taylor struggled to her feet, too weak to fight back, and the hijab flew from her head.

Taylor sat in the hard, straight-back chair, her head in her lap. Her female captor produced handcuffs and secured her arms to the back of the chair, leaving free only her right leg.

"You will be punished for not covering your head."

"But you knocked it off."

"You will see, whore."

Turning on her heels, the woman strode out of the room, leaving the door ajar. Taylor heard heavy steps approaching, and a tall man whom she had never seen before limped into the room followed by two younger thugs carrying AK-47s.

"So, whore. You have come to Iraq to kill Muslims?"

"I'm Second Lieutenant Maggie Taylor, United States Army . . ."

"Yes, yes, I know the rules of the Geneva Convention," he said in halting English with a British accent. "You will be sorry to hear that al-Qaeda in Iraq is not a signatory to that treaty."

Taylor's heart sank. She knew the Geneva Convention was not the only thing these savages didn't accept and the scale that measured her sanity tipped violently to the side of despair.

Chapter 16

Washington, D.C.

October 21, 2008

Congressman T. Wesley Dunn was fuming in his office in the Cannon House Office Building. Those terrorists had snatched his niece, the only daughter of his only sister. The Pentagon was stonewalling him, and his sister was calling him every ten minutes, demanding to know what he was doing about it. To make it worse, her husband, the still-rock-solid, former tight-end for the Tulane Green Wave, would arrive any minute to reinforce their disappointment in person. He'd never understood why his sister hadn't married an LSU man like any sensible Louisiana-born-and-bred woman. Well, at least his brother-in-law would be too worried about his daughter to repeat the wearisome story of how he'd made it to the last cut with the Saints and how, if he hadn't broken his ankle, he'd have made the NFL roster.

The army told him that Maggie had been snatched by al-Qaeda near an Iraqi tourist village she'd been guarding. Her driver had been executed on the spot, the clerks at the Pentagon had said, and the army was doing all it could to locate her. They'd told him everything—except when they were going to bring her home.

For years, Dunn had been on his sister's list over the scholarship he'd arranged so Maggie could get a four-year ride for her undergrad studies at Tulane. The ROTC deal he'd secured for her required army service after graduation, a detail he'd glossed over in discussions with both his sister and his niece. Since Maggie's capture, his sister had screamed at him in every conversation that her daughter should have been working on an archeological dig where she'd have been safe from being raped by savages.

Dunn screamed at an aide with a phone to her ear, sitting outside his office and holding for a colonel who was the army's liaison with Congress.

"What's the hold up? I want to talk to the secretary of defense right now. Do they know that I'm the fifth-ranking member on the House Subcommittee on Oversight and Investigations? I swear there's going to be an investigation into why they won't take my calls. You tell them if they don't respond with positive news in one hour, they're going to regret it."

Sometimes, Dunn regretted this whole congressional gig. His chances for another term were widely considered iffy, despite his being in a safe Democrat district. His big donors were unhappy that he'd been unable to deliver on an earmark for an overpriced sewer project in a strip mall development as part of the Katrina reconstruction. At least his party would be taking over the White House before long if the polls were right. Then, if his bid for another term was successful, he'd have more clout and these military clerks would take his calls.

Dunn was a natural-born salesman who could usually charm the chrome off a custom tailpipe. Some years back, he'd made a boat-load of dough selling the medical manufacturer's representative company that he owned, which had a contract with a small pharmaceutical firm. At the time, the drug company was delighted to have someone—anyone—out peddling its orphan drug, especially an independent contractor who worked on commission. But, then a Slovakian researcher discovered another use for the drug, and sales went up astronomically. Approached by a big pharma conglomerate that wanted to buy their small operation, the pharma firm tried its best to terminate Dunn's contract. Dunn sued both companies and settled for millions. He'd always said Louisiana had the best judges money could buy.

Now, with his niece a prisoner of al-Qaeda and his sister climbing all over his back, he regretted not having taken early retirement in New Orleans. Then, his greatest worry would have been whether he could get a good tee time. But he'd made the big mistake of deciding to jump into politics, and had become addicted to the power his office brought.

"One hour," he said to the aide. "One hour without a solid answer from the Pentagon, and I'm calling a press conference."

Chapter 17

The Condo, Northwestern Iraq

October 31, 2008

Twelve boring, solitary days had passed since my arrival at the condo—but it felt like a year. I'd read three novels, watched dozens of movies on my laptop, and run miles on the treadmill, but I was still bored to tears. It wasn't exactly solitary confinement, but it was close.

I sat outside the condo, on a smooth surface of the pile that functioned like a bench. The fake rock was so real looking that I still couldn't quite grasp that ATEC's mad scientists had fabricated it.

The day was sunny, and the daytime temperatures were now in the upper sixties. I knew from my earlier Iraqi tour that what they called the rainy season would come soon, but the desert didn't get much rain. There had been a few drops two days earlier but hardly enough to wash the dust off the rocks.

Back home, everyone would be donning Halloween costumes and knocking on neighbors' doors. Would I have any trick-or-treaters dressed up as terrorists? I was betting not—and even if I did, they sure weren't getting any of my limited supply of candy.

My mind traveled to other things happening at home. The World Series was over. Although I was a National League fan, I'd been rooting for the Tampa Rays to beat the Phillies. My dad had met one of their announcers, Dewayne Staats, on a flight once, and it turned out he was also from the St. Louis area. Dad and he hit it off, and Staats invited Dad and me to watch a Rays-Cardinals game from the broadcast booth when they played at Busch Stadium. That was one of the highlights of my youth. Now that football season was underway, I could get a few NFL games on Armed Forces Radio, but Rams games generally weren't aired because the team's record was about as potent as Saddam Hussein's army.

For me, being a short-timer in the army had been a lot like being a college senior. Just like when I was a senior and was looking past college, I'd given a lot of thought to the future and what I wanted to do when I finally left the army. Most of my contemporaries were already advancing, at least the ones who were still employed following the market melt-down. Several of the guys I worked with during my year as an analyst at AC Collins & Sons had already been promoted to vice president. Most of my schoolmates at The Barrington School for Boys and Girls who went to work for their fathers' companies had already been promoted to senior vice president. I was going to be starting late if I wanted to go into the investment banking business, so I'd lately been giving some thought to becoming an entrepreneur. I had the latitude of a financial cushion, so all I needed was a good idea. I had a good idea that I was sick of staring out into the desert as I was doing. But the bottom line was, I'd put in my time and just wanted out.

****

Looking out over the expanse of sand and rock, I saw the same thing I'd seen since arriving at the condo: nothing. I was wearing a shoulder holster with one of the 9-mm Sigs. I didn't think I'd need the pistol on such a glorious, solitary day in the desert, but the ATEC team had been clear that they wanted me armed when I left the condo.

Most people don't know that snipers are also experts with a sidearm. In fact, I'd finished first in my sniper school class with the sidearm. The other guys in my class said it wasn't fair, what with me being from St. Louis, where they thought everybody carried a gun. I convinced one of my more gullible buddies that everyone who crossed the bridge into St. Louis from Illinois was stopped for a gun check. If you didn't have a gun, they'd give you one, I told him. It was a little St. Louis humor.

Another broad misconception is that snipers function only as marksmen who kill the enemy from long distances. During my first assignment in Iraq, however, I spent most of my time gathering information, often behind enemy lines. We'd be clandestinely sent in before a major operation to scope out the situation before our guys were inserted. We sometimes spent days in a location, often hidden in plain sight, unable to move for hours. It took a lot of self-control, not to mention acting talent, to pretend to be a bush or a pile of leaves while the enemy went about its business nearby. So in comparison, with my current circumstances where I could call time out to eat and visit the bathroom, I had to admit that this was heaven.

****

Now only one-hundred-fifty miles from the condo, Lieutenant Maggie Taylor was shaken awake roughly by one of her captors. The hangover from the drugs the terrorists had injected before the move was worse than any she'd suffered at Tulane, which didn't win many football games but had never lost a party that anyone could remember.

She peered intently into the darkness, but she could tell only that the room she'd been moved to was smaller and colder than her original place of captivity. Taylor surmised that, given the temperature, she now must be farther north or perhaps somewhere in the mountains. She was glad to have the hijab, which at least kept some of her body heat from escaping.

Before Taylor could contemplate her new situation any more, the tall man with the limp and British accent who'd identified himself as an al-Qaeda official hobbled confidently through the door. During her earlier questionings, he had often struggled with her Louisiana intonations, which had effectively charmed so many Yankee men at Tulane. But this man was not charmed. Although he'd treated her with more respect than the rest of her captors, he'd slapped her on several occasions, telling her to speak English. What never failed to irk him, and trigger his slaps, was when Taylor said "y'all," which he understood to mean that she was going to yell.

"So, you are awake. You have been hiding information from me. That does not make me happy."

"I don't know what you're talking about."

"I am talking about your heathen uncle, the member of the infidel U.S. Congress. This T. Wesley Dunn has voted several times to attack innocent Muslims. I think the Americans will be willing to pay dearly to ensure that the niece of this important man does not lose her head, as she so justly deserves."

"My uncle won't deal with y'all, uh, I mean you people. He doesn't have anything to say about what happens to me. Only the president can make that decision."

"Well, since we do not have the president's niece, your powerful uncle will have to convince the president to give us what we want."

"What do you want?"

"An exchange for our comrades held in Cuba, of course."

"They will laugh at you."

"I don't think they are laughing. And we do not need to worry about this fool of a president for much longer. Americans are weak. They are afraid of war. They will elect a new man who seems to be more reasonable. Plus, he is a man who shares the same political party affiliation with your uncle."

"They won't do it."

"When they see you on videotape, explaining what we have planned for you, I think they will do what we ask."

"I'm not making any tape. I don't care what you do."

"I think a few days without food and water will change your mind."

Taylor wasn't going to subject her mother to seeing her on display, especially looking like this and especially without make-up. Leaping from the chair, she tried to slap him but was restrained by the chain. So she did the next best thing a Southern sorority girl could do to injure a man.

"You, sir, are not a gentleman."

"You will pardon me if I do not take seriously the opinion of a condemned whore. Perhaps you need another lesson in behavior."

As he left, he called for the female guard, who entered the room fondling the leather belt.

Chapter 18

The Condo, Northwestern Iraq

November 4, 2008

It was day sixteen in my exclusive, polylithic desert pad—not that I was counting. Back home, it was election day. I'd missed the chance to cast an absentee ballot. But, I was from St. Louis where I had no doubt someone else probably had already voted in my place. It didn't matter, the country was suffering from war fatigue, and any moron could predict the results, including AQ.

I'd started keeping a diary on my laptop, but every entry seemed to be the same: "Saw some rocks. It was windy. Generator worked. Had some crappy food." After a few days of that, I abandoned the journal.

I was beginning to think this was just another waste of taxpayer dollars, as well as my time. Most of the technology was off the shelf, but the sheer effort to prepare the site had to have cost a fortune. Guys with drill rigs going down a hundred feet had to blast away enough rock to fit the condo in place. Water and sewer lines had to be drilled, not to mention all the sensors, and it was all done in secret in only three months.

The condo itself probably hadn't been that difficult to build. It was basically an armor-plated mobile home that had been covered with a spray-on stone material. I'd finally succumbed to the temptation and used my knife to scrape away a little of the paint in a corner where I figured no one would notice. The stuff was about an eighth-inch thick, and the bare metal of the armor plate that had been spray-painted beige was visible underneath. They'd given me a five-gallon bucket of the stuff and a trowel in case the condo's exterior needed repairs.

Partly out of boredom and partly because it might somehow come in handy at some point, I had been getting to know the pile intimately, checking out all the nooks and crannies, and noticing which were in the shadows at various times of the day. I also had practiced with the automated gun sights for the dual M-107s, which I viewed as overkill. What kind of force did the engineers think I'd encounter here? Except for a few palm trees, cattails, and a couple of small boulders, there was no place for anyone to hide; and a target on the floor would be a sitting duck.

The speaker beeped, indicating that someone from Condo Control was calling me. It was also a heads-up that the camera would start broadcasting my image back to Kuwait. I really didn't like that camera just popping on with no notice.

"Novak, it's Skip Sallee, the doctor at The Farm."

"How are you, doc?"

"The question is, how are you?"

"If there are any pills for boredom hidden somewhere, tell me where they are and how many to take."

"No such luck, Novak. We need to do a quick physical if you have time."

"Time I've got."

The doctor asked me to zoom the camera out, so he could see me. The condo was chilly, but I stripped down to my boxers, the only clothes they'd given me that weren't the same color as the rocks on the pile.

At his direction, I attached some adhesive-backed sensors to my body at several locations for an EKG, which took just a few minutes. When he asked me to get the sphygmomanometer, I did a double take. Seeing my puzzled look, he explained that he was talking about the blood pressure cuff. I put the cuff on, and the doc said my pressure looked good.

Then I stuck a Bluetooth thermometer in my mouth and took my temperature. Normal. I pricked my finger and put several drops of blood on something that looked like a computer chip. Then I peed in a cup and dropped another sensor in it. Everything was relayed instantaneously to the doctor at The Farm. He said I looked good and that he'd get back to me with details on the test results.

I changed the camera so it would once again focus only on the area in front of the control panel. Although I'd spent considerable time looking for other cameras, I hadn't found any. These guys didn't strike me as the type who cared about my privacy, but they'd at least had the courtesy to build a wall in front of the toilet and shower.

I hit the exercise bike and then clocked three miles on the treadmill. My bad leg was throbbing, but I'd done my part to donate a few watts of power to the condo's battery reserve fund. Then I decided to tidy up the place before the generator kicked on and I could get my shower. Never knowing when company might pop in, I picked up some empty water bottles and a few dirty paper plates, and opened the trash chute to throw them away.

With no trash pickup in the desert, the guys at ATEC had been afraid that putting garbage in bags and then in the storage hold with the generator would stink after a while and attract the attention of anyone climbing around the pile. So while they were drilling holes in the ground for the drains and the makeshift heat pump, they bored a twelve-inch hole down about a hundred feet and capped it with a sealed steel cover that looked like one of those doors on a ship.

Once a month, I threw a heavy piece of concrete they had fabricated down the shaft to compact the garbage. Not terribly high tech, but it worked. With all the green-energy contraptions in the condo, I was surprised they hadn't installed a recycle chute. I wondered what they'd do when the hole filled up. But that would be somebody else's problem. I'd be long gone by then.

Chapter 19

The Condo, Northwestern Iraq

November 6, 2008

I was staring vapidly into the desert—the way I spent most of every day—contemplating the results of the election two days earlier and the deteriorating U.S. economy, which seemed headed into recession, maybe worse. The president, and the polls, had certainly been correct on the outcome. Well, it wasn't my problem; boredom was.

I was glad I'd brought my Remington 30.06 deer rifle on this deployment. It had been a while since I'd shot it, and having it with me brought back a lot of old memories. I decided it was time to zero-in the scope and have some fun. After my years of moving around, the scope—which I'd invested in during my leave between deployments—had to be seriously out of calibration. On a boredom-filled day some weeks earlier, I'd taken the rifle apart and given it a thorough cleaning using the kit in the condo's armory.

The Remington 700, which could take down a full-sized deer without a problem, was good in the hands of an average hunter out to three hundred, maybe four hundred yards—in my hands and with this scope, probably farther. Since it was only about two hundred yards from one end of the pile to the other, any unannounced visitor to the condo, man or deer, would be taking his life in his hands with my hunting rifle. And the .50-caliber sniper rifle I used on the job was five times as powerful.

Checking the rings on the Remington, I found them tight, and the scope height was good. I checked the scope from standing, kneeling, and

117

prone positions, and it felt right. I bore-sighted a spot on a soft piece of limestone about 100 yards away—I'd paced off the approximate distance during an early bout with boredom—and adjusted the scope.

When people see a sniper in a movie, they figure all he's got to do is put a target in the crosshairs and pull the trigger. But a sniper calibrates the scope for one distance, called zeroing in, and any shot farther than that distance requires fine-tuning.

I set the spot in the crosshairs and fired. It was off, left and a little high. I continued shooting and adjusting and by trial and error hit my limestone target dead on. No deer anywhere in Missouri would be safe when I got back home.

I ran my fingers up and down the Remington. A gunsmith at Fort Benning had told me I should refinish the wooden stock, but each scratch and mark brought back memories of hunting trips with my dad. I'd honed my shooting skills at sniper school, but my dad had given me my first lesson years before.

****

My dad grew up very poor in a small coal mining town in southern Illinois, about ninety minutes from St. Louis. I never met my dad's father, who died of a heart attack down in the mines when Dad was only nine, leaving my grandmother with two sons to raise alone, no savings, and only a monthly Social Security Survivors Benefits check. My grandmother died when I was two, so I have no memories of her. Dad's older brother, Uncle Jess, quit school at sixteen and, lying about his age, got a union job in the mines to help put bread on the table.

Dad was a good student—in fact, an excellent student. When he won a National Merit Scholarship at his small high school, his adviser suggested that he apply to Washington University in St. Louis, even then one of the top schools in the Midwest. The scholarship paid his tuition plus room and board, and Dad worked nights and weekends as a valet parking attendant at the nearby Chase Park Plaza Hotel to earn spending money.

He met my mother at a debutant ball. Mom was being presented to St. Louis society's born-wells at the Chase Park Plaza while Dad was being presented with the keys to their cars. Mom, who was attending Fontbonne College—back then a school for girls—just across the street from Washington University, recalled seeing Dad at a mixer they'd both attended. Just as she started to engage Dad in conversation, she was quickly shooed along by her father, who'd just learned that his daughter had not been voted queen of the ball. He rushed the family inside, intent on taking names.

My mom was the great, great, great granddaughter of a great, great, great patriarch of the Sumters, one of early St. Louis's most prominent families. Mom and Dad chose her maiden name for my middle name. Although the family had no connection to historic Fort Sumter of Civil War fame, they liked to claim a connection whenever they got the chance. The Novaks lacked the pedigree of Mom's clan, but I wouldn't change a thing about my family on Dad's side.

Great, great, great, great grandfather Sumter had made his fortune running arms from St. Louis for the Confederacy. He made another fortune after the war, when he and his son expanded the gun-running business into a barge concern that supplied rice from Arkansas to all the breweries in St. Louis and brought shoes and beer back down the Mississippi on return trips. The secret family lore said that back in those days, great, great, great, great, grandfather had supplied beer to many of the dry counties in Arkansas and Tennessee. Of course, that was never discussed in polite company.

There were still streets and buildings named after my ancestors. Unfortunately, after six generations, a depression, countless recessions, and too many dalliances to count, most of the family's wealth had been spent. My grandfather's trust paid for a comfortable life, but he still behaved as a wealthy scion, as he'd done his entire life. He felt ambition was beneath him. After all, being a Sumter, what more could a man aspire to be? In Fair Oaks, the exclusive village founded by the Sumters, breeding was more important that money.

My grandfather's two girls, my mother and my Aunt Mary, attended my alma mater, The Barrington School for Boys and Girls, just as grandfather and his father and grandfather had done before them. There wasn't enough free cash flow for the girls to attend Barnard College, as their mother had done, so they were sent off to Fontbonne, in hopes they would marry well.

Outraged when his youngest daughter decided to marry the heir to the estate of a deceased coal miner of Eastern European lineage, my grandfather did everything possible to end the relationship. He even went so far as trying to get dad's boss, Old Man Collins, to fire dad, but Mr. Collins refused saying he had shaken the boy's hand and a deal was a deal. But Mom persisted, and she and my dad were married the summer after he

119

graduated with a degree in finance. My grandfather was so angry that he refused to host the wedding reception at the venerable Fair Oaks Country Club—which was just as well, because his club dues were seriously in arrears.

Dad was hired right out of school at AC Collins & Sons, an old-line brokerage house with operations mainly in the Midwest. Dad worked as an analyst in the firm's investment banking department and attended the MBA program at Washington University at night.

Mom and Dad moved into a small starter home on the outskirts of Fair Oaks, which was a second scandal in my grandfather's opinion. Every Sumter going back to the late 1800s had lived within the city limits of Fair Oaks, leaving only to be buried because cemeteries weren't permitted within the municipal boundaries.

Dad was promoted after only a year, and two years later my parents learned I was on the way. It was a difficult pregnancy due to a previously undiagnosed clotting condition called Antiphospholipid Syndrome, and the doctors advised my Mom to watch her diet and to stay in bed as much as possible. The last month, she was confined to total bed rest, and Dad hired a day nurse to care for Mom. Two weeks before the due date, her doctors decided to take me by cesarean section and scheduled the surgery for the next day. But as Mom was packing her bag for her stay at Barnes-Jewish Hospital, she suffered a stroke and fell, striking her head on the floor. Dad rushed in and found her unconscious, called an ambulance, and an emergency C-section was performed at the hospital. The doctors delivered me alive, but Mom died on the table from the stroke.

Dad was heartbroken. The love of his life was gone, and a newborn baby had been thrust into his arms. My grandparents were also grief-stricken. My grandfather blamed my father, and I guess me, for the loss of his favorite daughter; my grandmother became prematurely frail almost instantly and died at fifty-two from what my grandfather always said was a broken heart; however, everyone knew the real medical issue was her liver.

Our relationship with the Sumters was almost nonexistent. They never gave me a birthday present or even sent a card. I guess the reminder that my birthday was the anniversary of the day their daughter had died was too much for them to bear. So I bore the middle name of a family dynasty that had pretty much exiled me at birth.

Maybe that's why the army picked me to be exiled out here: Maybe because I'm used to it.

Chapter 20

The White House

November 7, 2008

"They want me to do what?"

The president was fuming in the Oval Office. The election results and the crashing financial markets had already put him in a foul mood. Now this.

When he'd heard the milquetoast career diplomat's report, he'd kicked a waste basket about five feet in the air, narrowly missing a priceless 200-year-old artifact on loan from the Smithsonian. Two Secret Service agents had charged in, guns drawn, and he'd told them to stand down.

"These animals expect me to release all the terrorists at Gitmo in exchange for this young woman? They can't be serious."

The deputy assistant undersecretary of state who cowered on the sofa answered.

"Sir, we don't know if they're serious about all their demands. But if we don't give them something, they'll most assuredly execute Lieutenant Taylor."

"Where are you getting this information?"

"We've established a back channel with a cousin of the president of Syria."

"How much is that costing us?"

"The last accounting I saw, sir, was somewhere over two million dollars."

"And half of that is probably getting kicked back to the people holding our girl."

"He seems an honorable man, sir."

"Honorable. Yeah, that sounds about right. They know I won't do it, so they're going to run out the clock until the new man moves in and try to bilk us for money while they're at it."

"Quite possibly," said the career man from State, who was also looking forward to a change in administrations almost as much.

"That idiot congressman. What's his name? Dunn? He has to go on cable TV and blame me. Did he think we weren't moving heaven and earth to find his niece? If he'd have kept his trap shut, they might not have known she's related to him. He's made our negotiations that much harder."

"We think they'd have eventually figured it out," said the weasel from Foggy Bottom. "But yes, it might have been possible to do something else a little quicker. Now they think they're holding the key to the gates of Guantanamo."

"Well, I want that little girl out of there as much as anyone else, but that's one key they won't be getting from me."

"What are we doing about shaking the trees in Iraq?" the president asked, addressing the chairman of the Joint Chiefs.

"Most of our reliable sources have begun to disappear in anticipation of our withdrawal. Some have left the country, and others have gone into hiding; a few have been begging for asylum. They're afraid of being left hung out to dry on January 20."

"Gee, who'd have thought that would happen?" the president said sarcastically. "I want that girl back before I leave office. Authorize ten million dollars to any man, woman, child, goat-roper, or camel-driver who leads us to the girl."

The president looked at his chief of staff, journalist-turned-prosecutor Steve Higgins, who had the rep of being the president's personal BS detector. When the president had chosen a Midwestern U.S. Attorney to run the White House, the D.C. elites couldn't believe it. But when asked about his selection, the president had told one liberal reporter, "If Steve Higgins tells you it's raining silver dollars, the only thing you need to do is grab a bushel basket and get your butt outside as fast as you can." It was Higgins who had identified Novak as the perfect choice for the top-secret condo project, and had come up with the idea of the Medal of Honor.

"Any news from our friend in the condo?" the president asked.

"All quiet, sir. We keep hoping that maybe we can snatch someone important and use them as trade bait. But there's nothing yet."

"Well, let me know the second you hear anything."

The State Department civil servant asked for details about the condo, but the president changed the subject by abruptly kicking the waste basket again, signaling that the meeting was over.

Chapter 21

The Condo, Northwestern Iraq

December 20, 2008

Surrounded by what some days seemed like the world's largest sand trap, I regretted not bringing along my golf clubs so I could work on my sand game. My dad had learned to play golf in his twenties so he could go out on the links with his firm's clients, and he'd sometimes take me along. If you didn't learn the game as a child, he often said, you'd always play with a baseball bat swing like he had for the rest of your life. But he had worked hard at it and had become a ten handicap.

At a charity tournament once, Dad had won a raffle for a personal lesson from PGA touring pro Jay Delsing. A St. Louis kid, Jay had played his way from the public golf courses to the PGA. Eager for me to improve my game, Dad had insisted that I take his lesson. Playing eighteen holes with Jay cured me of any dreams that I might someday be a pro golfer. The man was quite simply on another planet.

I wondered if I could chip a sand wedge out of this trap and come close to a green on the other side of the pile. But if I was going to play golf out here, one of the fourteen tools in my golf bag would have to be a Barrett M-107.

A cool breeze was coming from the north, and the winds were picking up. The weather guys had predicted another wind storm later in the day. The weather in the desert was like everywhere else, with fronts moving in and out. The storms here merely lacked the rain, and the sand was always happy to fill in. At least after the storm, I'd be occupied inside for a while, cleaning off all the surveillance equipment and air filters.

I delayed going inside to batten down the hatches because I'd begun experiencing a little claustrophobia when I stayed inside the condo for more than about six hours. In a few months, the heat would make it impossible to sit and enjoy the view for more than five minutes. But, that would be my replacement's problem.

I'd heard from Major Shay that the man who'd replace me had started his training at The Farm. Shay said the ATEC folks wanted me to spend some time with my replacement on the video communicator as it got closer to his insertion date. With boredom really starting to get to me, even talking with my replacement sounded exciting. I felt like telling Control that nobody should spend more than a month in the condo if ATEC wanted the guy to remain sharp, but I knew they wouldn't care about my opinion.

I looked through my binoculars at some small, scattered piles of rocks off to the north, I tried to think where I'd hide if I'd been sent in as a sniper to take me out. The desert environment I was in now was a whole lot different from my first tour in Iraq, when The Dart and I were mainly on the upper levels of urban buildings. Unlike in the movies, where soldiers look for snipers sticking their guns out of windows, we'd set up about ten feet into a room. Our targets left their mortal planes, never knowing we were there.

Most of the rocks outside the pile were smaller and squat, the plants xerophilous and low-growing. From this elevation, I could see behind most of them. A professional like me dressed in a Ghille suit could lay on his belly in the open and never been seen. And here, an infiltrator would have to get by the motion sensors and cameras. It could be done by someone with army sniper training but probably not by amateur terrorists. I swept the ground again and was satisfied that I was alone.

Out of habit, I checked farther north where an abandoned road ran south into the desert. Built in the 1950s by an oil company that had done some unsuccessful wildcatting, the road was little more than an overgrown rock path now. It connected to a two-lane road that led to the nearest town, Ar Rutba, which, I was guessing, was about 150 clicks northwest. Ar Rutba was the crossroad of the main highways that led to Jordan and Syria.

Sitting there alone, I had an uncharacteristically strong desire to be around people again and fantasized about taking the dune buggy up to Ar

Rutba on Saturday night. Maybe hit a few bars. Take in a show. Pick up some souvenirs. Check out the local babes. At a hundred miles per hour, I could be up and back in a flash. But there'd be a big hole in the side of the condo with that big erector set hanging out. Not only would it probably blow my cover, but the brass wouldn't go for it, Congressional Medal of Honor or not.

Being out of range for a pizza delivery from Papa John's, I settled for going back inside and watching another light, airy romantic comedy, this one set somewhere in small-town civilization. As I watched, less than fully absorbed, I wondered what I'd do when I got out. Would my new life be light and airy? Would my problems be kids with bad report cards and lost little league games, or would I be eternally haunted by visions of the men I'd condemned through my scope as I dispatched them to the world beyond?

****

A little more than a two-hour's drive from the condo, just across the Syrian border, Adad Haneef was amazed at how quickly things had materialized. After a final, successful test flight of his stealth ultralight drone, which he had loaded with C4 and crashed into a remote Syrian military compound, his AQ-Syria superior told him to prepare a list of the tools and materials he'd need to assemble his stealthy aircraft in America.

Asu al Hamwi, the AQ-Syria man, hadn't given Haneef a chance to shoot off his big mouth and compromise the plan. After shooting Haneef's two assistants, al Hamwi had assigned an aide to fly to Paris with the self-proclaimed future president of Syria. There, they took a train to London and then flew to Mexico City, where another AQ operative met them.

The duo rented a small plane at an airport outside Mexico City and flew to Tijuana. The flight was rough, but it allowed them to skirt territory controlled by the drug cartels. At a hotel near what was left of the tourist part of town, they met up with a well-dressed Mexican man, who accepted a briefcase containing fifty thousand dollars in hundred-dollar bills.

Just before midnight, they got in a late-model Jeep Cherokee with California license plates and set out for the border. Looking at the fence that separated Mexico and the U.S., a nervous Haneef clutched the backpack containing his plans and expense money, and wondered how the taciturn man planned to get them to the other side.

The man stopped the Jeep at a dilapidated shack set a hundred yards or so from the border. As they got out of the Jeep, he heard a large generator grinding away nearby and saw a half dozen guards posted at various locations, all holding an automatic weapon. Wishing he, too, were armed, Haneef pressed his backpack more tightly to his chest.

Haneef and his handler went inside the facility and down into the basement, where they entered a long tunnel on whose sides were strung bare light bulbs as far as the eye could see. The tunnel was only about five feet high, so they had to bend forward as they moved. Haneef was uncomfortable in the confined space, which was filled with stale, moldy air, and stooping to walk made his claustrophobia even worse. He tried to stop a few times, but the Mexican kept shoving him forward, screaming at him in a strange language he didn't understand.

There is a phenomenon that says when confronted with a language you don't understand, you will reply with another foreign language you know. Haneef cursed the man loudly in French, but the Mexican apparently did not speak the international language of diplomacy and kept shoving him forward. Several times, Haneef became claustrophobic and the moldy smell filled him with nausea. When he suffered a panic attack, he struck his head on the wooden slats that served as the tunnel's ceiling. About fifteen minutes after they had entered the tunnel, they went up a ladder and stepped off into a warehouse constructed of corrugated sheet metal with opaque windows made of matching corrugated fiberglass. The moldy smell of the tunnel was replaced by the fragrant aroma of bales of marijuana that were stacked on pallets parked along one side of the building. More guards with automatic rifles watched them closely as Haneef gasped for fresh air.

A car whose make Haneef didn't recognize idled inside the warehouse, and Haneef and his AQ companion were quickly hooded without a word and shoved inside the vehicle as a large automatic door began to rise. They drove out of the warehouse and into the night, onto a two-lane, blacktop road. About ten minutes later, when they were nowhere near the warehouse, their hoods were removed and they were dropped off in a strip-mall parking lot, where another AQ operative was waiting.

This is the most powerful nation on Earth? Getting into America is child's play.

Of course, in his memoirs, Haneef would make this infiltration sound much more difficult and much more dangerous. No one would ever believe that gaining illegal entrance to the United States could be this easy.

Chapter 22

Lahore, Pakistan

December 22, 2008

The hotel suite had been rented two days earlier by a man posing as a visiting businessman from Lahore. After haggling over a discount, the man, who'd said that he'd need the room for three days, had paid the rental, along with a twenty-five-thousand-rupee deposit for incidentals, with cash. It was the slow season, and the clerk surreptitiously put the cash in his pocket after giving the bellboy a small gratuity to keep his mouth shut.

The man left through the front door, walked several blocks, and handed the room key to Abu Ahemed al Kuwaiti, who sat in the driver's seat of a white Suzuki SUV. Minutes later, key in hand, Osama bin Laden entered the hotel through a side door and made it to the suite without being seen. Exhausted after three days on the truck, bin Laden collapsed into a well-worn floral sofa that smelled of Turkish tobacco and was heavily stained with khat juice. He was looking forward to a good night's sleep after three days on the truck.

Although bin Laden wouldn't be able to venture out to a restaurant, at least this place had room service and the mini-bar was well stocked with Coke. He would spend the next few days resting before meeting with Asu al Hamwi, the Syrian AQ man.

It will be good to have a few days of peace and quiet away from the compound and all the wives and kids.

As expected, al Hamwi showed up for the meeting on the third day. Since his arrival in town the previous night, bin Laden's security team had

129

kept him under close surveillance. When the security force was satisfied that al Hamwi hadn't been followed, he was given a yellow windbreaker and told to leave the hotel and get on the back of a motorcycle parked in front.

As directed, al Hamwi walked out the door, directly to the motorcycle. After handing him a helmet with a dark visor and telling him to get on board quickly, the driver sped through the city, making quick turns and going the wrong way down several one-way streets. Suddenly, the cyclist zipped into a parking garage and sped up the ramp. On the fourth level, the bike stopped short, and a man standing near a van pulled al Hamwi off the bike and ripped off his yellow windbreaker and helmet.

The man, who was about the same size as al Hamwi, put on the windbreaker and helmet, got on the bike, which sped down the ramp, out the exit, and back onto the street. Al Hamwi was grabbed by a second man and thrown into the back of the van, which slowly exited the garage and headed to bin Laden's hotel.

Al Hamwi entered the hotel lobby and went up the stairs to the floor he'd been given. The portly man, his heart still pounding from the motorcycle ride, was out of breath when he reached the landing; there, AQ security grabbed and searched him. The zaftig man was then led up two more floors and into bin Laden's suite.

"Please sit, my brother."

"Thank you, my sheik."

"You are a good and godly man; peace be on you. Your work will help us immeasurably. I want you to tell Haneef to prepare three aircraft for the first mission. He will move them to locations I will provide later, all within driving range of each other, so he can operate the planes himself. We do not want to risk training anyone else and taking the chance of detection. The first two aircraft will carry heavy explosives. The third will carry a special cargo that must be handled carefully and that will not be given to him until the day of the strike. What is the report on Haneef's progress?"

"He arrived in California two nights ago and is being driven to the building we secured in Detroit. That is in Michigan, in the upper part of the country. We have found two tool makers, both devout, who were laid off from the auto factories. They will assist Haneef but will have no idea of our plan. Of course, they will be shot when they have finished their work. We will have no contact with Haneef until he arrives in Detroit with his security team in about two days' time."

"What about the equipment he required?"

"Everything was easily available, just as he said."

"Excellent, my brother. Excellent. These chemicals—the ones he needs for his magic paint—they will not sound alarm bells?"

"No, my sheik. They all have many innocent uses. We have men at universities who can order the material without raising suspicion. This paint is truly ingenious. It hardens fabric to form the wings and panels on the craft while it absorbs radar beams. If the energy can't bounce back, the radar doesn't recognize it."

"Excellent. And are you keeping him on a short leash?"

"Yes, my sheik. We will have several of our best operatives there twenty-four hours a day. He has no cell phone or computer, and he will not be allowed to leave for any reason."

"Good. I want him to be ready with the first three planes in early February. I cannot give you the dates or the target locations yet. We will meet again soon at the sacred sanctuary of our ancestors. At that meeting, you will receive the final instructions and my blessing."

"I understand, my sheik."

"Go now—and be careful. The infidels are trying their best to figure out what we are doing. They know something is coming, and they are questioning many of our associates. But the only one who knows is you, so they will learn nothing. They are also eager to see how things will change with their new leader, who will assume office in four weeks' time. They are in a bit of disarray. What super power allows itself to become so weak? I will never understand, but we will use this to our advantage. Now go with my blessing."

"Yes, my sheik."

A security man was called and led al Hamwi out of the suite and into a room down the hall, where he would be held until two hours after bin Laden's departure.

Once al Hamwi left the suite, bin Laden called two companions into the living area of the suite, where they sat around a small coffee table. An al Jazeera newsman was on the television screen, blathering about the new American president-elect.

"After the infidels install their more moderate leader," bin Laden told the men, "they will be lulled into assuming that relations with the Arab states will improve. But the man is weak and naive. I am almost expecting that he will send us subpoenas instead of drones. He will not have the stomach to come after us. In fact, I think it is highly possible that we can open negotiations and call off this whole thing. Wouldn't that be a coup? We could declare victory, get billions in American foreign aid, and all go back to our normal lives. Probably not possible, but it's a thought.

"We will give him a while and have a few Arab diplomats leak how good things are going to the press—perhaps tell them we are considering ending our jihad of terrorism. This should let their stock market get a taste of the era of good feeling that the infidels want so badly.

"The stock market will increase in value," bin Laden continued, "and we will place our short bets that the market will decline—on market indexes and a few selected companies—and we will buy future calls on gold and silver. We will use the new accounts in Switzerland; we can no longer use accounts in the United States because they have snooping computers that can pick up unusual trades.

"For stock cheats, they have all the weapons they need. For us, they plan to wage a war using diplomacy. When we hit them with our first aircraft, the media will stir up the fear of more impending attacks. The stock market will react but probably only slightly. We will not take our profits then. Once they are convinced that the first strike was a lone wolf, we will strike again. The markets will not like that one bit, but we will still hold onto our stock positions. We will wait until the special cargo is deployed, when you will see a market crash like no other since 9-11. Then we will transfer the funds out quickly and convert the paper into gold.

"I had a message from our fearless leader, the prince, today. He has agreed to join us at the sanctuary. We will work out the final targets for the attacks there. The man may be cheap and treat us like servants, but he is a financial genius. Soon, the economies of our enemies will crumble, and we will restore the caliphate. I've been trying out a few names. Abu, I know you favor 'the Islamic State,' but it just doesn't strike enough fear. We will keep thinking about it. Once the caliphate is established, who do you think the people will anoint as their leader? A faceless prince or the real face of the movement? Then we will see how he likes transferring all his wealth to the cause."

"Do you think it will be safe for us to travel to Iraq before the Americans start to withdraw? Remember, we will have to go back again a few weeks later so we can be there for the ritual five-day blessing." Abu asked.

"I think by then, they will have their attention looking the other way, to our brothers in Iran. As the Americans leave, the ayatollahs will start rattling their swords along the border. I don't think anyone will pay much attention to a few vehicles in the middle of the desert."

"I still don't like it," Abu said.

"We will be fine, my brother, and once we place our bets on the market crash caused by our strikes, we will have enough funds to take down our next target, those charlatan Saudi royals in my home country. When America loses access to that oil—well, I think we all know what that means. The fools have all the oil in the world, yet they won't drill for it. With the billions we will make, they won't be able to stop us. Now, tell me about this American woman soldier AQ in Iraq is holding. I might have a use for her."

Chapter 23

The Condo, Northwestern Iraq

December 22, 2008

I'd been ensconced in the condo sixty-five tedious days, and I started obsessing about the consumables I was living on, wondering when they'd run out. I watched the propane gauge closely. Without the generator, things could get pretty rough. But it looked like I'd have enough of the liquid gas to make it easily to the next resupply drop on January 3, perhaps even enough for a few extra days if the sun and wind cooperated. The output from the small wind turbines had been greater than the ATEC techs had expected, but the stormy weather meant the solar panels were yielding less. I needed a few sunny, windy days.

The resupply drop would rescue me from my state of desert privation in the food department as well. I started a list to send the guys at Condo Control, doing a mental check of what was on hand. I had plenty of cereal, soup and other canned fare, and of course, MREs, so I wouldn't starve. But my supply of fresh vegetables, bread, eggs, and bottled water was nearly gone, as were my cans of Coke. So I made a note on the list to up the order for my favorite cola.

I wondered if there was a McDonald's in Kuwait City. Regardless, pretty much out of the question. I considered what my chances would be if I asked them to get me a small Weber Kettle and a few bags of charcoal. After all, what's a condo overlooking the water without a barbecue on the deck? Like that would ever happen.

I had my shower, followed by my breakfast courtesy of Chez MRE. I checked the batteries, which had had their nourishment courtesy of Chef Generator. Everything was working properly. Another day in paradise.

I logged into my ersatz Internet and checked my brokerage accounts. I'd lived and died the market for years, but I hadn't paid much attention to it while I was deployed. I'd put my personal funds into very safe, boring bond funds before going into the army because I didn't want to worry about actively managing the funds while I was actively managing shooting people. That meant I'd been basically unscathed in the market upheaval over the past few months. But treasuries were paying a pittance now that interest rates had plummeted, so I used the condo-net to sell $300,000 in treasuries and buy some blue-chip stocks that had been hammered in the crash and paid predictable dividends. I still had about nine thousand dollars in cash sitting in my backpack, earning nothing, but somehow, I felt good having it—even though there wasn't so much as a hot dog stand within a hundred miles of the condo.

I was about to do some research on a few companies that might be takeover targets amidst the financial chaos when my email dinged. It was from Aunt Mary's son, my lurdane cousin Frederick, whom everyone at prep school had called Freddie.

All Sumter scions had first names that began with F for some historical family reason, and Freddie hated that he'd been stuck with that one. When my father named me Travis, you could hear the gasps from the Sumter side of the family; they'd all just assumed that I'd be named Fergus after one of my maternal ancestors.

It had been years since I had seen Freddie and here he was writing me when he'd been too busy to attend my father's funeral. Some excuse about being out of town and being unable to get back in time. I heard later that he'd been absent because he'd smashed a golf cart on the links at Fair Oaks Country Club after drunkenly sliding down a muddy hill on a cart-path-only day.

Dear Cuz,

Cuz? Frederick was the blue-blooded scion of the Sumter dynasty. His grandfather would turn over in his grave if he heard this product of Fair Oaks breeding and Barrington education use a word like cuz.

135

It's been a while since we've shared a brew and nosh.

Yeah, a while. The last time was probably at our high school graduation ten years ago. His dad had thrown a big wing-ding at Fair Oaks Country Club, and half the school was invited. Of course, I'd been in the other half.

I saw all the coverage of your medal thing. The Cat and I would have loved to have been there, but oh, well. . .

His younger brother's name was Felix, another family name, but everyone had called him The Cat—except, of course, my grandfather.

A few of us are getting together to work on the Barrington ten-year reunion. Go Bears! Can you believe it's been ten years already? It seems like just yesterday we were out there on the gridiron, tussling with those bad boys from John Burroughs and Country Day—me leading the way for you to get all the glory. Such is the role of the offensive lineman, but as Coach used to say, "There's no *I* in team."

There is, however, an *i* in idiot. It might seem like yesterday to someone who, unlike me, hadn't spent the last two and a half years lying in the freezing snow in Afghanistan or sweltering in the desert of Iraq, not to mention having to use a shovel to make a latrine, if there was even time to go. Yeah, time sure flies when you're taking a dump that freezes before it hits the ground.

And as a lineman, Freddie was indeed offensive. He rarely got in a game. Occasionally, if we ran the score up high enough, Coach would let him go in at left guard. His football nickname was Pancake because linemen from schools all over the St. Louis ABC League flattened him on almost every play. During our senior year in a game against Country Day, our first-string guard ripped his pants and had to run back to the locker room. Freddie was dispatched to fill in, and when the Country Day defensive line saw him, they started chanting, "Get the syrup. Get the syrup."

I'd set the school rushing record that day, but that didn't stop Grandfather Sumter, who never missed a Barrington game, from hobbling out on the track to put the Sumter backslap on Freddie's pads to congratulate him on his mop-up squad exploits.

136

Of course, everyone was talking about your award.

It was the Congressional Medal of Honor, Freddie, not some award.

And, of course, we're hopeful you'll be out in time to attend. Sally
Effingham, specifically, was asking me for details about you. She's
divorced now, you know, and the boys at the firm say she cleaned
her ex-husband's clock in the settlement. She's still quite a
knockout.

Sally Effingham had been my only real, steady girlfriend in high school.
We went together for a few months before her mother decided she should
have a more "normal" boyfriend—one with a mother who belonged to
the Fair Oaks Garden Club and had a standing reservation at the Zodiac
Room at Neiman Marcus on trunk show days. Or, at least a mother. Sally
told me her parents—she actually meant her mother—didn't like the idea
of my being home alone a few days each week while my dad was away on
business. It was too tempting for two teenagers, her mom thought. So Sally
dumped me, *tout de suite,* for a minor brewery heir a week before the prom.
I'd heard that she'd married a trial lawyer, one of those guys who advertised
asbestos lawsuits on television, but I hadn't heard about the divorce.

Please let us all know your plans. Everyone is interested in
hearing how our boy won the war—Sally especially. I hope you
don't mind that I gave her your email.

I'd have to think about that one.

If you're not interested, let me know. I think she always had
a thing for me, but I don't want to step on any toes.

Sally had a thing for Freddie? I may have had only one steady girlfriend,
and for a short time at that, but Freddie never had one date that I remember,
at least not one that his mother didn't set up with one of her friends at the
club.

Oh, and by the way, Cuz, my boss at the firm, Big Bob May,
you remember him from your time at AC Collins? Anyway, Big

Bob asked if when you get back home, you might see your way clear to attend a small reception the firm would throw in your honor. We'd invite a few clients and prospects, you know, do the schmooze. I know it's disgusting, but sometimes duty calls.

Yes, I'd noticed that.

Well, I told him I was sure you'd be up for it. I'll send you the details when you let me know when you're being released from the army. It would be a great help. Some of the boys are speculating the firm may be up for sale and, well, you know, anything I can do to be seen as bringing in new clients will help if a new man takes over.

Cousin Freddie had graduated, let's say, in the upper ninety-fifth percentile at Barrington. Despite his parents' herculean efforts and many influential friends, Freddie wasn't considered Ivy League timber. Even his dad's undergraduate alma mater, Brown, declined. Wait-listed by a small, liberal arts safety school somewhere in New England, he received the acceptance letter the day before graduation, saving his family the humiliation of having a child attending a state school. It had cost his father a last-minute donation of twenty-five thousand dollars, but face was saved. You couldn't put a price on that in Fair Oaks.

Freddie told everyone that he'd picked the school because they wanted him to continue his football career and that the coach there had said he might start as a freshman. I think there were six hundred kids in the entire college, more than half of them girls; with numbers like that, I think breathing was the only requirement to be a starter on the school's football team. But as it turned out, even his team, which had gone 1-9 the previous year, didn't need a guy playing left pancake.

Freddie graduated from college in five years, explaining that he wanted to take some additional courses he needed to get into med school. Freddie's dad was a surgeon, but my cousin received one of the lowest scores in the history of MCAT testing, not to mention that he apparently couldn't stand the sight of blood. He should try shooting people in the head for a living.

Freddie was never the same after his father left Aunt Mary to marry a twenty-five-year-old receptionist at a suburban ambulatory surgery center. It was humiliating for the entire family and the often-cited cause for

Grandfather's ultimate demise. Grandfather had been over the moon when his daughter had married a doctor. It was "Doc this" and "Doc that" with all his pals at the club. "Oh," he'd always say, "it looks like you have a little tennis elbow there, old chum; if you like, I'll put in a call to my son-in-law the surgeon."

When the cad ran off with a common trollop, grandfather developed iatrapistia, turning on the entire medical profession. He quit going to doctors altogether after the divorce, and his slow-growing prostate cancer got legs and tragically did him in.

After finally getting his bachelor's degree, Freddie returned to St. Louis and enrolled in an unaccredited MBA program that he was still trying to finish. Freddie had hoped dear old doctor dad might spot him the tuition and a reasonable stipend during grad school. But his dad was still sore about having had to bribe a third-rate school to get Freddie admitted. Plus his dad's trophy wife wanted a big family, and he now had two more tuitions to fund. He'd be removing gall bladders until he dropped, and he told Freddie to get a job.

Freddie moved in with his mom and set out to find honorable work befitting a man of his station. After the bigger firms had passed on Freddie, he'd gone to work for Big Bob May at Robert W. May & Company, a small, bucket-shop boutique that catered penny stocks to suckers with money.

Now, Freddie was saying that May & Company might be bought out. Had the mob suddenly opened a mergers and acquisitions department? Who else would want it? I'd sooner attend a reception for al-Qaeda than shill for Big Bob.

But the reunion and Sally Effingham? That, I might have to consider. I tried to imagine what she'd look like. But thinking about Sally while I was stuck here alone was the last thing I needed to do.

Take care, Cuz. See you soon. Oh—and don't forget to bring that medal with you to the reception. Ciao.

Ciao. I think that pretty much sums it up.

****

Lieutenant Maggie Taylor would have been glad to hear from anyone back home, even an idiot cousin.

After being in seven locations since her kidnapping, Taylor now knew the signs of when they were about to move her. The guards, especially Cruella—her name for the veiled matron who so enjoyed wielding the leather belt—would scream at her, shove her, and kick her. They wanted to terrorize her, break her spirit, make her afraid—and they were very good at it. Taylor had spent long hours thinking about how she'd kill Cruella if she ever got the chance. She wanted to rip that veil off Cruella's face and . . .

Taylor heard loud voices outside the door, then sounds of a scuffle and furniture being overturned, then screaming and a door slammed. Nothing like having your captors at each other's throats.

What if they kill each other and I'm left alone here? Will anyone ever find me?

Then she heard Cruella screech at someone. Whoever it was didn't answer but responded with the unmistakable sound of a hard-facial slap. Cruella screeched again.

Hit her again!

Taylor thought she'd been in her current location at least three days. One consolation was it was warm. But she'd lost all track of time, even the month. She guessed it was December, but it might be January. Had the new president been sworn in? Had her country just left her here with these sadistic savages?

She started crying softly, then began coughing. The coughing had started about a week earlier. She spat up something green and knew that wasn't a good sign. Taylor had lost about twenty pounds on the gruel and rancid water they allowed her. She was hungry and tired, but fear took her mind off food even though her stomach growled almost nonstop.

Taylor was weak and black and blue from the beatings, and she was beginning to lose all hope that the torment would ever end. She was trying to maintain her sanity by remembering people, places, images, and events from home—anything to keep from going crazy. She tried to pull from her memory the words of prayers from church, images of the colorful floats she'd seen in Mardi Gras parades, the names of the kids in her home room in high school. She spent an entire afternoon trying to recite the Greek alphabet, which she'd never quite learned during her college sorority days.

She felt her neck. They'd taken her dog tags. When she'd been inducted, she couldn't stand them, but she now felt naked without them. She didn't know, of course, that the terrorists had mailed her dog tags to her parents, suggesting that her uncle the congressman had better ensure that their demands were met.

Over and over, Taylor wondered what terms the terrorists had demanded for her release. An even bigger puzzlement was that they apparently thought her uncle could influence the president and his top advisers. That fool hadn't even been able to get her appointed to West Point. If she'd been a West Point graduate, she'd never have been shoved into a jeep to patrol dangerous streets without support.

No, Uncle Wes had to get her an ROTC scholarship that came with a free ticket to Iraq. She should have taken the partial scholarship that Louisiana-Lafayette had offered. Sure, she'd have had to work part time, but it would have kept her out of this mess. But the allure of the fancy private school, her daddy's alma mater, was just too tempting. Thanks a bunch, Uncle Wes. That man couldn't find his butt in the dark let alone have any success in international diplomacy. His election to Congress said nothing good about American politics.

Taylor rubbed her leg, which was raw from the manacle and chain, and hoped it wasn't getting infected. Then she leaned against the wall and closed her eyes.

Alpha, beta, gamma, epsilon—or is it alpha, beta, gamma, delta . . .

Chapter 24

The Condo, Northwestern Iraq

December 23, 2008

I decided to kill some time and shoot a box of 30.06 shells, so I went out on the loading dock. It was two days until Christmas—a day I'd always dreaded. Christmas was the one day each year that I saw my grandparents.

We never made the Sumter family's A-list Christmas Day open house, but we *were* allowed an annual pilgrimage on Christmas Eve. We'd arrive at the stone-and-brick house, nestled along a private lane on the Fair Oaks Country Club grounds, shortly after the dinner hour—we were never invited for dinner. An elderly maid would escort us to the warm, wood-paneled den, where a roaring fire blazed in the fireplace and a huge tree decorated with ornaments occupied center stage. We were told on every Christmas Eve visit that the ornaments had been in the family for generations. A warning not to touch the ornaments always followed the history lesson, after which Grandfather would brag that the tree came from the family farm. But everyone knew that the tree had come from the parking lot of a local Methodist church whose men's club sold trees every year during the holiday season.

Grandfather wouldn't admit that the family farm, along with the Michigan cabin and the Florida beach house, had been sold years earlier to raise cash for a margin call. The farm, which had been in the family for four generations, was now the site of two hundred "tar-paper shacks," as Grandfather privately called the tract homes, for blue-collar families.

I always enjoyed the Christmas cookies and eggnog, as well as the tree and decorations; Dad and I usually had only a small tree at our house. We'd sit in the overstuffed sofas, and my grandparents would pretend to be interested in the answers to the questions they asked me about myself for a half-hour. Then my grandmother, who had become quite feeble in the years following my mother's death, would give me my present. It was always under the tree, mixed in with the dozens of presents whose tags bore the names of my cousins. I never figured out if they thought I was too stupid to see all the gifts they'd bought for Aunt Mary's boys or if they wanted me to understand where I stood with them. I'd never give them the satisfaction. I'd accept their gift, give each of them my gift, and thank them politely. A week later, I'd dutifully send them a note telling them how much I enjoyed their present.

Then we'd leave and return to our small house on the wrong side of the city limits. I'd say the wrong side of the tracks, but trains weren't allowed within the Fair Oaks city limits either.

Dad always called it my mom's house, and even though he could have afforded a much grander home, he wouldn't have considered selling it. There, the two of us celebrated our own Christmas Eve after the obligatory "celebration" at my grandparents' home. I was twelve years old the Christmas my dad gave me the Remington carbine hunting rifle—about an hour after my grandparents had given me an ugly, polyester-blend sweater, a factory second from the JC Penney outlet store. I couldn't have been happier if Dad had told me there was a pony in the garage.

On Christmas Day, we always drove to my Uncle Jess's house in rural Southern Illinois around 10 o'clock so we'd be there for a Christmas lunch at noon. My uncle, who never married, lived a solitary life; he'd retired on a disability pension after being diagnosed with black lung from years in the mines. The Christmas that Dad gave me the Remington, my dad and uncle took me into the nearby woods after lunch to test my new rifle. Uncle Jess set up a target about fifty yards out, and I braced the rifle on a concrete post from a dilapidated fence that had run around the now-abandoned coal mine. The recoil knocked me backwards, putting a scratch on the brand-new wooden stock. I was shattered, but my dad and uncle laughed and told me the mark gave the rifle character.

As I looked out into the floor of the pile, I rubbed the scratch on the stock with my thumb. The wood had mellowed, and the scratch had become smooth over the years. I braced the weapon on a fake-stone ledge, scoped in a piece of wood near the pond, about 150 yards away, and pulled the trigger. It would take more firepower than I had in the condo's armory to blow away the ghosts of my Christmas past.

*****

I was feeling a little homesick, so to pass the time, I searched the condo-net for my old high school girlfriend, Sally Effingham, which slow-surfed me to bergersbeat.com, a site written by Jerry Berger, the dean of local gossip and news about St. Louis's rich and famous. I recalled that my grandparents would do *anything* to get a mention in Berger's column. The story I found was nearly a year old.

Socialite Wife Turns Plaintiff's Lawyer into Defendant

Noted local barrister to the asbestos-afflicted, Peter Varty, who recently won an eighty-million-dollar verdict in a trial in Madison County, Illinois—for those of you who can't figure one-third fast enough, let's round off his split at a little less than twenty-seven mil—was fleeced by his ever-lovin' ex, Sally, the former Sally Effingham, of the Fair Oaks Effinghams, in what some are calling one of the largest divorce settlements in recent memory. Courthouse wags are saying the former Barrington School debutant ankled the marriage with over thirty million clams when she produced emails containing explicit pictures Varty had sent to his paramour who—how should we describe her occupation? Let's just say that her employer is located on the east side and leave it at that.

Ha! Sally Effingham had been jilted for a stripper. That must have set Fair Oaks tongues to wagging. I was surprised she was planning to show up at the reunion. But I guessed with that size bank account, there was no reason to care what anyone thought of you.

The heiress to the Effingham family coin-operated, pay phone fortune, which shrunk considerably with the introduction of cell phones, also scored the family manse in tony Frontenac. The couple had no offspring, so at least Varty will be spared child support. At last word, Varty had moved into a downtown loft, apparently with better bridge access to the east side.

Wow. I wondered if a divorce settlement was taxable. I'd have to look that up. Either way, she was loaded. Made my lousy eight million look like spare change.

Chapter 25

Detroit, Michigan

December 23, 2008

Adad Haneef was freezing in suburban Detroit. He'd never known weather so frigid. The small gas heater mounted near the ceiling ran nonstop but didn't seem to ever take the chill off the filthy automotive machine shop that hadn't been used since Ricardo Montalban was selling Chryslers with Corinthian leather. The windows had been painted and very little sunlight came through, not that there was much sunlight anyway with all the snow storms. The facility had been rented through a commercial realtor who'd turned the utilities on and left the keys in the mailbox. Cash could do so many things in Detroit.

Haneef and his handlers slept in sleeping bags on the cold, concrete floor. At meal time, one of the guards would venture out and bring back what that they called fast food. Haneef liked the beef between bread slices, which they called hamburgers, as well as the onion circles and fried potato sticks; but he really enjoyed the fried chicken sold by something called Popeyes, located down the street. Even with the windows closed, he could sometimes smell the aroma of the delicious chicken being prepared. Haneef thought this type of business would do very well in Syria.

He'd seen next to nothing of America on the ride to Detroit. His handlers had kept him inside a van they'd picked up near Las Vegas, allowing him out only to use the restroom.

Haneef marveled at the snow, in piles three or four feet high outside the warehouse door and as far as he could see down the street; he'd never seen snow so deep. And he wondered about these people whose houses he'd seen on his drive through the city, which were lit up like a Pakistani big-rig. Outside many houses, blinking colored lights lit up the trees and outlined the roofs. The front yards of some houses even had displays of animals made of small light bulbs or life-size images of a fat man wearing a red coat. He didn't understand the point, but it was interesting despite being blatantly decadent.

The tools that had been secured for him were old but would do the job. He was pleased with the carbon composite material from which he'd fabricate the skeleton of the ultralight drones. Carbon was lighter and stronger than steel and had a reduced radar signature. The lighter the frame, the more cargo the small craft would be able to carry.

The orders he'd received from al Hamwi instructed him to prepare to finish production of his aircraft by the first week of February. It would be close, but with the design now perfected, he should be able to finish in time, *inshallah.*

He found the fabric that had been bought to cover the wings to be adequate. The material would be stretched over the camber of the wings very tightly, then shellacked to a precise degree of hardness, and finally covered with his radar-absorbing paint. The electronics he'd use to direct the plane, the cameras, and the controls, which would allow the landing gear to fall away after takeoff, were exceptional—better than anything he'd obtained in Syria. The engines, which had been ordered from something called eBay, were used but would fly. Anyway, they had to work only once.

Haneef's keepers had promised that the chemicals he'd need to make his special paint would be delivered soon. His paint was crude compared to what the Americans used, but it worked well enough. Lastly, the ultralight would fly low, well below the ability of most radar to pick up the craft. When possible, he would follow highways with large trucks that could confuse radar at low levels. His objective was for the craft to simply become lost in the clutter. In any event, even if the American radar picked it up, what could they do? He would launch the ultralights from locations only minutes away from their targets, so they'd be impossible to stop. He would be a legend.

Chapter 26

Near Abbottabad, Pakistan

December 23, 2008

Osama bin Laden was back inside the big rig's cramped cargo hold. They were traveling to a safe house to spend the night before heading back to the compound in Abbottabad.

He took a clean, disposable cell phone from the pocket of his robe. The Americans had technology to pick up his voice, but he wanted them chasing their tails. He'd often thought about getting one of those voice modulators that the prince used so he could use phones again, but it was much safer to simply stay off the air. He wanted to tweak their president as his term expired and the fool's promise to capture him ended in failure.

The call to the prince would be short. The prince would also be in a vehicle, most likely the Bentley that bin Laden coveted, and also using a throw-away phone. They'd both remove the batteries and destroy the SIM cards after their brief conversation.

The prince was the son of an exiled scion of the Saudi king, who'd been banished for dishonoring the royal family by killing a young girl while driving drunk in the middle of the day in central Riyadh. The death had been hushed up, the girl's family had been paid off, and the prince's family exiled to Paris, where the young prince had become westernized.

The prince, who had no interest in living the profligate life of his father, wanted his rightful place in the Saudi kingdom restored—and he was determined to have it, whatever it took. While his lazy cousins gorged themselves with the gluttony of palace life, the prince was making plans to turn what was left of his father's fortune into an even bigger one.

The king thought his besotted son by one of his homelier wives was simply a fool, failing to realize that the sot had taken advantage of the poor palace accounting system over the years to steal nearly a quarter billion in petro-dollars. The American accountants brought in to shore up palace finances found skimpy notations such as, "prince so and so took a large bag of money." Now the accounting was more professional, and although the princes still took bags of money, the amounts were much smaller and were accounted for according to Generally Accepted Accounting Principles.

The prince had never forgiven the king for denying him his birthright. Although he couldn't have cared less about religion, he was happy to use it as a tool to achieve his objective of overthrowing his estranged grandfather. And speaking of tools, he also was more than willing to use his childhood friend, bin Laden, for his purposes.

Bin Laden dialed the prince's number, heard the electronic ringing, and recognized the prince's voice: "Peace be unto you. How are you, my friend?"

"And to you. Everything is well with your servant?"

"We should have dinner soon. Perhaps the twenty-eighth?"

"That will be fine. Until then."

The twenty-eighth was not the date, although he knew security forces all over the world would scramble to identify the location of their meeting in six days. The prince's words told bin Laden that they would meet after sunset in the sanctuary, twenty-eight days hence.

Bin Laden and the prince had known each other since the days before the prince's family had been shown the door in disgrace. They'd attended school together, and their families knew each other well. When bin Laden had gone to fight with the Mujahedeen in Afghanistan, the prince had backed him financially—but there was always a price. It was the prince who demanded an American surface-to-air, shoulder-fired missile, which the CIA had given to bin Laden to take down Russian helicopters. The prince had it reverse-engineered and, through an insulated intermediary, sold the plans to the highest bidder—which turned out to be the CIA, but the check had cleared. When bin Laden had begun his fire-bombing routine, it was always with the consent and support of the prince, who would figure out how to profit from it.

Working with legitimate financial advisers all over the world, the prince had turned his inheritance from his drunken father into nearly twenty billion dollars. Although he was among the world's richest people, his picture was never on the *Forbes* listing of the world's wealthiest people. The prince had no interest in such things. The only picture he desired to see was of the corpse of his grandfather in repose. Once he controlled the Saudi family oil, he'd control the entire Middle East, and his family would finally bow before him.

Chapter 27

The Condo, Northwestern Iraq

December 24-25, 2008

Christmas Eve. No tree, no lights, no tinsel, no presents, no midnight church service. So far, however, it was a silent night, and I was looking forward to Santa's visit. The Santa I wanted to see, however didn't fly a red sleigh. This one flew a green army helicopter. But unfortunately, he wouldn't be coming for about ten days.

He'd better bring me some nice presents because I've been a really good boy.

I still wasn't used to Christmas without my dad even though more than four years had passed since the terrorist attack that took his life. I still felt guilty about his death. He'd been doing a stock offering for a firm in Central Illinois and asked if I wanted to come along on the European leg of the road show since my yearlong stint as an investment banking grunt was wrapping up. But my final interview with the University of Chicago was scheduled for the end of that week, so I'd begged off. But if I'd been there, I could have carried the woman he'd tried to save, and maybe he'd have made it out.

Our family doctor, who'd gone over the British autopsy, had said that Dad had coronary artery disease, even though he was relatively young and in good shape. But the doc had told me that it was nothing that a by-pass couldn't have fixed. They just couldn't get him out of the subway and to Wellington Hospital in time to save him.

To try to get out of my Christmas funk, I decided to check my emails—although I figured that no one would be writing to me on Christmas.

But Major Shay had sent me an article that had appeared in a left-wing magazine loved by the effete, intellectual elites. It was written by a liberal Ivy League professor, and it was about me. She was making the case that the U.S. was wrong to venerate military heroes with medals, and she'd used me as the poster boy. She talked about how many civilian fighters, not terrorists, I'd killed in cold blood from my "cowardly sniper lairs." Somehow, she'd found out that I was no longer at Walter Reed, which was the army's cover story for why I wasn't available for additional media interviews. A liberal congressman who'd gone to the hospital at her request had discovered that I was no longer a patient. The professor somehow postulated that I'd been transferred to a mental isolation ward because I couldn't cope with what I'd done.

I certainly was in isolation, and some people might call me crazy for taking this gig. But I guessed that I'd have to get used to the celebrity and the kooks like her that it attracted. Or maybe I'd had my fifteen minutes of fame, and this would be the last of it.

I had received emails from several agents, offering to represent me for media and public-speaking opportunities. There had even been a message from Jay Leno asking if I'd be a guest on his show. But I wasn't interested in commercializing the medal. That would be very bad form indeed, although it might be fun to be on *The Tonight Show*.

While the generator was doing its evening routine, I quickly zapped my dinner and washed out my clothes in the sink before quickly jumping into the shower. I was thinking about Christmases I'd spent with my dad when I heard the generator stop. Still covered with soap, I rinsed off quickly, stepped out, and saw the red lights on the control board flashing and the window into the cavity of the pile closing automatically. Major Shay was on the communicator, urgently calling my name.

"Novak? Come in, Novak."

"I'm here. I was in the shower. Are we having a malfunction?"

"Negative. A sensor under the road is picking up activity near the road, about a half-mile from the condo. Definitely a vehicle. Might be nothing, but we need to batten it down."

"Affirmative. The window is closed, and the generator is down. All gear is secure."

"I see your power supply is 80 percent. Hopefully, it's only a passing tourist. You can get through the night with 80 percent without any problem if we conserve, so don't worry."

The sun was setting. There was still some light, but it would be dark in a few minutes. I trained the telescopic infrared camera in the direction of the road and picked up some sort of SUV. Its lights were off, but I could see the vehicle coming my way. I activated several more cameras and watched the SUV turn off the deserted road abruptly and head straight for the pile.

"Are you guys getting this?"

"Roger."

"How do you want to handle it?"

"Let's see what he's up to."

"Roger that."

The SUV, which I could now make out as a Toyota, drove into an alcove of nearby small boulders and sat there. I kept the camera trained on the vehicle and zoomed in on the driver's side. I could see that he was alone.

"What do you think?"

"We're thinking it might be something, Novak. Let's let it play out. Maybe he's waiting for somebody else."

Just after the sun disappeared in the west, the SUV's door opened. The driver was wearing a sweater and had a backpack slung over his shoulder. He walked to the rear hatch, and as he bent slightly to remove a small box, his sweater rode up. I could see a pistol stuck in the back waistband of his pants. He then removed a long iron rod that looked like an elongated crowbar.

"You see the gun?"

"We see it, Novak. Keep the camera on him."

The man knew exactly where he was going, striding directly to the entry boulder. He shoved the lever under the rock that concealed the entrance to the pile just enough to squeeze inside.

I switched to a camera inside the rock maze that wound into the pile. The interloper now had a flashlight on and moved quickly through and into the cavity. I activated the interior cameras and picked him up as he entered the floor of the pile.

"If he knows I'm here, he isn't showing it. He's not trying to hide."

"Novak, there's no way he knows. See if you can zoom in on his face."

It took a while before he looked my way, but I finally got a nice, tight shot of him and sent it to Shay. He had a scraggly, untrimmed beard and a bad haircut, and appeared to be about thirty-five.

"We got it; we're running him through the system."

He walked around the pile, shining his light in all directions, and then headed for my side of the pile. He shined his light right on the condo but gave no indication of seeing a thing.

Now, he was right below me. I followed him via cameras mounted on the other side of the pile. He stopped near the wall, gathered some loose stones, and knelt to open the box. I zoomed in, half-expecting to see explosives. He'd need a bigger bomb than what was in that box to hurt me up here, but he had my full interest. I zoomed in tighter on the box.

"It looks like a camera," Shay said. "Shoot the box as tightly as you can."

I did and reported back, "He's setting up a camera." It was a Sony surveillance camera.

"Let's watch."

Next, he took a roll of wire and a small device, and strung the wire from the small box back to the camera.

"Get in tight. Looks like a motion detector," Shay said.

Shay confirmed it was a motion detector and explained that any variation in temperature would activate the camera. If someone walked by the sensor, it could distinguish between his temperature and the ambient air temperature, activating the sensor and turning on the camera.

"Got him ID'd. Anas al-Maqqati. He's on our most wanted list. He's Saudi, but he's been in Iraq for over ten years. Midlevel hit man for AQ-Iraq suspected of planning dozens of IEDs. And he was the go-to guy for suicide vests a few years back."

What we didn't know then was that he was also a bag man for the prince.

"I've got the guns sighted on him and ready to engage. Just confirm."

"No, no, Novak. We need to see what he's up to. We're redirecting a drone to your location. We'll follow him and see where he goes. Maybe we'll get lucky.

"Colonel Svoboda thinks, and I concur, that he's checking out the pile for something in the future. We'll check the camera for RF signals with the drone to see if it's broadcasting or if they're recording to an internal disk. We think he's recording to the disk and will come back later to check the camera for intruders. We're checking out the camera's specs right now. Kirkos says al-Maqqati is a distant relative of some minor Saudi royalty."

I watched the man walk back and forth between the camera and the sensor. Then he checked the screen to see if it worked. Apparently satisfied with his work, he concealed the camera under the stones and turned the sensor toward the entry maze. Anyone who walked in would trigger the camera.

The man walked to the pool and, after removing a prayer rug from his backpack, knelt in prayer. After he finished his prayers, he took off all his clothing and, despite the temperature being in the low fifties, pulled something out of his backpack and waded into the pool, heading for the deep end that abutted the east side of the pile.

I couldn't make out what he was carrying because his body blocked the camera's view. He was underwater for a long time, and I started to think that he'd drowned.

"What's he doing?"

"We don't know, Novak; maybe it's a ceremonial bath, like a baptism. He's going to be dead if he doesn't come up shortly. If the lack of air doesn't get him, hypothermia will."

Suddenly, his head popped to the surface, and he exited the pool carrying the same bag. Shivering, he shook off and dressed quickly.

"He's leaving."

"Let's make sure, Novak."

I followed him through several camera angles until he got back in the Toyota and drove back the way he came, again without headlights.

"The drone couldn't get there in time, but we have an AWACS trying to get him. Once he hits the sensor in the road, fire up the generator. You need to be at 100 percent capacity. Don't leave the condo until we figure out a few things. Stay inside and hang loose. Let's see what we get. We think this could be it."

I didn't bother asking if I was going to get Christmas Day off this year. I knew the answer.

****

After a restless night, I was up early on Christmas Day. No one dropped by for my Christmas brunch of ham and beans *à la* MRE topped off by a tasty can of fruit cocktail for desert. Our visitor's camera was still sitting there, well hidden. I was still stumped by our guest's sudden urge to go swimming the night before.

I suddenly heard Shay's voice come over the speaker.

"Okay, Novak, here's what we have," he began. "The drone has been circling, running through every part of the radio spectrum. We're sure the camera isn't broadcasting. That means it's recording to the digital card in the camera, and someone will have to return to physically inspect it. So we must be alert. Remember, it's probably set to document if someone has been inside. The specs say when tripped, it runs for fifteen seconds and then shuts down.

"We want you to put the ladder down, Novak, take your iPhone communicator, and use the video camera to give us a closer look. Then we'll decide how to play it."

"Affirmative. Any thoughts on our skinny-dipper?"

"We're mystified. One psychiatrist thinks he is trying to draw strength from the holy water, maybe some kind of purification ritual. We're still thinking about it. He must have been floating with his body underwater and just his face above water. But it was so dark, we couldn't tell."

I picked up the iPhone, put it in my pants pocket, and grabbed the shoulder holster and the nine millimeter. I was used to the long ladder now. After checking to make sure it was secure, I climbed down.

"Just to be safe, make sure to stay behind the camera."

"Roger," I said into my earpiece mic.

I found the camera the visitor had hidden under a few flat stones, lifted off the top rock, and focused the iPhone camera on the Sony device. Shay told me to stand by.

"OK," he said after a few minutes. "That confirms it's the model we thought. It's a surveillance camera—fairly new. It records to an internal card, in color during the day and infrared at night. It's meant for temporary outdoor work at places like construction sites, so it won't hurt it if it gets wet. The battery will probably run the thing for as long as two months, three tops."

They asked me to open a side panel and remove the SD card. It was a thirty-two-gig card which would hold a ton of video. I photographed the SD card, reinserted it into the slot, replaced the camera in its hiding place, and moved toward the back of the sensor.

"Stay behind it, Novak."

I sent video back to the condo's Intranet system, which microwaved it to the uplink on the neighboring pile of rocks that housed my uplink, and then onto Shay in Kuwait. I photographed the motion detector and uplinked the information to Condo Control.

"Pretty garden-variety motion detector. It's also made for outdoor use. Runs on a nine-volt battery that will last five or six months. The beam is adjustable, and our friend has it set to cover the entrance to the maze. So if you're behind it, you won't get picked up. Do you still have that digital camera you bought at Walmart?"

"Yes, I have a ton of pictures of sunsets and rocks."

"Good. If necessary, you can use the camera to reformat the card. That will erase anything if it catches you.

Shay told me to take the SD card into the condo and copy it on my MacBook. If we had to reformat the card, we could then replace the part where the guy had captured himself testing the card and walking out through the maze.

"We're going to drop you a couple of extra SD cards exactly like the one in the camera. If we screw up somehow, you can replace the card with a new one, and they'll never know."

"You're going to make an early supply run?"

"Negative. Can't risk it. A chopper will overfly the pile and drop it inside. You'll have to fetch it."

"How about putting in a Big Mac?"

Chapter 28

The White House

December 25, 2008

The president usually went home to his Texas ranch for the holidays, but this would be his last chance to spend Christmas in the White House. So he'd gathered his extended family for the final presidential celebration. After morning church services, the family headed back to the White House, dodging the flurries that promised to drop an inch or two of snow on the mansion grounds for a picture-perfect Christmas Day.

The president entered, and a butler took his coat and scarf. Steve Higgins, the president's chief of staff, stood nearby with a file full of papers.

"Steve, come on boy. It's Christmas."

"Mr. President, I think you need to see this immediately."

The two walked to the president's private office, bypassing the more ceremonial Oval Office.

"What do you have?"

"Sir, two things. We had company at the condo last night. A known AQ operative, a really bad guy, came in after dark and planted a surveillance camera. We think the AQ leadership is planning something soon. The boys in Kuwait think he was sent to make sure no one's staking the area out, which means they might be expecting some important participants. If this is true, we're possibly near another major attack. We need your approval to notify Homeland Security, the FBI, and state and local police, but in a way that isn't too revealing."

"Use the increased-chatter story. Nobody ever knows what that means anyway, or maybe that color-alert system. Even I can't remember what all the colors mean. Then turn our guys loose, and see what they can shake out."

"Yes, sir."

"I'm glad we have Novak in there. I think a lot of that young man. He's the kind of kid I'd have wanted for a son, if my wife and I had had one. You did a great job in finding him. How's he holding up?"

"They say he's bored to tears, but everything is going as planned."

"Good. What's the other thing?"

"Two nights ago, the NSA intercepted a very brief telephonic conversation from a moving vehicle in Pakistan to what they think was a moving vehicle in Monte Carlo. The spooks have definitely confirmed it was between bin Laden and The Boss."

"So he's finally sticking his head up for air?"

"Looks like it, sir. The NSA task force thinks they're planning to meet in five days. They were pretty vague."

"Shake and bake, Steve. Get these boys and maybe they can lead us to the girl they kidnapped. If I have to watch her idiot uncle on cable television one more time, I think I may have to check myself into Walter Reed."

Chapter 29

Detroit, Michigan

December 25, 2008

Adad Haneef was making steady progress. He'd fabricated the pieces that would form the fuselages of the ultralights as well as the struts that would support the wings. After work on the wings was finished, he'd begun running the control cables. Everything had to be wired precisely because the ultralights would be shipped in a panel truck and assembled and fueled on site. With three men, he estimated it would take less than an hour to assemble each one by snapping the sections together. Once the planes were constructed, Haneef would drill his two helpers in assembling the units until they had it down to a more acceptable time.

In the normal location of the cockpit, Haneef had installed a cargo hold. It looked odd with its angular shape, which was not particularly aerodynamic, but it was the one part, other than the wings and tail, that might reflect a radar signal. The fuselage would simply be the naked carbon supports. He knew he was going overboard with his concerns about stealth, especially on these first attacks. Nobody would be expecting them this time. But after they hit the first couple of targets, every duck hunter in America would be looking for ultralights.

Haneef was happy about everything except that Popeyes down the street was closed for Christmas. He had to settle for the little square grease burgers that gave him gas.

Chapter 30

The Condo, Northwestern Iraq

December 26, 2008

It was the day after Christmas. I had no football games to watch, no presents to return, and no relatives who'd be stopping by with late gifts bought that morning for 75 percent off. The temperature was 56°F, warm enough to take in some fresh air, so I was sitting outside the condo in the winter desert sun.

I'd set up the lawn chair I'd bought in Maryland, put on my earphones, and selected The Academy Is, a Chicago band I'd seen a few times while at the University of Chicago. I laughed every time I played their CD, *Fast Times at Barrington High,* which was obviously about a different Barrington High than the one I'd attended in Fair Oaks. I put my feet up on a ledge and sipped a Coke, thinking how much I'd rather have a beer.

Between sips, I glanced down to make sure I'd brought the M4. The M4 was the weapon most army personnel used in battle zones. A more compact, carbine version of the old M16 used during Vietnam, it was easier to maneuver in urban settings with their corners and other close-quarters situations. It was a fine and lethal weapon but nothing like the Barrett M-107 fifty-caliber rifle I carried. In the right hands, the M-107 is accurate to two thousand yards, although snipers have been known to hit targets farther than that.

The M-107, which has become the desired sniper rifle in armies all over the world, wasn't designed as a sniper rifle; it was engineered to stop vehicles and other equipment. The old sniper joke is that the zipper on

161

a terrorist's jacket is actually a piece of equipment. When fitted with the right scope, like the Leupold Mark 4 that was on the M-107 stored in the condo armory, it was a lethal killing machine—especially with a well-trained spotter like The Dart feeding you all the variables that would affect the round in flight. The bad guys in Iraq and Afghanistan feared the M-107 almost as much as the drones because they never knew when it was coming.

Hitting targets almost a mile away in the field was no easy feat, even with the latest technology. Although nothing like the computer-game 107 here in the condo, it was pretty accurate.

The last time I'd touched an M-107 was the day I was wounded in Afghanistan and The Dart was mortally wounded. I'd thought about him a lot since moving into the condo. Seven years my junior, he was the little brother I never had, and he followed me around like a puppy dog. He was great company on the many lonely, often dangerous, missions we endured together. He had a joke for any situation, and he'd tell it in an Arkansas twang that got me laughing even before he got to the punch line.

A spotter must be bright and understand a lot of math and physics. Although the Dart never made it to college, he was whip-smart. He'd scored a 29 on his ACT exam before being roped-in by the criminal justice system on a minor internet rap which resulted in his being given the choice of the army or Cummins Prison Farm. Sometimes he'd talk about going back to college, and other times he'd say he was going to be a lifer in the army. His hitch would have been up a few months after mine. I'd made it clear I was done with the army, and I think that made it harder for him to decide what he wanted to do. Then fate made the decision for him.

My earpiece beeped, bringing me back to the present.

"Condo, this is Cardinal." Cardinal was the chopper call sign they named for my favorite baseball team. "Do you copy?"

"I copy you, Cardinal."

"Condo, we've got your present all wrapped up and ready for delivery. We'll swing around, come in from the opposite end, and drop. We'll not slow down. Confirm."

"Roger. Try not to hit my swimming pool."

"We'll do our best. Confirm you are in receipt once it comes down the chimney."

"Roger."

The wind had died down, and I heard the bird making its wide turn, doing about fifty knots. Then I saw it drop down to about twenty feet over the pile. A drop master hanging out the door let go of a package attached to a mini-parachute, and it sailed right into the middle of the floor.

"He should be pitching for the Cardinals. I got it, thanks. Condo out."

"Good luck, Condo. Cardinal out."

As the sound of the helicopter dopplered into the Southeast, I quickly checked the cameras and sensors to make sure I was still alone, then anchored the ladder and lowered it over the side. The package had floated to an almost dead-center landing. The box felt heavier than I'd expected; I guessed they'd needed some ballast so it didn't float over the edge.

I covered my tracks with the palm frond and went back upstairs. The weather was becoming overcast, and I wanted to get back up before the sand started blowing. I went inside, closed the door, and set the box on the control panel. I sliced it open, removed the protective bubble wrap, and found a manila envelope on top. I opened the envelope, and three 32 gigabyte SD cards fell out along with a note.

> Dear Novak,
> I hope you have a Happy New Year. Good hunting.
> AH

Colonel Hunt. I was surprised he was still in Kuwait as he had told me he was heading back to Washington. I reached inside the box and carefully removed a small brick of dry ice, six frozen Double Quarter Pounders with cheese, and a six pack of Stag beer. Happy New Year, indeed.

****

Having been drugged and moved again—the second time in as many days, Maggie Taylor could hear traffic, car horns, and the call to prayer, suggesting that she was in a central city near a mosque.

The room Taylor was in looked like it had been some kind of business—perhaps a repair shop. There were windows, but only a few panes remained. The rest were boarded up, and she couldn't get to the ones that remained to look out, while she was chained to the trailer hitch on a white pickup truck at the far side of the warehouse-like room.

Cruella had warned Taylor that she'd take the belt to her if she screamed any more. But Taylor doubted that her sore throat would even allow her to scream. Feverish with a loose cough that was getting worse by the hour, she was worried that she might have pneumonia.

About two hours later, a boot kicked her in the ribs as she lay on her side facing a wall. She turned and looked up, expecting to see Cruella, but standing over her was the tall man who had taunted her about her uncle.

"So, whore," he said. "Soon it will be time."

"Time for what?" she said hoarsely.

"Time for you to make a video and confess your crimes against Allah and Iraq."

"I'm not making any video. I can barely talk, thanks to your incomparable hospitality."

Cruella stepped forward, belt in hand, to lash her, but the man stopped her.

"You will make the video. When you see the choice, you will make the right decision."

Taylor wanted to refuse again, but she was too feverish to argue anymore.

"Go, bring a doctor," the AQ official told Cruella. "Be sure he is trustworthy to us, and have him check her. She is of no value to us dead."

Chapter 31

The Condo, Northwestern Iraq

December 27, 2008

I finished off my second double-grease burger, which I'd zapped back to life in the condo's microwave. Going back to Spam and peanut-butter crackers would be tough once I polished off the rest of the Double Quarter Pounders in Hunt's package.

Although I was still on high alert, both physically and mentally, I couldn't figure out what the terrorist had been doing in the pool. I decided to take my binoculars out to the loading dock to take a closer look.

For the first time, I noticed that the water in the pool appeared lower by about six inches compared to when I'd arrived. I went inside, got my digital camera, and found a photo I'd snapped on my arrival day. Then I took a photo from the same spot and compared the two. Yep, the water was lower—maybe by even a foot. It was definitely depleting faster than they'd calculated. Had I taken too many cold showers thinking about Sally Effingham? Shay had said if the pool dried up, they'd chopper in more water. It looked like they might have to do just that.

Maybe this oasis wasn't fed by an underground spring. I could see a narrow, vertical fissure in the side of the cliff that dammed the back side of the pool. This crack hadn't been visible before the water level dropped. The ATEC engineers had told me the pool was about seven feet deep in the back and very shallow in front. They'd been down there installing the water intakes. Wouldn't they have seen anything there during the installation?

After telling the boys in Control that I was going down on the floor to clean the sand off the cameras, I headed to the pool to explore my discovery more closely. The cameras that trained on the pool, located on the opposite side of the pile, didn't monitor the area 24-7 because it would use up too much power. But I had no way of knowing when someone at Control would be watching, so I had to hope that the guys there wouldn't notice what I was doing.

I went to work on the cameras that captured the pool, directing them slightly away from the water. I walked to the edge of the pool, stripped, and waded carefully into the frigid water carrying a waterproof SureFire flashlight. I didn't know why someone at ATEC had thought I'd need a waterproof flashlight in the desert, but I was sure glad to have it.

It was only about twenty feet to the cliff, and once I moved into the pool a few feet, the bottom changed from sand to smooth stone. I walked until the water was just over my head, then swam the last few feet in the direction of the crevice I'd seen through my binoculars.

The opening in the wall was just large enough for a man to stand inside, I climbed onto a rock ledge so I could bob up for air and see back into the pile. I turned on my tactical flashlight and saw a ninety-degree turn going around a corner, which I squeezed around. I found myself inside an elevated cave. Steps were hewn into the stone up to a rock platform that was above the water level, surrounded by water on three sides.

I stepped up, into the cave, and saw a huge white tarp covering something very large. When I removed the tarp, I couldn't believe what I saw: a stack of boxes containing what looked like gold bars. I picked up one of the bars, which was marked "one thousand grams" and bore a marking indicating that it had minted by a bank in Switzerland.

Other boxes contained silver bars and sparkling jewelry. Stacked in neat piles were about three dozen large, rectangular crates, which I suspected contained artwork and other valuables. Then I saw what my recent "guest" had brought in his leather pouch: a Ziploc bag containing a stack of bearer bonds. I grabbed the bonds and two of the gold bars and headed back quickly the way I'd entered.

As I walked out of the water and toward my clothes, I heard Shay screaming at me over my army issued iPhone. I answered and said that I'd set the phone down to clean a filter. Shay told me not to spend too much time on the floor because we were still on high alert. I was dripping wet and freezing, and anxious to get back to the condo to dry off. He didn't have to tell me twice.

****

Two hours to the north, Lieutenant Maggie Taylor was dangerously feverish when the doctor arrived. He spoke no English, but his medical bag and stethoscope around his neck identified him. Taylor was happy to see a new face, even if she couldn't understand what he was saying. His presence also stirred a small ray of hope.

Perhaps he's been forced to come. Maybe he'll notify someone who'll rescue me.

But this doctor wouldn't call anyone on Taylor's behalf. His son had been killed by American soldiers in the fighting several years earlier. If the AQ guard hadn't been holding a gun on him, the doctor might have put Taylor to sleep permanently rather than treat her.

The doctor listened to Taylor's lung function and heard the congestion. He took her temperature, which her fever had spiked to one hundred two. He told the guard she was likely suffering from pneumonia, at the very least severe bronchitis.

"She should be taken to a hospital for more tests," the doctor said.

"No hospitals," the man shouted angrily. "You take care of her here."

The doctor reached into his bag for a syringe, which he filled with Azithromycin. He gave Taylor twice the dose he'd have administered to a patient with pneumonia then he handed the guard a generic Z-Pack with six 250 milligram pills, instructing that she was to be given two pills later in the day and one daily for the next four days.

The guard laughed as he accepted the pills, knowing that Taylor wouldn't be alive to finish them. But the pills would bring a good price on the black market, so he slid the packet into his pocket.

The doctor handed Taylor several Ibuprofen tablets to break her fever, which she swallowed immediately. As the medical man was looking for something else in his bag, the guard shoved the muzzle of his AK-47 in his ribs. The examination was over, and the doctor was ushered out. Taylor, still feverishly delirious, closed her eyes and fell into a sound sleep on the cold concrete floor.

Sometime later, Taylor was jarred awake by a loud screech of metal being ground. Away from her view, the tall AQ man was sharpening his sword. The next day, he would decapitate her and send a clear message to the infidels.

Unaware of her fate, Taylor took heart that she felt somewhat better. Her fever seemed to have broken.

Chapter 32

The Condo, Northwestern Iraq

December 28, 2008

The next morning, I was still pondering my amazing discovery. Had I found AQ's Fort Knox? If this was AQ's bankroll, allowing the army to confiscate it might put an end to the group's ambitions. But once sworn in, the new president would probably just turn the cache over to the corrupt Iraqi government, and it would be back in the cave within a week.

In business school, I'd studied the corporate raiders, the vulture capitalists, and others who play the game of business as a blood sport. I'd joined the army to put AQ out of business, but I figured any business transaction ought to at least pay a commission. The question wasn't whether I'd take anything. It was how much. I had plenty of time to decide what to do with what was left.

AQ owed me personally. What was I supposed to do? Hire Sally Effingham's ex-husband and sue them in Madison County Circuit Court? I decided I would just help myself and save the lawyer's one-third contingency fee.

I set the Ziploc bag on the control panel and took out the bonds. I'd studied bonds extensively in business school. The bonds, which had been issued in Costa Rica, were bearer bonds and as such weren't registered. No buyer's name was printed on the bonds, and by possessing them, I'd be the presumed owner. Although the U.S. government had outlawed bearer bonds in 1982—because they were regularly used by criminals, drug runners, and tax cheats—it appeared they were still in use offshore in places like Costa Rica.

Each bond had a term of ten years and was issued in the amount of $100,000. There were twenty on the nose, so I was holding $2 million in my hand. As the bond holder, I'd be entitled to interest at a rate of six percent—which would come to $120,000 a year. Two of the coupons attached to the bottom of a bond had been clipped and presumably surrendered for the cash interest payment, indicating that two years' interest had already been paid. So I stood to receive eight years of interest, or $960,000, and then the face value, $2 million, after eight more years had elapsed.

I picked up one of the gold bars I'd removed from the cave. It was a 1,000-gram bar, much easier to transport than the gold bricks typically shown in movies. Each bar was about three inches by an inch and a half, and about three-quarters inch thick. I grabbed my personal iPhone and did a quick calculation using an app. Each bar weighed a little more than two pounds. Not knowing the spot price of gold and unable to access the information without Control noticing, I guessed that each bar was worth somewhere around $26,000. But gold had been going through the roof since the stock-market crash, and I knew it was headed even higher.

****

The guard dragged Taylor to her feet, and shoved her to the bed of the awaiting truck. He chained her legs to the truck's walls, handcuffed her wrists to hooks in the floor, and threw a musty tarpaulin over her. She was flat on her back and instinctively turned her head to the side to breathe.

Taylor heard Cruella and her husband, the guard, loading items into the bed of the truck. Then she heard the loud squeal of the rusty track when the overhead door was jerked open. As the truck stared to move along the bumpy road, Taylor had to choose between breathing or banging her head.

Suddenly, she realized they were moving her without doping her—for the first time.

This sure can't be a good sign.

After they'd driven for almost two hours, the tall man from AQ told the guard, "Turn off here. The infidels always try to glean intelligence from our videos. Let them see what they can find from nothing but desert. We will shoot away from that limestone formation, and they will never be able to identify the location where we have killed her. And they will never beat the vultures to her corpse."

****

As I was still trying to figure out how to handle my incredible find, I saw the red light on the panel flash a split second before the alarm sounded. Shay was on the speaker. I quickly moved the bonds and gold out of the line of sight of the camera on the console.

"We've got company again, Novak. Same sensor out on the road, and it's heading your way. Train the camera out there, and let's see what we have."

"Roger that."

I flipped on the telescopic camera and zoomed in as close as it would go. All I could see was a cloud of dust. I followed the dust cloud as it got closer and morphed into a white pickup. Trying to see who was inside, I panned the camera to the left, but the dust was too thick.

Now what?

I hadn't had time to return the cameras to focus on the pool. If the hit man came back, Shay and his team would know I'd messed with the cameras.

The truck passed the range of the first camera, and I activated the next one, which picked it up. I started following the truck, panning as it slowed. But the camera stuck about halfway through its arc.

"It's stuck. I can't get it to move," I told Shay.

"I thought you cleaned them all out."

"I was doing that, but somebody told me to get back inside."

"Yeah. Okay. Turn on camera three."

Camera three should have picked up the truck as it left the second camera's range, but there was nothing.

"They must have stopped," I said.

"Novak," Colonel Hunt said this time from Washington. "We need you to put on your Ghille suit and go out and take a look."

"Yes, sir. Roger that."

I put my iPhone communicator in my pocket, scooped up my earpiece, and found the box with the Ghille suit in one of the storage bins. I quickly donned the suit, then opened the armory. Grabbing the Barrett M-107, I slapped in a ten-round, fifty-caliber magazine and clipped the nine-mike

Sig holster to my belt. Then I opened the door just high enough to slide under and closed it using a code on my communicator.

I crawled silently to the edge of the pile and saw the truck, motionless, about twenty feet off the road and maybe three hundred yards from the pile.

****

Cruella's husband unloaded a folding chair from the bed of the truck while Cruella set up a tripod with a small video camera mounted on top, then worked to level it on the uneven surface. The guard released Taylor from her chains, handcuffed her wrists behind her, pulled her out of the truck, and turned her over to Cruella, who dragged her to the chair.

"Today is the day for your confession," the guard said. "Today, whore, you will tell the world of your crimes and the crimes of your people."

"I'm not making any video for you. Never. And I'm not a whore, you filthy savage."

The guard put the barrel of his gun against her forehead, and Taylor started screaming.

"You will make this video, and you will confess your crimes," Cruella demanded. "If you don't, I will allow this man to do what he has wanted to do ever since we captured you."

"No! I won't do it! You'll just kill me anyway."

****

I saw them drag the woman to the chair. And I saw the sword the man standing behind her was leaning on.

"Control," I began. "I have the truck in sight. Four subjects; two males, two females. One female looks like a prisoner. They just set up a video camera. Hold on."

I scoped in on the woman in the chair and saw that she was wearing a torn brown T-shirt.

"Control, the prisoner's wearing GI-issue fatigues. Condo believes the prisoner is U.S. Army personnel—at least she's wearing our fatigues."

"Can you get a look at her face?"

"Negative. She's wearing a veil and keeps looking down. Control, it looks like they're forcing her to make a video. One subject has a large sword. I think they're going to behead her on tape."

"Are you sure?"

"I can only tell you what I see. One of them just slapped her and pointed to the camera. It looks like she's refusing to make the tape. Now the man with the sword is threatening her. I can hear her screaming from up here. Request permission to take out the bad guys."

"Condo, stand by."

"Hurry up! These guys aren't fooling around."

Within a few seconds, Shay came back. "Condo, permission to engage is denied."

"Control, say again?"

"Denied, Condo. Do not engage. We can't risk detection."

"Major, that's one of ours out there. You can't let them do this."

"Condo, permission is denied. Continue to observe and report."

"Roger. But this isn't right."

"That's not your decision, Condo."

I watched intently through my scope. The female soldier was screaming bloody murder, and the tall man was warming up with the sword. I reached up and muted my iPhone.

****

"You will confess," said the tall man, who now wore a black hood and held the sword to her neck.

"Please don't kill me. I'll make your video. I'll say anything you want, just don't kill me. I don't want my momma to see me like this."

"The whole world is going to see you die."

Taylor prayed out loud for a miracle, pleading to God for help.

"Your God will not help you now," the man said. "Where is your great, false God?"

The executioner raised the sword and took aim, tapping the sword at the nape of Taylor's neck as Cruella's husband pulled her hair to force her head down.

****

There's an old joke about MBAs: Ask an MBA any question, and the answer will be, "Well, it depends." The MBA curriculum at Chicago had taught us not only to be human "what-if spreadsheets," but also to weigh risk and reward.

With a sword literally hanging over the head of the imprisoned woman, I didn't have time to set up a spreadsheet on the situation. The risks couldn't be clearer. If I disobeyed a direct order, I could be a thirty-year prison sentence away from my discharge instead of just a few weeks. I also could put the condo project at risk, possibly costing my country the chance to get the terrorists responsible for 9-11 and the London bombing that killed my father. But the opportunity to save a fellow soldier tilted the balance sheet. I made the executive decision.

People think snipers always go for head shots. Sure, the most effective shot is to the so-called "fatal T" around the eyes, the nose, and the sinus cavity—cutting through bone, cartilage, and soft tissue. But this guy was moving, so I went for center mass.

If you get shot with a .50 caliber round, it doesn't matter where the projectile enters; you're usually done. The bullet from my rifle reached the would-be executioner three times faster than the report. The hole in his chest was impressive. The exit wound was even bigger. The damage to his vital organs as the bullet traversed his torso was massive and fatal. What was left of him was dead before he hit the ground.

I saw the prisoner look up through her tears as the guard was chambering his AK-47, looking for me in the distance and maybe wondering whether the infidel God might actually be the real one. Not finding me, he turned the gun on his prisoner. But his brain couldn't tell his finger to pull the trigger: it was no longer attached to his body. He'd made the mistake of giving me time to set up a head shot. Among my targets, there are only the quick and the dead. He was now among the latter.

Pistol in hand, the female terrorist had taken cover behind the truck. She peered over the top wall of the truck's cargo bed, yelling something in Arabic. The hostage buried her head in her lap as the explosion rocked the truck bed. She looked up just as her veiled tormenter went down. The .50 caliber projectile had penetrated the truck's double-steel sidewall.

****

I waited a few minutes, then radioed in. "Control, the truck has packed up and moved on, heading south." The direction covered by the broken camera.

"Maybe they were only rehearsing or trying to scare her," Shay said. Maybe they wanted to see if anyone hiding would reveal themselves. Probably just a coincidence and had nothing to do with us. We can't even be sure the prisoner was one of ours. Anyway, we couldn't risk exposure."

I could sense relief in the major's Pecksniffian voice that the execution hadn't happened and he couldn't be blamed for the woman's death. The plumbing business isn't the only one where it runs downhill.

"Control, I'm going to go take a look at that camera."

"Roger. Good idea."

I threw off the Ghille suit, grabbed an M4, and tossed the ladder over the outside cliff for my first venture outside the pile. The woman was outside the range of my iPhone communicator and I would briefly lose contact with the condo's Wi-Fi system, so I had to hurry. She saw me racing toward her and started screaming as she rocked the chair from side to side, trying to get free but tipping over sideways in the sand instead.

I checked the guard's pockets for the handcuffs key, found it, and freed the sobbing woman.

"Do you speak English?" I asked.

"I'm an American," she said in a Louisiana drawl.

"Me, too. Let's go. We don't have much time."

"Who are you?"

"I'll tell you later. We've got to clean this up."

"Clean what up?"

"Come on, quickly."

After dragging the guard's body into the bed of the truck, I put what was left of the dead executioner behind the wheel. Then I walked around the truck to get the woman. Her arm had been blown off, but she was still alive and bleeding out. Her 9-mm pistol lay a few feet away, and I picked it up and shoved it in my belt.

Now, what?

On seeing that the woman was breathing, the Southern belle coughed up a deep hack of phlegm and spit it in her tormentor's face. Then she grabbed the gun from my waist and emptied the clip into the woman, who could now add "dead" to her résumé.

"Help me get her in the cab."

I threw all their equipment, including the sword, into the back of the truck. Then I emptied their AK-47 into their bodies to camouflage their .50 caliber wounds. After removing the SD card from their video camera, I started the truck, jerking the steering wheel until it pointed the truck back into the nothingness of the desert, in the direction that was being covered by the condo's jammed camera. Grabbing a jerry can affixed to the tailgate, I splashed some gas in the cab, then slid the rear window open far enough to splash more gas through the opening. Using a sash from the headless man's robe, I tied the steering wheel straight, heading due south. I put it in low gear. The truck might travel miles before hitting something. By then, it wouldn't be my problem. As the truck moved on at about two miles an hour, I helped the woman to the ladder alongside the pile. She was too weak to climb, so I had to pretty much carry her. We finally made it to the top of the ladder, and I took her inside, set her down, gave her a bottle of water, and told her to stay put.

After inserting incendiary rounds in the M-107, I went back out and scoped-in the truck. It had gone not quite a mile. I had to keep recalibrating my aim, calculating distance and minutes of angle in my head, and using the legendary sniper Kentucky windage to adjust for the wind. I missed having The Dart at my side. Without a spotter, I needed five shots before a round went through the jerry can and ignited the gas. I heard a muffled explosion and watched until I could only see smoke as the truck disappeared in the distance.

****

"What is this place?"

"First, tell me who you are."

"Second Lieutenant Margaret Taylor. I'm an MP. They call me Maggie. I was kidnapped by these savages three or four months ago. I've lost track of time. What's the date?"

"December 28, ma'am."

"I was thinking it was January."

"You're the girl on the news. I was with the president the day they snatched you. He was very concerned for your safety."

"The president of what?"

"The president of the United States, ma'am."

176

"Yeah, sure. And you can forget the ma'am business. I am so done with all this army crap."

"No, listen. The president sent me here."

"How'd he know they'd bring me here?"

"No. Look out here."

I raised the window shade, and she saw down into the cavity of the pile.

"What is that? An oasis?"

"Exactly. There's intel that says shortly before every terrorist attack, the terrorists meet right down there by that pool of water. The army built this place and installed it so they could put a man here full time. I'm the first occupant."

"Who are you?"

"Sergeant Travis Novak, ma'am. I'm an army sniper and a short-timer. My hitch is up in a few weeks."

"I asked you to stop with the ma'am business, sarge. You just saved my life, so call me Maggie. Wait a minute. You're him—you got the Medal of Honor. I saw it on the internet right before they got me. You really were with the president."

"Guilty as charged."

"Well, do you have a radio or something? Can we call and get them to come pick me up?"

"There's a problem."

"What problem?"

When she heard that Control had been willing to let the terrorists chop her head off, she started crying again.

"So they were going to let me die out there while a perfectly capable Medal of Honor sniper was watching, ready to save me?"

"They have a lot invested in this place. They were afraid of being detected and blowing the whole mission."

"Gee, that makes me feel much better. So I was expendable."

"You know the army."

"What do we do now?"

"For right now, you stay here. I've got enough food until the next supply drop in a few days. I figure my hitch is up in a few weeks, and then I'll be discharged. Even if they knew you were here, they wouldn't risk coming for you. So we just keep it quiet, and you leave with me when they bring my replacement. When they find out you're here, they sure aren't going to give you back to the bad guys."

Taylor started coughing. "Sorry, I think I have pneumonia. A doctor they found gave me a shot yesterday, and I was supposed to start a Z-pack today. But I think it just drove off with the guy in the truck, the one missing his head."

I walked over to the medicine storage chest, pulled out a few drawers, and found five Z-packs. I tossed her one, got her a bottle of water, and then took a Z-pack for myself. If I caught whatever she had, it would be pretty hard to explain how I got a contagious disease in isolation.

"How long since you had something to eat?"

"A day or two. They gave me a bowl of rice; but I was so sick, I couldn't keep it down."

"I just finished my last Quarter Pounder, but I've got plenty of MREs and canned meats, crackers, and stuff like that."

"I'd kill for an MRE. Never thought a girl who grew up on New Orleans cuisine would ever say that."

****

ATEC had designed the condo for a single occupant, and a second person—especially a woman—hadn't been envisioned. The already claustrophobic condo became even tighter quarters.

Supplies were a concern. I'd have to watch the consumables. Maggie had already inhaled four bottles of water and two Cokes. Starved, she'd polished off three MREs, a can of soup, two cans of fruit, and several candy bars. I'd have to figure out how to order more food for the next drop.

Of course, the first thing Maggie wanted to do after eating was to brush her teeth and take a shower. Toothbrushes I had. Showers were my biggest concern; they used up water, and the pond was already down a foot. With no rain in the forecast for the coming week, we'd somehow have to make it work.

Nor was the condo designed with privacy in mind. I draped the small parachute that I'd retrieved from the Christmas drop around the open-ended wall to the recessed toilet and shower area. To provide each other some privacy, one of us could step outside the condo—but only if we were alone. Once the visitors arrived, we'd be sealed in. And although ATEC had spent millions on the place, a forty-buck bathroom exhaust fan had apparently been considered an extravagance.

After her shower, Maggie wanted to sleep, so I inflated the air mattress I'd purchased at Walmart for her and she was out like a light. I'd given her one of my size XL T-shirts and a pair of boxers that I'd fixed for her by pinning the fly shut and taking out a few inches of elastic in the waist. What was left of her uniform would be washed as soon as the generator was on again.

While Maggie was sleeping, I cleaned her up. She had several cuts and scrapes, and was loaded with bruises. A good-sized weal where somebody had punched her protruded on her forehead. When I saw the welts covering her legs and back, I wished I'd emptied my clip into the woman, too.

I was most concerned about her leg, where she'd been chained for months. After cleaning the wound and applying some antibiotic ointment, I covered it with gauze. I figured the Z-pack would prevent any further infection.

Her wounds and injuries would heal. As for any hostage, the big problem would be psychological. I was also concerned about how she might react to being confined inside if something went down.

Maggie slept in fits and starts. She'd sleep for a while, then wake up crying. Each time, I held and comforted her until she fell back to sleep.

When Maggie finally appeared to be in a sound sleep, I remembered the gold bars and bearer bonds that I'd left near the control panel and quietly put them in my backpack. So much had happened since I'd discovered the treasure cave, I'd had no time to figure out what to do with them.

****

The radio suddenly beeped, and Maggie bolted upright.

"It's Control," I explained. "Stay down and be quiet."

She nodded her understanding.

I was quickly ensuring that the control-panel camera was focused only on the desk chair when I heard Major Shay's voice: "Condo, this is Control."

"This is Condo," I responded.

"Condo, our aircraft found the truck in a ravine several miles southwest of your location. It had turned over and caught fire. We sent in a chopper, and our guys found three deceased, really shot up. A video camera that we retrieved must have been thrown clear when the truck rolled, but it didn't have a storage card. The camera was a little charred, but the internal memory had a few seconds of video that briefly showed the female in another location. We've confirmed it's the missing MP, but she was nowhere to be found."

"You think she did it?"

"Not sure what else to believe. She must have gotten the drop on them somehow. Or maybe they met up with some other bad guys who grabbed her. A female U.S. soldier is a valuable commodity to these guys, so we're looking for her now. We want you to keep your eyes open in case she comes back your way."

"Roger that."

I was happy that Maggie could hear that the army valued her and was trying to rescue her.

"The last thing we need," Shay continued, "is some girl wandering around spooking our guests."

Great. Just great, major.

I shot a glance at Maggie, who was giving the finger to the control-panel screen.

"Roger that, Control. I'll keep an eye out and advise. Condo out."

"Control out."

"So they don't care that I might be wandering around in the middle of the desert," Maggie said. "I might be wounded, or I could starve or die of thirst. Do they care? No, they're only worried that I don't spook their operation here."

"You make it sound personal," I said. "They wouldn't care whoever was out there. They only care about getting the bad guys they think are heading here. The rest of us are more than expendable. One reason I was selected for this mission is that I have no close living relatives."

"I'm sorry to hear that. What happened to your parents?"

"My mom died during childbirth. Her doctor told her she might die if she had me, but she didn't blink. She said she was having her baby no matter what."

"And your dad?"

"He raised me, and he's the reason I'm here at all—in the army, I mean. Dad was an investment banker at a firm in St. Louis. He was on a road show for a client company. . ."

"A road show?"

"A road show is what companies do when they file a stock offering. They spend about two weeks going from city to city, meeting with investors.

Dad, two guys from his company, and a woman who worked for the client were in London when AQ bombed the underground."

"Oh, my. I'm so sorry, Travis."

"Dad survived a blast in a nearby train car and tried to get the woman he was with out of the car. She was unconscious, and a fire at the far end of the car was getting closer. Dad started to carry her out. He got her about a hundred yards down the track when he had a massive coronary. He died in the ambulance on the way to the hospital.

"Travis, I'm so very sorry."

"Thank you. I'd been accepted to the MBA program at Chicago when it happened, and I swore that as soon as I got my degree, I was going to take out as many of the people responsible as I could. I figured becoming a sniper was the best way to get my revenge, and a general I knew pulled some strings to get me into sniper school."

"So that's why they sent you here? You're also expendable, and they knew you wouldn't hesitate to pull the trigger?"

I looked at her without answering. Of course, she was right. And having seen her battered body, I wanted to get those bad guys more than ever.

Chapter 33

Abbottabad, Pakistan

December 28, 2008

Osama bin Laden was in the backseat of a Suzuki SUV, uncomfortable under the blanket that was hiding him. He and his driver, his trusted aide Abu Ahmed al-Kuwaiti, had made the switch from the big rig about forty miles outside of town.

"How much farther, Abu?"

"About a mile, my sheik. Stay down. We're nearing that Pakistani military school; they're always wanting to stick their noses where they don't belong."

Having enjoyed his time away, bin Laden wasn't happy about returning to his prison-like life inside the compound.

"Abu, when we make the score after these next attacks, I don't care what the prince says. We're getting out of this slum. Maybe we'll get some plastic surgery and move to someplace where we can walk the streets."

"That   would   be   very   vain,   my   sheik."

       "Of course, you are right. But you must admit that we've given much to our cause. And what do we get for our devotion? Imprisonment in a low-rent villa. Remember when the prince said he was building us a villa? The man calls this a villa? Have you ever seen his apartment in Paris, or his villa in Tuscany? *That* is a villa. This is a hovel. And to make it worse, I can't even leave."

"But even the American president is said to be a prisoner in the White House."

"What I wouldn't give to be imprisoned in a place like that. Have you ever seen pictures of the White House? The man has only one wife, and the place is immaculate."

"I believe they have servants, my sheik."

"I suppose so. But I will wager that his wife provides him with good meals, not this dog crap we are fed here."

"Stay down; we're here."

"Oh, great."

Abu blew the horn, the gates opened, and Osama got out of the SUV and stretched his six-foot, four-inch frame. In a building not far away, a powerful telephoto lens on a CIA camera snapped a photo of him as he exited the vehicle.

"Home, sweet home," bin Laden said bitterly.

Chapter 34

The White House

December 28, 2008

The director of the National Security Agency, the secretary of defense, and the national security adviser were in the Oval Office, briefing the president. The leader of the free world was steaming.

"You're telling me that the girl—the U.S. soldier—these madmen have been holding for months appears right before our eyes, and you decide not to save her?"

The secretary of defense squirmed in his seat. "Sir, it happened very fast. The truck stopped. Our folks on the ground didn't know who she was until later. Novak said it appeared that the woman was wearing army fatigues, and he couldn't see her face. The man on the scene, Major Shay, thought it might be a trap to draw us out of the condo."

"Three bodies riddled with bullet holes sure doesn't sound like a setup to me. Do you think that little gal took them out?"

"We don't know, sir, but that's the easiest explanation. Somehow, she got hold of a gun and started shooting. She isn't a marksman, but being an MP, she knew her way around a 9-mm pistol. It looks like she shot the woman multiple times and then picked up something larger in caliber and took out the other two. Their bodies were burned so badly, it's hard to tell. It had to have happened fast. We didn't want to take the bodies back for autopsy in case someone was looking for them so close to the condo, so we just took pictures and DNA swabs and left the rest."

"What happened to her?"

"Sir, we don't know. The pickup truck overturned and burned. It must have been a bad crash because the woman even lost an arm. There were only three bodies there, all burned to a crisp. If the camera hadn't been thrown out of the truck bed, we wouldn't have known for sure that the prisoner was our missing soldier. The data on the hard drive was from some other location, and she was refusing to make a video confession. They must have been looking for a spot to make another video when this happened. She might be wandering around trying to find help. Or she could have been snatched by someone they met in the desert. Or, for all we know, she might have been shot and thrown out somewhere else."

"Let's assume for the time being that AQ no longer has her. Let's see if they keep pressing their demands. And nobody says a word to her uncle, that idiot congressman. You can be sure that loudmouth would hold another press conference, and her daddy would fly to the desert himself to take names and kick butts—and I can't say I'd blame him because we're sure not getting anywhere. Let's keep searching. It pains me to say that the chances of finding her out there are slim, but let's keep looking without drawing attention to the condo. Anything new on that front?"

Before responding, the director of the NSA opened a file and removed a sheet of paper.

"Sir, we're following up on that phone call between UBL and the Boss. We just confirmed that UBL was in Pakistan, in the middle of nowhere, and that his throwaway phone was bought in Islamabad. The Boss was in a car moving quickly through Monte Carlo, near the main casino, also on a burner phone. We're hearing a lot of chatter but nothing specific. Oh, and sir, the border patrol found a tunnel that crossed into California from near Tijuana. They caught a couple of low-level drug-cartel mules who said two Middle Eastern types came through the tunnel about eight days ago. We're circulating descriptions, but they could be anywhere by now. We don't like this one bit."

"Boys, turn up the heat. I will not have them launch another attack on American soil on my watch. Let's hope somebody else shows up in the desert soon. Sounds like that may be our only hope."

Chapter 35

The Condo, Northwestern Iraq

December 31, 2008–January 1, 2009

The helicopters had stopped their sweeps of the desert the previous day. They'd already given up on the drones with body-heat sensors that they'd used to search for Maggie before sending the choppers.

Shay said they feared she'd been killed in the gun battle or that another group of bad guys had snatched her.

"We've looked everywhere," he said from Control. "We've spent a couple of days looking out in the open, and we can't risk it anymore. If our friends see increased activity in the zone, they might get spooked."

"Well, let's hope she's holed up somewhere," I told Shay. "I'll keep my eyes open."

"Roger. Big plans for New Year's Eve tonight?"

"Roger, Control. I think I'll get a date, maybe have a few drinks, do a little dancing, and then maybe some fireworks at midnight."

Shay laughed. "Let's hope our fireworks start soon."

"Roger that. Condo out."

I shut down the communications system and swiveled the chair around to see Maggie. She was leaning against the wall, smiling. No longer so hurt by the army's betrayal, she was getting into the idea of putting one over on them. And her health had improved a lot. Her cough was gone, and her bruises were fading.

"So, Travis, you have anyone in mind for your New Year's Eve date?"

"Actually, I do."

"Who would that be, if you don't mind my asking?"

I quickly swiveled the control chair toward her, I took her wrist and gently pulled her onto my lap. Our first kiss lasted a very long time.

When we finally parted, I asked, "Does that mean you accept my invitation?"

"At OCS, they told us we're not supposed to fraternize with the help."

"That's too bad," I said, "because I've been saving a surprise for my New Year's date. But if you can't be seen with an enlisted grunt . . ."

"A surprise?"

"Yeah, I've been saving it for a while. But if you're not available, I might have to take the dune buggy out and pick up another girl."

"You're not going anywhere, mister."

Putting her arms around my neck, she hugged me tightly, then buried her head in my chest. Her hands found the replica of the Medal of Honor the president had given me.

"I think there's a special exception to the rule on fraternizing for enlisted men who've won this medal."

"Well, I'm sure glad to hear that."

"I accept. What time will you pick me up?"

I put my arms under her, lifted her up, and walked her backwards to the air mattress.

"Would now be convenient?"

"Now would be just fine. Travis?"

"Yes, Maggie?"

"What are the numbers on the back of the medal you wear on your dog tags?"

"If I told you that, I'd have to . . ."

I didn't get to finish the punch line to the old joke. Maggie was already smothering me with kisses.

****

Maggie fixed dinner while the generator ran and then took another shower, still trying to wash off the ordeal of her captivity. I actually liked having her with me. I was happy to be at the condo—for the first time.

Every day, Maggie was getting better. She no longer kept her head bowed all the time, was slowly gaining weight, and looked healthier. And each day, she appeared more beautiful to me.

187

True to my word, at ten o'clock local time, I produced my surprise: two cans of ice-cold Stag beer. I'd chiseled them into the large block of ice that provided the coolant for the fridge.

"Madam, we are out of champagne, but may I offer you a beer? You drink beer, don't you?"

"Honey, I went to Tulane University. What do you think? And where'd you get hold of a beer out here?"

Thinking about how much I loved her accent, I told her about Colonel Hunt's air drop. Then we popped the tops and went out on the loading deck to sit in the cool air and watch the new year creep toward us off to the east. The stars dancing in the clear desert sky were more beautiful than any crystal ball dropping in Times Square.

Maggie wouldn't leave my side. I couldn't tell if it was me, simple gratitude, or fear the bad guys would come back. But I wasn't complaining.

"Pick some music on my iPhone," I told her, and she selected "Do You Believe Me Now?" by Jimmy Wayne.

She complained that my iPhone didn't have enough country music and surprised me a bit when she knew all the words to the ones I had. We sipped our second beers and snuggled closely.

"May I have this dance, Maggie?"

"You may, sir."

We were dancing on the fake, flat rock when she suggested taking a walk down by the pool. I threw the ladder over the side, and we took our beers with us and walked toward the water. For a while, we sat on a small boulder, staying out of the line of sight of the cameras, enjoying the night. Our conversation was interrupted by the beep of the iPhone communicator.

"Novak," Shay's voice said, "there's company on the road. Where are you?"

"My New Year's Eve date and I are outside taking some air."

"Get back inside right now. Could be our boy."

I followed her up the ladder, which she now could negotiate by herself albeit pretty slowly. When we got up top, I told her to go inside, but she wouldn't leave me. I pulled up the ladder, then climbed to the top of the pile to take a look.

"Control, I have visual on the vehicle. It's too far away to make out."

"Roger, Condo, get back inside and button up. Let's see what this is."

"Roger that."

Maggie and I scrambled inside. The armored window shade had already lowered automatically, and the condo had gone to power-conservation mode. Maggie was tense and held onto my leg as she sat on the floor next to the leather recliner. I could tell she was afraid they might be coming back for her.

"Don't worry," I reassured her. "They have no idea we're here."

She scooted even closer to me while I trained the zoom lens in the direction of the alarm. Going to infrared, I recognized the vehicle as the same SUV that had come before. I told Maggie to remain absolutely quiet, and she nodded.

"It appears to be our friend," I reported to Shay.

"Roger, Condo."

The visitor didn't waste any time. A canvas bag slung over his shoulder, he made straight for the entrance to the pile. We followed him on various cameras as he took out his lever and moved the big rock to make his way through the maze and into the interior of the pile. Guided by the beam of a flashlight he held, he went directly to the video camera he'd hidden on his last visit, removed the SD card, and inserted another one.

Maggie started pulling my arm, silently mouthing something. I hit the mute button. "I'm kind of busy right now," I said.

"Travis, I think I left my beer down there. I set it down when I grabbed hold of the ladder."

"Let's hope he doesn't see it."

Our guest walked to the pool, just a few feet from where we'd been sitting a few minutes earlier. We hadn't had time to cover our tracks, and I was worried that if he saw and followed our footprints, they might take him straight to the beer can. Although he probably wouldn't find us, and there was no way he could get up to the condo without a long ladder, our cover would be totally blown if he found a still-cold can of American beer.

But our guy was focused on something else. As he'd done the first time, he prayed, removed his clothes, and waded into the pool with the canvas bag that he'd brought with him. He disappeared underwater for a few minutes, then resurfaced, got dressed, and walked to the entrance. I engaged the mic.

"Control, did you guys ever figure out why he does that?"

"Negative, Condo. Best guess is it is some kind of ceremony—like they get power from this holy water. Somehow, he must be coming up for breaths, but our psychological consultants are still baffled."

189

"Roger."

We followed the visitor on camera as he returned to the SUV. The bag appeared to have something heavy in it, but I didn't point that out to Control. Of course, there was no doubt in my mind what he'd put in the bag. He got into the vehicle and without turning on the headlights made his way back to the road. I saw the beams go on when the SUV was about a mile down the road. Then he disappeared.

"What do you think, Control?"

"I think once they see their SD card's blank, they'll think nobody's been here. He left the camera, so he might come back again before the big party."

We signed off, and I hurried outside and threw down the ladder. Sure enough, Maggie's beer was sitting there in full view. I grabbed the palm frond and retraced our steps, erasing our footsteps in the sand. Then I chugged the rest of the beer, crushed the can and stuck it in my pocket, and went back upstairs just as Iraq was ushering in 2009.

****

I climbed back up the chain ladder, and Maggie was waiting at the top in one of my sweatshirts, arms crossed in front of her. Without makeup, not even lipstick, she was 100 percent all-American girl, and she looked stunning. She reached down to help me up—an unnecessary but welcome gesture.

"Good news and bad news," I told her.

"What's the good news?"

"I found your beer, and he didn't see it."

"And the bad news?"

"The can was half full, and I finished it off."

She slapped my bad shoulder hard, and I winced.

"I'm sorry, Travis. Does your shoulder still hurt from being shot?"

"Yes, sometimes. I still have a little numbness."

She led me inside, lifted my shirt, and ran her fingers across my scar. Then she leaned over and gently kissed the jagged line.

"I can't imagine how you did it. A bullet in your shoulder and shrapnel in your leg, losing blood, and you can still carry a man like that. You really deserved that medal."

"I would trade it in a second if I could have saved my spotter."

"I know you would. You're a very good man, Travis Novak."

"The kind of man you could take home to meet your mother?"

"Oh, my. That would take some real finesse. Momma doesn't approve of mixed marriages."

"Of what?"

"Well, you being a Yankee and all."

I laughed and hugged her again. We closed the condo for the night, and I stuck a DVD in my laptop that she'd chosen. She'd picked out *Mr. Deeds*.

"Have you ever seen it, Travis?"

"No, I've been pretty busy the last few years," I said. But I'd actually seen it a dozen times.

"It's about this regular guy who inherits billions of dollars and wants to find the girl of his dreams the way his father had met his mother—by saving her life. He didn't want the money to get in the way of romance."

"I see."

"You're not worth billions of dollars are you, Travis?"

"Billions? Not yet."

"So what are you? Just a humble millionaire sniper?"

I decided not to tell her about the $8 million or the gold bars and bearer bonds, and to ignore her question.

I'll play Mr. Deeds a while longer.

"Oh, sure. I was issued a lot of stock options on the Iraq war, and I've made a ton shorting al-Qaeda. But I should have about six months' pay waiting for me when I get back. You should have a pretty nice balance in your account, too."

She laughed and started to slug my shoulder again but caught herself.

"Well, you sure saved my life. We met in probably the most unorthodox way any couple ever met."

"So, we're a couple now?"

"What do you think? "she teased, wrapping her arms around me and staring up with her gorgeous blue eyes.

I thought I approved wholeheartedly, and we fell asleep until six o'clock when the communicator beeped.

"Novak," Colonel Svoboda said from Control. "We need you to jump back down to the pool to check that camera and make sure he didn't leave anything other than the new SD card."

I climbed down the ladder, iPhone communicator in hand, and transmitted video of the new card, which was a different brand than the one he'd taken.

"Are you going to drop me a new one?"

"Can't risk it right now. With the activity of looking for the missing girl and our visitor, it's not worth it. Try to stay out of the camera's line of sight. We'll make your supply drop in three days anyway, and I'll stick a couple of new cards in that."

"Roger that, sir. I'm looking forward to that drop."

"Oh, by the way. We're getting a little modulation problem from your satellite uplink. While we're there, I'm going to drop down a technician to snap in a new module. It's a bit tricky, so I'm not sure you could handle it. He'll be in and out in ten, no more than fifteen, minutes. By the time you're done off-loading the tank and bins, he'll be finished."

"Ah, roger, that."

"We've got your request list here. Looks like you're eating for two these days. Better watch that waistline."

"Well, sir, with all this company I keep getting, you never know how long I'll be cooped up here."

"We've got it all here. They're getting your storage bins loaded. We'll be there on the third, barring any more company."

"Thank you, sir. I'm looking forward to it more than you can imagine."

"I'll bet you are, Novak. Control out."

Now what?

****

Maggie was waiting for me when I returned topside.

"What was that about?"

I explained to her about the surveillance camera and the storage cards, and then dropped the bomb about the technician stopping by for morning tea. She asked if I thought they'd find it strange if I asked them to include some makeup and a blow dryer.

"I think it's best that we tell them about you and let them take you out."

"But then they'd know you shot those animals."

She could tell I was concerned. I'd committed several very serious offenses, starting with disobeying a direct and lawful order from the president, which they might not overlook. Worse was that I'd breached my responsibility to keep the condo secret, a national security issue that might not even be in the army's purview. If the Justice Department had authority, it would be next to impossible for the president to interfere on my behalf. I explained my dilemma to Maggie.

"So if they find out about me, you might go to prison?"

"Maybe, maybe not. I think the president likes me, but he probably won't be happy about how I handled this situation. The new guy who'll replace him isn't particularly fond of the military. I just don't know."

I told her if she left with me on my last day in the army, I'd be out of their control. I figured I could just tell them I found her wandering outside the condo. I wasn't sure they'd believe it, but they couldn't prove my story was false as long as we both stuck to it.

"Then I'm not going."

"You want to stay here?"

"As long as you're here, I'm staying. I'll just make myself scarce when the technician drops in."

We looked around the pile for a place she could hide for the half hour it would take for the technician to do his thing. But there wasn't any place that couldn't be seen from the air. I thought about dropping her outside the pile, but I wasn't going to chance that.

"What if I stay in the bathroom?"

"You think a guy who just rode a bone-jarring helicopter for two hours isn't going to want to make the bathroom his first stop?"

"Then what do we do?"

I knew how much Maggie wanted to tell her parents she was safe and how anxious she was to get home. But she was willing to stick it out for my sake. It was a true Mr. Deeds moment.

I explained what we had to do and where she would hide.

Chapter 36

Abbottabad, Pakistan

January 2, 2009

Abu Ahmed al-Kuwaiti, Osama bin Laden's trusted confidant and courier, had stopped at a coffee shop after prayers. He liked to get away from the compound whenever he could, but this excursion was business mixed with pleasure.

The waiter at the busy cafe brought him a cup of strong coffee and several nankhatai cookies. Under the napkin on the small plate, Abu found, and palmed, a thumb drive from operatives in France. Communicating by computer drives was a pain, but it was safe.

On his return to the compound, Abu's cell rang. He answered it instinctively, momentarily forgetting the warning that had been issued on using a cell phone near the compound. An old friend and comrade from Abu's time on the battlefield in Afghanistan was wondering what he was up to. He was with the same people he'd been with before, Abu al-Kuwaiti told the man cryptically. Understanding that it was an inopportune time for Abu to talk, the caller signed off.

Though Abu regretted taking the call, the conversation had been very brief. With hundreds of thousands of calls made within the city and many millions in Pakistan, he told himself it was unlikely that the call would raise any red flags. But Abu didn't know about the NSA's new computer, Kirkos, and its ability to find needles not only in haystacks, but in entire farm fields of random data.

Dismissing the call from his thoughts once he was at the compound, Abu found bin Laden watching television in a room on the top floor. In the small, dark room, bin Laden was watching a 1970s American sitcom on VHS about a man who lived with two women who liked to show their flesh. The man pretended to be gay to deceive the landlord. What kind of a country, Abu wondered, would watch trash like this—although he had to admit that the show's theme song was catchy.

Their demise can't come fast enough.

Retrieving a laptop from the top of Osama's desk, Abu handed the computer and the thumb drive to the terrorist-in-chief.

"You put it in, Abu. I don't understand these machines. Maybe we should get one of those Apple computers. They're supposed to be easier to use, and they don't get viruses. The last time we hooked this up to the internet, your brother somehow downloaded that virus program, and the thing ran like molasses and sent letters about a weight-loss program to my entire address book. People who sit around dreaming up such unscrupulous tricks to invade innocent people's privacy should be found and shot."

The aide inserted the drive into the laptop's USB port and opened the file. He engaged the encryption program, and the prince's short message appeared on the screen:

> They will be busy with their transition on the 20th. Their guard will be down. We will meet at the sanctuary at eleven local time that night. I will give you the targets and the timeline then. Be sure your team in-country is ready. Allah will be pleased with our attack. All praises are due to Allah. How free from imperfection is Allah?

"Can you believe this guy, Abu? He hasn't seen the inside of a mosque since . . ."

Opening the door and interrupting bin Laden was Abu's brother.

"Those kids next door kicked their ball over the wall again," he told them. "I think they do it because you always give them money to buy another one."

"Give them a thousand rupees. All those kids have cell phones with cameras. We will all be dead if one of them gets a picture inside the walls and puts it on the internet. Go quickly."

Alone again with his confidant, bin Laden said, "We've got to get out of this place, Abu. It's driving me insane."

Chapter 37

The Condo, Northwestern Iraq

January 2, 2009

If it was possible to fall in love with someone in only a few days, it had just happened to me. And Maggie's willingness to put her life at risk by staying with me at the condo—after all she'd been through—told me she felt the same way.

Maggie was on the computer, reading the news. I'd told her she couldn't visit any websites that would be out of character for me, reminding her that Control watched everything I read. Bored, she kept asking if there was a way she could access her email account. The ding of my email box interrupted her third request.

"Honey?"

Now I was honey.

"Yes, dear?"

"Hon, you have an email here. You sure don't get many emails. As good-looking a man as you are, I'd think you'd have all kind of girls begging for your attention."

"I've told you that I don't have a girlfriend. See what it is, will you?"

"No girlfriends? Well then, who is Miss Sally Effingham? She sure seems very familiar with my new boyfriend."

"Uh . . ."

"Let's just see what little Miss Sally has to say."

I tried to tell Maggie that Sally was an ancient acquaintance, but there was no stopping her. Assuming a dramatic Southern-accented voice, she read the email out loud.

> My Dear Travis,
>
> It's been far too many years since we were last together. I think of the close, intimate times we shared during our years at Barrington often and fondly.
>
> I'm so proud of you and your accomplishments during your brave service to our country. I was telling Mommy just the other day about your medal. She agreed that of all my boyfriends growing up, you were the finest gentleman.
>
> Sadly, I married badly and am recently divorced from a horrible man who hurt me greatly. I am relieved to be out of that situation and ready to get on with the rest of my life.
>
> It's my hope that you'll be discharged from the service in time to attend the Barrington ten-year reunion this summer. I'm having an after-party at my home in Frontenac for the better people of the class. I certainly hope you'll be able to attend. If you get the opportunity, I'd welcome your response.
> Fondly,
> Sally Effingham
>
> P.S. If you wouldn't mind, please don't tell your cousin Freddie about my little get-together after the reunion. He's been badgering me to go out with him, but I'm not interested. He's becoming a pest. I hope you understand.
>
> XOXO
> S.

"Well, it sure sounds like Miss Sally is hot to get her hands back on the best boyfriend a girl ever had."

I told Maggie about how Sally's mother had made her break up with me and how Sally's husband had jilted her for a stripper. I had no interest in Sally at all, I explained to Maggie.

Walking the few steps to where I was sitting, she snuggled up next to me.

"I can't imagine that Miss Sally has anything I need to worry about anyway. What does she have that I don't?"

"Well, I hear she fleeced her ex-husband for $30 million in the divorce."

Maggie punched my bad shoulder as hard as she could and gave me a pout that I'd come to love.

Seizing the moment, I said, "It's time we had an important talk, Maggie."

"You're dumping me already? It's that snooty gold-digger Sally, isn't it?"

"To the contrary. It's you."

"You want her money, don't you?"

"No, I don't want her money. I don't even need it."

"Then what are you talking about?"

"I'll show you. But first, can you swim underwater?"

"I won the butterfly three years in a row at the country club before we had to resign because Daddy's business went south. And in New Orleans, you know where you end up if you go south."

I grabbed the flashlight and put my iPhone communicator and a 9-mm in a Ziploc bag, then inside a second bag for security. I couldn't chance being out of contact in case Control called or, worse, we had company. I lowered the ladder, and we walked to the pool, being careful not to cross in front of the surveillance cameras. I took off my pants and shirt.

"You fixin' to try to get me to go skinny dippin' here, Travis? I'm not saying 'no,' you understand, but it's a bit nippy for my taste."

The water temperature in the pool was about fifty, and she shivered as we waded in. I told her to follow me, and she held my hand as we went under and onto the landing. I put her on top first, then barely squeezed on myself.

"What are we doing, darlin'?"

"You'll see in a minute."

I could see the water level was down about four more inches. I no longer had to bob up to see out onto the floor of the pile. I switched on the flashlight and led her around the corner and up the stairs.

Stunned, she was silent for thirty long seconds before asking, "What is this place?"

"Best I can tell, it's an AQ vault. When the man comes in and goes underwater, he makes either a deposit or a withdrawal. I have no idea how much is here. They don't know about this at Control, and I'm not about to tell them."

She looked at the gold bars and then went to an old wooden box full of jewelry, some items in velvet boxes, others loose. Bracelets and necklaces with stones of various colors and sizes refracted sparkles all over the cave when Maggie aimed the flashlight on the box. Rooting around, she found a leather pouch, which she opened to find about four dozen loose diamonds, each one probably weighing at least two carats.

"We'll take the pouch back with us," I said.

She continued rifling through the jewels while I estimated the number of gold bars and looked inside some other boxes. Some had bundles of plastic-wrapped euros, others U.S. C-notes. I didn't bother taking any right then; we needed a plan first.

"Honey, look at this."

She was holding up an ancient wooden box that contained an engagement-style ring. The ring's huge round diamond had to be over three carats.

"Can I take it?"

"No, you can't take it from them."

"But, Travis . . ."

I took the ring from Maggie and slipped it on her ring finger. It fit perfectly.

"But I'm hoping you'll take it from me. Maggie Taylor, is there a chance in the world that you'll marry me?"

She threw her arms around me and smothered me with kisses.

"Oh, yes, Travis. I knew that first day we were meant for each other. I love you, Travis Novak."

"And I love you, too, Maggie."

She danced around, almost forgetting how cold she was. I took the diamonds and two more gold bars, and we exited the cave and were quickly out of the water. I grabbed my clothes and tucked them under my arm. Then I dragged the palm frond behind me to cover the footprints, not wanting to make the same mistake again.

We got inside, shivering, but no worse for the wear. I explained that we'd get her inside the cave when the chopper pilot radioed that he was about an hour out. She could take some dry clothes with her in a Ziploc bag and wait for the chopper to leave. And while she was there, she could take a more accurate inventory.

But Maggie was barely listening to me. She couldn't take her eyes off her sparkling new engagement ring.

****

I'd just asked Maggie to marry me, but I knew precious little about her. Once we were back in the condo, she told me about growing up as an only child in New Orleans. In high school, she'd missed the cut to be a cheerleader, but she'd excelled on the pom-pom squad—in the South, almost as good. She'd had several boyfriends, none serious.

Early in her high school years, her dad's business had hit rough waters.

"My daddy played tight end for the Tulane Green Wave. He got drafted by the Saints, made it to the last cut, and then broke his ankle. When his ankle didn't respond to surgery, he got hired on by a big Tulane booster who owned a corporate travel agency. Daddy signed up a lot of new clients, but the guy was cheating him on the commissions. After a while, Daddy started his own agency and was doing great—a lot of charters, Tulane away games and cruises and all. But people started booking their own travel on the internet more and more. After a couple of bad years, he closed his company and hired on with my Uncle Wes's medical sales company. Did I mention that my uncle is a congressman?"

"No, you forgot that part."

"Anyway, Daddy was doing great again. Then dumb old Uncle Wes went and sold the company to a bunch of Canadians who moved it to Toronto. To Daddy, the only thing worse than Yankees are Canadians, so there was no way we were moving to Canada. Mom was doing okay in real estate but not setting the world on fire, and sending me to college was looming. She read this article about military academies—what a great education you got and how it was all free. I had good grades, my ACTs were great, and I was involved in all types of things like the newspaper and Girl's State. I also was class treasurer."

"Good, we're going to need someone with money skills here very soon."

"Yeah, right, Sergeant MBA. Then Mom starts bugging Uncle Wes to get me appointed to a military academy. But he's getting heat from the *Times Picayune* about some twenty-three-year-old secretary he hired for like triple what a secretary should make. He was afraid if he appointed me—even to the Coast Guard Academy—the press would murder him. So he came up with this ROTC scholarship at Tulane."

She took a sip from a cup of coffee she'd made to warm up, then continued her story.

"The deal was, of course, that I had to serve after graduation. But school was free, and it's a very expensive and highly rated school. ROTC crimped my style a bit, what with all the drills and summer training, but I even got a stipend for spending money. It was a real help after Katrina. Tulane closed for the year, and ROTC got a bunch of us into SMU temporarily. That way I didn't miss any time off and graduated on time. Unfortunately, my major was archeology, and there's not much call for that in the army. They knew I was going to serve my time and bolt. Except—just my luck—there was a special connection between the military and archeology in Iraq. So they made me an MP and sent me out to patrol some ancient ruins, like the terrorists are going to blow up their own history. How stupid would that be? That's where those awful terrorists nabbed me. Now, I've got about nine months left in my hitch. We'll have to postpone our wedding, I guess, until I get out—unless you want to follow me to some dingy army base, sergeant short-timer."

"Unless I miss my bet, you're going to get out sooner than that."

We talked about how we'd get her out of Iraq and fix it so she'd be able to seek an immediate discharge at the same time.

"Travis, what are we going to do about all this money?"

I told her I was working on it.

****

I'd gone down to the generator storage hold to make sure everything was ready for the drop the next day. Sitting on a five-gallon bucket of the fake rock material, I began work on a plan.

It was obvious that we couldn't take the money out with us. If my story was going to be believed, Maggie would have to be found without much of anything on her person. I'd be going out on the copter, back to Kuwait, and I was certain they'd search me for anything that might reveal the condo's existence. Even if I could fit the bearer bonds and diamonds in the secret compartment of my backpack, there still was a risk that they'd be discovered.

An even bigger problem was the gold. I decided I could remove a cubic foot of gold without making the stack look noticeably smaller. I'd rearrange the stack, perhaps leaving some hollow spaces inside. I used the calculator on my personal iPhone to figure out how many thousand-gram bars would make a cubic foot. All those AP math classes my dad made me take at

Barrington made him a prophet. He'd always said they'd come in handy someday. A cubic foot of gold, I calculated, would weigh a little over twelve hundred pounds. Twelve hundred and four pounds, to be exact.

There are 19,264 ounces of gold in a cubic foot. The question was the price per ounce. I knew our country was printing money like hell was a half-block away. Then there was the war in the Mideast and the collapse of the housing market. All that was going to drive up the value of gold.

Low-balling the price of gold at $750 an ounce, a cubic foot of gold would be worth over $14 million. Counting the $2 million in bearer bonds and diamonds, figuring we could probably find some more precious stones, and including at least some of the cash, we'd have at least $25 million. After adding my own funds, I'd be in Sally Effingham territory without ever having to listen to her mother's vitriolic tongue. The problem, however, was getting it out of the cave and back to civilization

I leaned back against the wall, and the bucket of condo goop slipped out from under me. Suddenly, I knew exactly how I'd do it.

****

The chopper was scheduled to arrive the next the morning with a full tank of propane and my supply request. The Liquid Petroleum gauge indicated that there was probably enough propane for another week; conserving had paid off.

Control had asked me to let the generator run a few more hours than normal to reduce the tank's weight. It was a treat for both of us to enjoy long showers and to cook dinner without worrying about using too much power.

What I wasn't conserving was the supply of Coke. Maggie was a Diet Coke lover, so I'd ordered four cases to be dropped in the resupply. To explain the switch from regular to diet, I'd told Control that I was gaining weight and needed to watch my calories. We were probably the only couple on Earth that ever toasted their engagement with bottled water.

All I had to do to begin my new life was to skate by seventeen more days and then I'd be discharged. I hadn't contemplated having a wife so quickly, but I was very much at peace with the idea of having a family again. And Maggie and I would be a great team.

I was still concocting a cover story that would explain Maggie's presence when they came to ferry me out of the condo on the last day of my assignment. Maggie and I would have to have our stories down pat.

Seeing my beautiful fiancée typing intently on the computer, I rushed over to make sure she wasn't doing anything compromising. I smiled as I saw the email she'd written:

> Dear Sally,
>   Thank you for the invitation to the party. Regrettably, I won't be able to make it. Maybe I'll see you at the twenty-year reunion.
> Yours truly,
> Travis S. Novak

That settles that.

Chapter 38

The Condo, Northwestern Iraq

January 3, 2009

We woke up at five in the morning, and I called Control to reconfirm the drop time. Everything was on schedule.

Maggie and I had three hours to go and much to do. All was ready in the storage hold. After the generator had run, I disconnected all the gas lines and cables that connected the generator to the batteries so I wouldn't have to waste time with them later. Then I wheeled the storage bins onto the loading deck. If Control warned that we had company, I'd have plenty of time to get the bins back inside.

Maggie had picked out some of my clothes to take with her inside the cave. The temperature was supposed to reach sixty degrees later in the day, but it would be in the low fifties when she entered the water. She put the clothes and a towel into one bag and the flashlight, some extra batteries, and the 9-mm in the other. As an afterthought, she stuffed an empty bag inside in case she found something else small enough to bring out.

I got the call that they were about an hour out and told Maggie.

"Make sure you go to the bathroom before we leave the condo."

"Yes, Daddy."

"Don't get smart with me, young lady."

I left Maggie alone to finish getting ready and went outside with the binoculars to sweep the skies and the horizon. Nothing.

As I lowered the ladder, I yelled for Maggie, and we climbed down and made for the pool.

"If we get company, which I doubt will happen, you stay inside," I told her. "I'll handle it out here. I've got the capability to eliminate anything our visitors can bring in. If any of them happens to get inside the cave, don't hesitate; shoot him as soon as he hits the stairs. Just make sure it isn't me."

"Yes, sir."

"That's what I like—officers who know how to treat enlisted men."

"You have no idea how well I'm going to treat you. Just wait until our honeymoon."

"Don't distract me from what's happening today. We've got to get through this to have a honeymoon."

We held hands as we went under, and I got her safely inside. It was cold, and she told me to get out so she could change into the dry clothes in her Ziploc bag. I kissed her goodbye and headed for the floor. After dragging the palm frond on the ground, I climbed back up and into the condo.

I searched the condo from top to bottom to make sure nothing would hint at Maggie's presence. It looked clean. Actually, it looked too clean. Maggie was always tidying up. To make the place look more like a bachelor apartment, I scattered some stuff around. Then I went outside to wait for the choppers.

I did another sweep with the binocs. Still nothing. My radio beeped, and the pilot of the first chopper—which would lift out the steel pallet—checked in that he was five minutes out.

I heard the chopper's rotors and saw the bird swing around to come in from the south. The loadmaster, who was leaning out the door, waved to me as his voice came over my iPhone. "Did you call UPS for a pickup?"

Great. Another army comedian. There really ought to be a reality show.

As we'd practiced at The Farm, the pilot lowered the cables, I fastened the four ends to the hooks on the pallet, and signaled to him that it was secure. He started the hoist, and I guided the pallet up without hitting the exterior walls.

"Hold on, Condo," the pilot radioed. "We've got a visitor for you."

A man in a hoist, a box under one arm, was lowered slowly onto the loading dock. It was Captain Trey Mudge, the ATEC engineer I'd met when I arrived. I helped him out of the rig, the seat went back up, and the pilot moved out heading north.

"Good job, Condo," the pilot radioed as the chopper grew smaller and smaller in the sky. "Fed Ex will be here in ten. Adios."

"You look disappointed, Novak," Mudge said.

"Well, I was hoping they'd send a female technician: early twenties, gorgeous auburn hair, blue eyes."

"I'll tell them in Kuwait that you're definitely hallucinating. But let's move. I've gotta finish before the second chopper gets here with your resupply or you'll be having me as a house guest for a while. They think something's going down soon, so they want me and the choppers gone."

Going inside, he said, "Hope you don't mind, I need to take a dump first. Bathroom open?"

"Help yourself. I'll wait outside."

I stepped outside and checked my watch. When I heard the crapper flush, I ducked back inside to see him unscrewing a metal panel to the right of the window, remove a module, and insert a new one. He used a meter to adjust it, keyed the mic to test the module with Control, and they pronounced it fixed.

Handing me another care package, this one from Colonel Svoboda, he said, "The colonel told me it's training manuals. Feels like a six-pack. But that would be against the rules, not to mention against the law in Muslim country."

"Tell him 'thanks.' I'll start studying the manuals tonight. Say, why do they call you Trey anyway?"

In Fair Oaks, loads of guys were nicknamed Trey. They were the new money, *Trey* being an affectionate term for *the third*. Real old-money boys were generally the fourth or fifth, at least.

"I'm a poker player, and with not much else to do in Kuwait, we play a lot of poker. About eight years ago, I was back in the States and entered a poker tournament at Pala Casino Spa and Resort, not far from San Diego. I was on a hot streak and beat Jack McManus—you know, the big professional gambler—out of a quarter-million-dollar pot with a pair of treys. Bluffed the drawers right off him. I told the story to the guys at ATEC when I got back, and I've been Trey ever since."

We heard the second chopper, lugging its pallet of propane, approaching. The drop went off like clockwork. As soon as the pallet touched the floor of the hold, Mudge and I had the cables off, and a harness came down. Mudge quickly jumped on and headed up.

"See you back in Kuwait in a few weeks, Novak—maybe sooner if the big boys are right. Good hunting, bro."

I waved as Mudge was hauled inside, and the now-empty chopper made a fast turn over the pool, creating waves on the water. I hoped the noise hadn't scared Maggie.

The copter with my bins of food and supplies came next. Again, the drop went off without a hitch.

I waited a few minutes until the sound of the rotors had disappeared. Then I scanned the perimeter, lowered the ladder, and ran to the pool. Without taking time to remove my pants, I charged into the water and swam for the entry. I yelled to Maggie that it was me so she wouldn't shoot.

A huge smile visible on her face, Maggie was on her knees in a dark corner of the stone platform, rifling through a large, rectangular chest I hadn't noticed during earlier visits to the cave.

****

My fiancé the archeology major was carefully reviewing the contents of the chryselephantine cedar chest, which looked older than anything I'd ever seen. The lid was secured by ivory pegs, and silver coins and discolored papers were inside.

"What did you find?"

"There are papers in here, with Latin writing. I need to spend some time studying them. I'm pretty sure the coins are drachmas; I think they were either issued, or stolen by the Crusaders while they occupied Jerusalem. There are Arabic words on the coins, but they're also imprinted with a cross, the sign of Christianity. Control of Jerusalem went back and forth between the Christians and the Muslims. I remember reading that when the Pope heard that coins were circulating with Mohammed's name, he threatened to excommunicate anyone caught spending them. Rather than destroy the coins, Christian markings were added later. There must be several thousand coins here.

"I remember hearing about drachmas in Latin class."

"Drachmas, go back to the ancient Greeks. They were a form of measure that morphed into coinage. As the Greeks conquered surrounding countries, they brought their money with them. The Romans also used the drachma. You may remember from Sunday School that the Romans controlled this part of the world for centuries. As I recall, a drachma weighed a little more than an ounce, but these feel lighter. They might be a fractional coin, like a half drachma."

"With all this gold, we can't worry about half-ounce silver coins given the price differential."

"Honey, these coins are priceless. They're incredibly rare, and these all are in mint condition."

"We need to talk about this, but let's get out of here before Control starts looking for me."

Maggie put about ten silver coins, some of the papers, and several packets of jewels inside her empty Ziploc bag, and we raced back to the condo.

****

Maggie agreed with the plan I set out. Moving over a thousand pounds of gold would take a lot of trips back and forth, and a lot of time. But first, I had to prepare a place to put it all.

I retrieved the tool kit from its storage bin and took out a small sledge hammer and the largest screwdriver in the set. With an M4 from the armory and my iPhone in hand, I lowered the ladder over the outside of the pile. Maggie stood guard topside, listening for calls from Control and keeping an eye out for visitors.

The part of the sheer outer wall that I was looking for was about twenty feet from the ladder. It was the perfect color shading and already had a fissure about a foot long and three inches wide.

After putting a camouflage net from the dune buggy's survival kit over the work site to protect from drone or satellite surveillance, I went to work. I pounded the largest screwdriver I had into the wall as far as it would go and started to dig out the soft rock. Then I made two identical holes in the wall about six inches square and with the same depth.

I climbed back up to retrieve two hand grenades, pulled the pins, shoved the grenades into the holes, and ran for cover. The explosion was loud, but no one but us could hear it. The grenades created a jagged indenture, but it wasn't big enough. I got two more grenades and blew the wall again. I finished the job with the hammer and screwdriver, ending up with a roughly chiseled enclosure roughly three feet square. That was the easy part.

We'd agreed that Maggie would stay outside, and I'd be the mule. As a sniper, I was used to humping heavy equipment, so relocating the gold wasn't an issue. As I brought the bars out, she'd carry them to the ladder, and we'd pull the bars up later with a rope. We'd have to work on the far-right side of the pool, which I'd moved out of the view of the camera covering the water.

Twenty-five pounds, I'd figured, was the most I could safely take under water at a time, so it would take me almost fifty trips in and out to get the gold. I'd also take a little cash on each trip, and I'd promised Maggie that she could pick out some of the jewels.

We started early afternoon. I found a canvas ammo bag that I'd use to carry the bars. Each trip took me about fifteen minutes, so I decided to shoot for twelve trips a day. If we could buy four days before any visitors showed up, we'd be able to complete the job.

Chapter 39

The Condo, Northwestern Iraq

January 7, 2009

The previous day, at the end of my fourth and final trip to relocate the cache, I'd been shivering so badly that Maggie had to run into the pool to help me out. That last trip had taken me close to forty-five frigid minutes. I'd created a hollow section in the center by restacking the gold and turning some boxes on end. The terrorists would never notice that any gold bars were missing until they moved it, assuming they even knew how much was there in the first place. A greater concern of mine was that Control was getting suspicious, because I'd been outside every time a call had come in over the last four days.

The guys at Control were getting antsy. Kirk the computer continued to generate reams of predictions that something big was going to happen— soon. Kirk had been crunching all types of intel, telephonic and otherwise, and everything flashed red. If their theory—which had cost who knew how many millions of dollars to create the condo and then plant me here—was correct, the terrorists should be packing their bags and heading my way any minute.

Maggie and I spent the day lowering the gold outside the pile. Then I started stacking our "loot" inside the hole I'd blown in the wall. I put the gold in first, then shoved the cash and jewels around the edges. I'd taken enough cash, both dollars and euros, for what I planned plus a little more for contingencies I'd incur in getting the gold out.

Then came the tricky part. Maggie lowered the bucket of fake stone goop that ATEC had used to camouflage the condo. I shoved two large, flat stones inside the hole. They didn't fit flush but filled up most of the opening. Then I filled in the remaining gaps with smaller stones and covered the front of the stones with the stone putty. It was thick, almost like drywall compound, and I did my best to feather it in to match the texture of the cliff. Maggie insisted on marking the hiding place, so she took some of the magic paste and painted on a patch about two feet to the right side of our new wall safe. Then she cemented two heart-shaped stones she'd found to the wall.

"Two hearts alone in the desert," she said. "That's us. Two feet from two hearts."

We embraced passionately, and any doubts I had about this whirlwind romance were blown away by the sandstorm that was moving in.

As we climbed up, Major Shay was on the radio.

"Novak, what the heck are you doing out there?"

"Just a little patching, sir. That last sandstorm must have blown around some big rocks. I found a few places where your magic material was chipped. The stuff is really something. Once it dries, you can't tell that a repair was made."

"I'll pass that along to the boys at The Farm. But you'd better get inside now. The weatherman is saying another storm's on the way. It can't be much longer until you have visitors, and I want you rested. Lay off the work, and let's make sure we're ready for the big day."

"Roger that. Condo out."

Maggie had a scowl on her face. "I don't like that man."

"Oh, he's all right—if you can excuse his not letting me shoot those terrorists who were about to decapitate you."

"I'm usually a very good judge of people, and I tell you that he's not a good man. What do you know about him?"

"Not much. His father's a general. He's got a master's from MIT and did undergrad at Yale."

"That figures."

"If you ever meet him, you'll notice a nice scar on his forehead."

"Battle injury?"

"Lacrosse. I gave it to him in college a few years back. Knocked him out cold; of course, it was a clean hit."

"Lacrosse? In Louisiana, we've always thought of lacrosse as a sissy Yankee sport."

"I'd hate to see what the real men in Louisiana play."

"Football, silly, of course."

"Of course."

Chapter 40

The Condo, Northwestern Iraq

January 12, 2009

We awakened to an unusual sound for northwestern Iraq: the patter of rain. I checked in, and Control said a strong, cool, low-pressure system coming in from the Mediterranean was combining with the back side of another moisture-laden front from the Arabian Sea.

Walking out to the loading deck, I watched as the secret of the pool was revealed. Over the millennia, the water had found the path of least resistance. I saw several strong streams of rainwater rushing into the pool. It was as if every drop of rain that fell in the pile was ending up there. The more than one-quarter-inch of rain that fell raised the water level several inches.

Maggie came out on the deck to join me, and I put my arm around her as she melted into my side. She was blissfully happy and, for the first time in many years, so was I. She was excited at the prospect of getting out of the army early, marrying me, and, if things went as planned, being financially secure for the first time in her life.

She'd taken advantage of the quiet over the past few days to plan, and re-plan, our wedding at least eight times. The ceremony, she said, would be at her Lutheran Church in New Orleans, so she could show me off to all her friends. That was fine because there weren't many people I wanted to invite.

Maggie had hardly taken her eyes off her engagement ring, and she wasn't happy when I told her the ring would have to make the trip out in the secret compartment of my backpack. She relented after I convinced her how hard it would be to explain how she'd managed to keep a priceless, three-carat diamond ring from a gang of ruthless terrorists.

I spent more time working on a plan for hiding the wealth we'd someday spirit out of the country. I obviously couldn't just declare it at customs on reentering the U.S. The federal government was cracking down on numbered accounts in foreign banks, and there was talk that such clandestine accounts wouldn't even exist by 2010. But I'd thought of something and still had to flesh it out some more.

We read the news reports on the impending inauguration of the new president with interest. He'd be my problem for less than a day, so I wasn't really concerned—unless he wanted to raise my taxes.

I checked the sports scores. Barrington won its basketball game against John Burroughs, and Duke beat Missouri. The local news from St. Louis was about a lot of people I didn't remember.

I realized we'd have to decide where we'd live. Maggie assumed we'd live in New Orleans, but I wasn't so sure. Maybe we'd get a real condo on the Gulf coast. We'd have to talk some more.

I clicked the *Drudge Report* and was stunned to read an article announcing the new president's national security adviser. He'd selected Professor Christine Head, the horrible woman who'd written that hateful article about me and the medal. Unbelievable. She had no military experience, having never been through so much as basic training. The woman probably didn't know which end of a rifle expelled the bullet. She'd never even held a job outside academia. It was totally unthinkable that this woman could shape the president's view of how the military should be used.

After reading this news, I was even happier to be leaving the military. As the rain tapered to a drizzle, I didn't have a good feeling about what the future held for my comrades in arms.

Chapter 41

Abbottabad, Pakistan

January 14, 2009

Osama bin Laden's five-day trip from Abbottabad in the modified shipping crate had begun. It would be a difficult trip, but there was no other way he could get to the sanctuary until the Americans were gone from Iraq. The foreign devils were still in Afghanistan, so they'd have to skirt south and take the long way through Iran.

Abu Ahmed al-Kuwaiti and his younger brother, who were taking turns driving the jingle truck, would make minimal stops. A chase car with two bodyguards trailed behind. The truck's manifest said they were carrying explosives bound for Syria, so any Iranian border guards who stopped them along the way wouldn't suspect a thing.

His trusted confidant was trying to catch some z's while his brother was at the wheel, but bin Laden wanted to talk.

"You know, Abu, the prince could have made other arrangements for us. I guarantee you that he's not riding in the back of a stinking diesel-belching truck. I am sure he will fly his private jet into Syria and take a helicopter from there. You have to take your keffiyeh off to those American dogs. They may be decadent infidels, but when it comes to flying, that G-5 is one sweet plane."

"Perhaps we could stop in Tehran and spend a night in a hotel," Abu said. "I am certain Mahmoud would be happy to see you."

"Oh, please, Abu. Then I would have to stay up all night and listen to him brag about his nuclear bombs and how he took over that American embassy back in the seventies. How many times can a man hear that same story and not go crazy? He will want to rub my nose in it for hours. Really, I cannot think of any place I would want to stay less."

"I can."

"Well, of course, Abu, you mean that miserable dump back in Abbottabad. Trust me. As soon as we make this big score in the stock market, we are out of that place. How much longer before we get there?"

"We just left Abbottabad an hour ago. You aren't going to ask every ten minutes until we get to Ar Rutba, are you? I must get some sleep."

"You are right, my friend. You go to sleep. I will go back and review some videos I made for release after their new president is sworn in. I made a few practice tapes, but I am still not pleased with them. You know who makes a great video? Gaddafi. He's a little crazy sometimes, but you must admit that the man can orate like few others. They say this new American president is a great speaker, but he cannot hold a candle to Gaddafi."

"Osama, did you tell Dr. al-Zawahri that I need a new prescription for my blood pressure medicine? He is still coming, right?"

"Abu, how many times must I tell you that my number two, Ayman al-Zawahri no longer practices medicine. He is now a full-time terrorist. I brought in that woman doctor to live in the compound, but you refuse to see her because she is a woman. Well, that is your problem. Any guy who can scrounge up C4 explosives at the drop of a keffiyeh ought to be able to locate a few blood pressure pills.

"The famous Dr. al-Zawahri, the so-called soul of the movement. Can you believe that one, Abu? He is just waiting for something to happen to me so he can step into my sandals. Don't think that I don't know. Yes, he's a good number two operationally, but the man has no vision. Al-Qaeda would be bankrupt in no time with him running things. We'd probably be taken over by another terrorist group overnight—that would be a real hostile takeover. He is happy with the penny-ante suicide bombers that might get only a dozen people here and there. He is so fixated on the Jews, but we know the real action is in America. We need to hit targets that take out thousands. That is the only way to drive these invaders from our lands. Hit thousands, and they will crumble.

"9/11 was a brilliant strike, Abu. You think al-Zawahri could have dreamed up that one up? Or the prince? Give me a break. They are both using me. I am the real brains of the movement, and everyone knows it. Do you see *their* pictures on the cover of *Time* magazine?

"I am the face of the new caliphate. Your Egyptian doctor is just biding his time to take over, and the prince thinks I do not know his real motives. He wants to get even with his grandfather, the king. A new caliphate? I think he cares about nothing except planting his fat behind on that throne. I never liked him, even when we were in the madrassa together. He was always trying to get everybody else to do his work for him. 'My grandfather the king this,' and 'My grandfather the king that.' Did he ever once say, 'My father is a drunken thief?' No. He's been a user his whole life."

"Abu?"

But al-Kuwaiti wasn't interested in hearing bin Laden's peroration. He'd heard it all before and was sound asleep.

Chapter 42

The Condo, Northwestern Iraq

January 17, 2009

I'd be discharged in just three days, a minute after midnight on January 21, but still no sign of visitors. I was starting to think that, despite the intel, nothing was going to happen on my watch.

At least I'd found a wife on this otherwise uneventful assignment.

My replacement, a sniper named Greg Black, and I had spent some time on the communicator comparing notes. The highly-decorated Black, who was from near Fort Worth and a graduate of the University of Texas, seemed like a nice, bright fellow. Despite over fifteen kills in Iraq, he was understandably anxious about being dropped in, but I talked him through it.

I figured Black should be well on his way to Kuwait—might even be there now. There'd been talk about bringing him in a few days before my discharge, but with the intel still suggesting something was imminent, they couldn't chance it. More wind storms were also predicted, and the choppers didn't like the blowing sand.

That was fine. I wasn't sure how I'd have explained the five-foot, four-inch auburn-haired beauty I was hiding. Black probably would have been happy to keep his mouth shut if I'd told him she'd been staying at the condo but she was leaving with me.

My plan was going to work out fine. Maggie would show up outside the condo a couple of hours before the choppers brought in Black. They might be suspicious, but they wouldn't be able to prove a thing. Maggie and I would fly out together.

When a man makes a snap decision on a bride, sometimes he has second thoughts. Does she like football? Can she cook? —that kind of thing. But I considered myself a lucky guy to have found Maggie, and no unanswered question was going to change my mind.

My bride-to-be was sitting cross-legged on the floor, fondling my Remington 30.06 hunting rifle.

"I've been meaning to ask you about this rifle, hon. I'm pretty sure it's not government issue."

"Not hardly, although many early sniper rifles—the M40, for one— were based on that very gun. At sniper school, they told us a Vietnam-era marine sniper named Chuck Mawhinney still holds the marine record for 103 confirmed kills. He had over two hundred probables, all with a rifle pretty much like this one. This is my personal hunting rifle, a Christmas present from my dad when I was twelve."

"Why'd you bring it out here?"

"Just for fun. It'd been years since I'd had a chance to shoot it, and I figured I'd have plenty of time out here to get ready for deer season in the States."

"You hunt?"

"My dad and I used to go out every chance we got."

"We're duck people. Daddy shared a blind with a few guys from his football team. I used to go along sometimes, before I went off to college."

I had about four boxes of shells left, so I asked her if she'd like to shoot it. We went out on the loading deck, and she propped the rifle against her shoulder. The blast almost knocked her over.

"It's sure got a kick, boy."

"Yes, it does."

"Hon, you think we can go hunting sometime?"

If she'd told me right then that her father owned a liquor store, I'd have been certain that I'd found the perfect woman.

Chapter 43

The Condo, Northwestern Iraq

January 19, 2009

I was talking to Trey Mudge, engineer and poker champ, at Control. The generator had been running rough for a few days and was getting worse. The sand storms had depleted my supply of filters for the outside air intake vents now that I'd just installed the last one on the small GM four-cylinder engine that ran the generator.

The problem was, the sandstorms were throwing a lot of fine dust around. Mudge told me to try to blow the vents out with compressed air, but it wasn't helping. He'd decided I should turn the governor down and run the motor at a slower speed. It would increase the time needed to charge the batteries but wouldn't be so hard on the engine.

I'd changed the oil earlier in the day and told Mudge that I'd found sand in the oil pan. He said another generator was on order from the States, but it wouldn't be in Kuwait for at least a day. Mudge told me to try to get by for a few more days, and they'd possibly drop in a couple of filters by parachute while they fitted the new generator for the condo system.

Then Mudge told me a long-winded story about how, in the first Gulf War, the sand had affected our equipment, which had been designed for use against the Russians in Europe. They finally had to put women soldiers' pantyhose over the air intakes to keep the sand out.

Nothing like American ingenuity.

Mudge turned the mic over to Major Shay, and I confronted him about the plan I'd just heard from Mudge, which didn't seem to include a stop to pick me up as scheduled. "What's the plan for tomorrow? You know my hitch is up at midnight, and I've got a signed presidential order to that effect."

I was packed and ready to go, and Shay was giving me the diplomatic, Ivy League stall. I was getting a bad feeling.

"Calm down, big boy. We're working on it. The wind storms are really kicking up. Not only that. Your replacement, Black, has come down with some kind of a stomach virus. Been in the can since he got off the plane here in Kuwait."

"Well, get him a box of Imodium, pack an extra crate of Charmin, and get him out here."

"Look, Novak, there's a chance we might be a day or two late."

"Hey, I'm out of the army at 12:01 a.m. on the twenty-first. That discharge paper says local time."

"Well, if you want to take the subway and get off at Grand Central, I won't be able to stop you. Work with us, Novak, will you?"

"If I have to stay, major, it's going to cost you. I want an extra month's pay. That's fair."

"Novak, you've got $8 million in the bank, and you're holding me up for a few grand?"

"That's the deal. And that's a month's pay for every extra day I'm stuck out here. Otherwise . . ."

"Okay, okay. I'll get it done."

I signed off and felt Maggie's hand on my shoulder.

"Honey, did that horrible man say you're worth $8 million?"

"Darling, *we're* worth a whole lot more than that. All we have to do is figure out how to get it out of here."

****

Two hours northwest of the condo, as the couple was discussing strategies to move their retirement funds out of Iraq, Osama bin Laden's truck was slowing. The intercom from the cab buzzed, and al-Kuwaiti's brother told bin Laden and his confidant that they were entering Ar Rutba. It was as far as the truck would take them.

It had been a hard journey. Osama had needed to stop the truck numerous times to stretch his long legs, which cramped badly in the confined shipping crate. And he'd asked to stop at what seemed like every brazed-meat stand along their route. The amount of Coca-Cola that bin Laden could go through, despite his bad kidneys, always amazed Abu.

The truck parked at a loading dock inside a fenced lot, the same place where AQ-Iraq had last held Lieutenant Maggie Taylor. The terrorist and his crew would spend the next day in the warehouse until it was time to head for the sanctuary in the Suzuki SUV.

A local representative of AQ, Naveed Hussein, who'd been waiting for bin Laden's truck to arrive, greeting him warmly.

"May the mercy, peace, and blessings of Allah be upon you, my sheik," the regional AQ commander said.

"And also upon you," Osama said, stretching his lanky frame. "So where are you holding the girl?"

Hussein mumbled an unintelligible reply.

"Speak up. Where is the American whore?"

"I am not sure, my sheik. Usi took her off to make a video weeks ago, and we have not heard from him since. He said he was taking her into the desert to scare her into confessing, but we don't have the resources to look there."

"Well, that's just great. I was going to use her in a new video. The Americans will think twice about sending women here after they see one of their whores lose her head on cable news."

Osama made a mental note to look into whether such a beheading could be broadcast on pay-for-view. Money was tight.

"Do you think Usi is trying to ransom her himself?" bin Laden asked.

"I certainly hope not. He said they would be back later that same day. Those two awful people from Karbala, that man and his foul wife, were with him. They took off in my best pickup truck, and I had to send two men into Jordan to steal a new one."

"Try to find him. I want to take the woman back with me."

"Yes, my sheik."

"Now, please have your wives prepare a meal for us. And tell me, Naveed, is there a Coke machine in this warehouse?"

****

Shay was still being vague about when they'd send a chopper for me, but I wasn't going to let up. After all, a deal was a deal. I was about to call him—and apply the negotiating skills I'd learned during my MBA studies—when the alarm sounded. It was Shay on the horn.

"Company coming down the road, Novak," Shay said.

"Roger, Control. I'll scope him with the camera."

I'd been trained to stay calm under pressure, but I suddenly realized that I was all that stood between the woman I loved and the world's most dangerous killers. Things were totally different now that Maggie was with me.

It was the same white SUV, driving slowly to the condo. I watched the vehicle park in its usual parking place and saw the same guy—Anas al-Maqqati, according to that computer, Kirk—get out of the vehicle and head straight to the camera. The hit man removed the card in the camera, then his clothes, and waded into the pool with his bag.

"He's doing it again," Shay said.

"I'd sure like to know what he's doing," I said.   Of   course,   I suspected that, just as Maggie and I had done, he was making a major withdrawal. The AQ cave did not have the same rules limiting what dollar amounts had to be reported as American banks.

When he emerged with the bag, I was worried that he'd noticed some of the cache was missing. But he gave no indication that he suspected anything; he walked to the camera, replaced the card, and returned to the SUV.

As the SUV and hit man disappeared into the night, Major Shay was starting to panic. "That settles it, Novak. You're going to need to stay put a few more days. The computer models are swearing it's going to go down any minute."

"Just remember, major. A month's pay for every extra day I'm here."

"Yeah, okay," Shay said. "Ten thousand snipers in the army and we have to pick the one with the MBA. Control out."

Chapter 44

Detroit, Michigan

January 19, 2009

Adad Haneef had finished the first of the three ultralights, and his heart was pounding with excitement. At nightfall, the plane was disassembled and loaded into the back of an extended white Ford panel truck.

Haneef felt good getting out of the dirty warehouse to take the ultralight for a test run. He rode in the back of the truck with his two helpers while the AQ handler drove. They took I-75 south to State Route 50 and then went south on U.S. 23 at Dundee. There was a small airfield near their destination, and Haneef hoped if the ultralight was picked up by radar, it would be mistaken for the local airport traffic.

The truck pulled off on a deserted side road where the snow had recently been plowed. It took only twenty minutes to attach the loose parts to the body and unfold the wings. The helpers snapped the landing gear in place and wheeled the craft onto the flat, rural road. Haneef had put two hundred pounds of bricks in a box in the storage compartment to simulate the explosive cargo the ultralight would carry on its mission.

He pressed the remote start button, and the engine roared to life. Haneef wasted no time in revving the engine, and the craft took off into the wind, working flawlessly. He checked the cameras sending back the signals that would guide him to the still-unknown target, double-checked all the instruments, and brought the craft in for a landing. He didn't dare drop the landing gear, as he'd do on the mission. There wasn't time.

One of the guards uploaded a coded message on his cell phone to a Yahoo account registered to a student somewhere in Ohio. The student then posted a coded message on a new messaging service called Twitter, which was read by an al Qaeda official in Syria.

They were back at the warehouse and hard at work in less than ninety minutes. They still had much work to do and little time.

Chapter 45

The Condo, Northwestern Iraq

January 20, 2009

It was 4 p.m. local time, and we were locked down tight. In Washington, D.C., the president-elect would soon take the oath of office and become the commander in chief. But Maggie and I had much more immediate issues to think about.

The generator now coughed worse than Maggie had when she'd arrived with pneumonia. It seemed to be taking three times as long as it should to charge the batteries, and I was praying it wouldn't die on me. Earlier, I'd radioed Mudge about the problem, and he'd told me to shut it down for a while, even though we were barely at 60 percent battery capacity.

The sky was overcast, so the solar panels weren't of much use; the sun was going down anyway. I was worried about the batteries, but there was nothing I could do about it. We turned off everything, including the heat pump system, which made the condo very stuffy and uncomfortable.

Maggie was at the computer, and I was about to tell her we had to conserve battery power when my email dinged.

"Hon, you have an email. Want me to read it to you?"

"You're not going to be one of those kinds of wives, are you?"

"It's from somebody named BigEagleCIC. What kind of a name is that?"

She began reading the email out loud. At least it wasn't from Sally Effingham.

Sergeant Novak,

This marks the last day of service for both of us. I understand you may be stuck there a few extra days, but I assure you that you'll be officially discharged tomorrow, January 21, at 12:01 a.m. local time.

They've briefed me on the visitor. Our best minds believe something will happen soon. I can't tell you how glad I am that you're manning the station. I'd love to get this guy before I leave, but I realize that may not happen. I regret that we couldn't find that young girl they're holding. I pray every day that she got away safely, but there's no trace of her.

I've spent the morning signing notes to a lot of people who all want a piece of history. You're getting the only email. I'll print it off, sign it, and put it with that cufflink picture I'm holding for you.

This will be my final message to you until you return home. Please know that I'm proud of you, and remember what I told you at The Farm. I hope you haven't lost that medal I gave you.

I'll see you soon. You have my personal thanks and the best wishes of a grateful nation. Godspeed, Sergeant Novak.

CIC

"Is this really from the president?" Maggie asked when she finished reading.

I told her it was, and tears streamed down her cheeks as she reread the president's words, silently this time.

****

Despite the conservation measures we'd initiated four hours earlier, the power meter was down to a little over 40 percent. I was counting the minutes until midnight and my new freedom when I heard the unmistakable sound of a helicopter overhead. If Control was sending in a chopper to get me, I didn't know what I'd do about Maggie. With five hours to go until my discharge, I was still within the army's legal grasp.

I had to get an answer fast and radioed Shay in Kuwait to find out what was going on. "Why didn't you tell me you were sending a chopper?"

"What are you talking about?"

"A chopper's hovering outside. I can hear it, but I haven't been able to train a camera high enough to see it."

"Novak, it's not one of ours. Hold on."

My first reaction was relief that I wouldn't have to do a fast tap dance to explain Maggie's presence in the condo. But quickly realizing that this could be the real thing, I started sweating.

As I swept the pile with the cameras, I saw a spotlight shining on the far side, near the pool. Two men—who even from afar looked like professionals, not amateur AQ fighters—were repelling down ropes to the top of the pile across from my location.

The chopper shined its light on the pile, temporarily blinding my cameras, then lowered carefully into the cavity of the pile and touched down. Two other men unloaded a large box, then jumped back on board and the chopper lifted off.

"AWACS says it's a civilian French model," Shay said. "It must have flown below the radar. They've got it now."

As I heard the chopper's rotors fade in the distance, I knew this was the denouement of my journey to avenge my father's death.

"Control," I reported, "I saw two operators repel onto the top of the pile. These guys are pros, and they're still on site. Repeat. Two operators are still out there."

"Roger, Condo. This could be it. Stay on them with cams."

****

Traveling to the sanctuary in the white Suzuki SUV were bin Laden, his trusted confident Abu, and the two body guards. A stolen pickup driven by the Saudi hit man, with Abu al-Kuwaiti's brother riding shotgun, followed behind.

The group met up with a small truck transporting the two top men in AQ-Syria, and bin Laden got out of the SUV briefly to receive a message he'd take to the prince. The ultralight craft worked perfectly, the men told bin Laden, and the plan would be ready for action in early February.

The prince will be very pleased to hear this news when he arrives at the sanctuary.

As the AQ-Syria team fell in behind, the entourage left the highway, doused their lights, and crept over the abandoned road toward the sanctuary.

****

The prince wasn't as paranoid as bin Laden, but he still was cautious. Rather than use his personal limo, at 1:15 p.m. Paris time, he'd exited his luxury apartment building in the sixteenth arrondissement through a service door and walked several blocks to a hotel. There, he'd caught a taxi to a small airport north of the city. The prince's bags had been delivered to his Gulfstream V earlier in the day.

Once the prince had boarded the plane, it had taken off on a heading toward Turkey. When the plane was over the Alps, the pilot had canceled the flight plan and changed the destination to Damascus, Syria.

The prince had sent two security men ahead to ensure that the sanctuary was secure not wanting to depend solely on his hitman cousin. Once the plane landed, he'd make contact with them and decide whether to deplane or to instruct his pilot to return to Paris.

****

I extinguished all the lights except the screens on the console and zoomed in on the two men on the ridge across from the condo. Behind me, Maggie was suiting up. She had on what was left of the blood-spattered camos she'd been wearing when I found her, a tactical vest, and a 9-mm rig. She was chambering an M4.

"Hey, be careful with that."

"Don't worry, hon. I know how it works."

Shay asked me for a close-up of the two visitors. I got a pretty good shot, although it was kind of grainy with the waning crescent moon intermittently blocked by storm clouds. They were unloading a box and removed two Heckler and Koch carbines along with several boxes of ammo. My heart skipped a beat as I saw one of the men pull out a Dragunov, an old but deadly sniper rifle used by the Russian army.

What are Russian snipers doing here?

I watched as they set up a hide, repelled onto the floor, and checked every square inch using powerful flashlights. After a half hour, apparently satisfied that they were alone, they climbed back on the ridge directly across from me.

"We've got them," Shay said. "They're former Russian Spetsnaz and usually work for hire for Russian oligarchs. Their specialty is standoff assassinations. We're running this by our boys at the CIA. This really doesn't sound like AQ."

"They're up in their hide—looking out, not in. I can take them out any time you say."

"Stand by and stay buttoned up. We think they're the advance party. Hold on a sec. AWACS intercepted a transmission in Russian from your location. The message is, 'The table is set.'"

Game on.

****

An hour later, just after 10 p.m., it was getting close in the condo. I was sweating the power meter, because using multiple cameras was eating up the juice. The battery was at less than 30 percent capacity, and I wasn't sure when I'd get a chance to run the generator—or if it would even work. We were using only the systems we needed to monitor our guests, except when I activated the air intake blowers from time to time to get some fresh air.

Suddenly, the two Russians walked carefully around the top of the pile, seeming to be looking for anyone in hiding. When the smaller of the two climbed directly over the top of the condo—and us— Maggie squeezed my hand and jumped slightly as he landed hard on the loading deck just outside our door. We both breathed a deep sigh of relief as we heard him climb up the cliff and continue on his journey. They both were making the circuit, I guessed, to be sure the other didn't miss anything. A few minutes later, the bigger guy stumbled down onto the loading deck and over the top of us, going in the opposite direction.

Once they were satisfied, they repelled down to the floor, unpacked a small tent—the kind that pops up—and quickly installed it at the far end of the pile near the pool. Then the Russians returned to their hide on top, as Maggie and I continued to watch and wait.

Chapter 46

Washington, D.C.

January 20, 2009

It was 11:00 a.m. on Inauguration Day. The president had a few minutes alone before he and his wife would host the brief, traditional tea for the incoming president and the new First Lady. The two couples would exchange a few niceties for ten minutes or so before boarding the presidential limousine for the short ride to the Capitol.

It was almost as chilly in the room as the twenty-five-degree temperature outside given the icy feelings between the president and his successor. The president had been highly insulted by the new man's attempts to issue orders before taking the oath of office. The new man had been elected by slamming the president's failure to end the wars and capture Osama bin Laden. For his part, the president-elect was miffed that he'd have to put on a happy face for a man he not only considered his intellectual inferior but whom he disrespected for what he, and others in his party, regarded as a miserably failed presidency.

The president's aides had conducted most of the briefings for the newly elected administration over the previous few weeks. The outgoing president had personally shared a few issues of substance with the next occupant of the Oval Office. The bulk of their discussions, however, had been filled with inconsequential chit chat.

This farce of a tea can't end fast enough.

WASHINGTON, D.C.

****

The two couples stopped at the side of the limo so the photographers could get some shots. The president allowed the other three to seat themselves in the limo, then turned and gave a final wave to the White House staff, most of whom had tears in their eyes.

On the trip up Pennsylvania Avenue, the Secret Service driver maintained a precisely-planned, slow speed for the benefit of the crowds lining both sides of the street. The two men and their wives smiled and waved. As the car reached its destination, the wives were escorted inside, and the president grabbed his replacement's arm.

"There's one more thing you need to know," the president said. "Osama bin Laden is a puppet—nothing more than a front man. We've never been able to uncover the name of the top man we refer to as 'the boss.' All we have is a voice print. If you want to stop al-Qaeda, you need to find him. Here's an envelope with the names of the people who can fill you in on this. Good luck."

The president smiled to himself as he strode into the Capitol, leaving the soon-to-be leader of the free world speechless for the first time in his life.

****

If the *Daily Beast* ran a feature on the twenty best-looking babes of the new administration, Professor Christine Head wouldn't be among those profiled. She was a plain-looking, bespectacled, thirty-eight-year-old with dowel-pin legs and limp, stringy hair who'd been too busy as a member of the left-wing commentariat to have a social life. At least that's how she explained her single status to her mother. And if she felt ridiculous in the pink, puffy-skirted ball gown she'd bought at a funky, second-hand store on Boylston Street in Boston, it was with good reason.

At first, she was insulted to have been assigned to attend this late afternoon inaugural ball at the Capitol Hilton instead of one of the more prestigious affairs that would kick off in prime time. But when she'd found out that a certain Emmy Award-winning cable-TV reporter would be covering the Capitol Hilton event, she'd decided the evening might end up working out perfectly.

One man had shown an interest in her since she'd become an adviser to the campaign in early 2008. Robert Meyers—the rising cable-news star featured in *The Hill*'s year-end piece on the most eligible bachelors in the political press, who'd won accolades from the liberal press for his daring wartime reporting from Afghanistan—had called and emailed her often during the campaign. He was suave, good looking, and intelligent—unlike, she thought, Kevin Stroyeck, the stiff, buttoned-up Navy commander who'd been assigned to stick close to her at the ball in case of an emergency.

Dating Meyers might be a conflict in view of their jobs, but she'd worry about that later. Tonight, she resolved to enjoy herself; there'd be plenty of time to change America's militaristic image tomorrow.

She'd find Meyers, chat him up, and maybe even invite him back to her new Georgetown townhouse for a nightcap. She envisioned clipping a *Washington Post* gossip-column snippet about their romance to send in a White House envelope to her mother. That would shut her up.

What a remarkable D.C. power couple we'd make.

Her plan for the evening now worked out in her mind, Head looked around at the others at the gala soiree. The high-rollers with their trophy wives in their ten-thousand-dollar gowns and glittering diamonds made her sick. It'd been necessary, of course, to take their money during the campaign, but the president had promised her that they'd have no influence in his administration. She couldn't wait to see their faces when they figured out they'd elected an honest man who couldn't be bought.

When the band struck up "Hail to the Chief," the president and First Lady walked on stage to an ear-splitting ovation. His remarks were brief. There was a toast, and the crowd went wild as the couple danced cheek-to-cheek amidst a waterfall of balloons and confetti falling from the ceiling. She hoped the president would put all this hoopla behind him and shift quickly out of campaign mode to tackle the hard work of refurbishing American's tarnished international image. This man loved to campaign.

Head almost fainted when the president pointed to her in the crowd and gave her a presidential wave. Head could tell that the president was having a great time. She could also tell that he was getting loaded; he didn't handle his liquor very well. Neither, in fact, did she, and she'd already downed four champagne cocktails for the liquid courage to invite her cable-journo stud home. There'd also been that quick joint—well, two—in the cab on the way over.

Head looked over at the press pool and saw Meyers flash his trademark high-wattage smile, which had to violate any number of EPA regulations on global warming. The crowd around him was cheering while he talked to an invisible anchor back at the cable TV news studio. He looked so handsome, so authoritative. He was a Cornell man, but he looked so delicious that she could overlook that.

It appeared to Head that Meyers was wrapping up his live shot speaking to an anchor back in the studio. She started working her way through the packed ballroom to be in position to grab him for a brief chat. A firm hand on her shoulder stopped her short of her goal.

"Excuse me, ma'am."

It was that pesky navy man Stroyeck, standing in front of her with a half dozen medals on his formal dinner dress uniform.

"Not now, please," she told him. "I need to speak to someone."

"Ma'am, it's the situation room. They need you there ASAP."

"It will have to wait."

"Ma'am, the secretary of defense is asking for you. He says it's a matter of the highest national security."

"Incredible! Go get the car and meet me out front."

The national security adviser thought she could still get to Meyers on her way out, to set something up for later that evening.

"The car is waiting, ma'am, with a police escort. If you please, ma'am." The navy man repeated, "It's a matter of the highest national security, ma'am."

Chapter 47

The Condo, Northwestern Iraq

January 20-21, 2009

It was 11:45 p.m., and sixteen minutes was all that remained in my enlistment. But I clearly wasn't going anywhere; truth be told, I didn't want to. I was still concerned for Maggie's safety. But, I wanted a shot at the brains behind the terrorist attack that had taken my dad's life. Literally.

"AWACS reports inbound chopper," Shay said from Control. "We think it's the same one, but the transponder's been turned off. ETA fourteen minutes."

"Roger that, major. We're down under 25 percent power, Control."

I looked at the screen and saw the two Russians on the top of the pile scanning the horizon, probably for the chopper, too.

"Understand," Shay came back. "AWACS reports the chopper just sent another message in Russian: 'Party lights.'"

The Russians slid down the ropes onto the floor of the pile and began placing light sticks in the ground to guide the chopper inside the pile. The sticks were barely in the ground when the chopper flew over the top of the condo and set down softly inside the illuminated landing zone. Two armed men jumped out of the chopper and quickly scanned the area. Then one of them spoke into a mic on his collar, and a stout, hedgehog-like man dressed in a flowing black robe stepped out and went directly to the tent that had been set up by the pool.

"That's got to be the boss, Novak. It's imperative that we pick him up with the shotgun mic for a comparison with the voice prints we've got. That's the only way we'll be able to identify him as the boss."

"Roger, Control."

Colonel Hunt came over the speaker from the White House Situation Room, taking over from Shay.

"Novak, let's talk tactics here. We've got six people there right now. Four are going to be trouble. The pilot is probably ex-military, given the way he hugged the desert floor on the way there, but he won't be a ground warrior. Then we've got the boss. My suggestion is your first targets should be the two men on the ridge, who are in a position to do the most damage. Then pop the other two. We'll have to see if bin Laden shows and who he brings. We'll make that call from here. The new national security adviser is on the way here now."

Oh, great. She'll probably demand my medal back.

"Although, ideally, we'd like to take the boss alive, that's not going to be feasible. Three choppers loaded with Delta Force operators are standing by, but they haven't been able to take off because of the sandstorm that's moving between you and them. It's not like we have MPs there who can arrest him, so you know what to do."

I glanced at Maggie, who was smiling knowingly. At least one MP was here, but after her treatment at their hands she had no intention of arresting anybody.

"Roger that, colonel. Standing by."

****

The digital clock on the control panel displayed 12:01 a.m. local time. It was January 21, 2009, and I was a free man. I'd also just earned an extra month's pay.

About five minutes later, Shay was back on from Control.

"Novak, two vehicles just hit the road sensor. We need you to activate the infrared camera. Make that three vehicles."

I powered up the outside cameras, consuming even more precious power, and saw the white SUV followed by a small truck. A third vehicle, also a pickup, had pulled off the road. The SUV and the truck pulled into the same spot the hit man had used previously, and four men, one very tall, exited the SUV. Two others got out of the truck and followed close behind. I activated a camera that would get them as they came through the maze.

"Confirmed. The tall one is bin Laden. We're running the others through the facial database."

"Roger."

The terrorist we thought was the boss appeared from inside the tent and walked a few steps to greet bin Laden. I had a shotgun mic trained on the two and was getting an instant translation through a channel on my headphones. They skipped the traditional Muslim greetings.

"My prince," bin Laden said.

"Osama, my friend, it has been too long, much too long."

The two men retreated inside the tent, making the microphones useless for eavesdropping on their conversation.

"Digital voice match confirmed. The man bin Laden called 'prince' is the man we know as the boss."

"Roger, Control. I have a clear shot at the two snipers. I can take them both out on your command and then work down."

"Hold your fire, Novak," Shay said. "The NSC is on the way. We're anticipating command approval momentarily."

Chapter 48

Situation Room, The White House

January 20, 2009

The new president had been crystal clear during his election campaign that he wanted to change America's militaristic image in the worst way. So, that is exactly what he did. He'd appointed as his NSA, Christine Head, Ph.D., a professor of political science with an emphasis on international relations.

The national security adviser wobbled into the situation room on her fresh-out-of-the-box high heels, which had started to wear a blister on her heels ten minutes after she'd put them on. The president had left clear orders that all national security matters would be run by Dr. Head. And if the president's direct order wasn't enough, no one wanted to interrupt him anyway. He was obviously getting smashed and he had a throbbing left hand after spending the afternoon signing a stack of documents reversing most of his predecessor's executive orders.

The secretary of defense, who'd agreed to stay on until his replacement was confirmed, introduced Dr. Head to Colonel Hunt. The colonel gave her a rapid-fire summary to bring her up to speed.

"Ma'am, what we have here is a top-secret facility that we constructed in a remote location in the Iraqi desert. This op was run directly out of the Oval Office. We have a man inside a high-tech fortification we call the condo. He has guns trained on Osama bin Laden and a man we believe is bin Laden's superior and chief financier, whom they call 'prince.' We've used a snippet of the prince's voice print to ID him definitively as the real power behind al-Qaeda. We'd like to notify the president to seek permission to take them out."

"I'm a bit overwhelmed, colonel. You say Osama bin Laden isn't the head of al-Qaeda? That sounds quite preposterous."

"I assure you it's accurate. The former president told me that the new president has been briefed, if you'll just call him."

"I'm sure you were told many things by your former president. Where is this place exactly?"

"It's in western Iraq, in the desert, masked as part of a rock formation."

"And you want the president to order the murders of these two men, criminals though they may be?"

"No ma'am, not just those two. We'd like to get them all while we can, ma'am, because they are all very bad people. If you'll just call the president . . ."

"I can assure you, my good colonel, that the president is very busy right now. And even if I called him, there's no way on Earth that he'd summarily authorize the cold-blooded executions of these men. This is a law enforcement issue for the Iraqi government. Contact them and have them pick up these people."

"Ma'am, there isn't time for that. The Iraqi government is probably three hours away from the condo even by helicopter, and a sandstorm is moving in as we speak. If we don't take them out . . ."

"We, colonel, no longer take human beings *out*. This country no longer does that type of thing."

"But, ma'am, you don't understand. These people meet at this location only days before they launch a major attack. In five days, they'll likely unleash a savage assault of some kind on our country."

****

"Situation room, this is Control. The boss and bin Laden finished their private discussion and are out of the tent. The shotgun mic just picked up bin Laden telling two other subjects identified as members of AQ-Syria that the targets are three large retail stores in Illinois, one in the Chicago suburbs. They're to be hit with drone-controlled ultralight aircraft carrying heavy explosives. One aircraft will carry something they called 'the special cargo.' We suspect that means a dirty bomb."

"Who is that? "the national security adviser demanded.

"Ma'am," Hunt replied, struggling to maintain his cool, "that's Condo Control, in Kuwait."

"Well, there has to be another way. We are not—I repeat, not—killing those people in cold blood."

"Situation room, we have more information. The ultralights are being assembled in a warehouse in Detroit. They apparently have a Syrian team in-country. We're requesting permission to fire."

"Who is speaking?" the national security adviser asked.

"Major Robert J. Shay, ma'am, with ATEC."

"Major Shay, you are directed to stand by."

"Yes, ma'am."

"Colonel, who is the man you have in this place at this condo?"

"Sergeant Travis Novak, ma'am, one of our best army snipers. He was recently awarded the Congressional Medal of Honor."

"That man? That's preposterous. I heard he's in a mental ward."

"No, ma'am. He's been at the condo in Iraq for months."

"Well, I think Sergeant Novak has murdered quite enough people for one lifetime. Patch me through to him."

Chapter 49

The Condo, Northwestern Iraq

January 21, 2009

I had a shot sequence ready to go; the bad guys wouldn't know what hit them. But with all the cameras and microphones operating, the power was down well under 10 percent. Time was running out.

What are they waiting for?

"Sergeant Novak?"

"This is Condo."

"Well, Sergeant Condo, this is the White House. I'm Dr. Christine Head, the president's national security adviser, speaking to you from the situation room. I'm giving you an order on his behalf. You are to hold your fire and wait for Iraqi law enforcement to arrive."

"But there's no one within hours of here, and a sandstorm is on the way. These people could leave any minute. They have a chopper, and they could...."

"Sergeant Novak, are you in the habit of questioning your superiors?"

"Well, lady, my enlistment expired an hour ago. You're talking to someone who now holds the highest office in the world: a U.S. citizen. The last time I checked, civilians don't take orders from bureaucrats. And if you don't have the guts to take out these scumbags who've killed tens of thousands of people all over the world, including my father, I can assure you that I do."

"Young man, you are to stand down. Do you hear me?"

"Say again. Our power's running low. Say again, White House."

"Don't pull that old B-movie line on me, young man. Stand down, I tell you."

****

I lined up the two Russians, and in less than five seconds they were both dead. The new gun system worked better than advertised. I was transfixed. Nothing else mattered. It was my intention to turn their sanctuary into a charnel house. I tried my best to keep my emotions in check. These were the people who had killed my father. They were going to pay. I looked down, and the rest of the rats were scrambling for cover. I popped bin Laden's two guards who had tried to find refuge behind a rock, and I was looking for the prince.

****

I heard Dr. Head's loud screech in my headphones as she watched in real time as I took out the four terrorists. When she'd finished screaming, she asked, "Colonel, isn't there a way to disable that place?"

"Ma'am, it's kind of . . ."

The voice of my loyal pal, Major Shay, broke in.

"Ma'am, we can disable the systems remotely from Control here in Kuwait."

Next time I see you, Major, you'll think that bruising I gave you during that lacrosse game was a love tap.

I reached under the panel, yanked the cable connecting the control console to the satellite dish, and then popped two more. I was on my own now—I was no longer in touch with The White House, or Control.

The power meter was flashing red, but I was determined to kill as many of them as I could. I told Maggie to get on the stationary bike and start pedaling, hoping it would generate enough juice to allow me a few more shots.

The prince and bin Laden were crouched behind the tent, so I couldn't get a good bead on them. But they weren't going anywhere. The pilot had dived for cover under the chopper, and the others were blindly firing pistols and an AK-47.

Chapter 50

Situation Room, The White House

January 20, 2009

"Major Shay, he is still killing them. Why haven't you disabled the equipment?"

"We're trying, ma'am. But either Novak must have disconnected the line from the satellite input to the control panel, or the condo power system may have run out. We've been having generator issues. Without that, our signal can't reach the guns."

"Isn't there any other way to stop him? This is going to create an embarrassing international incident on the president's first day in office. I assure you he isn't going to like this one bit."

"Well, there is a way," Shay said. "We wired the condo with explosives in case it was infiltrated. It works on an independent radio beam, but..."

"Then blow it," the national security adviser ordered.

Colonel Hunt stood up, glared at the woman, and said with a break in his voice, "That's a loyal, decorated U.S. soldier in there; a national hero; a holder of the Congressional Medal of Honor. You can't . . ."

The professor, who wasn't used to being contradicted in her classroom, interrupted the colonel.

"The way I see it, colonel, this criminal, this murderer, this Novak, is by his own words a civilian trespassing on a military installation. He's an illegal alien in a sovereign nation, and he's in violation of international law for killing those men. Blow it."

"Give me one last try," Hunt countered. "Give me just three minutes."

"As you wish, colonel. But in three minutes, I'm ordering you to blow it, Major Shay."

"Yes, ma'am."

Chapter 51

The Condo, Northwestern Iraq
January 21, 2009

Suddenly, I heard a blaring audio tone coming out of the short-wave receiver. An exasperated Colonel Hunt came over the speaker.

"Novak, I am your direct commander. I am giving you a direct order. Do you understand, son?"

Using the small, attached mic, I responded, "Roger, colonel."

"If—within three minutes—you do not stand down, the consequences will be dire. Do you read me, son?"

"Roger that, sir," I said to the device. I didn't know if Hunt could hear me, but I wasn't going to wait around to find out.

I threw down the mic; picked up my Remington, backpack, and a case of bottled water; and ran to the door. I heard Colonel Hunt continue to plead over the shortwave.

"Throw all the MREs you can in this sack in thirty seconds," I told Maggie.

"What's going on?"

"They're going to blow up the condo. We've got less than three minutes to get out."

Maggie threw a few supplies in the bag, and I told her to forget the rest. She grabbed an M4 and a pistol and met me by the door.

I tried to open the door and punch in the code for the storage hold just as the batteries went dead. I threw the manual override switch, and the generator powered up—still sputtering but spitting out enough juice to run the door.

****

Alerted to our location by the noise of the generator, the terrorists started shooting in our direction. A few shots pinged off the rocks nearby. I got Maggie down into the storage hold just as the generator gave up the ghost. I pressed the detonator and dived on top of her as the five-second delay counted down.

The charges blew the side panel off the cliff, and we were looking fifty feet down and out into the desert. I told Maggie to get on the dune buggy and buckle up, threw the supplies in the rear, and checked my watch. Less than two minutes.

I cranked up the dune buggy and let it idle. Then I grabbed my Remington and climbed back up on the deck.

"Where are you going, Travis? We've got to get out of here."

"I've got about a minute, Maggie. Hang on. I'll be right back."

I crawled up to the loading deck and looked down at the floor far below. The prince was slithering like a snake in the sand, trying to get to the copter. I scoped him in with my deer rifle and introduced a 30.06 slug to the sphenoid bone of his skull. I'll bet that cleared out his sinuses. The result wasn't as pretty as I'd have achieved with the Barrett M-107, but he was as dead as any twelve-point buck. There was no time for me to get the others.

I jumped down, got in the driver's seat, and put the buggy into "descend" gear. The flat bumper on the front of the buggy moved into the giant roll of track, and it began to push forward like it had done during my training at The Farm. The only difference was that we were about three times higher.

Belted in and holding on for our lives, we pushed off with nothing between us and the ground but a thin, carbon-fiber track. I was praying that we'd hit the floor before the explosives detonated. Maggie was emitting a scream like someone being chased by an ax murderer.

We were halfway down to the floor when the Saudi hit man and Abu's brother, started their truck. They drove straight for us, and Maggie opened-up with her M4, slowing them down momentarily.

247

When we were about three feet from the ground, a massive blast tore through the condo. Our erector-set track dislodged from its mounts above, and we fell the last few feet. The buggy bounced several times on its huge tires and, remembering Captain Klingel's instructions, I put it in drive and floored it as condo debris from above started raining all around us.

****

I guided the dune buggy away from the pile as fast as I could and still keep the tires on the ground. The tires took the terrain, a mix of sand and rocks, with ease but not without frequent bounces. Taking out my 9-mm pistol, I put a round through the emergency locator beacon transmitter. I didn't want the army knowing I'd survived, at least not yet.

We were taking incoming fire from the pickup, which was struggling to keep up. I slowed down and told Maggie to switch seats with me, which was a tricky maneuver. Once she gained control, I racked the general-purpose machine gun affixed to the roll bar and opened fire. The belt-fed gun spit spent shells everywhere as I guided the tracer rounds into the cab of the truck and quickly blew it out of the race.

"That was too close," I told her. "Let's put some distance between us and that place."

Maggie floored it. I could tell she was scared but nonetheless enjoying driving the buggy. Who wouldn't?

When we were a couple of miles from the condo, we stopped to see if anyone was behind us. I didn't see anything, and we made for a small rock outcropping. I offered to drive, but Maggie said she had it covered.

We reduced our speed to conserve gas and our spines, making it easier as well for me to keep a lookout behind us. Still nothing.

Then, I heard it. The prince's chopper roared directly over us at some fifty feet, leaving a trail of sand and dust in its wake. There was no doubt that the pilot had seen us; he was making a wide turn to come back. Colonel Hunt had been right. The pilot was good. I was certain he was ex-military—whose, I had no idea.

I loosened the case containing the Stinger shoulder-fired missile that was bolted behind the seats, jumped out, and told Maggie to pull in behind the rocks. The chopper wasn't armed, but with their automatic rifles, the two AQ passengers could shoot until they got us. They wouldn't be expecting the SAM, but I only had one shot.

As I'd expected, the terrorists went after the buggy. Shooting from a chopper isn't easy, and these guys weren't snipers, but anyone with an automatic weapon can get lucky. They came around slowly with the door open, and Maggie opened-up with the machine gun. But she had no experienced with the weapon, and the ammo belt quickly ran out.

She grabbed her M4 and fired until the magazine was empty. Then she produced the 9-mm we'd taken from her captors and started shooting with it. She had to dive behind the rocks as rounds from the chopper found the range.

The chopper banked steeply and came around for another try from a better angle. I flipped the power switch and acquired the target. The SAM left the tube in a loud bang and a whoosh. Seconds later, the French bird exploded into a desert flambé and fell from the sky, narrowly missing my girl.

I ran to Maggie, who was hopping from foot to foot, hugging herself to control her frantic shaking.

"Honey," she said, "that was the most exciting thing that's ever happened to me. But I was so scared, I almost wet my pants!"

Chapter 52

Situation Room, The White House

January 20, 2009

Dr. Christine Head glared at Colonel Hunt.

"The lives of those men are on your head, colonel. If you'd have let me blow the place when I wanted, they'd still be alive."

"The world is a better place with them dead. But you've killed one of the finest soldiers to ever serve in the United States Army. That one is on your head, Dr. Head. Novak took this mission at the direct request of the president. The man wears the Congressional Medal of Honor . . ."

"Please, I'm weary of hearing about your military tchotchkes, Colonel Hunt. That man was a mass murderer, and you are an insubordinate menace. Your career is over."

"I'll agree with you on that part, lady. Mr. Secretary, I hereby resign my commission. I will not serve in any army commanded by traitors who kill American soldiers for the benefit of some twisted international fantasy."

"Expect to hear from the Justice Department very soon, colonel," the national security adviser spat.

Hunt kicked over his chair and stormed out. Looking for support, Head turned to the secretary of defense but found none.

"Tell the president, Dr. Head, if you ever get around to sobering up, that he will have my resignation in the morning. May God save the republic."

Chapter 53

Syro-Arabian Desert

3:10 A.M, January 21

I checked the GPS compass system on my iPhone and then shut it down. I had a full battery charge but no charger, so I'd have to be judicious with the phone.

I'd earlier bookmarked the coordinates of the pile to be sure we could find our way back to make a withdrawal from our Pile National Bank safety deposit box—someday.

The GPS told me that we were about an hour's drive south of Highway 10, the main east-west highway that joined Baghdad and Jordan. There was nothing in any other direction that would be reachable without refueling.

We found a cave in one of the smaller limestone formations that was large enough for the buggy and decided to hole up for the night. A powerful wind storm was predicted for morning, and I didn't want to get caught in it.

The food and water we'd brought with us would last a few days. The buggy had a survival kit, but it was stocked for only one person; so I had to get Maggie out soon. I took a thermal blanket from the kit, and we snuggled together and tried to get some sleep.

About two hours after things had gone bad, we'd heard choppers whizzing overhead. Were they were looking for us or the bad guys? Probably both.

****

The next morning, satisfied that the choppers weren't coming back, we talked about our plan. I figured at least some of our troops would begin leaving Iraq later in the day. Some news reports had said the threat to leave had merely been campaign bluster by the new president. I was betting, however, that at least a symbolic number would be moved out to allow the press to hype the departure into a big story.

The buggy's survival kit contained a map of the region. I surmised that the exfiltration would be through Kuwait. The main highway there was Highway 8, which ran from Baghdad all the way south to the Kuwaiti border. I figured U.S. troops leaving the western part of the country, near us, would make the drive east on Highway 10 and then pick up Highway 8 heading south. And even if the new president didn't order the withdrawal to begin immediately, there'd certainly be army traffic on the main road.

With that in mind, we spent the day in the cave practicing Maggie's story. The army wouldn't be able to break it if she stuck to her guns—and as I'd seen firsthand, she was really good with guns. Maggie had over twenty-five million reasons to turn in an Academy Award–winning performance.

Maggie had kept as a souvenir the CZ-75, Czech-made 9-mm pistol she'd used to finish off Cruella, and she'd somehow had enough presence of mind to grab it when we escaped the condo. She'd be found with the pistol, a key part of the plan we'd concocted. After firing at the prince's helicopter, she was down to one round, which would make her story even more believable. I could almost hear the media: "Our heroine was down to her last bullet when she was rescued in the desert."

As I'd learned in B-school, packaging is everything. After spending hours driving in the desert, no one would be able to tell if Maggie had been in the desert a month or a day. I also had in my backpack some of the ancient coins she'd found in the cave. She'd use a few of the coins as props, adding a little more spice to her tale.

****

We left the cave at sundown. I used the compass on my iPhone to set our course and the map to identify landmarks—which I'd learned to do in sniper school. It took us almost two hours to find Highway 10. We

252

parked behind a rise with some large rocks and a few scrub bushes, and I covered the buggy with the camouflage netting from the survival kit and camouflaged it with some brush and desert foliage for good measure. We spent the night waiting for the troops to pass our location.

Around six the next morning, I started watching the highway using the small binoculars from the survival kit. Before long, we saw a caravan of six heavily loaded, army M35 deuce-and-a-half cargo trucks, led by a Humvee, speeding toward us. When the convoy was about a mile away, I splashed some water around Maggie's mouth. Then she took a handful of sand and pressed it to her mouth to add to the effect.

I kissed her sand-covered lips, told her I loved her, and positioned her on her hands and knees along the side of the road. As I started to retreat to my hiding place, I realized that I had forgotten one thing and I ran back to Maggie.

"Give me the ring. Hurry."

"Oh, please, Travis . . ."

"It'll blow the whole story. Don't worry. You'll get it back, I promise."

"I love you, Travis."

"I love you, too," I told her. "Keep to the story, and everything will work out—I promise." And I hurried back to the brush to watch. I figured the army drivers would see her, knowing they'd been trained to be alert for roadside bombs.

The trucks were approaching at about forty-five miles an hour. Maggie raised her hand and waved pitifully at the convoy. It took a few seconds for the sight of her to register with the driver of the lead HUMVEE. The convoy stopped a safe distance down the road from her to ensure it wasn't an ambush.

First Sergeant John Stiles, a national guardsman from Windsor, Missouri, jumped out and pointed his M4 at her. His partner trained a roof-mounted chain gun in her direction.

"Identify yourself," he said in Missouri-accented Arabic.

Maggie faked a struggle to her feet and then fell down to her knees and said, "I'm an American. Help me, please."

Stiles radioed to the convoy commander and advised him of the situation.

"What's your unit?" Stiles asked her.

"Sixteenth MP Brigade out of Bragg. I was kidnapped and escaped. Please help me."

Not yet convinced, Stiles said, "Stand up and raise your hands."

Maggie got to her feet, feigning a great struggle, and raised her hands. Then Stiles ordered her to lift her shirt so he could check that she wasn't wearing a bomb. He shouldered his weapon in earnest when he saw the pistol in her belt.

"Slowly, reach back and drop the weapon."

Maggie complied, laying the pistol on the asphalt. Stiles nodded toward a truck, and two soldiers who'd been waiting behind it ran out to get her. While I lay hidden only a few feet away, she collapsed theatrically into the arms of the first man. To the other man, she rasped in that Louisiana drawl that I loved, "Pick up that pistol will you, sweetie? I'm going to want to hold on to that. "

I watched with mixed emotions as they drove off with my girl. I knew the radio was already sending word of her rescue. By the time she reached Baghdad, my future in-laws would have been notified of the good news. My future uncle-in-law, the congressman, would be holding a press conference giving credit for Maggie's discovery to his fellow party man, the new president. The new president would gladly accept Maggie's uncle's thanks, and the former president would say a sincere prayer of thanks down at his ranch. I, however, would be alone for the next part of the trip, which wouldn't be quite as easy.

Chapter 54

Washington, D.C.

January 21, 2009

As the newly inaugurated president and his wife were returning to the White House from the last inaugural ball, word came that the secretary of defense had resigned. When, in a second relayed call, the president heard why the secretary had quit, the limo had just passed through the White House gates.

The president told the limo driver to stop, mumbled an excuse to his wife, got out of the limo, and walked to a secluded area on the White House lawn trying to sober up. There, he lit up a Marlboro Red that he'd taken earlier in the evening from a pack carried by his body man and took a deep drag on the cigarette. When he'd finished the cigarette, he flipped the butt onto the lawn and walked inside, hoping the First Lady wouldn't discover that he'd never really kicked the habit.

Dr. Christine Head, now sober but still slightly high, was in the White House situation room. She still wore her wrinkled ball gown but had taken off her high heels. Along with the director of the CIA, the chairman of the Joint Chiefs, and the president's chief of staff, the national security adviser was awaiting the president's arrival.

When the president walked into the room, the three other men stood, but Head remained seated and stared blankly at the conference table.

"I want an explanation of what went on here," the president said, taking the place at the head of the far end of the table.

Shifting uncomfortably in her seat, the former professor started babbling about a secret assassination squad that the military had established, and how the sovereignty of Iraq had been violated.

The president stopped her in mid-sentence, asking, "Christine, why didn't you call me?"

"Sir, they made no sense at all—saying that bin Laden was just a puppet and that there was some . . . some . . . wizard behind the screen that they called his boss, or some poppycock to try to justify their . . ."

"Christine, that's all true. I just found out about it yesterday."

"Why didn't they tell us sooner?"

"Maybe they didn't want that cable newsman you've been mooning over to make it the day's lead story."

"But, sir, I never . . ."

"Stop it, Christine. It's not helpful."

"But, sir, these people were killing civilians."

"Christine, we're at war with those people."

"I told them to stop, but they kept killing them."

"Christine, we've been friends for a long time, and you were a great supporter of the campaign. That's why I'm going to give you a graceful way out. In one month, you will announce that you miss academia and are offering your resignation. Until then, you will not attend any more briefings. If anyone asks, tell them you are ill. Do you understand?"

"But they were killing people . . ."

"You're excused, Christine."

The president waited for her to leave the room before resuming.

"Now, gentlemen, let's talk about how we can clean up this mess."

The chairman of the Joint Chiefs reported that the video feed before the condo was blown up showed bin Laden running for the pile's entry maze. By the time the choppers carrying Delta Force arrived, there were only dead bodies, which were flown to Kuwait for autopsy and identification. Bin Laden's corpse was not among them. The president said he'd cover himself by merely announcing that a high-level AQ official had been killed in a successful operation—with no mention of either the prince or Novak's death at the order of Dr. Head.

The chairman also told the president about the rescue of the female soldier who'd been kidnapped months earlier. The chief of staff—who'd always seemed able to make lemonade out of any crisis—interjected that the story of the rescue would deflect press attention from any leaks about the fiasco at the condo. The president agreed.

The president ordered the entire condo project classified and buried in the depths of the darkest federal archives. It would come to light, he estimated, about a week after the truth about the Kennedy assassination was released. Crisis averted—and meeting adjourned.

****

At the Key Bridge Marriott in Arlington, Virginia, across the Potomac River from the White House, Colonel Ansley Hunt had finished a hearty breakfast—the last meal, he figured, he'd be charging to the army. He planned a leisurely drive back to Fort Benning, followed by a quiet, well-deserved retirement. It was clear things would change quite a bit with the new administration now in power—had already begun to change—and Hunt wanted no part of it.

Back in the room he'd occupied for the past few weeks, he quickly finished packing his clothes. Then he checked the room's safe and retrieved some cash, his 1911 .45 automatic, Novak's Congressional Medal of Honor and the gold cufflinks the president had given him. He put the medal and cufflinks in his briefcase, wondering what he should do with them. The boy had no family. Maybe he'd ask the sniper school to construct a fitting memorial to Novak that included the medal.

Hunt couldn't wait to hear the cock-and-bull story the government came up with to explain how Novak died. If Novak were still alive, certainly the boy would have established contact with him by now.

As Hunt was zipping his bag, he heard a sharp knock on the door. He looked through the peephole to see two army officers and a thirty-something civilian in a Sears Roebuck suit. He opened the door, and the senior officer, a lieutenant colonel with JAG insignias, asked to speak with him.

The two army lawyers identified themselves as Lieutenant Colonel Benton "Tad" Armstrong and Major James Hackett. Hunt recognized the men's names. The two were the army's chief prosecutors of high-profile deserters. The civilian didn't bother introducing himself. He just barged in with the two army officers, wagging his finger at Hunt.

"Boys, I was just now fixing to check out of here. What can I do for you?"

The lawyer from the Justice Department, who belatedly introduced himself as George Riecan, told Hunt he was in big trouble. Specifically, he'd more than likely be indicted for complicity in the murder of multiple foreign nationals. The civil servant began citing the federal statutes that Hunt was accused of violating.

Hunt, who'd heard more than enough, interrupted Riecan.

"Sonny, save your breath. I was in the service before you made the move to pull-up Pampers. If you want to indict me, I'll personally drive you by the federal courthouse on my way out of town. If you were here to arrest me, you'd be traveling with a couple of burley MPs or maybe a few FBI agents wearing blue windbreakers.

"You and I both know the last thing the president wants to do is to indict a man who will tell the world how his drunken national security adviser blew catching or killing bin Laden and then killed a holder of the Congressional Medal of Honor. I figure every television news show in America will want me as their guest. Hells bells, Fox News will probably give me my own show with a salary of $1 million a year. How does "The Ansley Hunt Show" sound to you, sonny?

"You're here to try to scare me into something, so let's hear what it is."

The trio explained the deal, which was detailed in a document they'd brought for his signature. Hunt would retire immediately with a full pension. He'd also sign a consulting agreement with a security company that they identified. Hunt figured, but they didn't say, that the company was owned by the CIA. He'd get five thousand dollars a month for ten years, plus full health and dental benefits and a 401(k) with a 50 percent match. There was no mention of vacation, as he'd be on call and could work from home—meaning that he'd probably never hear from anyone in the company other than receiving a direct-deposit to his checking account once a month. Finally, he'd have to keep silent on all classified operations in which he'd participated during his army career.

They told Hunt he could return to Fort Benning to collect his belongings, after which he should make himself scarce for a while. Hunt knew the game they were playing, and he didn't like it. But he knew he couldn't beat the federal government. And there was nothing else he could do for Novak. Taking a pen from the plastic protector in the breast pocket of the young lawyer's wrinkled jacket, he signed the document.

Chapter 55

Ar Rutba, Iraq

January 22, 2009

Abu al-Kuwaiti was bringing bin Laden up to date while attending to his brother, who'd suffered several broken ribs when the pickup was riddled with 7.62 x 54 mm NATO slugs from the dune buggy's machine gun. The Saudi hit man hadn't been as lucky; he'd died behind the wheel. Going through the deceased man's pockets, al-Kuwaiti had found over five thousand dollars in cash. He'd also found several hundred thousand Euros in the Saudi's bag. But the trusted confidant's memory proved much poorer when it came to telling bin Laden about the six gold bars he'd discovered.

Shaking his head, bin Laden said, "What you've shared with me, Abu, is just the way it goes. A low-level operative was walking around with more money than we've seen in years. I have six hundred Euros and a Krugerrand sewn into the hem of my robe, and this man—whose name none of us even knows—had more money than he could ever spend.

"Guard what you found carefully, Abu, because we are going to have to lay low for a while. The prince may have been a phony, but he never failed to come through with cash when we needed it. Now that he is dead, we will need a more aggressive fund-raising effort. I will get to work composing some messages appealing to our supporters and you will need to find a safe courier to deliver the messages before we leave Ar Rutba. And we need to step up our kidnappings for ransoms as well.

"Speaking of kidnappings, Abu, has that American female soldier been found?"

"I just heard the news, my sheik. The Americans rescued the girl this morning.

Abu continued. "It was unfortunate that Dr. al-Zawahri did not make it to the sanctuary. We could have used him to help with my brother and the others who were injured."

"Abu, the man is like every other doctor in the world: always running behind. I received word from him in this morning's messages, inquiring about my safety. The worm only wanted to know if I was still alive so he could grab the reins. He doesn't fool me a bit. He said he was a few miles away, saw the explosion, and turned back. Only Allah knows where he is now."

With finances now a top priority, bin Laden began typing away on his laptop, begging for cash. He wondered how he would finance the new home he so desperately wanted without being able to place his bets in the stock market. Now there would be no attack and no insider-trading windfall. With the two AQ-Syria men killed at the sanctuary, he had no way to contact the team in America. The compound in Abbottabad might be a real dump, but at least it was safe.

The terrorist stopped typing and turned to his confidant, who was preoccupied with changing his brother's dressings.

"You know, Abu," bin Laden said, "when we were at the sanctuary, I had a strange feeling that we were close to a massive fortune that slipped through our fingers.

****

The al-Kuwaiti brothers were bragging about their heroics of the previous night to a local AQ man.

"I tell you," Abu said, "we were pinned down by American snipers—maybe ten, probably more. I'm sure they were SEALS. The prince's professional guards lasted only a few seconds. But we are al-Qaeda, and our courage and faith allowed us to stand up to them. We blew up their hiding place, killing all but two."

"Yes," said the younger brother. "I was outside the sanctuary with that Saudi hit man. I was never very comfortable around that guy, but when we heard the attack begin, we rushed to help. Then we noticed this new American weapon, unlike anything we have ever seen. It was like a dune buggy, but—don't ask me how—they drove it off a towering cliff. Then the thing stopped in midair and fired at us before slowly dropping onto the sand and speeding off. We gave chase, of course, but our AK-47s were no match for their machine gun. They got the hit man, and the truck rolled. Someday, we will find those mongrels and they will pay."

"A flying dune buggy with a machine gun," the AQ man said, shaking his head in disbelief. *Next you will be telling me that unclean pigs can fly.*

Chapter 56

Detroit, Michigan

January 22, 2009

Adad Haneef's guard and keeper, Kareem Hassan, had arrived in Detroit as a teenager. His early education in a Pakistani madrassa hadn't provided him with many marketable skills, unless hating infidels qualified. During a summer trip to visit relatives in Pakistan, he'd been recruited and radicalized by AQ.

Hassan liked his current assignment of keeping the ultralight operation secret and on schedule. He also liked the expense money he was able to skim. What he did not like, however, was Haneef's obsession for Popeyes chicken. Every day without fail, Haneef said, "Kareem, go get us more of that chicken." Hassan had walked in the bitter cold to order the family meal so many times that he'd stopped counting.

And here he was again, for the umpteenth time, sidling up to the Popeyes counter to place his order and remind them to put the hush puppies in the box. He told them they had forgotten the last time and he was still hearing about it. The order came to a little over thirty-eight dollars, and Hassan opened his wallet and pulled out a hundred. A hundred-dollar bill was remarkable enough in this section of town. But TyWayne "Tire Tool" Washington, who was waiting impatiently for his two piece with red beans and rice, almost choked when he saw the wad of bills inside the man's wallet.

Tire Tool took his meal to go and got into a Cadillac Escalade driven by his cousin, Ronald, who went by the handle "The Flamer." The Flamer tried to grab a drumstick from the box, but Tire Tool slapped his hand away.

The pair was part of a local gang called Woodstoned Nation, a combination of Woodward Boulevard and the purpose of the dope they sold. Tire Tool figured the man with the fat wallet was a member of another gang. The dude looked Middle Eastern but he could be from El Salvador. Tire Tool had never been much for physiognomy, but geography was a different story entirely. The guy was on his block, and that's what mattered to Tire Tool. Nobody in Detroit but gangbangers and auto executives had that kind of dough, and this cat didn't look like he was running the Ford plant.

Tire Tool and The Flamer followed Hassan back to the warehouse and watched him enter the side door. The two cousins walked down the side of the building and tried to look inside, but the windows had been painted over.

"They be cuttin' dope in there right now. I can feel it," Tire Tool said.

"Naw, they be eatin' that grease."

Tire Tool agreed that The Flamer was probably right, so it was the perfect time to bust in and make clear the neighborhood rules on profit sharing.

The back entrance to the place had large, old-fashioned wooden doors that met in the middle and swung into the building. A flimsy latch was all that kept them closed. The Flamer revved the stolen Escalade and rammed it through the doors, which opened like a book. The two gangsters batted away the now spent air bags and jumped out, guns drawn, and started yelling, "Where's the dope?"

Hassan, who had just prepared a paper plate with a breast, a thigh, and a side of slaw, yelled something the bangers didn't understand and lunged for an off-brand AR-15.

"Who'd you think you is? al-Qaeda or somethin'?" The Flamer hollered.

Then the Flamer plugged Hassan with a Kimber .45 ACP that he'd lifted from a house in Grosse Point.

"Take that, al-Qaeda. You think you tough? This here ain't no desert. This here Detroit. Didn't y'all see all the snow?"

Tire Tool capped Haneef's two helpers. And as Haneef dived for his backpack with his plans and cash, he caught a double tap in the neck and skull.

The two bangers didn't find any dope, but they did score several thousand in cash and the off-brand AR-15. After considerable discussion, Tire Tool and The Flamer concluded that they couldn't fit an ultralight in the Escalade, Tire Tool saying he'd always wanted one. They'd made a pretty good haul, so they decided to blow—but not until The Flamer had grabbed a drumstick from the half-eaten family meal.

Chapter 57

Highway 10, Near Ar Rutba, Iraq

January 22, 2009

I waited until dark so I wouldn't run into any army colleagues. The army wouldn't travel at night except in convoys of overwhelming strength, and I was betting they'd already turned in their token appearance for the media earlier in the day. About eight o'clock, I set out for Ar Rutba, the only spot on the map close enough for me to reach before the buggy ran dry.

A sign indicated that Ar Rutba was twenty-one clicks ahead. The buggy was down to an eighth of a tank of fuel, so I'd have to get gas somewhere or abandon my ride. I didn't know if driving fifty-five would make the LSV more fuel efficient, but I tried to keep the needle there. Worst case, I'd siphon somebody's tank or steal a car; I was from St. Louis, after all. I didn't pass a single car until I saw a tall minaret in the distance that I figured was in Ar Rutba.

When I saw a radio tower, I pulled off the road about a quarter mile into the scrub. Powering up my iPhone, I got three bars of service and let it download my email. Then I heard the ding.

Two messages. The one from my cousin Freddie told me that, because I hadn't responded about his reception, he'd been let go from the firm. I guess it had to have been my fault. It couldn't have been his—he was a Sumter.

The other message was a pouty, two-sentence missive from Sally Effingham telling me how disappointed she was that I wouldn't be at the reunion. She'd hoped we could pick up where we left off at Barrington. I was glad Maggie wouldn't see that one.

I took the miniature medal the former president had given me and turned it over in my palm. I decoded the numbers the way he'd shown me and dialed the phone number it revealed. The line rang several times, and I considered calling back later. But as I was about to disconnect the call, a Texas-accented voice answered.

"Yes?"

"Sir, this is Sergeant Travis Novak. The former president gave me this number and said I could call if I ran into a jam."

"Where are you, Novak?"

"Highway 10. Outside Ar Rutba in western Iraq. I'm about seventy miles from Jordan, which is where I'm heading. I need help crossing the border."

He asked me to spell the name of the city, and I did.

"Will this phone work to get back to you?"

"Yes, but I don't want to leave it on."

"Turn it on at the top of the hour. I'll get back to you."

"Yes, sir. Thank you, sir. Can I ask who this . . ."

The line went dead.

I checked the time and powered off the phone. I had about forty-five minutes until the call would come, so I decided to make a quick trip into town to try to find fuel. Then I remembered I'd never asked Captain Klingel at The Farm if the LSV took regular or premium.

I drove slowly back to the quiet highway. A bus passed, and none of the passengers even looked at me. I guess the Iraqis had all become numb to guns and war. At a small gas station ahead, a flatbed truck with a large shipping container on the trailer was fueling up at a lone diesel pump on the far side of the lot. The truck was lit up like a honky-tonk bar in the Ozarks on the first Saturday night after payday. Closer to the center of the lot, two gas pumps were in front of a ramshackle concrete-block building. A white SUV was getting gas at one of the pumps, and a pickup truck was starting to pull away from the other. I watched as the pickup parked near the flatbed.

I pulled up to the now-vacant pump and told the attendant to fill it up. He didn't understand English, so I pointed to the pump while he stared at the machine gun.

****

Abu's brother was saying goodbye to Naveed Hussein, the local AQ man, when he saw the LSV.

"That's the infidels' new magic machine," he said excitedly to the AQ man. "Look, he's putting gas in it."

He quickly called his brother, who answered the intercom in the crate. "What is the problem? Talk slower so I can understand you."

"He's here; he's here."

"Who is here?"

"The cur from last night, on that chariot that can stop in midair."

The elder al-Kuwaiti had wondered if his brother had concocted the story of the flying chariot to cover for his failure at the sanctuary. Or perhaps he'd taken too many narcotic pain killers. He looked through a small peephole in the crate and saw the buggy.

"Osama, do you hear that? The American army is outside."

Abandoning his computer solitaire game, bin Laden grabbed a pistol.

"My sheik, it's only one man. My brother says he is one of the dogs from the sanctuary."

"If he doesn't bother us, let's just move on," bin Laden said. "There might be more of them nearby. Let's get moving."

Receiving the instruction to move out, the younger al-Kuwaiti embraced Hussein through the cab window. Then Hussein got back in his pickup and pulled to the side of the lot as the flatbed rolled onto the highway heading east, and the white Suzuki SUV followed behind.

****

I bought a few liters of bottled water and some candy bars. Iraqi gas stations apparently didn't sell potato chips. I asked the man if he had any Coke. He pointed to the truck that was pulling out and said, "Coke, coke." I didn't understand what he was talking about, but I wanted to get out of there. I grabbed a Pepsi, gave him a hundred-dollar bill from the secret compartment in my backpack, and went out to my ride.

I strapped in and took off, heading west toward the junction of the two highways. I had to ensure that I took the left fork; the right one would take me to Syria. I was looking for a place to pull off to get my bearings when I noticed headlights behind me. I sped up and so did the lights. As the road went down a hill and the lights momentarily disappeared, I whipped the buggy off the road and floored it. About three hundred yards off the road, I turned the LSV around facing the road and flipped off the lights.

Checking my watch, I had only ten minutes before check-in. I powered up the phone and rechecked the signal. Only one bar of service.

Whoever was following me didn't pass by as I'd expected. I heard a crack coming from the road—first one, then a short burst—and saw the sand in front of me explode. As I floored the buggy and came back around toward the road, I saw a man running back to his pickup, lugging an AK-47.

This wasn't what I needed right now. I still had Maggie's M4, but the magazine was spent. The machine gun needed a fresh ammo belt, but it would wake the entire town anyway. And the guy was too far away for a pistol shot.

All I had within reach that made any sense was my Remington hunting rifle—and I wasn't sure if the scope was still zeroed in after the jarring ride through the desert. There were five shots in the magazine. But there was nothing I could use for cover, and he'd just emptied his second clip and was starting on a third.

He was still too far from me for the AK-47 to be very accurate, but I was trapped. With homes behind me, I couldn't fall back. And I didn't want to get caught in the town, which was an AQ hotbed.

Instead, I drove closer to him, jerking the buggy to make it harder to hit. When I was about a hundred yards out—the distance to which I'd zeroed the Remington's scope—I jumped off the buggy, dived to a prone position in the sand, and chambered the Remington. I scoped in the truck's rear-view mirror, knowing I'd miss, but the glass would show me which way the rifle was off.

My trial shot was too far left by two inches. As I suspected, the scope had been jarred, knocking it out of calibration. Without the tools, time, and ammunition to zero-in the scope, I'd have to compensate.

I waited until he stuck his head up and carefully took aim, when my phone rang.

I put my phone on speaker. It was the man from Texas.

"Novak?"

The guy in the pickup fired off a burst that hit ten or twelve feet in front of me.

"Novak, are you all right?"

"Hold on a second, please, sir."

I sighted in the shooter's head and compensated for the scope. In south St. Louis, many of the old-time neighborhood taverns serve brain sandwiches, usually with a lot of mustard. It would probably be a while before I'd be able to eat one of those again.

"Sir, everything's fine now. Just fine."

Epilogue

To this day, I still don't know the name of the man who answered when I called the phone number the former president had given me. He told me to drive to a GPS coordinate just my side of the Jordanian border. After wiping Maggie's fingerprints off the buggy and hiding it, I walked several miles to the meeting spot. The army never told me if they found it. But I had presidential permission to use any available military transportation following my discharge and the last time I checked, that dune buggy was owned by the army.

A car with two Americans inside, their faces hidden by dark shades, pulled up in front of me. I assumed they were CIA, but I never asked and they never said. For all I cared, they could have been from the Salvation Army. As we approached the border crossing, I pulled my passport out of my backpack, which they were surprised that I had. That saved them the fifty dollars they'd planned to use to pay off the border guards.

In Amman, we stopped at a store specializing in western clothing, and I bought some new clothes. Then, my escorts drove me to the airport, where we parted company. I threw the condo-colored fatigues and boots I was wearing in a trash can, swearing to never wear that color again. I showered in the pilot's lounge before using my AMEX Platinum Card to charter a small jet to Geneva, Switzerland. It cost a fortune, but I had one—and it would soon be even bigger.

I checked into a five-star hotel and bought some even better clothes in the boutique in the lobby. After a brief trip to buy a laptop at an Apple Store nearby, I returned to my hotel room for a long, well-deserved sleep.

The ring of my cell phone interrupted my nap. The caller, a lawyer who identified himself as Dennis Huneke, told me that a mutual friend had asked him to help me out. He said there would be no charge for his services. There was no question in my mind who that mutual friend was.

I recognized Huneke's name. He was a powerful Washington, D.C., lawyer, and a fixer who, with his brother Edward, had made a fortune in real estate and ownership of professional soccer teams around the world. It was said that he pulled more strings in D.C. than Geppetto.

Huneke asked me how I wanted things with the government resolved, and I told him. He said he'd get back to me.

After setting up my new computer, I logged in to an email account I'd told Maggie to set up when she got back home. The email address was twoheartsaloneinthedesert@charter.net. Of course, Maggie picked the name. (She still has the account. If you ever want to send her an email, she would love to hear from you). A draft message was waiting for me, and I opened it anxiously.

> Travis,
>
> I'm hoping with all my heart that you're reading this message, which I'm sending from Baghdad. I'm safe but worried sick about you.
>
> They checked me out at the army hospital and said I was in remarkable shape for someone who'd spent all that time in the desert. Still, they're sending me to Germany for some further tests.
>
> I told them what you told me to say: I lived in a cave near some nomads and left the cave after dark to steal food and water. After the nomads moved on while I was sleeping, I got lost and finally stumbled on the guys on the highway.
>
> As we expected, they asked a lot of questions about how I escaped the terrorists. I told them I faked passing out, grabbed the 9-mm when the woman was trying to rearrange my handcuffs in the back of the truck, and started shooting them. The truck flipped when I got the driver, and I jumped out before it caught on fire. Then, I said, I grabbed their AK and made sure they were dead. Having the gun was a nice touch.
>
> When they asked for more details, I said I'd been out of my mind for much of the time and couldn't remember. They didn't press it. You were right: they were really happy to have me back. And when they saw the coins, I think that sealed the deal.

Of course, they also asked how I got kidnapped. Travis, I didn't tell them about looking for the stupid carpet. I just couldn't. Instead, I said my interpreter had asked the driver to pull over, and they jumped us. They said my interpreter was found with his throat slit the day I disappeared. His family said he'd gone along with the kidnappers because they'd threatened to kill him—and all his family—for collaborating with the Americans if he didn't agree to betray me. I feel terrible that I got my driver killed, and I'm going to see if I can do something for his family.

My parents said my uncle will pull some strings to get me an early discharge, just like you said. I hope to be home in New Orleans in a few days, after they're done checking me out in Germany.

We have a whirlwind romance to start, Travis, so come to me as soon as you're able. And I want that ring back. My finger feels very bare without it.

I love you more than anything on this Earth, Travis. Be safe.

Love,

Maggie

****

I rented a car and drove east to Liechtenstein, to a private bank run by one of my father's old clients. Debt had put the world economy into crisis, and I decided I was going to use debt to solve my dilemma.

Dad's banker friend listened intently as I outlined my proposal. Maggie and I would put the bonds, gold, diamonds, and most of the cash in a safety-deposit box in his bank, as collateral on low-interest loans he'd make to a company I'd form. If I didn't repay the notes on time, he could remove the balance due from my box. It was the perfect private-equity model; it was our equity, and we intended to keep it very private. If our company made money, I told the banker, we'd declare it and pay taxes.

My proposal wasn't strictly legal, but neither is trying to blow up a U.S. citizen. The banker went for it. I put the two million in bearer bonds, the diamonds, and four gold bars in our new safety-deposit box and drove back to Geneva.

273

Back in my hotel room, I called three guys I'd worked with in the special forces who'd become private contractors after leaving the military. After I explained the job, they told me what they needed and said it sounded like a piece of cake. I promised each of them $100,000 in cash from the "contingency fund" I'd expropriated from the Bank of al-Qaeda.

I trusted the three men, but I was less than honest with them. They thought they were working for the CIA. Faced with the prospect of the CIA hunting them down, I figured they wouldn't be tempted to pop me and grab our retirement fund.

Two of them were to meet me in Amman in two days using air tickets I wired to them. I sent the third man to Cyprus. Then I flew back to Amman, where I checked into a hotel, hung a do-not-disturb sign on the door knob, and made myself scarce.

The two ex-Green Berets flew into Amman the next day, and we rented an SUV. After renting a fast fishing boat in Cyprus, the third man, a former Navy SEAL, made for the international waters off Lebanon.

My two new companions and I crossed the border into Iraq and then retraced my steps on Highway 10. I'd programmed the location of the pile on my phone's GPS, so we easily found the abandoned road leading to the pile. It was a piece of cake, and I felt entitled to a little cake after months of eating MREs.

The pile was empty. Somebody had picked up the rubble from the condo. Maybe ATEC had a secret rubble-collecting machine. Who knows? It was impossible to tell that anything had ever been there.

I found the two heart-shaped stones in the pile wall, eyeballed two feet over, and cracked open my makeshift vault. It was all there. I was tempted to check the cave behind the pool, but I was in a hurry to get out of Iraq. Maybe Maggie and I would sneak back someday to see if the cache was still there. Right then, though, it didn't matter.

We loaded the SUV—replacing the spare tire under the rear floorboard with the gold and hoping we didn't get a flat on the return trip. The three of us were back in Jordan within two hours.

Getting the loot out of mostly landlocked Jordan was another story altogether. The only part of Jordan that was wet was a thin strip of land near Aqaba and the gulf of the same name. But taking that route would have meant navigating dangerous waters off many hostile Arab countries and possibly encountering pirates. In any event, our navy kept a close watch there. Going west through Israel was out because the Israeli border guards were sticklers for checking for secret compartments and contraband in vehicles arriving from Jordan. Likewise, I didn't want to risk driving through Syria or Lebanon. And having just shot the prince, I figured I probably wouldn't receive a hero's welcome in Saudi.

I made a reservation for a week at a resort in Tripoli, Lebanon. It was a luxury destination that attracted the Middle East's glitterati. That gave me cover to book a helicopter to briefly cross Syria and then enter Lebanese air space. I packed the gold in small, fifty-pound boxes, which would be easier to manage.

The pilot of the heavily loaded chartered helicopter filed a late-night flight plan for Tripoli. Once we cleared the shoreline, we dropped down below radar coverage and went directly to Sanani Island, an uninhabited part of the Palm Islands just off the Tripoli coast. In less than thirty minutes, we unloaded our cargo onto a rocky beach and then into the rubber raft the ex-Navy SEAL had brought in from the fishing boat that was anchored nearby.

The copter then zipped to Tripoli where, if he'd been asked, the pilot would have said he'd wanted to have a look at the nature reserve on the Palm Islands on his way there. For the cash I paid him, the pilot was willing to take the risk—but we ran into no trouble. Four days later, we brought everything ashore in Italy on the raft in the dark of night.

After the boredom of the pile, this part of the salvage effort was gut-wrenching. I paid the men with AQ dollar-denominated C-notes, and they shook my hand and said they hoped we'd work together again soon. Then I made a nerve-racking eight-hour drive north from Italy, being cautious not to exceed the speed limit, all the way to Liechtenstein. There, I deposited the fortune that I felt Maggie and I had more than earned in our safe-deposit box.

The next day, I flew to London and checked in at the Berkeley Hotel in Knightsbridge. I was catching a nap when the Washington fixer, Huneke, called my cell.

"Here's the deal," Huneke said. "They'll forget the whole thing. You're officially out of the army. You will tell anyone who asks that you were in the hospital rehabbing your leg since receiving the Medal of Honor. You'll get an honorable discharge, your back pay, and a 50 percent disability pension. I asked for 100 percent, but I threw them that bone to make them feel they'd won something. No books. No interviews. No screenplays. The entire matter is classified, and if you say one word about it, they'll put you in Leavenworth."

"They said that?"

"They always say that. They'd probably just put you in the Congressional Medal of Honor section of Arlington National Cemetery if you start becoming a problem."

"Can I go home now?"

"There's one more thing. They want to be able to use your services from time to time on a contract basis."

"The army?"

"The Company. They apparently were impressed with how you handled your escape, especially your loose interpretation of orders."

"I'm kind of through with that life. I'm a peace-loving investor now."

"They were really firm on that part. It keeps your mouth shut, if you get what I mean."

"I don't like it, but I'll worry about that later. They'd better not need my services very often."

"Yeah, sure. And to answer your question, you can go home whenever you want. I also got you that extra month's pay for every day beyond your retirement date. The direct deposit should have already hit your checking account."

****

I called my AMEX concierge to book a first-class flight to New York, and went down to the lobby to get something to eat. I was asking the bellman how to get to the Euston Square tube station—the stop on the London Underground where my dad died—when I noticed a *USA Today* newspaper on a coffee table. What had grabbed my attention was a photo of Maggie on the front page. A long article accompanied her photo.

President to Award Medal to Kidnapped U.S. Soldier

In an unusual move, the White House announced today that Lieutenant Margaret Amerson Taylor, who spent several months as a prisoner of al-Qaeda during her service with the U.S. Army in Iraq, will receive the Congressional Medal of Honor this spring, in a ceremony at the White House.

Lieutenant Taylor, who served in the army Military Police, was kidnapped in an ambush last October and held for ransom by al-Qaeda. Her captors threatened to kill her unless the United States met their demands, which both the former and current presidents refused.

She was beaten repeatedly while the terrorists attempted to force her to make a videotape in which she denounced her country. A video camera obtained by the army contained footage showing Lieutenant Taylor in an unknown location, refusing to make the video while being threatened with decapitation by a hooded, sword-wielding figure. The lieutenant managed to grab a pistol from a guard, kill her three captors, and escape by leaping from a moving, flaming truck.

Taylor lived in the desert for several weeks. Using her army survival skills, she hid in caves during the day and pilfered food from passing Bedouins at night. Last week, she encountered U.S. Army troops, and was taken to an army hospital.

Lieutenant Taylor, who earned a bachelor's degree in archeology from Tulane University, in her hometown of New Orleans, received an ROTC commission following graduation. She made a significant archeological discovery while on the run, finding several coins dating back to the Crusades in a cave where she took shelter. Archeologists have hailed the coins as amazingly well-preserved examples of coinage during the Crusades.

The auburn-haired beauty said she is unable to remember the location of the cave in which she found the coins because she was delirious much of her time in the desert.

In announcing the award, the president said, "Lieutenant Taylor epitomizes the courage and skills of female American soldiers. Her performance and heroism should put to rest any questions about a woman's right to choose to serve in combat in the U.S. military.

Military historians say the timing of the announcement was highly unusual since the military generally conducts exhaustive due diligence before the prestigious Congressional Medal of Honor is awarded. This marks the second Medal of Honor awarded in expedited fashion in the past year, possibly signaling that on today's digitally covered battlefield, timeframes may be accelerated. A presidential spokesman said that standard procedures were waived because the circumstances were "so extraordinary" and "her valor and heroism so compelling." Much of the evidence of Lieutenant Taylor's heroism, he said, has been classified.

Of course, everyone knew the reason the new president waived the rules. Sure, he probably did want to promote women in the military. But awarding the medal to Maggie—and classifying all information about her experience—made it pretty much impossible for any inquisitive journalist, or anyone else for that matter, to figure out the army had been willing to let the terrorists kill her.

****

As far as the rest of the world was concerned, I met Maggie for the first time a few weeks after her return, when we appeared together on a popular cable TV show. The true story, known only to the two of us, was that Maggie wanted me to come down to New Orleans—begged me to come—and I wanted desperately to go. But for the time being, we had millions of reasons to keep our relationship secret. So our only communication was via our secret email account.

I was in New York renewing some business school acquaintances, trying to get current on the stock market. I intended to make some serious cash, which was going to take some serious catching up. The guys I caught up with, at least the ones lucky enough to still have a job after the crash, weren't very different from my cousin Freddie. Although they worked at the white-shoe, big-bulge firms, they also wanted to capitalize on my status as a recipient of the Congressional Medal of Honor. They'd say, "Have dinner with me and my boss. Maybe there's a spot for you here." But the translation was, "It'll make me look good—but why in the world would we hire a dope who wasted the country's most coveted MBA degree by joining the army?"

The real reason behind my visit to New York was that Maggie, who was in the city on an army press junket, was scheduled to appear on the *Robert Meyers Show*. The army had orchestrated a month-long dog-and-pony show for Maggie to boost its female ranks before presenting her with the medal and granting her early discharge.

I'd decided to take advantage of the opportunity to see my fiancée and to "meet" her publicly. I anonymously emailed the producer of the show, saying the other recent recipient of the Medal of Honor was in town and staying at the Waldorf. Since my story was responsible for Meyers' Emmy Award, I knew they wouldn't be able to resist. An hour later, the show's booker called me with an invitation for me to appear that evening as well. I hesitated the appropriate few seconds before saying I'd be delighted and agreeing to be at the station at 5:30 p.m.

The producer "introduced" Maggie and me in the green room. My gal was perfectly coiffed and manicured, and all her scrapes and bruises had healed. I'd never seen Maggie with makeup on, and she was even more beautiful than I remembered. I slipped her the ring as we shook hands for a little too long perhaps, but the producer didn't seem to notice.

Then Meyers came into the room to speak briefly to the two of us. He extended his belated condolences, remarking that losing my friend had been a lousy way to win the medal. He didn't mention anything about it being a lousy way to earn a cable television news program.

During the twenty-minute on-air interview, Meyers let us each tell our story and called us heroes. Then he asked what we planned to do now that we were returning to civilian life. I said I was ready to find the right woman, get married, and settle down. A family, kids, a dog and cat—the whole nine yards—sounded appealing. Maggie chimed in that settling down and raising a family appealed to her, too.

Well, Meyers hit that softball clean out of the park. We both were single and available, he told his TV audience, and we'd make a very handsome couple. He insisted that we go to a fancy steakhouse for dinner after the show, on him on our first "date." Meyers promised to keep his viewing audience updated on our progress as a couple, jokingly giving us the name: Mr. and Mrs. Medal of Honor.

At the dinner, Maggie and I agreed that we kind of liked the sound of Mr. and Mrs. Medal of Honor. And we agreed as well that the steaks at Smith & Wollensky were a big improvement over the MREs we'd lived on at the condo. I found Maggie's smiling face and Southern drawl, however, as enchanting as ever.

From that day on, we were a celebrity couple. The public had seen us meet with their own eyes. Even the army loved the publicity. Our secret was secure.

Four months after our TV appearance, we were married at Maggie's Lutheran church in New Orleans. Her parents had happily accepted our offer to pay for the wedding after we assured them we'd use back pay that we'd both saved. They'd have choked if they knew what the wedding ended up costing.

Maggie invited all her old friends from high school and her sorority sisters from Tulane. She had a big extended family, including her nincompoop uncle, who was disappointed that we hadn't asked him to be the master of ceremonies at the reception.

I'd finally tracked down Colonel Hunt, who agreed to be my best man. He was living quietly on a lake in Windermere, Florida, where he spent his time fishing and playing golf at Bay Hill with an attractive realtor who lived nearby.

The former president and his wife did their best to stay in the background at the ceremony and reception that followed. But all the other guests wanted a photo with the former residents of the White House, so they were kept busy graciously complying.

Robert Meyers—who, as far as the world knew, had been responsible for introducing us on his TV show—flew in from New York with a film crew. I heard one of the producers tell a cameraman that she expected the viewing audience for his next show, which would feature Meyers' exclusive report on our wedding, to set a new rating record for the show.

I, of course, had no close family, so I'd asked the catering staff to set two empty places at the head table. During the toasts, I toasted my bride and then turned, held up my glass to the two empty places, and toasted my parents *in absentia*. I had eight years of Latin. So, sue me. I hoped they were proud of me—not so much for stealing the money, of course, but for finding the perfect wife.

Just as the dinner service was about to begin, the country club manager asked me to step outside the ballroom. There was a problem at the door, he said. I thought that the gaggle of reporters that had camped outside might be trying to get in. Instead, it was my cousins Freddie and the Cat, who were haranguing the Secret Service, demanding admittance. The poor saps, both then and still unemployed, had driven all the way from St. Louis, just assuming they were invited. I should have sent them packing, but I let them stay. Freddie pulled a camera out of his pocket and made straight for the former president, while the Cat went in search of the open bar. I was certain their wedding gift was in the mail.

We spent our honeymoon cruising the Greek Isles. When we sailed out toward Cyprus one day, I was tempted to dock and sneak back to the pile of rocks where we'd met. But that would have to wait.

****

On our return from our honeymoon, we bought a real condo—this one perfectly visible and without gun turrets—on the Gulf shore. It was close enough to New Orleans for Maggie to visit her parents and friends when she wanted but far enough away to short-circuit unannounced visits from her uncle (who'd mentioned using us as props in his next reelection campaign).

We spent our time there, entertaining her family and friends and getting to know each other better. After hearing how her father had almost made it to the NFL for the eighth time in two weeks, it was time for us to move on to our new place in Connecticut, which would be our home base. I wanted to tell her dad that I'd almost shot Osama bin Laden, but even that wouldn't have topped an NFL story in Louisiana.

In Connecticut, I had an office in Stamford, near the train station. We also took a small flat in London so I'd be closer to our banker in Liechtenstein. Maggie moved from the Southern Ivy League to the real one for the fall term at Yale to work on a master's degree in archeology. It's nearly impossible to get into Yale but a lot easier when two of your three letters of reference are from a former or sitting U.S. president. I still have the bruise on my leg where Maggie kicked me when I asked if she wanted me to get her a reference letter from Yale alum Major Shay.

Our celebrity status brought business opportunities out of the woodwork. Funds brought us lay-up, late-stage deals, and the cash was pouring in. We were on everyone's initial-public-offering allocation list, which usually meant free money and there were even requests for me to manage people's accounts. I declined that part. We made a killing investing in a new laser eye surgery company started by Dr. Frank O'Donnell, the Johns Hopkins ophthalmologist I'd met at The Farm. We got in a private placement shortly before O'Donnell's company went public and made a very lucrative quick flip. That opened the door to even more deals that people brought to us almost daily.

I had a small staff that included Colonel Hunt, who joined us as a consultant. When he asked what a consultant did, I told him if I needed a tee-time, I'd assume he was already at the golf course. Other than that, I told him, it involved cashing a check for ten grand every month. He said he'd become quite accomplished at cashing checks, but he'd prefer direct deposit. He'd more than earned it because, after all, neither Maggie nor I would still be alive without his warning.

****

Maggie and I had more money than we could spend—including our military disability and Medal of Honor pensions, which Maggie insisted go into a savings account for our future children. I didn't think they'd need it, but I didn't argue. I did remind her that the children of Medal of Honor recipients aren't subject to a quota if they want to apply to a military academy—even, presumably, if they had a simpleton congressman for a great-uncle with a penchant for hiring twenty-three-year-old secretaries.

I didn't acquire any more gold, except in those red and blue boxes from Cartier and Tiffany's. All the jewelers at those storied establishments who saw Maggie's ring marveled at its craftsmanship. They'd never seen anything like it—and, of course, they never would again.

As I expected, the price of gold doubled over a short period, giving us an even larger line of credit. The banker in Liechtenstein introduced me to a fabulous but unscrupulous jeweler named Stefan Schrader to help me bring home the gold bars in our safe-deposit box. Schrader had a side business of melting down gold bullion and turning it into items that can skate through customs. On each trip to Liechtenstein, I still return home with three or four leather belts with solid gold buckles. Schroeder created a mold to make the plastic inserts of those leather-covered Tumi luggage handles in twenty-four carat gold. I even have a collection of solid gold Visa Gold Cards.

I'm pretty sure that Schrader is stealing a few grams out of each gold bar I give him. When I've called him on it, he's blamed it on "shrinkage"; but he and I both know it's larceny. Anyway, my cost of goods is zero, so I can afford a little shrinkage. I'll be a very old man before I bring all the gold home.

****

We got invited to the former president's ranch for a barbecue, and he cooked up St. Louis-style pork steaks on the grill. I loved them, but Maggie said they were too fatty. It was our first spat.

By that time, the new president had figured out that Iraq was more complicated than he'd calculated, and his "rapid withdrawal" didn't go quite as planned. The public, however, was used to campaign promises being broken. And most Americans were more worried about losing their homes and retirement accounts than the Iraq war.

One such family lived in Orlando. Maggie arranged to anonymously pay off the mortgage on the family home belonging to the parents of her deceased army driver, PFC Spanky Stafford. Every month, a thousand dollars in cash appears in their mailbox. On her return, Maggie had met with the boy's family and spun a yarn about their son's brave effort to defend her from the kidnappers. Her story got PFC Stafford the Silver Star, which was awarded posthumously and given to his parents. They had the medal framed and put it next to his picture on their television set.

I also paid a visit to The Dart's parents in Jonesboro, Arkansas. They didn't need any money, but I told them I was funding a scholarship for returning veterans in his name at Arkansas State. It made them very happy, and I even got a ride in the finally restored Dodge Dart.

****

A man from the Company visited me at my office once. He said he was just touching base and wanted me to know they were serious about the deal that Huneke had told me about. I told him my aim was pretty shaky after my last assignment, but it didn't seem to change his mind. Maggie said she'd refuse to let me take any of their assignments unless she got to come along—which I wouldn't let happen in a million years. I'd have said "for a million dollars," but Maggie could pay that many times over.

I received two interesting letters from home. The one from my alma mater, The Barrington School for Boys and Girls asked me to be their commencement speaker. I accepted. The letter from Fair Oaks Country Club, the club that had blackballed my father at my grandfather's request, informed me that I'd been nominated to stand for membership and had been approved by a unanimous vote of the membership committee. I passed on that one.

Connecticut issued special Medal of Honor license plates for Maggie and me. The plate on my Mercedes SUV reads "MR," and the one on her flashy red Corvette reads "MRS." Any time we park our cars outside next to each other there is always someone stopping to snap pictures with their cell phones.

Maggie and I can't make the hundreds of appearances that veterans groups ask us to make each year, but we do what we can for the troops. On the Fourth of July alone, we had over a hundred invitations to ride in parades. Maggie was thrilled when we were invited to ride on a float in the Krewe of Muses parade the night before Mardi Gras. That parade has come to be known for the decorated shoes that are thrown from the floats. From our stations on the float, Maggie and I threw several hundred decorated army boots to the cheering crowd. It was the hit of the parade.

The curiosity about Mr. and Mrs. Medal of Honor has only gotten stronger as our battlefield exploits are embellished by reporters and television shows that can't seem to get enough. There's even talk of a movie about Maggie's escape, and she obsesses over which actress will be chosen to play her. I'm not sure there's an actress in Hollywood who could have given a better performance than Maggie gave—first, to the troops who "found" her and then, to the officials and staff at the army hospital in Iraq.

Maggie became a volunteer at the history museum in New York, where her now-famous coins became a popular exhibit whose write-up describes the rare coins as well as Maggie's heroism while in the desert. If they only knew. The curator told her he expected the new government in Iraq to demand the coins back. If that ever happens, it would be okay. Maggie and I know where we can get more.

****

Major R. J. Shay was exiled from ATEC to a desk job at the Pentagon. He got the message that he'd not be chosen for promotion to lieutenant colonel, so the long line of Shays who made general would end with him.

Shortly after his discharge, Shay took a position with a New York venture fund that ran a portfolio focused on novel technologies to produce green energy. During his interviews with the fund, he probably bragged loud and long about how he'd put a man in an energy-efficient mobile home on a mountain in the middle of the desert.

I followed Shay home one night and found he was living in a walk-up on the Upper West Side, a bit unusual for an Ivy League man who hadn't gone to Columbia. I kept an eye on him for a few days. A sniper is never seen if he doesn't want to be seen. He was in the habit of jogging through the neighborhood and into the park each night after work. I found a sporting goods store on Columbus Avenue, bought a lacrosse stick, and waited for him one night. As he chugged around the corner and cut through the same alley he always took, I stepped out from behind a dumpster and whacked him in the gut with the stick. He went down babbling that it hadn't been his fault and how he had just been following orders. I told him that excuse stopped working after the Nuremburg Trials. I told him if he ever so much as mentioned my name again to anyone, I'd be back, and not with a lacrosse stick.

Professor Christine Head went back to her beloved, insular world of Ivy League academia. Her position as department chair had been reassigned to another professor, so she found herself humiliated teaching freshman-level classes. She lived in further humiliation for having so quickly been the target of the new president's opprobrium, and speculation on the reasons was rampant. Even worse, that cable newsman, Robert Meyers had stopped returning her calls. I gave her a few months and phoned her office. Using my best Middle Eastern accent, I told her I was an aide to Osama bin Laden, and we blamed her for killing the prince. When she least expected it, I said, her home would be blown up with her in it. The woman who told the world I'd been committed to a psych ward ended up in one herself for most of the spring semester.

The murders of Adad Haneef, the should-have-been future president of Syria, and the others in the Detroit warehouse remain another unsolved Detroit mass homicide for that city's police and the FBI. The FBI took the ultralights back to a lab, where they tested Haneef's magic stealth paint and discovered that it actually *increased* the ability of radar to pick up a signal.

TyWayne "Tire Tool" Washington, CEO of Woodstoned Pharmaceuticals, LLC, and his COO, The Flamer, continue to operate a thriving drug dispensary on select Detroit street corners. And they still frequent Popeyes, especially on nights when the special is an eight piece with two large sides.

As for Osama bin Laden, he made it back to Pakistan following the debacle at the sanctuary. He may have hated the prince, but as they say, "You don't know what you've got until it's gone." Money became tight for the terrorist and his collaborators, and any thoughts he had of getting out of the compound in Abbottabad decomposed faster than the prince's unembalmed corpse in the desert.

His flatbed truck—owned by a shell corporation that in turn was owned by the prince—was repossessed by the prince's estate, making Osama a prisoner in his own compound. Osama believed he'd never be found at the compound. After all, so many years had passed since 9-11, and, he wondered, *how long could these people hold a grudge, anyway?*

Osama became complacent and resisted Abu's pleas to build an escape tunnel, saying the noise would disrupt his family life. But his three families and more than a dozen children were a constant headache. His children wanted everything that kids everywhere want and got into the normal mischief that all kids get into. The man who'd tormented the world had no peace.

The brief cell phone call that Abu had taken from his comrade months earlier had set off a cascade of events that eventually led the infidel SEALS to bin Laden's door—or roof. When faithful Abu al-Kuwaiti and his brother went down in a hail of gunfire defending bin Laden from the Navy SEALS, the man who had terrorized the world worried about how poorly the hovel he lived in would reflect on him. As he cowered behind one of his wives, bin Laden's last thoughts in this world were of the seventy virgins who awaited him. He hoped at least a few of them knew their way around a vacuum cleaner. But most frustrating was that he knew somewhere al-Zawahari, the Egyptian quack, was smiling.

****

Maggie has been true to her word and treats me like a king. She still sometimes has nightmares that interrupt her sleep, but she seems to be getting better. I suggested it might help her to talk to someone, but she always says I'm the only one who understands.

The victims I dispatched during the war still sometimes visit me in my dreams. But the face of the prince never is never among them.

Maggie and I finally got to go hunting together. I took her to see my father's small hometown in Southern Illinois, where our visit turned into little more than a walk in the woods. Neither of us felt like shooting anything anymore. My rifle, which I'd sent to a gunsmith for refurbishing following our drive off the pile, arrived looking no worse for wear. I wondered what it would be worth if it people knew it was the rifle that had killed the brains behind al-Qaeda. But, I killed him. Guns don't kill terrorists; snipers do.

An old sniper once told me that the rigorous concealment training he'd received at sniper school left him constantly looking for safe places he could hide. I didn't suffer from that anymore. I'd found my safe place.

Author's Notes

The story of one man against the world has been told for centuries. This is my take with a different twist.

The Congressional Medal of Honor is one of the few untarnished gems of our society. This story fictionalizes how the medal could be used to achieve political objectives. We should all hope that both sides of the aisle avoid the temptation to do what is described in this book. There is no doubt it will be harder to resist as digitized war coverage becomes more immediate and dramatic.

To the best of my knowledge, the army does not have an ATEC, however it should. All the technology used existed during the period covered by the book. The ophthalmic laser sighting technology I used, actually happened, but in reverse. The tracking software on the excimer laser which is used in LASIK surgery," was actually adapted from the "Star Wars" technology used to shoot down missiles. I reversed the process for the condo's weapon system. Frank O'Donnell, MD was very involved in the development of that industry. For those looking for Fair Oaks, Missouri, it is also fictional, as is the Barrington School for Boys and Girls.

Anyone who has ever written a book knows it quickly teaches you how little you really know. I would like to express my appreciation to the many friends who helped me understand the story was a good one and then helped me hone it into a better one.

Many thanks to my early readers: John Borchers, Dennis Svoboda, Trey Mudge, Chris Carenza, Steve Higgins, Tad Armstrong, Chris Head, RJ Shay, Steve Straus, Chris and Becky Arps, Rachel Stack, Major Chris Ianni, and Lane Holmes. This group convinced me my early draft was worth the effort required to get to this point.

I have never been to Iraq and this didn't seem like a good time to make my first trip. I depended on two Iraq War veterans who were there during the period described in the book, Major Chris Ianni, USAF and Cpl. Lane Holmes, USMC, for a reality check to make sure I wasn't too far off-base. I wish to thank them for their military insights and for their brave service to our country.

All authors require many names for their characters. I made up some of the names including those of the two main characters who are amalgams of many people I have known and are purely fictitious. The Arabic names were taken from internet lists of common Arabic names and are all fictitious. I named many other characters after friends and acquaintances. There is no connection between the character and the name. I simply wanted to share this adventure with them. I want to thank Ansley Hunt, Maggie Taylor, Frank Bono, John Borchers, Dennis Svoboda, Trey Mudge, Travis Aylward, Steve Klingel, Chris Carenza, Steve Higgins, Eugene Bode, MD, Frank O'Donnell, MD, Skip Sallee, MD, Bob Meyers, John Stiles, Vito Modica, Tad Armstrong, Hon. James Hackett, Ronald "The Flamer" Behrhorst, George Reican, Glenn "Spanky" Stafford, Karen Keller, Dennis Huneke, Ed Huneke, and Paul Jenkins for allowing me to use their names. I especially want to thank Chris Head, RJ Shay, T. Wesley Dunn, John Towell, Peter Varty, Steve Schrader and the late, Robert W. May for allowing me to use their names as villains. In real life, they are great people.

Thanks also to PGA professional golfer and Fox Sports Analyst, Jay Delsing and Tampa Rays announcer, Dewayne Staats, both good friends, for appearing as themselves.

Thanks to my real-life former CFO, B. Charles Bono III, CPA, MBA for teaching me about MBA's. He saved me a lot of money on tuition by telling me the only thing you need to know to be an MBA is to answer every question by saying "well, it depends." I'd also like to thank the many investment bankers, analysts and fund managers I worked with over the years who helped a liberal arts major learn the intricacies of finance and the ways of Wall Street without ever having taken a business class. People always ask if I enjoyed it and I always say, "yes, twice a month," but otherwise, it depends.

Thanks to Vic Kreuiter for lending his expertise on country music.

I want to thank Dennis Svoboda who has taught foreign languages at schools all over the world including the Middle-east. Dennis introduced me to the phenomenon that people will revert to a foreign language they know when confronted with a language they don't. Dennis also taught me to never underestimate the intelligence of a foreign speaker just because they have an accent when speaking English. In the book, I have the Arabic characters using accents only when they are speaking to English speakers. There is no accent when they are speaking to each other.

Every author thinks their work is perfect. It is the job of editors to gently tell them it isn't. I would like to thank Chris Head, the greatest English teacher at Edwardsville High School since the legendary Margaret Warmbrodt, for the long, thankless hours she spent on early corrections. Book editor Donna L. Brodsky, took a book that was much too long and showed me how to structure it much more clearly, making it a much better read. I had the last crack at the manuscript, so any errors were probably mine.

The cover art was done by one of America's premier illustrators and my good friend, RJ Shay. (www.rjshay.com).

Authors often talk about the typeface used in their novels. I really don't think anyone cares about type, one way or another, so I am not going to even bother with mentioning it. If this bothers you, feel free to complain to the publisher.

JJK
St. Louis, Missouri
July 4, 2017

About The Author

John J. Klobnak is an entrepreneur and former CEO of a publicly-traded company. He is a graduate of the prestigious College of Arts and Sciences at Southern Illinois University at Edwardsville, where the English Department always has a better year than the football team. He lives with his family just outside the city limits of Fair Oaks, Missouri.

Travis and Maggie will return soon as Mr. and Mrs. Medal of Honor begin their lives as civilians. If you want to be notified of the release date, please send me an email at klobnak.books@charter.net.

Made in the USA
Columbia, SC
23 July 2018